AND STILL, SHE STAYED QUIET

Dheeraj Kumar

For every woman who stayed quiet –
not out of weakness,
but out of strength.

For those whose silence held storms, truth, and courage.
This story is yours.

For those who carried the weight of others.
For those who were judged but stood tall.
For those who spoke and were silenced.
For those who endured without applause.

For every woman who stayed quiet –
not out of fear,
but for reasons the world may never understand.
This book is for you.

Chapter 1

Usha Rathi belonged to one of the poorer families in Chandrapur….where walls were thin and bricks lay exposed, held not by strong cement but by the strength of the people within. On the other side of those walls, the bonds between hearts were strong enough to keep the house standing. Here, hearts were thick with true feelings, rooftops whispered memories, room walls guarded secrets, and silence echoed with unspoken prayers.

Homes here wore memories like a faded dupatta, draped tightly, worn daily, never discarded.

There was no grandeur in her world, no chandeliers, no sweeping staircases.

But there was warmth.

There was turmeric on skin, marigolds on doorways, gods framed on cracked walls, and a kind of love that spread slowly, like perfume rising in the summer heat.

Usha was born from that love, softened by it…but not dulled.

She carried her father's silence, her grandmother's spine, and her sister's softness.

Each thread in her dupatta told a quiet story…of sacrifice, of dreams postponed, of pride never spoken aloud.

Her eyes did not seek the stars, nor did she dream of gold.

She guarded the soil beneath her feet.

Rathi House was painted in hopes and chipped corners. Inside lived Roopa Devi, Usha's grandmother, her silver braid woven with memories of Partition and poetry, her silver earrings whispering of the past.

There was Anika, her twin, whose smile could make sorrow disappear, and whose eyes noticed what others missed.

And Ameet Rathi, their father... a man of few words, whose walk bore the weight of the world, guarding his daughters like roots anchoring a tree.

That morning, joy had bloomed early.

It was Anika's wedding day.

The scent of haldi mingled with incense.

Bangles clinked like temple bells.

Sarees rustled as neighbors arrived, laughter tucked in their dupattas.

Shreya's voice floated from a borrowed Bluetooth speaker wrapped in tape.... like a blessing pressed onto vinyl.

For a few hours, happiness wore jasmine garlands and danced barefoot through the rooms.

But by noon, the colors began to blur.

A call came.

The voice on the other end crackled:

"Keval Pandit...... died... he didn't make it."

Silence fell — not like a whisper, but like thunder.

Keval Lal, the wedding priest, was gone.

The man who had known every auspicious hour, every chant, every thread that stitched tradition.... was no more.

Panic unfolded like a broken fan.

Guests whispered.

Aunties speculated.

Some said it was a bad sign.

"I'll go," Usha said.

Her voice was steady, though something trembled inside.

"I'll find another pandit."

She didn't wait.

She ran.

Not noticing the street.

Not noticing her sandals biting into her feet.

Not stopping to catch the yellow dupatta that slipped from her shoulder….waving behind her like a banner of hope.

She ran.

Through narrow lanes.

Toward the temple.

Toward something she couldn't name.

But in truth…. she ran for her sister.

The sky had turned a bruised orange.

She prayed it would hold its tears.

✦ ∞ ✦

Across the city, in a mansion the colour of privilege, the Rai house stood tall and immaculate… everything the Rathi house was not.

A small family in a mansion so vast, it felt like living inside their own private city.

Here, the roof was too high to hear a heartbeat.

The walls didn't hold warmth….they shone, they reflected, but they never absorbed.

The air smelled of expensive perfumes, air fresheners, and carefully plated food.

And love?

If it lived here at all, it lived quietly.

Hidden.

Almost shy.

Vikrant Rai was a man of responsibility.

Business ran through his veins.

His calendar ruled his life.

He believed money could buy emotions, buy solutions….that everything had a price tag.

He believed in logic, not in love. Not in tradition. Not even in God.

Born into legacy, raised in politics and power, he had learned early that emotions were best kept behind boardroom doors and bulletproof glass.

His father, Kunaal Rai, rarely smiled unless cameras or shareholders were watching.

His mother, Anjali, found comfort not in touch or hugs, but in temple rituals and the horoscope section of the newspaper....her belief in astrology never wavering, even from her wheelchair.

And Karishma, his sister, She was like the first diya in the temple: small, steady, glowing in her own way.

She didn't know much about tradition, but followed it anyway... like a strand of hair falling on your face without reason.

She didn't believe in fate, but she still read the stars in the newspaper every day.

That day, Karishma was pacing restlessly, her heels clicking sharply against the marble floor.

"Brother, the pandit isn't answering the phone," she said, her voice tight with urgency. "And...and, Maa says today's a bad omen."

Vikrant let out a dry laugh, muttering something only he could hear.

Anjali clutched the edge of her dupatta, her eyes darting between the two. Then she turned to Karishma.

"It's bad times," she whispered. "Something feels wrong in this house.... And we need to speak to the pandit before it gets worse."

She looked at Vikrant, her voice softening this time.

"I know you're worried about the business..."

Vikrant rolled his eyes.

"It's not bad luck, Maa. It's business. Our competitors are strong....but this time, we're stronger. We're prepared."

But Anjali didn't respond. She lowered her gaze, wrapping her fingers tightly around the edge of her Sari. Then, without another word, she wheeled herself away….as fast as she could.

Karishma instinctively stepped forward, wanting to stop her, but Anjali had already turned the corner.

"Please," Karishma said, turning to Vikrant, her voice trembling. "Can you go to the temple? Maa only wants you to go. She believes that if you call the pandit and do the pooja with your own hands… things will settle. Please, bhai… for her. For me."

Vikrant sighed.

"Fine," he muttered. "I'll go to the temple…..if that's what it takes to shut everyone up."

As the sky melted into a bruised orange, and birds returned home in quiet lines, Usha stood alone….just outside the temple, on the raised stone platform that circled its heart.

The new pandit had promised to finish one final pooja, then come for Anika's wedding.

She waited… palms joined,

her heart praying louder than any chant around her.

Every second mattered.

Her sister's smile was on the line.

Her father's dignity.

Her family's fragile happiness.

And then…..Footsteps.

Polished leather on old temple stone.

Vikrant Rai appeared.

Crisp clothes. Sharp walk.

A look on his face that didn't ask permission….it expected obedience.

He moved toward the sanctum.

Usha saw him and called out, her voice clear:

"Excuse me, listen…… your shoes. Please remove them."

Vikrant didn't look at her.

"I need the pandit," he said flatly. His voice gave nothing away.

Usha stepped forward.

Her throat burned, but her voice stayed steady.

"But…. he promised us first."

The pandit appeared just then, having completed his pooja.

His eyes moved between the two of them…..Usha and Vikrant.

And then, he chose.

He moved toward Vikrant.

The silence that followed was loud……like thunder with no sound.

Usha didn't plead.

She didn't beg.

Her dignity wouldn't allow it.

But this was her sister's wedding.

Her family's moment.

Her home's only joy after years of quiet sacrifice.

So her heart tried anyway.

She looked at the pandit again.

Her lips didn't move.

But her eyes asked everything.

Tears slid down her face… silent, steady… as if words had failed her completely.

She swallowed the ache in her throat.

Steadied herself.

And whispered:

"But… we need you at my sister's…."

Vikrant cut her off.

"That doesn't matter. I need him.

He's coming with me."

Tears continued falling from Usha's eyes....heavier now.

Vikrant saw them.

But his voice stayed still.

Usha looked at the pandit.... straight into his eyes.

Her lips trembled, but her voice found its way through the storm in her chest.

"But..... but you promised," she said softly, like a wound speaking aloud.

"Now that promise means nothing... because, because you saw power?"

Her breath caught. Her hands clenched the edge of her dress.

"Is that power greater than the power of God?"

She blinked back another wave of tears.

Her vision blurred.... not just from tears, but from everything she no longer wanted to see.

She didn't look at Vikrant.

Instead, her gaze lifted to the temple.... to its silence, its stone, its sky.

It was as if she was asking God a question she already knew had no answer.

The night sky above remained calm, clouded.

But not a single drop of rain fell.

Inside her, though....the storm had long begun.

And it wasn't just a storm.

It was a flood. A drowning.

And she stood in its center ...quietly shattered.

Vikrant watched her.

Still silent.

His heart wanted to speak, to call her.

His hand even twitched... rose halfway.

But pride pulled it back.

And the moment passed.

The pandit stepped closer.

"Shall we go?" he asked.

That was it.

Usha didn't argue.

She didn't say another word.

She turned.

And walked away.

Her shadow trailed behind her....like a torn plastic bag mistakenly carried, dragging along the dust.

She didn't look at the sky to blame God.

She didn't glance back at the path home.

She wasn't broken because the pandit had gone with someone else.

She was broken because she knew.... without him, the groom's family would not wait.

Each step grew heavier.

Each heartbeat slowed.

And still... she walked.....

✦ ∞ ✦

She arrived home, hoping to still find music, laughter, someone arguing over too much sugar in the tea.

But silence had taken root.

The door creaked open.

No anklets.

No laughter.

No wedding songs.

Only Roopa Devi, still as stone, eyes hollow.

"They left," she whispered. "The groom's family. They said the day is cursed. They said... Anika brings bad luck. The wedding is off."

Usha's body didn't fall.

Her soul did.

She sank to the floor near a broken garland, jasmine petals scattered like the remnants of a dream.

Her fingers reached out to touch them.

They still smelled sweet.

But now… they meant nothing.

The house was dry.

The street was dry.

The sky… still dry.

But inside Usha Rathi…… A storm began.

A quiet, wordless, endless storm.

And for the first time in years…

She cried not through tears … But through Silence.

Chapter 2

In the quiet corners of the Rai Mansion, Vikrant Rai was not thinking about Usha.

He didn't see her face in mirrors.

Didn't lie awake tracing regrets across the ceiling.

He never tried to remember what he had done that day.

Never wondered what it meant for the girl whose voice never reached him.

What if he could've heard her?

What if he had listened....truly listened.... to what she never said aloud?

But Vikrant never knew what he didn't know.

And that was the cruellest part.

His world was made of glass and ego....clean, structured, unemotional.

He believed in logic. In control. In himself.

Emotions were inefficiencies.

Love was a word he left for the films his sister cried over.

To Vikrant, the world moved forward. Always.

And people.... especially people like Usha...were names in passing.

Not chapters.

Not even footnotes.

He never turned back to see whose life cracked beneath his footsteps.

But the universe......

It's made of soft collisions.

✦ ∞ ✦

It was one of those mornings where the clouds flirted with sunlight, and the air smelled like something unfinished.

Vikrant's car moved quickly along the familiar road near the temple.

"Rahul, I said close the Australian deal. Just draft the………"

Screech.

A sudden brake. A slip of breath. The phone fell.

And, she was there.

Usha.

Standing still. At the edge of the road. Her cream dupatta brushing the stone gently like…..like the wing of a memory.

She wasn't moving.

But something in her stillness screamed.

Their eyes met.

And for a second…

The world forgot how to pretend.

She didn't step back.

Didn't look down.

Didn't fold herself into apology like tradition had taught her.

She looked at him.

Straight into him.

In her eyes….Not fear.

Not longing.

But war.

Grief.

Resentment.

A quiet scream: *You have no idea what you ruined.*

He stepped out slowly. Words caught in his throat.

"Are you… are you okay?"

The question wasn't arrogant. It was… tentative. Human.

And…Usha blinked once.

Twice.

And then turned.

No word. No nod. Just a soft retreat into silence.

But something shimmered in the space where she had stood.

A silver chain.

Simple. Old. Nestled between mud and memory.

Its pendant…..an infinity symbol…..caught the fading light, whispering stories of promises never spoken, and bonds that refused to break.

Vikrant stared at it. Then bent, hesitated, and picked it up.

It was light in weight……but heavy in presence. It didn't belong in his hand. Not because of the dirt……

But because it wasn't his.

Still, he didn't drop it.

He turned it in his palm, as if trying to make sense of its shape, its meaning, its story.

He didn't know…. That it had once belonged to Usha's mother.

That Usha had worn it every single day since her death.

That it was her anchor, her prayer, her inheritance.

And today…

She'd let it fall.

He placed it gently in the glove box.

Closed it.

But his fingers lingered.

Why did I pick that up? he asked himself.

Why does it feel wrong to keep… but impossible to return?

He shook his head.

"Leave it," he muttered. "Not now. Not her."

But even as the car moved again, even as his phone rang and business resumed….The chain lay quiet.

Pure, yet heavier than silver.

✦ ∞ ✦

Some silences are soft.

They hum like lullabies in the quiet of night wrapping themselves around memories and rocking grief into sleep.

But some…some silences scream without sound.

They stand between two people like locked doors, like words never spoken, like glances never returned.

The silence between Usha and Vikrant was the latter.

Days had passed since the wedding that never was.

But time… it did not heal.

It only learned how to layer more dust on wounds that still bled beneath.

Usha moved like a ghost in her own home, a shadow that remembered it once used to be light.

She arranged tea trays for visiting families her father now met, trying to rewrite Anika's future as if it could be unbroken. She held her sister's hand through heartbreak, sewed back the smile on Roopa Devi's tired lips, and told the neighbours, *"Everything happens for a reason,"* even when her chest felt like a crumbling temple.

But when night came…..And the house finally exhaled its sorrow,

And everyone drifted into uneasy sleep,

And the wedding songs stopped haunting the corners….Usha sat by her window, tracing invisible raindrops on glass.

It hadn't rained since that day.

And yet, she felt soaked… always.

Drenched in a sorrow no one else could see.

Her mind, stubborn and cruel, always returned to that one moment.

Not the pandit.

Not the rejection.

But him.

Vikrant Rai.

Because it had started with him.

He took the pandit.

He spoke those words that ended everything.

And because of him, the wedding never happened.

Her sister's dreams scattered like marigold petals in the dust.

Her mother's silence turned to sobs.

And Usha…..Usha was the one who had to hold the pieces.

So no… he didn't matter.

Not anymore.

Not after what he caused.

But still… for one fleeting second,

he had.

She hated that memory most of all.

The moment at the temple.

The crowd behind them, the decision just made,

and him…. standing there, not smug, not cruel, but… still.

His hand had reached out.

Not with pride.

Not with power.

But something harder to name.

Guilt, maybe.

A hesitation.

A pause in a man who had just broken her world.

She had turned her back.

She had to.

Because even then, even after everything, her heart had paused too.

Not out of affection.

Not out of hope.

But because even the ones who hurt us most...

sometimes leave behind the deepest silence.

And just as that memory faded

….. **she froze.**

Her hand flew to her neck.

The chain.

Her mother's chain.

Gone.

She looked down, touched again harder.

Bare skin. Nothing.

It was the last thing her mother had left for her.

A thread of protection, of presence, of love.

And she had lost it.

In the chaos, in the running, in the breaking…. she couldn't even protect that.

A whisper cracked inside her.

She hadn't even noticed it slipping away.

Not until now.

And somehow…

that felt like losing everything all over again.

Chapter 3

There are men who speak their hearts aloud.

And then there are men like Vikrant Rai.

Men who tuck vulnerability behind the folds of expensive suits.

Men who speak in strategies, not sentiments.

Men who believe that to say *I'm sorry* is to surrender a part of their spine.

He wasn't heartless.

Just armoured.

He didn't lack feeling.

He just didn't know what to do with it once it arrived uninvited.

The silver chain sat in his drawer…still, silent, unassuming.

Untouched, yet never forgotten.

It had no voice, yet echoed her absence louder than grief ever could.

And in his thoughts, it pulsed…..steady and relentless like a heartbeat he couldn't quiet.

At night, when the city dimmed and his family drifted into cold sleep, he would sit at the edge of his bed, open that drawer, and look at it.

A small thing.

Old.

Tangled slightly.

No diamonds.

No shine.

No value in the world he lived in.

And yet……And yet…

It weighed more than any gold bar in his father's safe.

Maybe because it carried grief.

Maybe because it carried her.

He wanted to return it. He needed to.

But not like some apologetic stranger.

Not like a man begging forgiveness.

Because he was Vikrant Rai.

And she, Usha Rathi, was the girl who had walked away from him... like he was the one who didn't matter.

His pride twisted inside him like a blade.

So, instead of walking up to her doorstep, he did what men like him do best, he created distance and .... he called it dignity.

He picked up his phone and called the one person who never asked "why."

Satish.

Childhood friend. Creator of chaos. Owner of Chandrapur's most charming stationery and gift shop.

"I need a favour," Vikrant said, keeping his voice flat.

"I'm listening my friend" Satish replied, the smirk audible.

"I want to return something... but not directly. She wouldn't take it from me."

"Romantic? Or dangerous?" Satish teased.

Vikrant didn't answer.

Satish laughed. "Let's make it fun then. What do you say... a game?"

The streets of Chandrapur whispered curiosity.

Posters hung from lamp posts and grocery shop windows. Pastel-coloured with curled edges and soft fonts:

Missing Something Precious?

Join the Lost & Found Lucky Draw!

Tell us what you lost, when and where.
If it matches an item in our collection……
You win it back.
And as if that weren't enough…. a surprise gift.
The city came alive with stories.
A boy missing his cricket ball.
A girl searching for a stolen doll.
A man asking about his wife's gold ring.
But Vikrant wasn't looking for them.
He waited.
Quietly.
Anxiously.
He called Satish twice a day. "Anything yet?"
And every time:
"Not yet."

✦ ∞ ✦

Usha went back to the temple.
First in the morning. Then again at dusk.
She searched the steps.
She asked the pandit.
She walked around the peepal tree with folded palms, looking in grass and dust and corners of stone.
She searched with the desperation of someone trying to find a part of herself.
That chain wasn't just metal.
It was her mother's last gift.
Her anchor.
Her ritual.
Her prayer.
Losing it felt like losing her all over again.

When she was returning from her third search, shoulders slumped, her soul a little hollower…..a boy approached at the temple gate.

"Sister," a stranger boy said softly, holding out a folded flyer. "This might interest you."

She almost waved him away. Almost.

But something in her breath told her to take it.

Later that night, under the flicker of a yellow bulb, she opened the flyer.

Missing Something?

The words glowed softly.

Her heart skipped.

Could it be…?

Could the world still be kind?

The next morning, Usha walked into the store… cautious, guarded. Sleep hadn't visited her, only fragments of thought and the weight of what was gone.

Her fingers trembled slightly as she filled out the form, each letter shaky, as if even her handwriting no longer trusted the world.

"*A silver chain.*

Old.

Rusted in memory.

Its pendant….a delicate infinity symbol, worn smooth with time.

Lost at the temple steps two days ago.

My mother's.

The last thing of hers I ever wore.

The last thing that ever held me."

Satish read the form slowly.

His eyes softened.

He smiled....not teasingly, but gently. Like someone who knows the real value of things.

"Thank you," he said. "If it matches, we'll call you."

✦ ∞ ✦

Vikrant's phone lit up.

Satish.

"We got one," he said. "She described it perfectly. Her mother's chain."

There was a pause on Vikrant's end. Then...

a breath.

Then something rare..... A smile.

Soft. Real. Quietly blooming on a face that hadn't known peace in days.

"Good," he said.

"And the surprise gift?" Satish asked.

Vikrant looked out the window.

The city was melting into golden dusk.

But in that light, he saw not the skyline.

He saw her eyes.

He thought of the silence between them. The unsaid words. The weight of moments he didn't know how to name.

"Give her something she'd never expect," he said finally.

"What's that?"

Vikrant's voice lowered.

"Give her back the most beautiful gift her mother ever gave her." He looked away, the ache settling in his chest.

"That chain... it's not just silver. It's memory. Protection.

It's the one thing I had no right to take.

Return it. That's the most priceless gift."

Chapter 4

The room was dim lit only by the soft flicker of a lamp and the silent strength of two sisters holding each other like the world outside had vanished.

Anika clutched a worn photograph of their mother....faded, creased at the edges, but held as if it still carried breath.

As if she could hear her mother breathing through it.

As if letting go would break something inside her.

"She left too early," Anika whispered, her voice trembling, as if she was speaking from the inside of her own chest. "We never even knew what it felt like... to be truly loved by a mother. We're the unluckiest people."

Usha didn't speak.

She didn't need to.

Instead, she leaned in, wrapped her arms around Anika like the ocean does the shore.....quietly, deeply, endlessly.

No permission asked.

No explanation given.

Sisters didn't need words when pain was loud enough.

At the doorway, Ameet Rathi stood still.

A man worn by time, softened by sorrow. His daughters were women now....grieving something they never truly had. Watching them like this tugged at something ancient inside him.

Regret, maybe.

Or perhaps just helplessness — the kind only a father knows, when he's done all he could..... and it still wasn't enough. He kept watching. His eyes wanted to say what his lips couldn't.

But the words stayed buried.

Then....he lifted his gaze, as if he'd fought something within himself.... and wasn't sure if he'd won, or lost.

Usha's hand lifted to her chest, her fingers brushing against the cold touch of the silver chain, now back where it belonged....over her heart.

Her voice broke the silence, gentle but unshakable.

"Papa... is there another photo of Ma? One where she's wearing this chain? I... I want to see her with it. Without her, it...it feels... incomplete. And.... did she put this chain on me herself?"

Ameet's eyes softened, the kind of softness that arrives when memory meets guilt. In just one breath, she had asked all the questions he had carried his whole life... or maybe the ones he thought he had buried long ago.

"That photo you have... it was taken before you two were born. Back then, I was still working shifts at the factory. I saved for months to buy her that chain. It wasn't much. But to her... it was everything."

From the adjoining room, Roopa Devi stepped in....slowly, like she was walking through old rain. Her eyes looked far away, somewhere in the past where ghosts still lived.

"There was heavy rain that day," she began, her voice low and distant, like a breeze remembering a storm. "Your father was at work. And your mother... she was alone with me. She started screaming.....suddenly. Her legs couldn't move. She collapsed and I panicked. I thought the baby was coming early. I...I didn't know what to do."

Her voice began to crack like dry leaves underfoot.

"I ran... ran through narrow lanes and puddles... I called the nurse from the hospital. But by the time we returned..."

She paused.

A long pause.

The kind that holds more than words can carry.

"There was so much blood. She must've tried to crawl. Tried to reach for something. The floor was cold… and she was gone."

The silence that followed was the kind only grief understands.

The kind that doesn't ask to be broken.

It just sits there….like ash, like rain, like memory.

Roopa's voice dropped to a whisper.

"We…….we could only save you both. Usha and Anika. Twins. Crying, breathing, alive. Born together… bound in ways even blood can't explain."

Usha's breath caught.

She turned instinctively, looking at Anika….not with questions, but with a feeling. A pull. As if the story now belonged to both, more deeply than ever before.

She touched the chain again…..except this time, it didn't feel like jewellery.

It felt like weight.

Like love.

Like inheritance.

Ameet stepped forward. His voice cracked around the edges.

"This chain… it was hers. Her memory. Her love. She couldn't place it around your neck herself…but it belongs to you now. Keep it close. You carry her strength… and her love for your sister, too."

Usha stood and walked to her father, hugging him tightly. Her tears soaked into the shoulder of the man who had been both father and mother. A quiet sob, shared without shame.

Anika stepped forward too, silent but present wrapping her arms around them both.

Three souls.

One silence.

One love.

Two girls…..raised as one soul. Bound not just by blood, but by something even holier than fate.

"I'll keep it safe, Papa," Usha whispered.

Then....something stirred inside her. A soft knock of curiosity.

"But Papa... who was the nurse? The one who brought us into this world?"

Ameet hesitated. His eyes shifted......subtle, but enough.

Roopa answered first. "Leave that... it was long ago."

"No," Usha said gently, but firmly. "Please. I want to thank her. If she's still around."

Roopa looked down. Wringing her hands like prayer beads.

"She's... not here anymore. She passed away."

Anika, ever tender, asked softly, "What was her name?"

Ameet opened his mouth. "Her name was Na—"

"Namu," Roopa interrupted, quick as lightning. "Her name was Namu."

Anika smiled faintly, pressing the photo of their mother to her chest. "Namu...thank you. You saved my sister."

Usha's voice followed, quiet and teary. "You saved my sister too."

Across the room, Roopa and Ameet exchanged a glance.

A look of shared weight.

Of secrets too old to confess.

Of truths that sat in the throat like stones.

Anika kissed the photo gently. Her face calmer now....but her silence carried a sorrow too deep for words.

Usha looked at the picture again. Something always felt... off. A detail she had noticed, but never asked about.

"Papa," she asked, eyes still on the image. "There's a date written behind this photo. I always wanted to ask."

Anika turned it around carefully. "1st October," she read aloud.

"What's special about that day?" Usha asked.

Ameet's breath hitched.

Roopa answered too quickly. "It's just a date, beta."

"But it's not anyone's birthday," Usha continued. "We've never celebrated anything on 1st October. Our birthday is 28th August."

Ameet cleared his throat. "Maybe... maybe it was the day we picked up the photo from the studio. Or when it was taken. Don't overthink."

He turned, a bit too fast.

"I'm hungry. Come. Let's eat."

"Wash your hands, Papa!" Usha called after him, trying to laugh, to lighten what had darkened. "We'll serve the food."

He nodded and left the room, his back straight.....but his silence louder than the rain that had once fallen

Roopa didn't follow.

She stayed. Alone with the photograph.

Her trembling fingers brushed the date gently....*1st October*.....as though stroking the past itself.

And then, when no one else was listening...

She whispered something the walls already knew.

A name.

A memory.

A truth still buried in the rain.

And softly, as if speaking to the silence itself ..... And still, she stayed quiet.

As if some stories were never meant to be spoken....only remembered.

Chapter 5

Steam curled on the mirror, warping the edges of a face that liked his lines defined.

Vikrant Rai stepped out of the bathroom, towel slung over his shoulder, water clinging to his collarbones like unfinished sentences. He rolled his shoulders, cracked his neck, and walked into the room with the precision of a man who made to-do lists in his sleep.

And then….he stopped.

The air had changed.

It was still… but strange. Heavy, like memory. Sharp, like incense. The scent of burning mustard oil, of camphor curling into the corners, brushed against him like a prayer he hadn't asked for.

His eyes darted across the room, landing quickly on the source.

A diya, glowing quietly on his bedside table.

Small.

Sacred.

Uninvited.

Its flame flickered with calm defiance, casting a slow dance of shadows against the minimalist walls he preferred cold and plain.

His jaw tightened.

"Karishma!" he bellowed, snatching the diya, the metal warm against his fingers. He stormed downstairs, the flame shaking with every step but refusing to die.

✦ ∞ ✦

Karishma was decorating the banister with marigolds, her wrists jingling, her eyes bright with the kind of chaos only younger sisters could wear with pride.

She looked up and grinned. "Good morning,…. Brother! Why are you already fighting the universe?"

Vikrant held out the diya like it had insulted him. "Who put this in my room? I told you I hate this smell!"

She took it gently from his hand, cradling it like an apology he didn't know how to give.

"Panditji's suggestion," she said sweetly. "Seven days. A diya in your room every morning…..for clarity, peace, and positivity."

"I already went to the temple that night. I called the pandit like you wanted. I even tied that stupid red thread." He lifted his arm….the thread dangling like a memory he didn't believe in.

"But this smell?" He shook his head. "I can't wake up choking on devotion."

He turned on his heel.

But moments later, from the top of the stairs…..his voice thundered again.

"I can still smell it! Karishma, don't ever do this again!"

Karishma just smiled, turning back to her marigolds. The scent of sandalwood and rebellion followed her like perfume.

Anjali Rai sat with quiet poise. Her hands rested on her lap; her shawl folded with meticulous elegance. The wheels of her chair barely creaked anymore.

She looked up. "Why is Vikrant shouting this time?"

Karishma grinned without looking up from her phone. "Because a diya dared to disturb his personal ecosystem. We almost lost him to peace."

Just then, the front door clicked open.

Kunaal Rai stepped inside, checking his watch out of habit, his eyes always five minutes ahead of the room.

He sniffed the air. "Why does it smell like a temple in here?"

"Your daughter's lighting fires," Anjali said dryly. "Sacred ones."

Kunaal looked at Karishma. "Did your mother take her blood pressure tablet?"

"I did," Anjali replied before Karishma could roll her eyes.

"And what are you doing?" he asked his daughter.

Karishma smirked. "I was busy lighting positivity in a very negative bedroom."

Later, Karishma…. unfazed, made a quiet call to Panditji.

"Pandit ji, Vikrant is refusing the diya," she said, half-laughing. "You'd think we asked him to do Tapasya in the Himalayas."

The pandit chuckled. "No problem beta, Perhaps the house itself needs something stronger. What do you think of a Maha-pooja?"

Karishma lit up. "Awesome, What dates are good?"

She waited as pages turned. The soft rustle sounded like fate flipping through itself.

"Three options," he said. "16th September 23rd September… or… 1st October."

Karishma walked to the dining table, where Vikrant now sat scrolling through emails, sipping black coffee like it owed him answers.

"Bro? Pandit ji says 16th, 23rd, or 1st October for the Maha-pooja. Can we confirm?"

He didn't look up. "I'm packed all month. Australian clients, investor meetings. Honestly, let's skip it."

Anjali spoke then….soft, firm. "What about 1st October? That's free, isn't it?"

Vikrant paused.

Something inside him almost stirred. A flicker.

But it passed.

"I guess... yeah. It's open."

Karishma smiled and raised the phone. "Pandit ji, we'll go with 1st October. Please block it."

There was a pause on the other end. Not long, but not nothing.

Then the pandit replied slowly.

"1st October... yes. That would be perfect."

✦ ∞ ✦

Behind them, half-hidden in the hallway, Kunaal Rai had returned.

He had heard the date.

And the date had stopped him.

1st October.

The words froze in the air. He didn't move. He didn't breathe.

His gaze rose....slowly.....toward the sepia-toned family portrait that hung above the pooja room.

It was a beautiful frame.

Dustless. Ageless.

His eyes narrowed.

His jaw tightened.

"No," he said sharply.

Everyone turned.

"Ask the pandit for another date," Kunaal added, quieter now but firm. "Not the first."

Karishma blinked. "But Papa, what's wrong with....."

Before she could finish, Vikrant....without lifting his eyes...spoke again.

"No. It's fine. Book 1st October."

The room fell into a strange silence.

Long. Heavy. The kind that left a taste behind.

No one noticed the way Kunaal's expression changed.

Not anger.

Not fear.

Something else.

A shadow pulling at the corners of his face. His fingers curled slightly against his palm.

His breath shallowed.

His eyes flicked….once…..toward the pooja room, then to the stairs, as if something were waiting for him at the top.

Outside, a soft wind stirred the curtains.

It slipped into the house through the open window.

It carried with it the smell of camphor... and the echo of something older.

A truth.

Unspoken.

But not forgotten.

A truth named 1st October.

Chapter 6

Usha stood at the entrance of Satish's Shop, her fingers circling the silver chain around her neck... her mother's chain.

Recovered like a forgotten prayer.

Returned like fate hadn't forgotten her.

And yet... something about it felt too exact.

Too precisely timed.

Too carefully wrapped in coincidence.

Inside her mind, the memory returned... sharp and strange.

That day at the temple.

The heat. The ache. The emptiness of her neck.

She had been searching.... desperate, frantic .... when the boy appeared.

A stranger. Young. Still.

He hadn't spoken much.

Just stepped out of nowhere, like an echo taking form.

And handed her a folded piece of paper.

"For missing things," he had said,

before vanishing into the crowd like smoke.

She had thought it was a joke.

But days later... the chain had arrived.

Wrapped carefully.

Without a name.

Without a sender.

It felt like someone had played every move

just to place the chain back in her hands.

She stepped inside.

The bell above the door chimed..... not cheerfully, but like a quiet warning.

Satish looked up.

His grin, usually easy and bright, flickered for a breath.

"Usha ji! Everything alright?" he asked, wiping his hands on a cloth as he came around the counter.

She smiled .... polite, calm.

But her eyes held something sharper than curiosity.

"Yes.... I just came to say thank you. I received the chain yesterday." Then, a pause. "And to ask... did you ever find out who returned it?"

Satish blinked....only for a second. Then he scratched his head, voice casual.

"Ah, well... one of our staff must've found it near the temple. It was in the lost-and-found box. Probably someone just passing by."

Usha tilted her head slightly. Still watching him.

"It's strange how perfectly the contest matched. The location. The date. The description."

Satish chuckled, but it didn't land right. "Fate has strange hands, doesn't it? Some people don't like being known. They do their part and vanish quietly."

She studied his face.

Behind the warmth in his tone, something flickered.

"Well," she said at last, voice softer, "thank you anyway. This chain... means the world to my family."

After she left, Satish exhaled and dropped into his chair behind the counter.

He opened his phone.

One message still blinked on the screen:

Did she take it?

He didn't reply.

He just smiled...slow, knowing.....And locked the screen.

✦ ∞ ✦

Vikrant sat alone, surrounded by silence that felt too loud.

The clock ticked above him, marking time that refused to move.

His eyes stared at the same front page for ten minutes.

He hadn't turned the page.

His thoughts circled the same face.

Usha.

The girl with the storm behind her silence.

The girl who had walked away once…..and never looked back.

Karishma passed by the open door. She paused, leaned against the frame, arms folded and knowing.

"Still pretending you're not serious?" she asked, amused.

Vikrant blinked, slowly returning to the present. "I'm serious."

"Serious about what?" she stepped in with a smirk.

He looked away. "When did you get here?"

"Oh, so now you're talking to yourself?" she teased. "Or hiding something from your sweet sister?"

He didn't answer.

That silence told her more than words ever could.

She narrowed her eyes playfully. "Thinking about someone? Maybe… a girl?"

He scoffed. But it lacked weight.

"Karishma, you know me. Business only. There's no girl."

"Yes, Bro," she said with a raised brow. "That's why you've been reading the blank page of file since I came upstairs."

She walked away, laughing.

But Vikrant stayed.

Alone.

With a chain.

A name.

And a silence that kept echoing.

✦ ∞ ✦

The television murmured in the background.

Anjali Rai sat still in her wheelchair, her eyes fixed and sharp beneath the veil of age.

A breaking headline cut through the quiet:

"Unidentified body found in forest…..estimated 7 days old."

Anjali's fingers gripped the armrest.

Her eyes didn't blink.

Just then, Kunaal walked in, removing his watch like clockwork.

"How are you feeling today?"

She didn't answer right away. Her voice was low….almost distant.

"They found a body. In the forest. Said it's been lying there for a week."

Kunaal's steps faltered for a breath.

Then resumed.

Anjali turned her wheelchair toward him.

"Last week," she said slowly, "I…I saw blood on your coat."

Kunaal looked at her. "That was nothing. The car hit a stray dog."

"There was no damage to the car," she replied calmly. "Vikrant drives it too. He would've noticed."

His face changed.

"Are you accusing me?"

"I'm asking questions," she said, her voice now cold. "Because silence doesn't erase what we remember."

He said nothing.

But the silence in the room grew darker.

✦ ∞ ✦

Anika tossed the newspaper aside.

"Of course. Karishma Rai tops the medical entrance. Is there anything she doesn't win?"

Roopa Devi stirred the curry quietly. "She has her life, dear daughter. We have ours."

Anika sighed. "I wanted to be a doctor."

Usha entered, a glass of water in hand. "Doctors don't just treat. They save people. They change stories."

Roopa didn't respond.

Usha leaned against the table. "Someone saved us too. Right? Namu... she was a nurse?"

Roopa's stirring slowed.

"Yes," she said. "But Usha... don't say her name again."

"But why?" Usha frowned. "She helped us...."

"Leave it," Roopa snapped, sharper now. "She moved away. Long ago. It's forgotten."

The silence that followed wasn't ordinary.

It sat heavy in the room.

Like something buried.

Like memory refusing to stay dead.

Just then, Ameet entered. Usha turned to him, opening her palm. "It broke again."

He looked at the chain. "Same joint?"

She nodded.

He smiled faintly. "We'll fix it."

But his eyes didn't quite meet hers.

Usha lay awake.

The darkness pressed against her skin like questions.

Roopa's voice.

Papa's silence.

The way the word Namu tasted like fear in the house.

She turned toward Anika, sleeping softly beside her.

She reached out. Held her gently.

"I wish we could go back," she whispered. "Just once. To see Ma. To ask the things we were never told."

A single tear slid into the night.

In the side room, Roopa sat at the edge of the bed, staring into a past that refused to stay still.

Ameet stood by the window, eyes fixed on nothing – or maybe something only he could see.

"They're asking about the woman" she said quietly.

He didn't turn.

"They always would."

Their silence... spoke louder than any truth.

"That woman saved both," Ameet said, voice low, words weighed down.

"She was the one who saved them. And yet we don't speak her name. That hurts me more than anything."

Roopa looked up; eyes lined with a grief she had long stopped naming.

"No," she said softly.

"You saved them.

And that woman just….."

Before she could finish, Ameet cut in.

"Stop," he said, sharper than before. We have to bury it again…. just like we've been doing for years. I don't know why this wind keeps blowing the dust off….. again."

A long pause filled the room – too long to be comfortable, too short to forget.

Then he added, almost a whisper:

"Some truths are like dry sand …. one gust of wind, and they're gone."

✦ ∞ ✦

As the early morning sun filtered through the trees, Usha stepped into the temple. Her mother's chain rested against her heart, warm beneath her shawl.

The city was still asleep.

She lit a diya.

Folded her hands.

"Devi Maa," she whispered. "Anika wants to become a doctor. We don't have the means. But she has the heart. Please… show me a way."

She turned to leave.

And then……A voice.

Familiar.

Unexpected.

"You come here often now."

She turned.

Vikrant.

He stood still.

The usual hardness in his eyes was gone – replaced by something else.

Something… softer.

Usha didn't blink.

Her fingers brushed the silver chain at her neck.

"You rich people can buy pandits," she said, voice steady, "but you can't buy God from us. Yes, I come here. To speak with my Devi Ma. And I believe she's with me… no matter who caused what, or what the world throws my way. She will protect."

He took a small step forward. Not fully.

Just enough to mean something.

"I didn't mean to…" he said.

"I was just… going to the office. And…..thought…"

He paused.

Didn't know how to finish.

Didn't need to.

Because in that moment…. there was no Rai.

No ego.

No pride.

Just a soul.

Just a heart.

And a silence that spoke louder than words.

"You rich people pray for your business, "Usha said softly.

"Maybe that's why you're here. Maybe you have an important meeting today…"

Then, quieter …. kinder …. she added;

"And yes…. you have the right to pray to Devi Maa.

She helps everyone."

Vikrant remained silent.

He hadn't stopped the car to pray for a deal.

He hadn't come for a pandit.

He hadn't come to prove anything.

He didn't even believe.

But something inside him had whispered…..Maybe she'll be there.

The girl with the silver chain.

And she is.

He didn't say a word.

But in that stillness, his silence was the loudest truth he had ever offered.

Chapter 7

Usha walked back from the temple, her shawl fluttering behind her like a thought that wouldn't leave her alone. The prayer on her lips had faded, but something else echoed louder now.

Vikrant's voice. His calm gaze. His unexpected softness.

But her heart fought back.

"Rich men have ego," she muttered under her breath. "They think they can buy anything. Even a blessing. Even the pandit. First, they make mistakes. Then they return with folded hands."

Her lips pressed together.

She knew that look…..the kind that dressed sympathy in tailored shirts. The kind that reached out only after they'd already walked away.

Her phone buzzed.

Anika.

"Usha, Papa didn't eat anything. He left in a rush this morning."

Usha glanced around the street. "I'm near the market. I'll stop by the shop."

The scent of warm ghee and syrup greeted her …. as if the sweetness had found its own scent. Inside the sweet shop, her father stood over a large pot of bubbling syrup, carefully dipping golden jalebis with slow, practiced grace.

"Papa," Usha asked, stepping closer, "why didn't you eat?"

He looked up, sweat on his brow, kindness in his eyes.

"The shop key was with me. The other workers were waiting. I had some cookies with tea. That's enough."

Usha watched the jalebis swirling in the syrup.....circles within circles, golden patterns forming in silence.

"You make sweets the way you raised us," she said softly. "With patience… and love."

Ameet smiled faintly. "Here….pack some. Anika loves jalebi."

He wrapped them in newspaper, folding each corner with fatherly precision.

"But hide them from your Daadi," he whispered. "Her sugar was high last night."

Usha chuckled, tucking the parcel under her arm. But just as she turned to leave, her ears caught the low murmur of two old men sitting near the window.

"Forest… where they found the body?"

"Yes, near the old Rai factory."

"No one's gone there since it shut down. Cursed land. My father once saw a skeleton hand near that place."

Usha froze……like a river that had suddenly turned to ice.

A shiver traced its way down her spine, quiet but undeniable..

"Anika! Papa sent jalebi!" Usha called as she stepped inside.

From the kitchen, Anika shouted, "Hide some before Daadi sees!"

Too late.

Roopa entered with damp hands from the backyard. "Jalebi….?"

Anika giggled. "Daadi, your sugar level!"

"I only want one!" Roopa pouted like a child.

"No," Usha said, playfully stern. "Doctor Anika's orders."

As Usha opened it, her smile faltered.

The syrup-soaked sweet touched a headline.

A spiral of jalebi…. golden, sticky…..now curled over words soaked in red.

Sweetness kissing blood.

Like a spiral of sugar and silence…. now stained.

A headline bled through, like a ghost rising beneath it:

"…….well-known pandit Keval Lal… reported suicide…."

Usha's fingers trembled.

She turned slowly to Daadi.

"This….. this is the same pandit who was supposed to come for Anika's wedding."

Roopa's smile faded.

Her eyes searched for something….. memory, maybe. Or escape.

"I thought he died in an accident….." Usha whispered.

Anika's face turned pale.

"That day ruined everything," she whispered.

"The groom's family left. They said I was cursed… because a pandit died."

The jalebi now tasted like ash.

Warm, but hollow.

Sweet… but ruined.

At night, Usha sat by the window, watching the sky.

It was too still... like the calm before a storm.

Her fingers traced the chain around her neck…..her mother's memory, her unanswered question.

The factory.

The forest.

The nurse.

The suicide.

Each memory pulled at a thread buried deep in the seams of her life.

She turned to her sister sleeping nearby and pulled the blanket gently over her.

"I wish I could go back, Didi," she whispered. "Back to your wedding day. I'd fix it all. I swear I would."

✦ ∞ ✦

The television murmured in the background, another news update about the forest body.

Karishma walked in, carrying a bowl of night soup.

"Which forest are they talking about?" she asked.

Anjali glanced at the screen. "It's …. it's far."

But Vikrant, seated at the table with his planner open for tomorrow's meeting, looked up. "Isn't that near our old factory?"

No one answered.

His phone rang.

He picked up, eyes still on the planner.

"Reschedule all my meetings." He said, flatly.

"But sir….the international clients…"

"I said reschedule."

He hung up.

Anjali looked at him sharply. "More important than business?"

Vikrant stood slowly.

"Yes."

Anjali's heart skipped. For a second, she wondered….does he know?

About Kunal?

About the blood?

But Vikrant only smiled lightly.

"I'm planning something. Our Karishma topped the city. I want a celebration."

Anjali let out the breath she hadn't known she was holding. "Oh. That's… wonderful."

He smirked. "You looked like you thought I had a secret."

Before she could answer, Kunaal walked in.

"Yes. And now you have a party to host We need to start preparations tomorrow, and it's already late tonight.... so get some rest.."

Anjali met his gaze.

And behind her calm eyes…. questions stirred.

✦ ∞ ✦

Late at night, Usha sat by the window, the silver chain cold against her chest.

Its pendant….an infinity symbol, small and timeworn…..rested just above her heartbeat.

She looked out at the night sky, as if it might whisper the truth the living would not.

Somewhere between the scent of syrup and ink,

Between half-spoken stories and headlines wrapped around sweets….something was stirring.

The past wasn't a road behind them.

It was the ground beneath their feet.

And they were already standing in its centre.

Chapter 8

The scent of sugar and ghee wrapped around the sweet shop as if someone had let it drift freely into the air. Orange-yellow jalebis hissed in hot oil, curling into shape, their syrupy sheen catching evening light.

Ameet Rathi, kurta stained with sweetness, flipped the final batch into a tray. His hands moved with the care of a man who had spent his life raising daughters….with patience, gentleness, and quiet grace.

Just then, the shop owner rushed over, phone in hand. "Ameet Bhai! Rai House called again. The party has already started. We delivered everything except the sugar-free box for the lady of the house."

Ameet frowned, wiping his forehead. "For Mrs. Rai, right? I packed that already."

The shop owner held up the small gold-wrapped box. "They left this behind. Now who can take this?"

He looked over at Usha, who was arranging trays behind the counter.

"Usha beta…," he said, "can you take this to the Rai residence? Everyone else is gone. Just hand it over and come back. It's close."

Usha hesitated, her hand tightening around a spoon. "Papa… the Rai house?"

He nodded. "You'll be back in ten minutes."

She finally nodded, accepting the gold-wrapped box. Took the box in both hands …. and held it like something heavier than it looked.

✦ ∞ ✦

The Rai mansion shimmered with lights, its garden glowing with fairy lights and rich laughter. Guests clinked glasses, music floated on the air, and the walls of the house held years of legacy beneath their polish.

Usha stepped cautiously through the gates; the box gripped like a fragile truth. A servant spotted her and waved toward the house.

Karishma, dressed in green silk and gold bangles, descended the steps with the kind of elegance only privilege could afford.

"Oh….from the sweet shop?" she asked warmly.

Usha nodded. "Sugar-free jalebi."

"We were waiting for this! Come inside."

The marble floor under Usha's sandals felt like another world… too bright, too echoing. Her eyes skimmed over the gathering… until something quiet drew her gaze.

A hallway near the pooja room.

A wall lined with photographs.

She walked toward it, pulled by something she couldn't name.

There….between black-and-white frames and dusty factory portraits….one photo caught her eye.

A group picture. Factory workers lined up in front of a building.

The gate behind them read: *Rai Factory*.

She leaned in.

One woman stood beside a man in a golden frame.

Her face was slightly turned, her eyes soft…. lit with a kindness that tugged at something deep inside Usha.

Something about that woman…. felt like a whisper from a memory she never lived.

She wore a soft smile, the kind that felt like it had waited years to be remembered.

A silver chain glinted at her collarbone…. its pendant, an infinity symbol. The same shape. The same delicate curve of metal.

Usha stared.

The pendant was identical to that one she kept …. the one that once lay against her own chest.

Her fingers brushed it gently, as if seeking answers through touch alone.

That chain. That face.

The woman's features were gentle, framed by dark hair and the ease of someone at peace.

Usha didn't know her….or didn't think she did.

But something about her shimmered with familiarity.

As if the chain was trying to say something.

As if it recognized her…even if Usha couldn't.

Before she could think further, a voice cut through her stillness.

"Some memories."

She turned sharply.

Kunal Rai stood near the frame, hands in pockets, eyes unreadable.

Her voice shook. "What are these photos?"

Kunal stepped beside her, calm as always. "Old memories. My old factory days."

Usha's eyes didn't leave the photo. "That woman… she's wearing the same chain I have."

Kunal opened his mouth, but before he could speak….

"Hi."

Vikrant's voice.

She turned.

"You?"

Kunal raised a brow. "You two know each other?"

"Yes," Vikrant said.

"No," Usha said at the same time.

Vikrant cleared his throat. "We met… at the temple."

Kunal's smirk deepened. "You, at a temple? Really?"

Before Vikrant could respond, a voice called from across the hall.

"Kunal! Come meet the others!"

With a nod, Kunal left.

Usha turned back to the photograph, unsettled. Her fingers itched to reach out and touch the glass.

Vikrant moved beside her. Quieter than usual.

Karishma returned with a small envelope. "Here's the payment. And, Thank you."

Vikrant looked at Usha. "Stay. It's just a party."

"I have to return the change to owner," she said quickly. "And it's getting dark."

"I'll drop you."

She hesitated.

Karishma offered a soft smile. "Please. He'll get you to shop safe."

Usha nodded.

The car hummed down quiet streets, its headlights chasing the shadows.

Vikrant drove in silence…..until finally:

"You weren't wearing the chain today."

Usha blinked. "You noticed?"

He kept his eyes on the road.

"The first time I saw you… you were wearing it. That chain. Have you….. got it back?"

She smiled faintly.

"It keeps breaking. I left it at home today. I can't afford to lose it again."

Then suddenly…a pause. A breath caught.

"But…" Usha turned to him, her voice sharper now.

"What did you say? How do you know I got my chain back."

Vikrant stiffened, hands tightening slightly on the steering wheel.

He tried to mask the slip, forcing his tone into something casual....almost annoyed.

"How do I know it's your chain?" he muttered.

A deflection.

A poor one.

Usha turned toward the window, the question still echoing inside her.

Neither of them spoke again.

When they reached the shop, Usha stepped out.

She paused, turned back. "Thank you. For the ride."

He didn't respond.

But he didn't drive away either .... Not until she had disappeared inside.

"Who dropped you?" Ameet asked, lifting his head.

"The man hosting the party," Usha said. "His sister asked him to."

Ameet only nodded.

"Your Daadi and Anika are waiting. Go on."

As Usha walked home through the moonlight, her thoughts spiraled.

The photograph.

The chain.

Kunaal's words.

And beneath it all....Vikrant.

She tried to shake the thought off.

Did he help return the chain?

"No" she told herself.

Why would he?

He didn't even know how to speak gently.

He had ruined her sister's wedding.

He didn't believe in feelings, in rituals, in memory.

So how could he possibly understand what that chain meant?

And yet...

He knew.

He had noticed she wasn't wearing it.

He mentioned the chain.

And somehow …. he knew it had come back to her.

She stopped under the dim glow of a streetlamp.

The chain wasn't on her neck. She hadn't worn it today.

It sat tucked away in her drawer – safe, quiet, almost forgotten.

But his words hadn't been a guess.

They had been too certain.

Why would someone who doesn't care... notice what I'm not wearing?

And more importantly... How did he know it had returned?

She touched the space just above her collarbone…. bare.

But the question pressed deeper than the chain ever had.

She walked on, slower now, as if each step carried her closer to something she hadn't yet dared to name.

As Vikrant stepped through the gate, a boy came running.

"Sir! Someone left this for you."

Vikrant raised a brow. "For me?"

The boy nodded, handing him a plain envelope.

It had no stamp. No sender.

Just his name.

Vikrant opened it slowly.

Inside….one torn piece of paper.

A single sentence:

"It all starts from the factory."

His eyes narrowed.

"You saw who left this?"

"No, sir. It was near the gate."

The street was quiet. Still.

Vikrant tucked the note into his pocket.

Party music still played in the background as he stepped inside. He tossed the envelope onto a side table and headed toward the garden.

Karishma saw him do it … her heart fluttered.

Was it from that Jalebi girl?

She picked it up.

Opened it.

"It all starts from the factory."

Her smile disappeared.

She hurried to find Anjali, who sat with a glass of apple juice by the window.

"Maa…" Karishma whispered. "That forest body. The factory. And now this note. What's happening?"

Anjali's expression shifted… Slowly…. as her eyes settled on the message written on the note.

Her fingers tightened around the glass.

"Some stories," she said softly, "are better left where they belong."

"But Maa…"

Anjali didn't answer.

She stared past the window, into the dark.

And somewhere…deep inside her…. A date stirred.

A name.

A memory wrapped in fire.

She whispered it like a curse no one else should hear:

"Not again… not after all these years."

Chapter 9

The report was still warm from the printer when Inspector Rajeev took it. He didn't sit. He stood by the table, flipping through the first few lines…his eyes narrowing.

Partial document recovered: *Anika Rathi's Kundli.*

Fingertip traces: *Pandit Keval Lal.*

He paused.

A chill moved through the room….subtle, but certain.

Rajeev muttered under his breath,

"A pandit leaves to conduct a wedding….. ends up in the dark forest. And someone else dies that same day.

No one goes that deep in … and the body…… found seven days later. Cause of death: heart attack."

He didn't wait.

He pulled out a fresh case folder, wrote across the front:

RATHI FAMILY - FOREST INCIDENT

and slipped the report inside.

Then, without hesitation,

he drew a red line through the suicide report filed days ago, and in bold, heavy ink, he wrote:

REINVESTIGATE - Potential link to forest body.

Foul play suspected.

The knock wasn't loud, but it brought everything to a pause.

Roopa opened the door. She didn't flinch at the sight of the officer. Behind her, Usha and Anika stood quiet in the hallway.

"We're revisiting a few files," the officer said. "Some routine questions about your daughter's wedding day."

Roopa gave a brief nod and stepped back.

The officer checked his page.

"Did Pandit Keval Lal take anything from your home that evening?"

Roopa frowned slightly. "Yes. He asked for Anika's Kundli. Said he wanted to double-check the wedding Muhurat."

"Did he return it?"

She shook her head. "No. He never came back. We waited. Later, someone from the temple said he had died."

The officer scribbled, closed the pad, and left with a polite nod.

The door clicked shut. The house fell still.

Anika spoke first, her voice low. "Then how did the Kundli end up in the forest?"

Usha didn't answer. She stood near the edge of the hall, her fingers tracing the edge of her kurta.

She wanted to have an answer. She wanted to make it all make sense…..for Anika, for herself.

But nothing about this felt simple anymore.

The chain lay coiled on her pillow, as if it didn't belong anywhere else. The pendant caught the light …. not from the bulb overhead, but from the moon slipping in through the window.

A cold, quiet glow.

Usha lay on the bed beside Anika, her eyes fixed on the chain.

She didn't reach for it.

Not tonight.

She just kept staring.

Her mind kept circling back to the photo in the Rai house … the one placed near the pooja room.

The factory workers.

That woman.

That chain.

It was identical.

Usha had never seen that woman before.

And yet……something about her felt familiar.

Uncomfortably familiar.

She lay down slowly, the chain still resting between her and the blanket.

The one on her pillow…. hers.

The one in the photo …as if it was calling her.

As if both were parts of the same story….. and she had only one piece.

She faced the wall, but didn't close her eyes.

Sleep didn't come easily.

It came only when her body gave up trying to understand what her mind couldn't explain.

Late at night in police station, Rajeev reopened the file labelled "Death: Pandit Keval Lal."

It was still new signed off just few days ago.

He glanced through the original incident report again. It was too neat.

Too quiet for a man found dead in his own home… with a spiritual document missing.

Rajeev's voice was barely a murmur.

"What looked like suicide… now feels like murder."

He pulled out the summary and marked the bottom corner:

Blood sample ….. unknown. Not yet matched.

Then added a single line above it:

Link to forest case. Re-examine timeline.

✦ ∞ ✦

Vikrant hadn't opened the envelope again. It lay on the desk like it was watching him.

Instead, Vikrant opened his browser and typed: *Rai Factory* into the search bar.

Old news clippings came up. Faded photos. Articles about textile exports and machinery upgrades.

Then the rest.

A blog post: *The Factory That Whispers. Rumours of screams at night. A girl in red, seen walking near the boilers.*

One forum entry claimed the factory was built on an old graveyard. Another referenced a string of suicides in the early 2000s.

And buried deep in a local industry blog was the only formal mention:

Rai Mill shut down after an internal incident. Records not retained.

Vikrant leaned back in his chair.

He didn't say anything.

But he didn't need to.

This wasn't a place forgotten by time.

It was hidden...deliberately.

Morning light slipped through the sheer curtains of the Rai house. The tea tray sat untouched.

Karishma scrolled through her phone, eyes distant.

"You're glued to that screen," Vikrant said, trying to break the silence.

She smiled faintly. "Just replying to someone special I missed at the party."

Anjali sat quietly beside them. She hadn't said a word all morning.

Then the house servant stepped in. "Inspector Rajeev is here."

Rajeev entered with a file under his arm. Calm, precise.

"Kunaal Rai," Rajeev said evenly. "May I ask where you were on the evening of 13th September?"

Kunaal raised a brow. "Why?"

Rajeev opened the folder with calm precision.

"We've received CCTV footage. A parked car near Pandit Keval Lal's residence captured your vehicle. You and your driver were seen entering at 5:05 p.m. You both left twenty minutes later."

He flipped to the next sheet. "At 5:37, the pandit's wife returned home. He was already dead. There was also an unknown blood sample found in the room."

Across the room, Vikrant looked up sharply.

"You went to the pandit?"

"Yes," Kunaal replied, unfazed.

"Your mother and Karishma wanted you to meet the pandit, so I thought I'd go see him."

Rajeev's gaze stayed steady. "Was he alright when you left?"

"He was alive," Kunaal said.

Rajeev lowered his voice slightly.

"We found a few drops of blood on the floor of his room."

Kunaal reached into his pocket and calmly pulled out a handkerchief.

"Narayan cut his hand."

"How?"

"A stray dog ran across the road," he said.

"Narayan tried to pull it away and scraped his palm."

Rajeev nodded once. "We'll need to speak to Narayan. And test the blood sample."

"Of course."

"Did you visit the family after the death?"

"We did. Paid our respects."

Rajeev closed the folder. "We'll continue this later."

He left with a quiet nod.

The moment stretched in the stillness that followed.

No one moved.

The air felt heavier than before.

Anjali sat in her wheelchair, unmoving…. but not unnoticed.

She hadn't spoken a word throughout the exchange.

But now, her fingers curled slightly against the armrest.

She didn't look at Kunaal.

She didn't need to.

Her silence said everything.

And in that silence … layered with history, betrayal, and knowledge she hadn't yet spoken …. she became the quiet the room couldn't ignore.

And still, she stayed quiet.

✦ ∞ ✦

Evening had settled like ash.

Vikrant stood in front of the photo wall. The same one Usha had paused at.

The factory. The workers. The woman with the silver chain.

And his father. Younger. Smiling.

He didn't touch the frame.

Just stared.

He hadn't seen it before. Not like this.

Not as a beginning.

Outside, the wind shifted.

A slow breath moved through the streets.

Not loud.

Not sharp.

But enough to carry things.

Somewhere beyond streetlights and shopfronts and houses with locked doors… the forest still waited.

Chapter 10

The morning sun spilled softly over rooftops and rusted gates, touching the city's quiet corners with pale gold. Usha stepped outside, sandals pressing into the warm earth, dupatta pulled snug across her shoulders. The sky was clear, but inside her, clouds moved differently.

Since the pandit's death, her thoughts hadn't been still. The wedding that never happened. The Kundli found where no one had taken it. The forest. The silence. The chain.

She didn't believe in coincidences anymore.

The temple smelled of incense and burnt ghee. Aarti had just ended, and soft bells still echoed in the air. Usha folded her hands before the goddess, placing a diya at the marble steps. The flame flickered against the breeze, steady despite the world.

She turned toward the elder pandit sitting near the arch...his white beard moved gently with the wind, his eyes clear despite age.

"Pandit ji..." she began, softly. "Do you know why Keval Lal... ended his life?"

The priest's gaze dropped. His fingers paused over the rosary beads.

"He was a quiet man. Gentle. No debts. No fights. No enemies. But sometimes..." He paused, searching for words. "Some people carry weight inside that others never see."

Usha nodded slowly. The answer didn't settle anything. If anything, it made her feel heavier.

"I hope the police find the truth," she said.

As she turned to go, her eyes caught a familiar figure. Satish stood beside a tall, graceful woman placing marigolds on the tray. Her braid hung over one shoulder. Her expression was sharp, watchful.

Usha approached. "Namaste, Satish Bro."

Satish jumped, startled. "Oh! Usha ji…namaste, namaste!"

The wife of Satish turned. "Who is she?"

Satish hesitated. "She's… uh… a friend of a friend."

Then added, too quickly, "I mean, she was the contest winner."

Usha's eyes narrowed slightly. "You just said 'friend of a friend.' What did that mean?"

He scratched his head, forcing a laugh. "I just meant the item you lost… it was returned by someone. Someone I didn't know. Or you didn't. That's why… friend of a friend."

The explanation stumbled over itself, like a lie dressed as confusion.

Usha didn't argue. She just gave a quiet smile.

"Namaste, Bhabhi."

And she walked away….without turning back. But something in her chest had shifted.

✦ ∞ ✦

On the way home, she passed a small bookstore she'd never noticed before. A narrow glass window displayed stacks of exam guides and second-hand textbooks.

Inside, behind the counter, stood Anika….her head lowered, flipping through a worn medical prep book.

Usha stepped in.

The air smelled of dry paper and ink. Wooden shelves leaned under the weight of used books. She moved quietly through the aisles.

Anika looked up. "Didi? What are you doing here?"

"I saw you through the window."

"I'm just checking some prep books. Maybe I can get a scholarship if I try. You know fees are hard... but ...but books are a start."

Usha smiled and hugged her sister gently. "We'll figure it out. Devi Maa is watching."

As they moved toward the counter, something on the bottom shelf caught Usha's eye. A thick, dust-covered book with the spine almost torn. She pulled it out.

History of the Forest and Factory – by Samar Dev

The name struck something inside her.

She turned the cover. The pages crackled like old leaves.

"This forest is not just trees and roots. It holds bones, silence, and stories too long buried.

It began with a fire. Some say it was man. Others, God."

Usha's hand paused.

Anika peered over her shoulder.

"Looks like a local myth book."

Usha shook her head slowly, eyes fixed on the cover.

"No. I've seen this man before."

Anika raised an eyebrow. "Where?"

Usha's voice dropped, uncertain.

"I....I don't know. Maybe somewhere in the Rai house. Maybe in one of the factory worker photos. But I can't remember where."

The shopkeeper, having overheard, stepped closer.

"That one's been here for years. Never sold. Self-printed. People say the writer wasn't a real author, just some reporter. He vanished."

Usha didn't let go of the book. Her fingers gripped it tighter.

"I'm taking it."

Anika laughed softly.

"When did you start reading books?"

Usha gave a faint smile.

"I still don't like books. But...this one's different."

She looked down at the worn cover, her thumb brushing the edges as if the pages were breathing.

Then, barely a whisper… "This isn't a storybook. Not really."

She held it like it held something back …. something meant only for her.

And as they walked to the counter, the light caught the spine of the book just right.

Old. Faded. Waiting.

Because some books are bought.

And some books…. find you.

✦ ∞ ✦

The house was quiet. Anika had fallen asleep beside her textbooks. The book lay on Usha's lap, open beneath the glow of a table lamp.

"An ancient forest tribe believed their ancestors lived in trees. Each tree held a name. Each gust of wind carried a voice."

She flipped the page.

An illustration glimmered in the light….. a pendant. A twisted infinity symbol.

She froze.

It was the same as her mother's chain.

"Symbol of the Forest Tribe. Said to protect the bearer through bloodlines."

She looked down. The chain lay beside her pillow, broken but still whole.

She turned another page.

"Long before the Rai Factory was built, a tribe lived on that land.
Then, one day…. they vanished.
No trace. No farewell.
Some say the land was cursed.
Others believe they returned to the soil … becoming part of it.

Years later, the factory rose over what was once sacred ground.

But the soil never forgot. "

Her eyes raced across the text.

"Workers reported strange visions. Voices in the machinery.

In 2003, a journalist ... Rekha Kapoor ... uncovered tribal relics buried near the foundation: ritual blades, bark carvings, altar remains.

She vanished on October 1st.

Last seen entering the forest.

Some say the tribe took her back.

Others... say it was the ghosts. "

Usha slammed the book shut, her heartbeat thudding loud in her ears.

The room felt suddenly smaller.

Her calendar sat beside the lamp, quiet and unbothered – except for the red circle drawn around the date.

October 1st.

She looked at her reflection in the mirror.

And for the first time, she didn't just see Usha Rathi.

She saw the end of a story that had started long before her name was ever written.

She reached for the silver chain …. the one her mother left her.

Held it tight, her fingers trembling slightly.

And then, barely above a breath, she whispered:

"Why does it feel like you're trying to say something? "

"Why does it feel…. like someone wants me to find something?

She paused.

The chain was cold ….. but it pulsed like it remembered more than she did.

"But what is it?"

She didn't know.

Not yet.

But in that moment, Usha no longer felt like the reader of the story.

She felt like the page being turned.

✦ ∞ ✦

Dust danced in the morning air. Teacups sat untouched on the glass table of the Rai mansion's vast living room.

Karishma guided Anjali back to her room, just off the main living space.

The wheelchair moved smoothly across the marble floor.

Anjali sat upright ..... quiet, composed, her expression unreadable.

Morning light touched her face, not to fade her, but to reveal her stillness.

She didn't speak.

But she noticed everything.

Kunal walked past them, phone in hand.

"Start the car," he said to Narayan. "We're leaving."

Inside, Karishma opened the window. A breeze slipped through the curtain, knocking something off the shelf.

A photograph fluttered to the floor.

She picked it up. A young man stared back....smiling, thin, eyes sharp with ambition.

"Ma...who is this?"

Anjali's hand trembled slightly as she took the photo.

"Your Mamu. Samar."

Karishma stared. "Samar Mamu? You never spoke about him."

Anjali looked out the window.

"He disappeared a long time ago."

Karishma's voice dropped. "Disappeared?"

Anjali didn't answer right away. Then softly, she said, "Some stories come when they're ready."

Karishma looked back down at the photo.

The man's face was unfamiliar, but something in the way he stood….felt like a shadow she'd seen in her mother's silence.

She whispered his name under her breath: *"Samar Mamu."*

And she didn't know … at that same moment, in another part of the city, Usha was turning a page beneath a flickering lamp, her thumb frozen over a name printed on a dusty book cover: *Samar Dev.*

Two daughters.

Two houses.

Two timelines, unknowingly walking toward the same breath of truth.

And between them, a silence that had waited long enough.

Chapter 11

Vikrant sat at the edge of his bed, holding his wristwatch, letting it roll slowly between his fingers.

But his eyes weren't on time.

They were somewhere else… lost in memory, stuck on a face.

Not just any face.

A girl.

A chain.

A chain that had once meant nothing… forgotten in a drawer…. but now echoed with weight the moment he saw it resting against her skin.

He let out a dry laugh.

"Usha."

She came to him in flashes… her silence,

her eyes, the quiet way she carried herself without knowing the effect she left behind.

He tried to shake the thoughts off.

But they stayed.

Like a sentence that hadn't found its full stop.

Suddenly, he stood.

Tossed the watch onto the bed.

"Who cares," he muttered."

"She's…she's just some girl."

But his voice didn't match his eyes.

And even he knew it.

His phone buzzed.

A message from Satish.

She met me at the temple again today.

Vikrant began typing, almost without thinking:

What did she say....

His fingers hovered over the send button..... paused.

The words blinked back at him, too eager, too telling.

He didn't press send.

His hand lowered slowly, and the screen dimmed with the weight of what he didn't ask.

He told himself it didn't matter.

But his silence said otherwise.

He locked the phone and slipped it into his pocket....as if that could lock her away too. But the thoughts of her moved freely inside his mind .... uninvited, uncontainable, like light seeping through cracks, he didn't know he had.

He stood still for a moment, jaw tense.

Then he walked away, like he hadn't just read her name.

Like it didn't echo.

He told himself he was trying to forget her.

That....she was just another unfinished sentence.

But somewhere deep down, he knew he wasn't forgetting.

He was remembering .... without knowing why.

And trying, so hard, not to care.

In Karishma's room, the door stood half open.

She sat cross-legged on a chair near the bed, a textbook open in front of her... but unread.

Vikrant passed by and noticed Karishma sitting in silence, lost in thought.

He paused at the doorway.

"What are you doing?" he asked gently.

Karishma looked up. "Trying to study. Actually…just…just thinking."

"About?"

She hesitated. "I found out today Ma had a brother. Samar. And nobody told me. Not you. Not her. Not Papa."

Vikrant stepped inside slowly. "She mentioned him to me once. Said he was close. But Papa didn't like him. Said he wrote something… something against the family, something against the business."

Karishma's voice sharpened. "So that made him vanish from our story?"

"She never spoke of him again," Vikrant said. "It was like he never existed."

Karishma crossed the room slowly, her expression unreadable.

Then she turned and walked back, holding the photograph out carefully.

"He did," she said softly. "And I think Ma still remembers him. "

Vikrant took the photo. His fingers stopped mid-air. "Where have I seen this face before…?"

The answer lingered just beyond reach.

✦ ∞ ✦

Usha sat on her bed, the book open in her lap.

Her thumb traced the edges of the author's photograph…. worn, faded, but unsettlingly familiar.

"Why do you look familiar?" she whispered.

His face stirred something in her…. a memory, perhaps.

Or maybe something she hadn't yet lived but already started to feel.

And then….quietly, almost at the same moment, in two different corners of the city, two voices… Usha's and Vikrant's… spoke the same words.

"Satish's shop."

A few moments later, Roopa entered the room, her dupatta slung over one shoulder.

Usha, startled, instinctively slipped the book beneath her pillow.

She didn't think.

Her body moved before her mind could catch up… as if hiding it meant holding onto something sacred.

Then, with a steady but heavy voice, she asked, "Did you take your medicine, Daadi?"

Roopa nodded. "Yes, But call Anika. She went to buy vegetables."

Usha reached for her phone. "Anika? Where are you?"

"On my way home," Anika replied.

Usha turned back. "She's coming."

Roopa sat down with a tired sigh. "Tell her to bring eye drops. My eyes are flickering today. Feels like something bad is going to happen."

Usha stilled at that.

A flicker…. in the eyes, in the air, in the space between past and present.

Then she stood.

"I'll go myself," she said, already reaching for her bag.

But this…. this wasn't just about medicine anymore.

Her feet moved with purpose.

Because now, finally, she had a reason…. a real, spoken reason….. to return to the shop.

To the place that held pieces of a story she didn't understand yet.

To the beginning of an answer that had waited too long.

✦ ∞ ✦

The little bell above the door jingled.

Vikrant stepped inside. The shop smelled of paper, incense, and old dust. A slow breeze passed through the open shutters.

Satish looked up from behind the counter. "Hello dear……"

"I need to ask you something," Vikrant said, pointing to a painting on the wall. "This. Do you know who that is?"

Satish squinted. "My sister……she painted it. She passed away a two years ago. She used to sketch faces from memory. Never gave him a name. Just called him the man with fire in his eyes."

Vikrant stared at the painting, unease settling into his gut.

The bell jingled again.

Usha stepped inside, holding a small cloth bag. She stopped when she saw him.

"You?" she said.

Vikrant gave a nod. "Hello."

His voice was even, but something shifted in him when she walked in. He looked away….to a row of soaps, to a shelf of perfume….but his mind kept turning back on her.

Satish smiled. "My two favourite visitors, at the same time. Must be a special day."

"What brings you here?" Vikrant asked.

"Eye drops," Usha replied. "For my grandmother."

The moment stretched…not awkward but filled with something unspoken.

Vikrant gave a quiet smirk. "It's not a chemist's shop, you know."

Usha didn't respond.

Then her eyes caught the painting on the wall.

She stepped toward it, her breath shifting. "That's the one…"

Vikrant moved slightly aside, watching her.

"What do you know about it?" he asked.

Usha hesitated. "It just felt familiar. That's all."

"And you?" she asked, looking at him. "You came here to ask about it?"

"It's personal," Vikrant said, his voice tight.

She lowered her gaze and brushed her hand against the glass counter.

A sharp hiss escaped her lips.

Blood.

"You're bleeding," Vikrant said, stepping forward. "What were you thinking?"

"It's just a scratch….."

He pulled a tissue from the counter and gently pressed it against her palm.

"What if it had been deeper?"

Usha watched him. Not just his hands, but his face. Something inside her tried to place him….not the man others described, but the one standing before her.

Was he merely ego?

Was he defined by class?

Or was there a deeper essence within?

Their hands touched. Their eyes met.

The space between them shifted.

Satish watched from the side, a quiet smile on his lips. "Ok then, let me get a Band-Aid."

Outside, a white police jeep pulled into the lane.

The bell rang once more.

Inspector Rajeev stepped in, his gaze landing on them….Vikrant holding a tissue to Usha's hand, her eyes wide.

"Rai sahib and Miss Rathi," Rajeev said with a dry smile. "Funny how I always find you two where silence breathes secrets."

Usha stepped back, covering her hand with her dupatta. Vikrant straightened.

"What are you doing here?" Vikrant asked, his tone flat.

Rajeev walked forward. "Don't act too innocent, Vikrant. Your father's still under watch. The investigation isn't over."

Usha turned sharply. "Investigation? What are you talking about?"

"This is not your business," Vikrant snapped before Rajeev could speak.

Usha looked at him.

And in that moment, something inside her settled. The softness in his voice was gone. The distance, real.

She had seen another face.

Rajeev's voice cut through the silence. "Your lover boy here….his father was the last person to see Pandit Keval alive. Minutes later, the man was found hanging."

Usha froze.

The words didn't fully land at first … they echoed instead, sharp, distant, not real.

She opened her mouth, but no sound came.

Then a constable burst through the door, breathless. "Sir! Another body. Forest site. Same place."

The air in the shop shifted.

What had been a place of quiet suspicion suddenly felt heavier… charged.

Usha's heartbeat quickened, her fingers curling slightly around the edge of the counter.

The world around her didn't move, but something inside her did.

Rajeev turned slowly, eyes narrowing.

His voice was low, but it carried weight. "Looks like the forest has more to say."

He glanced toward the door, "And this time… it's not whispering."

The silence that followed didn't settle.

It lingered.

Like breath caught in the throat of something still watching."

✦ ∞ ✦

Kunaal drove the car himself... for the first time in years.

The gates of the Rai mansion creaked open, and the car rolled in slowly, deliberately.

He stepped out alone, his gaze brushing past the garden ... not looking for anyone, but hoping no one was looking.

Karishma stood near the marigolds, a basket of flowers in her hands.

She turned as he approached, her brow lightly furrowed.

"Where's Narayan?" she asked.

Kunaal paused...just a second too long.

"He... took leave," he replied, avoiding her gaze.

She watched him walk past her, toward the house.

There was something strange in his pace.

Not rushed. Not calm.

Measured. Heavy.

And his expression... too composed.

Like a man holding his breath behind his eyes.

The doubt didn't leave her.

It clung to her.

Settled into her chest.

Because in all the years she'd known him,

he never drove himself.

And now he had.

Alone.

And carrying something

he wasn't ready to say.

✦ ∞ ✦

Usha sat beside Anika, folding clothes slowly. Her fingers moved, but her mind wasn't here.

"What are you thinking about?" Anika asked.

Usha smiled faintly. "Nothing important."

Anika noticed the bandage. "What happened?"

"Satish's shop. A scratch."

Roopa entered, drying her hands. "Did you get the eye drops?"

Usha blinked. "I forgot."

"You're always forgetting. Anyway...your father's aunt came. There's a boy for Anika. Owns a chemist shop in Indore. They might visit tomorrow."

Usha looked at her sister. "Are you happy?"

Anika gave a small smile. "Yes."

But her eyes hesitated.

Usha didn't say anything more. But something tugged inside her.

A girl who once dreamed of saving lives might now marry a man who sold ointments and bandages.

✦ ∞ ✦

Vikrant stepped through the doorway and paused, the weight of the evening pressing down on him. His jaw was tight, knuckles whitening around the edges of his coat.

In the living room, Kunal sat in an armchair, cradling a chipped teacup as though it were just another ordinary night. Steam curled from the rim.

Vikrant's voice was slow but steady. "Where were you today?"

Kunal set the cup on the saucer with a soft clink. He met his son's eyes evenly. "At the farmhouse. And now you're questioning me? Your father?"

Vikrant drew in a slow breath, exhaling it like a shield. "I'm not questioning you. I'm worried." He let the word linger between them. "They found another body today. And one more thing...where is Narayan? I heard you drove yourself back.

Kunal's shoulders eased fractionally. "Narayan said he had some work to finish, so I let him go. I drove back alone."

At that moment, Karishma slipped into the room. She stood in the doorway, silent, her presence a quiet testament to the tension that hung in the air. She didn't speak, but lingered long enough to feel the sharp stillness settle over them.

Outside, the wind picked up among the trees. Leaves whispered against one another, and for the first time, the forest felt less like a silent witness and more like a living, breathing thing….watching, waiting, aware of the darkness creeping closer.

Chapter 12

The forest didn't move.

Fog coiled around the roots, low and steady, like breath held too long. The birds had gone quiet. Even the wind passed carefully between trees, as though afraid to touch what lay on the ground.

Inspector Rajeev stood still, coat buttoned tight, staring at the second body.

Male.

No ID.

No wounds.

Eyes closed, limbs still.

A face untouched by violence...yet something about him disturbed the earth itself.

A constable approached, holding a sealed pouch. "Sir, burnt paper. Found twenty feet from the body."

Rajeev opened it. Ash clung to the plastic. Words floated between blackened edges:

Kundli... Nakshatra... Birth time.

Another link. Another thread back to the pandit.

"Two bodies," Rajeev muttered. "Both with traces of astrology. Same forest. No marks, no blood. But something keeps tying them here."

The forensic officer spoke beside him. "We'll check if it matches the paper at the earlier site."

Rajeev nodded. "Do that."

Then he stepped away and dialled. "Get me full mobile data on Kunal Rai. Calls. Locations. I want to know who he's speaking to...and who he's not."

The line crackled. Somewhere deeper in the forest, a crow screamed once and fell quiet again.

✦ ∞ ✦

Vikrant sat on the sofa, a folder open in his lap, his gaze distant and unreadable.

The phone on the table buzzed with an ongoing conference call. A voice on speaker droned on.

"If you have doubts, raise them now. Final report goes out by tomorrow."

Vikrant ended the call and leaned back, exhaling through his nose.

Karishma entered, balancing a tray. She placed a cup beside him.

"Do you think Papa's hiding something?" she asked quietly.

He didn't answer immediately. "I don't know. But he's too calm. Detached, even."

Karishma nodded. She had felt it too.

In the kitchen, the cook chopped onions slowly. The knife thudded against the board.

"Where's the rest of the vegetables?" Karishma asked.

The cook looked up. "Narayan didn't return. And no one else went."

Karishma's brows tightened.

She returned to the living room. Kunal sat by the window, reading the newspaper as if the world beyond the headlines didn't exist.

"Papa, where's Narayan?"

He didn't glance up. "At work."

"He wasn't there yesterday either."

Kunal paused. "He'll be back. Don't worry."

But Karishma was already worried. And that pause… it had lasted a beat too long.

Anjali wheeled in from the corridor. Her voice was soft, almost distant. "Where's your brother?"

"He left," Karishma replied. "Said he had meetings all day."

Anjali turned toward the wall, eyes resting on the calendar.

"October 1st is near," she whispered. "We'll go to the temple. Panditji said it's auspicious."

Karishma gave a small nod. "We'll go, Ma."

But the word auspicious no longer felt like a promise.

It felt like something waiting in the dark.

In the Rathi the house, Anika stood at the kitchen counter, slicing cucumbers into thin rounds. Usha folded clothes nearby, but her hands moved without thought.

"You're thinking too much again," Anika teased.

Usha blinked, her voice lower, distant. "Some people… they act like they care. They say all the right things. But when the moment changes… so do they."

Anika smiled faintly. "Then stop thinking about them."

Usha's voice dropped. "I'm trying."

Roopa entered, holding a bright, pressed saree.

"Usha, iron this one. The boy's family is visiting. We must look proper."

Usha nodded. "Yes, Daadi."

"They're decent people," Roopa added, more to herself than anyone.

Anika gave a small smile. "Hmm."

Usha turned to her. "But is this what you want?"

Anika didn't answer immediately.

Her dreams were quiet ones…never shouted, never demanded.

She hadn't asked for palaces.

She wanted to learn, to heal, to wear a white coat and understand the human body not for profit, but for kindness.

Maybe marrying a man who owned a chemist shop would bring her closer.

Or maybe it would just pull her further away.

"Maybe what I want," Anika said slowly, "was never meant for me."

Usha stepped closer and hugged her tightly.

"Don't say that" she said. "Dreams don't ask for permission. They ask for belief."

Roopa stood by the doorway, saying nothing. But her eyes lingered on the two girls….longer than usual.

Behind her silence, something stirred. A memory. A name. A fear she had folded and hidden long ago.

Inspector Rajeev sipped his tea, cold and bitter.

A constable entered with a folder. "Timeline checks out. Kunal Rai was at the pandit's house. Phone location confirms it. Then he headed home. No suspicious calls on the way"

Rajeev flipped the file open.

"And what about the forensic report on the body?" he asked.

"He ate laddu before dying. It was on her mouth. Confirmed by lab."

"No ID on the second man?" Rajeev asked.

"None. Died of heart attack. Nothing abnormal."

Rajeev frowned. "again, heart attack…."

There were no answers.

Then the phone rang.

"Inspector Rajeev?"

"Yes."

"This is SP Chandrapur. The case is being transferred. Inspector Aryan Jha will lead. You'll assist him."

The call ended without pause.

Rajeev leaned back in his chair.

He hadn't been pulled off the case.

But the current had changed direction.

✦ ∞ ✦

The black SUV pulled to a stop. The engine clicked off. From the passenger door, a tall man stepped out—shirt sleeves rolled, shoes dusty, eyes sharp.

"Aryan Jha," he said calmly.

Rajeev greeted him. "Welcome to the district's most polite haunting."

Aryan didn't laugh. He scanned the crime scene with quiet focus, then moved past the markers and crouched by the base of a tree.

"We've confirmed both men died of heart attacks," Rajeev offered.

"Maybe fear did it. People still talk about that forest... say it's haunted. Some villagers claim they saw something with their own eyes … years ago."

Aryan didn't reply. His hand skimmed the ground, slow and focused. After scanning the area, he paused – his eyes narrowing at a patch of disturbed leaves. "Check there," he said, pointing.

A constable moved in, checking carefully into the soft soil.

"Sir!" he called a minute later, holding up a small object...mud-caked, half-tucked into a piece of tissue.

A cigarette butt.

Aryan's eyes sharpened. "Bag it. Send it straight to the lab."

Rajeev watched him. "You think that's your thread?"

Aryan stood. "The forest may hide things. But people....people always leave something behind. We can't write *ghost* in a report ....but we can run the autopsy again. Deeper this time."

✦ ∞ ✦

Karishma sat in the garden, the last light of day spilling across her lap. She scrolled through her phone, smiling faintly, the way she used to before things got complicated.

Inside, Anjali opened a drawer. Her hand hovered over a worn photo.

Samar. Her brother.

His eyes still full of the fire he carried.

She picked it up, then set it back.

Then picked it up again.

Outside, the wind tugged at the leaves.

Karishma looked toward the door where Kunal had just walked in.

Something in the way he moved felt different.

But no one said it.

Not yet.

✦ ∞ ✦

Usha sat beside Anika again. The tea tray rested between them. Anika poured two cups, gentle and practiced.

Usha watched her sister...not just with eyes, but with memory. They were twins, but today, Usha felt a step behind.

Anika was being measured by people who didn't know her. Who never would.

Usha's hand brushed the bandage on her finger. It had begun to fray.

She remembered how Vikrant had looked at her ... like she was fragile, but not weak.

Like he wanted to speak... but didn't know how.

As if something in him had cracked .... but hadn't learned to break open yet.

Then Rajeev's voice echoed back, sharp in her mind:

"There are loose threads around his father. Be careful who you trust."

The warmth of that memory pressed against the cold edge of suspicion.

She felt both at once.

And that ache ... the kind that comes from believing someone, just a little too much... settled behind her ribs.

Anika handed her a cup.

"Hot," she said gently.

Usha took it with a faint smile.... but her eyes had already hardened with resolve.

Her voice was low. Steady. Certain. "I'm not done yet."

Not with the truth.

Not with the forest.

Not with the girl she used to be... and not with the woman she was becoming.

Chapter 13

Laughter floated through the living room....thin, nervous, brittle at the edges. The kind of laughter that tries to cover up the weight in the room. The prospective groom's family sat on the beige sofa, worn but polished, surrounded by trays of tea and homemade sweets.

Ameet's smile held steady, hopeful. Roopa moved with care, her hands trembling only slightly as she poured chai into delicate cups. The air smelled of sugar, cardamom, and something unspoken.

Rajpal sat beside his parents. He was tall, neat, and soft-spoken...his smile respectful, but rehearsed. His father wore a well-pressed white kurta; his mother sat straight in a regal blue saree, scanning the room with practiced judgment.

Anika sat quiet, eyes downcast, draped in a soft peach salwar. Beside her, Usha stayed alert, gaze steady.

"So, Anika," Rajpal's mother asked, "what do you enjoy doing in your free time?"

Anika opened her mouth, but Usha spoke first, voice smooth and steady. "My sister has always loved biology. She dreamed of becoming a doctor. Still does, if given a chance. And she makes the best masoor dal I've ever had."

Rajpal smiled. "I run a chemist shop in Indore. It's small, but consistent. I love south Indian films."

His mother glanced around. "This is your house, right? Not rented?"

Roopa lifted her chin. "It's ours. Brick by brick, memory by memory."

Usha added without flinching, "Our father works at a sweet shop. Wakes before sunrise every day."

The mother gave a tight nod. Tea was refilled. Sweets passed around. For a moment, the room softened. Laughter returned. A sliver of what could be a future shimmered quietly between glances.

Then came the sound of tires on gravel.

A police jeep stopped outside the gate.

Two officers stepped out....Inspector Rajeev, followed by a taller, leaner man.

Inspector Aryan Jha.

The name cut through the room like a cold gust.

The air shifted.

"Police?" Rajpal's mother murmured, her voice sharp with disbelief. "During a marriage proposal meeting?"

Rajpal glanced at Anika – but his father was already on his feet.

"We should go," he said curtly. "This is clearly not the right time."

Roopa stood quickly.

"Please.... Don't misunderstand..."

But the mother was already reaching for her purse.

"We ignored the last sign. The pandit died. Now the police? She's cursed."

Anika didn't speak.

Didn't move.

One tear slipped from the corner of her right eye ... but this time, it didn't stop there.

Her lips parted slightly,

but no words came.

Just a quiver in her breath.

The kind that arrives not with shock ... but with the exhaustion of hearing something too many times.

Cursed.

She had heard that word before.

The day the pandit died.

The day her wedding fell apart like it never mattered.

The day relatives stopped meeting her eyes

and started walking past her like guilt with legs.

It wasn't just an old belief.

It was a fresh scar.

And today, someone had ripped it open …. without flinching.

More tears followed.

Quiet. Uncontrolled.

She didn't wipe them.

She didn't try.

She just sat there – not proud, not composed.

Just…..breaking.

Softly. In front of everyone.

And no one truly saw it.

Because she didn't scream.

Because she didn't fight.

And still, she stayed quiet.

Rajpal hesitated, gave her a soft nod. "Bye, Anika."

And the door shut behind them.

Ameet sank into a chair, his face blank. Roopa turned her head toward the gods, lips moving in silent prayer….or quiet grief.

Anika walked to her room.

Not because her heart was broken…but because curses have loud mouths, and the world listens too quickly.

Usha turned toward the officers, her tone sharp. "You could've waited."

Rajeev met her gaze evenly. "We didn't know. We're sorry."

Aryan stepped forward, gentler. "Truly. We regret the timing. But this matters."

Roopa's voice was stiff. "Ask what you came to ask."

"We're following up on the suicide of Pandit Keval Lal. A burnt piece of paper was recovered near the unknown body in the forest … it turned out to be a Kundli. Anika's Kundli. We believe… there's a pattern."

Roopa's fingers clutched her shawl. "I told all this before."

"It may mean nothing," Aryan said gently, his voice careful.

"But if you remember anything…anything unusual on the wedding day… a strange visitor, odd behaviour when you spoke to the pandit, an argument — anything at all. Please let us know."

Ameet's voice was low, rough. "We gave him the Kundli. He never came back."

Aryan nodded. "That's all for now. But if anything, else comes back to you… we'll return."

✦ ∞ ✦

The room was dim. Just the hallway light leaking through the half-open door.

Usha sat beside Anika, who lay curled toward the wall. Her breath was quiet. But her eyes….when she spoke….were tired in a way that had nothing to do with sleep.

"Di…" Anika whispered. "Am I really cursed?"

Usha pulled her close, arms wrapping around her shoulders. "Don't ever say that."

"They looked at me like I was… marked," Ankia whispered. "Like I ruined everything."

"You didn't," Usha said softly, her voice like shelter. "You're everything they're not. Strong. Kind. Brave. Beautiful. My sister."

Anika said nothing more. But her head rested on Usha's shoulder. And in that silence, the weight finally slipped….for a moment.

✦ ∞ ✦

Anjali sat by the window; hands wrapped around a warm cup of water. The breeze teased the curtains.

"Where's Vikrant?" she asked.

Karishma placed a tray on the table. "In his room. Came late."

"And Narayan?"

"Still missing."

Kunal entered just then, unbuttoning his collar. "He's at the farmhouse. He'll be back tomorrow."

Anjali nodded slowly. Her gaze shifted to the calendar. "The 28th. We have the pooja soon."

Karishma replied, "I'll remind Bhai."

In his room, Vikrant tossed his files onto the bed, sighing. "I need tea!"

He called out, loud and dramatic, "Sister! Tea!"

Karishma's voice echoed down the hallway. "After dinner, drama king!"

He smiled to himself. "Fine, then come down for dinner."

And for once, there was laughter in the Rai house.

Just a little.....but enough to feel like something was healing.

The board was lit with dim amber light. Threaded photos. Printed reports. Red strings stretching across locations and names.

Aryan stood still, flipping through the lab file. Rajeev leaned beside him, holding cold tea.

"Anything new?"

Aryan tapped a page. "Both bodies. No IDs. No phones. No wallets. No missing person reports match. Nothing."

"Then who were they?"

Aryan laid a printout flat. "Here. First body....traces of neurotoxin in the lungs. Second body...same toxin, but through the stomach."

Rajeev looked up. "So, the first inhaled it. The second ate it."

Aryan nodded. "Unfiltered cigarette, laced with a slow-acting nerve agent. Not over-the-counter stuff. Rare. Custom."

Rajeev frowned. "So, both died of heart attacks—because the toxin stopped their hearts?"

"Exactly. The poison triggers acute cardiac arrest. Looks natural unless you're looking for it."

"And the sweets?"

Aryan tapped the next page. "The laddus were laced too. Second victim had the same toxin….only orally. They wanted it to look soft. Spiritual. Harmless."

Rajeev's voice dropped. "And that cigarette butt?"

"Same residue. Same compound. Whoever smoked it…..died"

Rajeev stood slowly. "So, we're looking for someone who poisons through smoke… and sweets."

Aryan added quietly, "And knows these woods well. Like they've walked here forever."

They both stared at the board.

Three deaths.

A forest with secrets.

And a trail just beginning to smoulder.

Chapter 14

Light slipped through the windows like a visitor unsure of its welcome. The pale gold touched Anika's walls, warming the paint, but it couldn't reach the weight in her chest.

Roopa sat on the edge of the bed, folding a lavender dupatta, smoothing the creases over and over again.

"Your father didn't eat," she said softly, eyes fixed on the cloth. "Left before sunrise again."

Anika frowned, tying her braid. "But.....but I made less oily paratha. He said he was washing his hands."

Roopa shook her head. "He's not angry, dear. He's... grieving. When the world calls a daughter cursed, it doesn't just hurt her...it tells the father he failed her."

By the window, Usha sat quiet. Her hands picked at the threads of a cushion, but her mind was elsewhere threading its way through the name Samar Dev, through Satish's painting, through pages that whispered truths buried too long.

Anika stood suddenly. "I'll take breakfast to Papa. He shouldn't be working empty."

Usha stood too. "I'm coming."

Roopa gave a nod. "Don't stay long."

Ameet stood behind the counter, wrapping sweets in clean butter paper, moving like a man who couldn't stop or he'd start to feel too much.

When the girls entered, he blinked in surprise.

"Papa, sit," Anika said, setting down the tiffin. "Your favourite paratha. And mango pickle."

"I already had tea," he replied.

"Tea isn't breakfast," Usha said with a faint smile.

"You're the one who taught us that."

They sat in the backroom, on low stools near the sacks of sugar and flour. The meal was quiet, but not tense. For a few minutes, the silence felt like peace instead of pain.

When they rose to leave, Ameet touched their shoulders.

"I'll be okay. Go on."

Outside, the sun filtered through tarpaulin roofs and hanging spice garlands.

"You head home," Usha said. "I need to stop somewhere."

Anika didn't ask. "I'm off to buy vegetables anyway."

✦ ∞ ✦

The bell chimed. The shop smelled of agarbatti and old ink.

"Ah, Usha ji," Satish said warmly. "Back so soon?"

She offered a brief smile. "I wanted to ask again. That painting…..who was the man?"

Satish followed her gaze. "Still haunting you, that face?"

She didn't look away. "Vikrant Rai asked about it too, didn't he?"

He blinked. "Yes, same day you cut your hand. How's that healing?"

"Fine," she said quickly. "Why was he asking?"

"Same reason as you, I guess. Curiosity. I told him the truth…my sister painted it from a dream. She never knew his name. Just said he had fire in his eyes."

Usha stared at the canvas again. The colours had faded slightly at the corners, but the face held something fierce, something… unfinished.

"I've seen him," she murmured.

"Me too," Satish looked at the painting. "Sometimes I think he's watching me right back," he said, studying the face of painting.

"Look at it... he looks angry. Like he's about to attack me."

He let out a short laugh …. but it didn't quite reach his eyes.

Usha's voice came from behind him, calm but pointed.

"Then why do you still hang that angry man on your wall?"

A pause.

"Because your sister painted it," she added softly.

Before Samar could reply, a woman entered.

Satish greeted her. "Namaste, Kalyani ji."

Usha stepped back. "Thank you. I should go."

"Come by anytime," Satish said, kind as ever.

Outside, the brightness of day felt dimmer. The threads in her mind were pulling tighter.

Why had Vikrant asked about the painting?

Had he seen the same face in the shadows she was chasing?

Anika stood at a vegetable stall, voice soft but firm.

"These potatoes aren't fresh. Not for sixty."

The vendor began to protest, but her tone made him switch to tomatoes instead.

Across the street, a white police jeep slowed. Aryan Jha sat inside.

"That's her," he said to the driver.

He looked again….the red Bindiya, the hair escaping a loose braid, the quiet intelligence in her eyes.

Not cursed, he thought. Not even close.

"Stop the jeep."

He stepped out casually, hands behind his back, and walked to the stall.

"Tomatoes should be red, not sad," he murmured, glancing at the pile.

The vegetable seller forced a chuckle. "Yes sir. Best batch!"

Anika sighed. "Forget tomatoes. Just give me potatoes."

The bag in her hand tore suddenly. Potatoes rolled across the street.

Aryan crouched quickly. "Allow me."

He picked them up one by one, dusted them gently, placed them in a fresh bag.

"These are fine. But give her firm ones," he told the vendor. "She deserves the good ones."

He handed the new bag to her.

She looked at him. His uniform was crisp, but something in his eyes was not.

"I wanted to say sorry," he said. "About yesterday. We didn't mean to ruin anything."

Anika hesitated, then took the bag. "Thank you."

"Better potatoes," Aryan smiled. "Better lunch."

Anika blinked...and to her surprise...smiled back.

Then she turned and walked away.

Aryan stood a moment longer.

Then returned to the jeep.

✦ ∞ ✦

The gate creaked as Rajeev stepped in. A woman came out, drying her hands on a faded towel.

"Yes?"

"Inspector Rajeev," he said, flashing ID. "We need to ask about Narayan."

Her eyes cooled. "He doesn't live here. We're separated."

"Divorced?"

"Yes. No calls. No visits."

As Rajeev turned to leave, his phone buzzed with a video call.

It was his wife, holding their baby. The infant cooed and waved a tiny hand at the screen.

Narayan's ex-wife peeked over his shoulder.

"Your child?"

Rajeev smiled. "Yes. One month old."

She took phone and looked at the screen. Her voice softened. "Beautiful. May Mata Rani protect him."

Her eyes shimmered, but she stepped back into her house.

Rajeev walked back to his car and dialled Aryan.

"Sir. Narayan hasn't contacted his wife. They're not in touch."

Aryan's voice came clear. "What about his house?"

"Checked. His mother says she hasn't seen him in five days. Kunal told her he sent Narayan on an errand."

Aryan was silent. "Where did he go after the farmhouse?"

Rajeev's voice dropped. "Exactly."

"Send teams," Aryan ordered. "One to sweep the farmhouse perimeter. Another down the forest trail. Ditch to ditch. And pull Narayan's last cell tower ping. Something's missing."

Rajeev hung up.

The sky was turning orange, a soft flame behind the trees.

But the answers weren't coming with the sun.

They were waiting in the shadows.

Chapter 15

The sun hovered low above the Rai farmhouse, casting long shadows over cracked walls and rusting iron gates. The place, once proud, now wore age like a scar. Its silence wasn't peace...it was the kind that comes after things are buried.

Inspector Rajeev and Aryan Jha stepped out of their vehicle. The scent of old wood, dried hay, and damp earth filled the air. Underneath it all....something colder. The faint trace of something unspoken.

The peepal trees near the porch stood tall and twisted, their roots clutching the ground like secrets unwilling to let go.

Aryan knocked once.

A servant peeked from the side door. No words, just cautious eyes.

"We're from the city police," Aryan said, holding his badge. "Routine check."

The man disappeared inside.

Moments later, Kunal Rai appeared....hands damp, sleeves rolled to the elbows, and his expression calm, calculated.

"Officers," he said, nodding. "What brings you here?"

"Follow-up visit," Rajeev replied, voice casual. "May we?"

Kunal held the door open. "Of course."

As they stepped in, Rajeev scanned the hallway...the mud-splattered floor, the documents on the table, the faint scent of smoke.

Then, from behind the hedges, movement.

A figure. Watching.

"Stop," Aryan said sharply.

Narayan emerged.

Dusty.

Pale.

Still.

"Mr. Narayan," Rajeev said, walking forward. "Weren't you missing?"

Kunal stepped in smoothly. "His phone fell in water. During work. He's been here....handling land papers and permits. He does more than drive."

Narayan nodded, but his eyes never met theirs.

Aryan observed. He noticed everything....the twitch of fingers, the lack of eye contact, the nervous pulse in Narayan's neck.

He said nothing.

But he didn't forget.

✦ ∞ ✦

The knife moved rhythmically on the cutting board. Anika chopped potatoes with steady hands. Usha rinsed coriander beside her, the scent of earth and green sharp in the air.

"He surprised me," Anika said suddenly.

Usha looked up. "Who?"

"That inspector. He came to the market. Helped with the vegetables. Apologized."

Usha stilled. "Aryan?"

Anika nodded, her voice soft.

"He wasn't what I expected."

Usha smiled faintly but didn't reply. Her thoughts wandered....to the portrait at Satish's shop, to Samar's name, to the feeling that each path she followed was somehow leading to the same locked door.

✦ ∞ ✦

The city unfurled before them in golden patches of light and shadow. Vikrant drove with one hand resting lightly on the wheel, the other tapping against the steering in rhythm with the FM radio hum.

Karishma sat beside him, scrolling. "You drive like the roads owe you something."

He smirked. "They do. Especially when you're in the car."

She rolled her eyes. "We're stopping at the temple. Ma reminded me. October 1st is close."

He nodded. "We'll stop."

Then his phone buzzed. It connected automatically to the car's Bluetooth. Karishma turned down the radio.

Satish's voice filtered in, crackling slightly. "Bhai, Usha came again. Asked about the painting."

Karishma glanced sideways, one eyebrow lifting in quiet surprise.

Vikrant straightened in his seat. "The same sketch?"

A pause. Then Satish's voice again, steady and knowing. "Yes. Curious like you. Thought you'd want to know."

The call ended. Karishma turned to him, grinning. "Usha. The jalebi girl?"

Vikrant smiled, amused. "She's more than that."

"She made you smile like that. That's enough of an identity."

Then her tone changed. "What's with the sketch?"

Vikrant exhaled slowly. "It looks like someone we knew. Samar Mamu."

Karishma's eyes widened. "The sketch........it's him?"

"Yes," Vikrant said quietly. "But Satish doesn't know. Now Usha's asking too."

Karishma's smile faded. "That's not a coincidence."

Vikrant's voice was quieter now. "No. It's not."

✦ ∞ ✦

The board on the wall glowed under a single yellow bulb. The smell of stale tea and paper hung heavy in the air. Threads of red string crossed photos and names, maps and timelines.

Aryan stood still; arms folded. Rajeev sipped his third cup of tea, the silence between them thoughtful, not tense.

The board read:

Body 1 - Male. Age 25–27. Poison.

Body 2 - Male. Age 21–22. Same poison.

Pandit Keval Lal - Found hanging. No poison.

Kundli - Burned. Belonged to Anika Rathi.

Rajeev broke the silence. "Maybe it's simple. Pandit meets one of them. The guy dies. Pandit panics, burns the Kundli, kills himself. Guilt. Fear."

Aryan didn't turn. "Then explain the toxin. This isn't panic. It's too exact."

Rajeev looked again at the notes. "So, what are you saying?"

"Same neurotoxin in both victims," Aryan said. "It causes a rapid but silent heart attack. No marks. No struggle. But deliberate. Controlled."

"Smoked and eaten," Rajeev murmured. "First one through a cigarette. Second through sweets."

Aryan nodded. "They didn't know they were dying when they did."

He walked to the photos of the half-burned Kundlies.

"Why carry the Kundli into the forest? Why burn it there?"

Rajeev shrugged. "Psycho killer. Ritual maybe."

"Or a symbol," Aryan said. "A sign. Forest. Fire. Paper. Smoke. Someone's leaving a pattern."

Rajeev leaned in. "Then who gave them the poison? And why would they take it willingly?"

Aryan's eyes narrowed. "They didn't know. That's the point."

He paused.

"Maybe one thing connects them… Pandit Keval.

Maybe he knew both men.

And now… he's dead."

Rajeev's voice was grim. "Took the secret with him."

Aryan's fingers traced a path on the board.

"No," he whispered. "He didn't take it. Someone made sure he wouldn't tell it."

They stood there, beneath the hum of the ceiling fan.

Quiet and focused.

And then Aryan said, almost to himself, his eyes fixed on Anika's Kundli.

"Someone's burning the past. But they left one ember alive."

Chapter 16

The temple stood in quiet reverence....its marble steps dusted with sandalwood, its corridors humming with prayers. Golden bells swung gently overhead, and incense trails curled in the air like memories.

Vikrant stood a few steps away from the crowd, arms crossed, distant. The bhajans rose and fell around him, but they barely reached his ears.

His thoughts wandered...drawn back to a rain-slicked evening. Usha.

That storm in her eyes. That stubborn calm in her silence. The way she clutched that silver chain...not like an ornament, but a thread holding her to something deeper.

A soft smile curved across his face.

He didn't even notice the boy until their shoulders brushed.

"Oh! I'm sorry," Vikrant said, steadying him.

"It's okay..." the boy grinned, already disappearing into the crowd.

Vikrant froze.

That grin. That boy. That voice.

The boy who'd handed him the letter that night outside the gate.

"Let's go?" Karishma's voice pulled him back. She appeared beside him, red tilak still fresh on her forehead.

"Do you still have the party video?" he asked, suddenly focused.

Karishma smirked. "Want to see Usha again?"

He gave her a look. "It's not about her."

"Right," she teased, unlocking her phone. "I think I still have it. Why?"

"The boy. The one who gave me the letter….I think we can see who placed the letter. Maybe we can spot something in the footage."

Karishma paused. "Still haven't figured out who sent that letter?"

"No. That's what's bothering me," Vikrant said. "Now Usha's asking questions about Mamu. Even you only learned about Samar a few days ago. So how does she know his name?"

Karishma's smile faded. "You think she's hiding something?"

"I don't know," he said quietly. "But I want to know how it all connects."

She looked at him carefully. "Should we meet her?"

He shrugged. "You can meet her."

She smirked. "And what would I say?"

"Tell her you love jalebi."

Karishma burst out laughing. "I didn't even eat it. That was for Maa."

He shook his head. "You'll go. I'll just… come along."

"Oh, of course," she grinned. "Coincidence."

Vikrant looked away. But inside, something pulled him forward.

Not just curiosity.

Something he couldn't name yet.

The dining table glowed under a soft yellow light, the smell of ghee and cumin still fresh in the air.

Roopa sat with folded hands as Usha placed a bowl of dal before her. Anika arrived from the kitchen with warm rotis wrapped in cotton cloth.

"You girls eat," Roopa said gently. "I'll take my time."

"You haven't been eating properly either," Anika added, pouring water into glasses.

Usha gave a tired smile. "There's too much on my mind."

Anika raised an eyebrow. "Like that chain? You were miserable when it got lost. Then one day, it's just… back."

Usha paused. "Yes. Like magic."

"Or a gift," Anika teased. "Someone clearly cares."

Usha looked down. "Don't be silly."

✦ ∞ ✦

Later, in room, Usha sat near the window, holding the chain. The pendant swung slightly in her fingers, the silver catching lamplight.

"You're thinking about him," Anika said softly.

"I'm not thinking about Vikrant."

"I didn't say Vikrant," Anika replied, smiling. "I said the one who returned the chain. Don't lie."

Usha looked away. "I don't even know who it was."

"But you feel something," Anika whispered.

Usha didn't answer. She only stared into the darkness, the chain warming in her palm.

Later, Usha lit a lamp and reopened Samar's book. The pages whispered history and loss, but no new clues. No hidden marks. Just questions.

Her eyes moved to the wall.

A photo of her mother….smiling, forever still.

Beside it, the chain now hung from a small nail. Its shape cast a soft shadow.

Usha pressed her forehead to the frame.

"Ma," she whispered, "why do I feel like everything….this chain, the painting, the book, him…is part of the same story?"

Her voice trembled.

"I don't want to feel this… but I do."

From outside came Anika's voice; "Papa's home. Let's come outside."

Usha blinked away the tears forming.

"Coming," she said, barely louder than a breath.

✦ ∞ ✦

A desk lamp flickered in the corner. The room was mostly quiet, save for the slow ticking of the wall clock and the occasional rustle of papers.

Rajeev sat slouched, a half-eaten samosa beside him. His tea had gone cold.

Aryan stood before the investigation board, arms folded, eyes narrowing as he examined every pinned clue like a map leading nowhere.

"Your tea's dying," Rajeev said dryly.

Aryan didn't move.

"Samosa too. Cold food makes cold thinking."

Aryan finally turned. "Tell me something…if you were burdened by guilt… real guilt… would you kill yourself at home?"

"Depends on the guilt….But no. Why would I commit suicide?" He let out a dry laugh.

"Pandit Keval burns a Kundli in forest. Then he goes home. Then hangs himself. All in one day."

"Or" Rajeev said slowly, "someone else burned the Kundli."

Aryan paced. "Then Body Two…same poison. Same method. No resistance. Another Kundli found. Why repeat the pattern?"

"Someone's hiding a truth… or trying to create a pattern," Rajeev murmured.

Aryan stared at the whiteboard. "This time, no pandit died."

He grabbed a marker and drew a triangle:

Body 1

Body 2

Pandit Keval

"There's a fourth point we're missing."

Beneath it, he scribbled:

Pandit registry review

Check Roopa Devi and Ameet Rathi family links

"We need to see if another pandit was marked."

Rajeev looked up. "You think the Rathi family is part of this?"

"I don't know," Aryan said, voice steady, "but, the forest is connected to them. And someone doesn't want us to find out why."

✦ ∞ ✦

The house had gone quiet.

Outside, the wind-swept leaves along the path. Inside, a low glow from a corner lamp cast shifting shadows on the walls.

Vikrant sat cross-legged on his bed; his laptop open. The video from the party paused mid-frame.

There she was….Usha.

Mid-step.

Her dupatta lifted by a breeze.

Her brows furrowed, surprised by something unseen.

He stared at her face. He didn't understand what pulled him in. Maybe it was the way she looked at the world…..not wide-eyed, but aware. As if she had already been hurt… and still dared to stand.

Karishma walked in with a mug of tea.

"Still watching her?" she teased.

He fumbled, trying to close the video … but couldn't. "No, I was just…." he stammered. "Sure," she grinned. "She's cute though."

"She's not cute," he muttered.

"You were literally staring."

She tapped the spacebar. The video resumed.

"It paused," she smirked. "Cute."

Vikrant laughed, finally. "Maybe my finger slipped."

Karishma smirked. "Just tell her."

He didn't answer. She walked out, humming.

Vikrant stared at the screen again.

It wasn't just a letter.

Not just a chain.

It was a feeling. One that didn't make sense but refused to leave.

She was mystery and resistance and grief and light...all tangled together.

And he wanted to know what came next.

Even if it undid everything, he thought he understood.

Chapter 17

The house moved in its quiet rhythm....Roopa sweeping dry leaves from the veranda, Anika pulling sun-drenched clothes from the line, and Usha restacking the kitchen shelves with a kind of distracted precision.

Then came the knock.

A soft chime. A second knock...gentle but certain.

Usha wiped her hands on her dupatta and moved toward the door.

A delivery boy stood on the threshold, holding a brown-paper-wrapped package. "Parcel for Rathi House," he said, glancing at his phone.

Usha tilted her head. "Parcel?"

He handed it to her.

No logo.

No sender.

Just a carefully written address, and something handwritten beneath it ..."To be handled with care."

Anika turned from the courtyard; her sleeves rolled past her elbows. "Another mystery gift, Usha ji?" she teased lightly.

But Usha didn't laugh.

Her eyes narrowed as she examined the writing. Then her lips softened into a faint smile.

"No," she said. "This...this one isn't for me."

Anika stepped forward, her tone shifting. "Then... who?"

Usha walked to her and placed the parcel in her hands. "It's for you, Anika."

Anika froze. "Me?" She looked down at the package, hesitant. "There must be some mistake…"

"There isn't," Usha said gently. "It's yours."

Anika's hands trembled as she held it, the paper cool against her skin. "Who would send something… to someone like me?"

Her voice broke quietly. "How can anyone send a gift to a girl the world called cursed?"

Usha sat beside her, resting a hand on her shoulder. "Let's find out."

Anika unwrapped the package slowly.

Inside:

A set of brand-new medical entrance books….crisp, clean, never opened. Physics. Chemistry. Biology. A small pouch of gel pens. A folder filled with neatly handwritten notes. And atop them all, a notebook adorned with real pressed wildflowers.

A note was tucked beneath the cover:

"For the dreamer who never stopped dreaming."

Usha turned to the boy. "Who sent this?"

He shrugged. "I don't know. No name. I picked it up from the parcel desk."

And then he left.

The silence that followed was tender.

Anika stared at the books, her fingers gliding across the pages like they might vanish.

"But… who?" she whispered.

Usha offered gently, "Maybe Rajpal. The boy who came with the Rishta. Maybe he…"

But Anika shook her head slowly.

Because in her heart, she didn't hear Rajpal's voice.

She heard someone else.

Calm. Measured.

A voice that had once bent to pick up her scattered potatoes in a crowded market.

Inspector Aryan.

✦ ∞ ✦

The office was already busy….phones ringing, printers humming, and the faint static of a music player in the distance.

Rajeev entered with purpose; a file tucked beneath his arm. Aryan stood in front of the board, unmoving, eyes on the triangle of names and threads.

"We got the names," Rajeev said, placing the file on the table. "The two unidentified men…Anas Ali and Rakesh Sharma. Friends. Both from Hyderabad. Local police contacted their families."

Aryan turned. "And?"

"They arrived in Chandrapur a day before they were found dead. No confirmed bookings, no check-ins. Their phones….silent now…but call data is being pulled."

Aryan leaned closer to the board. "What brought them here? Why this town? And how did they cross paths with Pandit Keval Lal?"

Rajeev exhaled. "Something held them here. And it didn't let them leave."

✦ ∞ ✦

Preparations had begun for the temple pooja on October 1st.

The scent of dried mango leaves and sandalwood filled the courtyard. Narayan was back, unloading brass thalis and garlands under Karishma's sharp direction.

In the kitchen, Anjali and Karishma rolled laddoos together, their hands moving in rhythm as they hummed a soft bhajan… a melody that lingered in the air like memory.

In his room, Vikrant sat with his laptop open....but the meeting screen had long frozen.

His eyes weren't on numbers or presentations.

They were on a memory.

Usha, mid-laugh.

Hair loose, brushing her cheeks.

That unguarded moment, the kind she didn't even know she gave, looped in his mind like a secret only he was allowed to keep.

And for a second, he forgot how to blink.

From the hallway, Karishma's voice carried in. "Bhai?"

He didn't answer.

"I was thinking….."

He smirked faintly.

"Don't think. Dangerous things happen when you think."

"Shut up." She paused.

Karishma walked up and stepped into Vikrant's room.

"I was thinking…. we should invite Usha to the pooja."

Vikrant turned slightly. "Why?"

Karishma shrugged. "I want to meet her again."

Vikrant rolled his eyes. "You want to see your Jalebi Girl."

She laughed. "Yes, your friend"

Vikrant laughed.

"She's not my friend… but if you want to invite her, tell Narayan. He'll find her address and pass along your message."

Karishma nodded, "That's a good idea. And maybe we can talk to Usha about Samar Mamu… why she was asking."

"Yes…" Vikrant replied softly.

But inside, it wasn't just about the painting.

It wasn't about Samar.

It was the quiet pull in his chest...the simple, unexplainable happiness at the thought of seeing her again.

Not to question.

Not to confront.

Just.... to be near her.

✦ ∞ ✦

Sunlight streamed through the window into Anika's room. The floor was cool beneath her feet. Her hands still smelled faintly of haldi and soap.

She walked toward the small wooden desk and sat down. The notebook with the pressed wildflowers still lay unopened.

She picked it up, held it close for a moment, then gently opened the cover.

A folded letter slipped out.

The handwriting was slanted, precise. It wasn't decorative...it was real. Like the words had been written with care, not flair.

She unfolded it.

If you're reading this, take a breath.

Let it settle deep in your chest.

Let it remind you... you're still here.

And that matters more than you know.

Always smile.

You are not cursed.

You are the echo of resilience.

Your hands ... they were made to heal,

to comfort,

to create.

Your mind .... it was meant to shine,

to wander,

to imagine,

to change the world ... even if only in one quiet corner at a time.

Keep walking. Keep dreaming.

Even on the days it hurts.

Even when the world feels heavy.

Especially then.

Because the world needs you.

It may not say it.

It may not know it yet.

But it does.

And I see you.

Always.

— Someone who believes in you, completely

Anika's hands trembled.

Tears welled …. not from shame, but from the unfamiliar ache of being seen.

Of being remembered.

The old voices … the ones that whispered she wasn't enough, that she was a burden … faded into something softer.

Quieter.

Not gone, but no longer winning.

For once, someone had reached into her silence…

and placed hope there.

She closed the notebook.

Held it close to her chest.

And smiled … not because she knew who had sent it, but because someone believed she could.

Chapter 18

The golden dusk spilled over the Rai mansion like molten saffron, glazing the marble floors and casting long shadows across corridors steeped in memory.

Outside, marigold garlands swayed gently in the breeze, their fragrance mingling with the curling scent of agarbatti rising from brass stands in the courtyard.

Inside, the mansion held its stillness.

In the main dining hall, Karishma sat at the wooden table near the window, head bent, her pen moving slowly across the guest list.

Every now and then, she paused …. chewing on the pen cap, her mind somewhere between the names and the weight of what those names once meant.

Nearby, Kunaal and Anjali sat with their evening tea.

No words exchanged.

Just the quiet presence of people used to holding silence like furniture – always there, always settled.

Above them, behind a closed door, Vikrant remained in his room, caught in the middle of a business meeting,

unaware that downstairs,

time was moving differently … slow, watchful, and waiting.

After a long stretch of quiet, Anjali spoke. "Karishma, it's been over two hours. Go call your brother. I need to discuss the rituals."

Karishma nodded and climbed the stairs.

Anjali glanced at the paper Karishma had left behind and passed it to Kunal. "Look through it."

Kunal read aloud softly, "Pooja Guest List – 1st October."

His voice faltered ever so slightly on the date. He paused.

Anjali noticed.

She reached out and placed her hand gently over his.

"That date never came again," she said.

"Time covered it in dust. People forgot.

What happened... with us.... with this Rai family... it's over. It's gone."

Kunal nodded.

But his eyes lingered on the page....

Inside, he whispered to a silence only he could hear:

How can I forget?

It never left me.

That day is still here....beneath the dust, beneath everything.

He looked at Anjali, his expression calm, but something in his gaze distant.

And inside his mind, the words returned:

You still don't know.

What happened that day...

Wasn't just dust covering memory.

It was the kind of secret

that hides itself from the world—but never from us.

And even now...

that secret is still breathing.

Still watching.

Still waiting to be found.

And someone...

someone out there,

is still trying to uncover it.

And then, Vikrant and Karishma came down the stairs together.

Anjali looked up with gentle smile. "All done?" she asked.

"Meeting ran long," Vikrant replied, brushing his sleeves.

Karishma handed him the list.

"Here. Read it. I added one special name at the end."

Vikrant scanned the paper ... and stopped.

"You added her?" he asked, trying to sound annoyed... but the effort fell flat.

Karishma tilted her head playfully. "Yes. I added your new friend, Usha."

He scoffed. "Your friend."

She grinned. "Fine. Ours then.

And...you didn't stop me."

He didn't reply.

But a faint smile tugged at the corner of his lips.

Inside him, something shifted.... a quiet anticipation

he wasn't ready to name.

His eyes dropped to the list again.

There ...there were so many names...

but only one stood out.

He read her name once.

Then again.

And then... the paper disappeared.

What remained

was her.

Not the ink.

Not the list.

Just her.

Her name blurred into the page, and from it, her face began to form.... soft, unfinished, but alive.

And in that quiet hallucination, he saw them... three or four strands of her hair, loosened by wind, drifting across the words... as if weaving through the letters themselves, stroking the silence between syllables, moving gently across the shore of a paper filled with names....

yet carrying only one.

To anyone else, it was just a list.

To him, it was her.

Beside Vikrant, Kunal glanced at the same paper…. but he wasn't looking at the names.

His eyes had frozen on the date.

1st October.

And for him,

the page didn't carry people….

it carried silence.

The kind of silence

that had been buried long ago….but never fully gone.

The words on the paper

seemed to echo something

he couldn't quite name… a sound between memory and warning,

between truth and dust.

It was as if the letters were whispering,

reaching for him,

ready to speak….

But before the echo could form,

Kunal looked away.

And just like that, whatever the page was trying to say

fell quiet again.

Two men.

Two silences.

One page.

One was seeing a girl

he hadn't stopped seeing.

The other was staring at a day

that never truly ended.

✦ ∞ ✦

The breeze danced lazily through open windows, fluttering the sheer curtains. In the courtyard, the air smelled of soap, dried cotton, and the faintest trace of roasted cumin from dinner earlier.

Usha and Anika sat near the clothesline, folding sun-warmed laundry.

"You're thinking about it," Anika said, without looking up.

Usha blinked.

"Thinking about what?"

Anika folded a dupatta, voice soft but certain.

"The invitation. You should go. It's not far."

A few hours earlier, Narayan had come to the door….awkward but polite….handing over a gold-edged envelope.

From Karishma Rai.

You're invited for the pooja.

She….insisted.

Usha hadn't said much then.

Now, she sighed.

"I just don't know why they'd want me there."

Anika smiled gently, that knowing kind of smile.

"Maybe someone wants to see you.

Someone who cares…. more than you think."

Usha didn't answer right away.

Her hands paused over the folded cloth.

"Maybe I want to ask Vikrant," she said quietly,

"about the sketch…. and about the girl in that photo.

The one who wore this."

Her fingers rose instinctively to her neck….

but stopped.

There was nothing there.

Anika met her eyes and tilted her head.

"Then wear it.

Maybe someone's waiting to see that chain…

and when they see it on you, they'll know how to find you."

Usha looked away, toward her room.

The silver chain sat on the table— snapped at the clasp again.

Quiet. Barely noticed.

Like the past.

But in her silence,

there was no doubt.

She would go.

✦ ∞ ✦

The air in the station was thick with humidity and the scent of old paperwork. A single desk lamp cast a long shadow across Aryan's desk.

He leaned near the window, phone to his ear.

"Yes, Maa. I ate," he said, smiling faintly. "No, I'm not skipping meals. I'll try to be home for Diwali. Promise."

As the call ended, Rajeev walked in with a file.

Aryan raised an eyebrow. "New?"

Rajeev handed it over. "Names confirmed. The two victims…. Anas Ali and Rakesh Sharma. From Hyderabad, but their families didn't know they came to Chandrapur."

Aryan flipped through the pages. Two ID photos stared back at him.

"Anas' mother Fatima thought he was preparing for job interviews. Rakesh's mother Rajeshwari had already reported him missing two days before the forest incident."

Rajeev placed two more photos on the desk. Slightly creased, torn at the edges.

"These were found in Pandit Keval's old cupboard. His wife found them this morning while clearing out old things."

Aryan's gaze sharpened. "Anas and Rakesh…. why would a pandit keep photos of two strangers like them?"

"No call records from his number. But both men attended last call from Chandrapur"

Aryan stilled. "Who?"

Rajeev looked up slowly. "A landline registered to Satish's store."

Aryan stepped back. "Satish?"

Rajeev nodded. "We visit first thing tomorrow."

✦ ∞ ✦

The shutter groaned as Satish pulled it down halfway. Behind him, the outer tube lights flickered, casting a tired glow across the room. He turned back to clear the day's accounts when a faded note slipped from his hand.

He bent down to pick it up…. ready to crumple it without a second thought.

But then he saw it.

One number. Scribbled neatly.

Beside it, small message note…..simple reminders, almost forgotten.

He stood still for a moment, the paper soft between his fingers.

Then his eyes shifted slowly toward the old wooden register, locked and untouched for months. Something in him hesitated.

His gaze lifted.

To the sketch on the wall.

The man with fire in his eyes.

The man his sister had drawn from memory.

Still watching.

Still there.

And suddenly, it didn't feel like just another night.

✦ ∞ ✦

The books were neatly arranged beside the bed, the notebook with wildflowers resting on top like something sacred...almost breathing.

Anika picked it up, opened it gently, and pulled out the folded letter once again.

Her fingertips brushed the inked words, as if her touch could read the face behind them.

She didn't need a name.

Some part of her already knew....

who had written this.

Who had meant it.

She closed the letter with care,

held the notebook to her chest,

and whispered.... "I don't know who you are....

but I believe you.

And I know.... you meant these words."

As she placed the book back on the side table, a quiet thought stirred in her chest....*what if it wasn't who she thought?*

What if someone else had sent it...?

But who would do that?

Her eyes drifted to the photograph on the wall...her mother, smiling in stillness.

Anika stared for a moment longer than usual.

And then, in a voice barely more than breath,

she whispered to the silence:

"Why do I feel...

like it was him?

Why does my heart say...

the inspector sent this?"

It wasn't certainty.

But it was something deeper.

A pull. A knowing. A quiet echo between heartbeats."

✦ ∞ ✦

Inside, Ameet sat alone, the room steeped in a silence that felt too personal. He wiped his hands on a napkin, absentminded, lost in thought. That's when he noticed the envelope on the table....left behind carelessly by Usha.

He picked it up.

Invitation: October 1st – Mahapooja at Rai Residence.

His fingers froze mid-motion.

The paper suddenly felt heavier than it should.

His hands stilled.

Something flickered behind his eyes....regret, maybe.

Or memory.

Or guilt that had been buried deep, so deep it only stirred when it was called by something as simple as a date on a card.

His throat tightened.

The room seemed smaller now.

That date... it didn't just mark a day on the calendar.

It marked a wound.

It called him back to a moment he wasn't sure he had the strength to revisit.

And he didn't know if he was ready to answer.

Or if he ever would be.

✦ ∞ ✦

Karishma placed earthen diyas into the pooja corner of the Rai hall, one by one...lining them like stars waiting to burn.

The flames had not yet been lit,

but her face already glowed ... as if the diyas had drawn their warmth from her instead of fire.

She picked up one gently,

cradling it in her palms.

Her gaze fixed not on the flame—but on the cotton wick,
still white, still untouched.
And yet….. in her eyes, it was already burning.
From across the room, Anjali watched her.
"Did you invite your friend this time?"
Her voice carried both curiosity and memory.
"You said you missed someone last time."
Karishma didn't look up.
Still watching the diya, she whispered…. "Yes…… I tried again."
And just like that,
her smile faded….quietly, like a flame that never got the chance to rise.
She placed the diya back on the floor.
A soft breath escaped her.
The room felt too still.
Too wide.
Too empty.
Like someone was missing.
And then— a single tear slipped from her eye,
falling straight onto the cotton wick.
No fire.
No oil.
Just a drop of her.
She quickly wiped her cheek.
Anjali turned toward her. "What happened, Karishma?"
Karishma blinked fast.
"The thread of the cotton…. it went into my eye," she said quietly.
"It's stinging."
Anjali began to roll her wheelchair forward.
"Let me see."
Karishma lowered her gaze, wiping the corner of her eye again.

"No, Maa.... I just pulled it out. It's fine now."
She looked down at the diya... the cotton still damp with her tear.
And softly,
only in the silence of her own chest,
she whispered: *"Thank you. You saved me."*
And still...
she stayed quiet.

Chapter 19

Morning light spilled into the courtyard like liquid gold. Strings of marigold and jasmine hung from the balconies, swaying gently in the breeze. Incense smoke curled and drifted in slow spirals, mixing with the scent of ghee lamps and rose petals. The house breathed tradition…steady, sacred, timeless.

Pandit Ji, seated cross-legged before the havan, murmured mantras as flames crackled softly, the holy fire glowing like a sun reborn in clay.

Guests trickled in, their silk sarees rustling, their whispers gentle. The Rai mansion shimmered with its usual elegance….but it was a different kind of moment that turned heads.

Usha entered, dressed in soft cotton. No sequins, no gold. Just presence.

Like wind through leaves….she arrived unnoticed but couldn't stay unseen.

From the far end, Vikrant spotted her.

And something in him paused.

A calm. A shift.

But he turned away, quickly, like a boy caught looking.

Karishma noticed him.

She walked toward Usha, her smile easy. "Hi. I invited you, remember?"

Usha returned a quiet nod. "Yes. I wasn't sure if I should come."

Karishma laughed gently. "Well, you did. Which means you were supposed to."

Usha looked around, taking in the symmetry of the mandap, the glow of brass lamps. "It's beautiful," she murmured. "We've never had anything this... grand."

Karishma glanced sideways. "What do you do?"

Usha hesitated.

"I finished my studies last year,"   she began, voice low.

"I've been trying to apply further, but... for now, I'm just at home."

She looked down for a moment...a flicker of discomfort in her silence.

Not shame. Just the weight of being someone

Who's always putting herself second.

"We're a simple family," she added quietly. "Things are tight.

So…. I…I help around the house."

She looked up, a small, soft smile trying to break through.

"And my sister…she wants to study medicine.

Her dream matters more right now."

Karishma brightened. "You're the pillar of your family. What you're doing at home…that's not nothing, Usha. And look at me,"

she laughed,

"I can't even cook biryani. But I'm sure you'll help me someday."

Her eyes drifted to the silver chain around Usha's neck….

its soft shine catching the light.

"Wow… this is so pretty."

Usha looked down at it, touching it gently.

"It's a little dull now.

But it's the last thing my mother gave me.

It matters more than how it looks."

Karishma's smile softened.

She nodded, her voice lower now.

"Then it's not just pretty…..It's powerful. And you…. you look beautiful in it."

From a distance, Vikrant watched. Pretending not to. But watching anyway.

Then he walked over.

"Do you know when this pooja ends?" he asked dryly.

Karishma smirked. "It's your pooja, Bro. You're the one burning in it."

He sighed. "Too much smoke. I feel like a stuffed samosa in a tandoor."

Usha raised an eyebrow, whispering silently to herself.

"So... this is the famous Rai prince.

Irritated by smoke and divine rituals. "

Her gaze lingered, amused.

"What kind of man doesn't believe in pooja?

Look at his sister.....so calm, kind, full of warmth.

And then there's Mr. Ego.....

strange, stiff, and allergic to anything sacred. "

Karishma interrupted her thoughts with a grin.

"Vikrant, you didn't even say hi to Usha.

He needs reminders from others that his friend is here... and that he should say hi."

They both turned to her at the same time.

"Friend?" they said in unison.

And then.... they smiled.

Not because they meant to.

But because in that single word,

they saw each other differently....

and didn't know what to do with it.

The bell above the shop door jingled sharply as Inspector Rajeev entered, two officers behind him.

Customers quickly stepped aside, sensing the tension.

Satish looked up from the counter, startled. He stepped back, nervous.

Rajeev walked up, voice calm but serious.

"Satish," he began, "we've confirmed something. The last calls received by Anas and Rakesh… both came from your landline."

Satish's face went blank. "I… I didn't call them. I swear. I don't even know them."

Rajeev opened a file, slid it across the counter. "Look."

Satish leaned over. His eyes scanned the printed call logs…..two numbers, two outgoing calls from his phone. Both answered. Both traced to the victims.

His throat went dry.

Rajeev's voice dropped lower. "Tell me, why did you call them?"

Satish blinked. Then pressed his fingers to his temple, trying to remember.

A flicker. A moment.

Then it surfaced.

"That day…" he murmured, "Pandit came in. He looked tense. Said he needed to make a quick call. I told him he could use the landline."

Rajeev narrowed his eyes. "And you didn't think to ask who he was calling?"

"No," Satish said, shaking his head. "He didn't say. Just made the call and left. Didn't even thank me."

Rajeev paused, then asked, "What about the second call?"

Satish tried to think. He looked at the date again — from the call logs. Then he checked the shop bills. His eyes moved slowly…. and then, something clicked. He remembered. Something.

"There was a girl," he said. "She came in later that day. Didn't speak….she handed me a note. Said she was mute."

"What did the note say?" Rajeev asked.

"It said, 'Please call this number. Tell him his father wants to meet at the usual place. Tomorrow.'"

"You called?"

"I did. I thought she was just delivering a message. She looked scared. Young. Harmless."

Rajeev nodded slowly. "You planning to install CCTV?"

"I was. But I never did," Satish admitted.

"Can you describe the girl?"

"Long hair. Face half-covered with her dupatta. Very fair. Slim. And… beautiful. That's what I remember."

"You'll come to the station," Rajeev said. "A sketch artist will work with you."

Satish nodded. "Yes. Of course."

Rajeev pulled out his phone, stepping aside.

He dialled Aryan.

"According to Satish, he didn't make the calls himself……Pandit and a stranger girl used his landline. The girl handed him a note, Pandit looked anxious."

The house was quiet.

Anika dried her hair under the sun, the scent of rose soap clinging to her skin.

Roopa was still at the temple. Ameet hadn't returned.

A knock at the door.

She opened it to find Aryan Jha….calm, as always.

"Everything alright?" she asked, surprised.

He nodded. "Just thought I'd stop by."

"Papa's not home."

"I can wait," he said. "If you have tea."

Anika smiled slightly. "Sugar?"

"However, you make it."

While she stepped away, Aryan walked in, eyes falling on the open books. Medical guides. Notes. A notebook with pressed wildflowers.

"You're preparing for entrance?" he asked.

Anika nodded. "Someone sent these. A stranger."

"Strangers don't usually send study material."

She glanced over her shoulder. "I thought of returning them."

"Why?"

"Maybe they weren't meant for me."

Aryan didn't say anything.

Anika walked into the kitchen, a small confusion blooming in her chest.

"Then... he didn't send the books?"

The thought unsettled her.

"I was wrong…. Wasn't I?"

But even as her mind tried to reason, her heart wouldn't accept it.

Something didn't add up.

Something still felt…. his.

A few minutes later, she returned with tea and a plate of biscuits.

Aryan took the cup, then paused.

"They came to the right address," he said quietly.

Anika met his gaze….. quiet, questioning, searching.

He smiled… soft and simple.

Like a secret meant only for her.

"Don't return what's already yours, Anika ji.

And don't stop dreaming."

Then he turned and walked away…. his presence lingering like the warmth of sunlight

just after it fades.

She stood alone in the hallway, tea in one hand…hope in the other.

And for the first time in a long while, neither felt too heavy to hold.

✦ ∞ ✦

Rajeev knocked gently.

Pandit Ji's widow opened the door, eyes hollow, frame smaller than before.

"We found some evidence," Rajeev said gently. "Your husband kept photographs of two men...both of whom are now dead. Did he ever mention them to you?"

"No," she whispered.

Aryan arrived, holding photos. "You gave us these. They were in his cupboard. These men were found dead. In the same forest your husband visited."

She shook her head. "I didn't know. I swear."

"If anything comes to you....anything at all," Aryan said gently, "tell us."

They stepped outside.

Aryan's voice dropped. "Rajeev....inform Hyderabad police. Tell Fatima and Rajeshwari. They deserve to walk through this."

Rajeev nodded.

The wind stirred the street.

But not all ghosts wore chains.

Some walked with old names and old debts still breathing.

✦ ∞ ✦

The pooja neared its final chants.

The fire leapt higher, its glow dancing across the marble courtyard.

Pandit's voice echoed like a bell...sharp, sacred, unwavering.

Usha stood quietly, her eyes fixed on the flame.

She adjusted her dupatta at the shoulder,

her mind far from the chants echoing around her.

"Everyone's focused on the pooja...

How can I ask about the painting?

Or the woman in that photograph?"

The questions circled gently, unanswered.

She didn't' move much….just stared ahead,

her fingers slowly tracing the edge of her infinity pendant,

as if it held answers her lips couldn't voice.

And all the while, she remained unaware of the gaze that never left her.

Vikrant, now seated in the second row, saw everything.

He leaned slightly toward Karishma and whispered,

"She couldn't wear something better?

That dress looks like a dry leaf blown onto fresh grass."

Karishma didn't flinch.

She simply smiled.

"And yet…. you can't stop looking."

"I'm not looking."

"You are."

Vikrant exhaled, his jaw tightening. "I'm just saying… she doesn't belong here."

Karishma's voice dropped, soft as incense smoke. "Oh really? But you invited her."

She looked at him, eyes steady. "She's like a story you tell yourself not to read…. but you do. Again. And again."

He didn't answer.

He couldn't.

Because some stories… you don't find them.

They find you.

And once they do…

they never really let you go.

Chapter 20

The pooja had ended. The scent of marigolds clung to every surface, mixed with sandalwood smoke and the echo of mantras now fading into memory. Laughter drifted through the hall as guests offered final blessings and filtered through the iron gate....silks rustling, hands folded, conversations fading behind.

Inside, the stillness returned like a hush settling over the house.

Usha stood by a carved pillar; her fingers curled around the end of her dupatta. She watched Vikrant from a distance. He stood near the guests.....smiling, composed. Hands behind his back. Clean posture. Clean lies.

He belonged to a world of polished shoes and polished manners. And she didn't.

She turned her eyes away, but something caught her gaze....a large, golden framed photograph on the far wall.

A woman stood beside a man. Her sari was wrapped in grace. Her face was calm. And around her neck, an infinity pendant....silver and unmistakably familiar.

Usha stepped closer.

Behind the woman, a man stood in a police uniform. Rigid. Expression unreadable. He looked like someone the past hadn't quite let go.

"Do you need help?" a soft voice interrupted.

It was Anjali.

Usha blinked. "No. I was just looking at this woman. Who was she?"

Anjali's eyes dimmed a little. "A friend. Her husband was an inspector. They died in a car accident. Years ago. Along with their newborn child. Mata Rani keep their souls."

Before Usha could ask more, a voice called Anjali from the corridor. She gave Usha a small smile and walked away.

Vikrant appeared just then, adjusting his kurta sleeves.

"You love old photographs?" he asked casually.

Usha gave a small smile. "Curious, maybe."

"How's your hand?"

She pulled her dupatta back and showed the faint pink line. "Almost gone."

He nodded. "That painting in Satish's shop. You asked about it?"

Usha hesitated. "Yes. I saw the same face in a book... in the author's picture."

Vikrant's voice dropped. Low. Weighted.

"That's Samar. My Mamu."

Usha froze.

Not dramatically...just a subtle stillness, the kind that settles when memory brushes too close.

"Your Mamu?"

The question left her lips before she could soften it.

He nodded once, eyes fixed ahead.

"He died in a car crash. My mother survived.... but she never walked again."

A breath.

"They never found his body."

She said nothing. Not yet.

"My father says he betrayed the family. That he wrote things—about the business. Lies."

His jaw clenched.

"But Maa.... she still talks to his photo. Like she expects him to speak back."

The silence that followed didn't ask to be filled.

It just.... lingered.

Like the scent of something once burning.

Usha didn't speak.

Didn't blink much.

Then...without warning, without words....she reached for his hand.

Not tightly.

Not timidly.

Just enough to say I heard you.

And I stayed.

Warmth passed between them...quiet and brief.

Like recognition.

Like something half-remembered.

Then she let go.

Soft. Quick.

And before either of them could say another word....

the chain slipped from Usha's neck.

A fragile fall.

A whisper of metal against the air.

Vikrant moved before he could think.

One quick step.

One sure hand.

He caught it....just before it met the ground.

And for a moment, he held it in his palm like it meant everything.

Like it had always meant everything.

His breath caught.

Why did I reach for this?

Why does this... feel like mine to protect?

The chain was hers.

But something about it...about her....made him feel responsible.

Made him want to shield the pieces she never asked anyone to hold.

Then her voice came.

Sudden. Sharp.

Like glass cracking under pressure. "If you knew it was broken... why did you wear it?"

Vikrant looked up.

But Usha didn't.

She was already pulling the chain from his hand, her touch gentle... and distant.

She turned without a word, walked through the archway, and disappeared into the hush of the hallway.

Vikrant stood still.

Motionless.

But inside....his mind whispered:

I broke her again.

Like the chain.

Delicate. Precious. Unspoken.

And once again....I let it fall.

✦ ∞ ✦

Rajeev entered Aryan's office. The investigation board behind Aryan was crowded with threads and photographs. Names circled. Red pins punched through time.

"Message from Hyderabad," Rajeev said. "Fatima and Rajeshwari.....their sons never knew each other. Different circles. No communication. They're shocked."

"But both connected to Pandit Keval," Aryan replied. "Call logs. And their photos in his cupboard."

Rajeev nodded. "We may be looking at something bigger than the forest."

He handed Aryan a printed sketch. "Here's the drawing. The girl who came to Satish's shop."

Her face was partly covered in the sketch. Eyes visible. Dupatta draped across the lower half.

Aryan stared at it. "Can we digitally lift the dupatta? Clean the sketch?"

Rajeev replied, "Yes. Facial estimation software can reconstruct occluded features using surrounding ratios…..jawline, eye position, cheek structure. We run it through a deep-image enhancer. Then match against database."

Aryan nodded. "Do it. Quietly."

Rajeev stepped back. "Understood."

Aryan's eyes didn't leave the board. "Now we dig deeper. Into Pandit's past. His connections. His debts. I want everything."

"Today itself," Rajeev said firmly.

✦ ∞ ✦

The air was thick with heat. A still, burning hush had settled in the small lanes of Chandrapur.

Anika stirred lemon water in the kitchen. Roopa sat under the awning on a Charpai, waving an old newspaper in her hand as a fan.

"It's too hot today," she muttered.

Anika walked out with a steel tumbler. "Lemon water. You'll feel better."

Roopa accepted it, sipped slowly. "You girls… always looking after me."

Anika smiled. "We should get ration today. It's already the 1st….."

The glass slipped from Roopa's hand.

Water splashed across the cracked floor ….. like blood rushing through old veins.

Anika rushed to her.

"Daadi? What happened?"

Roopa clutched her head, forcing a weak smile.

"I'm fine… the lemon water was just too cold."

But inside, something was burning.

Not from today's heat ….. but from something older.

A memory.

A guilt.

Or maybe something she never dared to name.

Anika picked up the broken glass.

"It's okay. I'll make another. Just sit, rest a bit."

Roopa's hands still trembled.

As Anika walked toward the kitchen,

she kept glancing back ….. watching her grandmother through the small kitchen window.

And then, almost too softly to hear, she whispered:

"The water wasn't cold…… I know.

But what you're hiding…

It's something else, isn't it?

Why do you always go quiet….

whenever we say that date? "

It wasn't anger in her voice.

Just the kind of ache that grows

when the truth begins to knock ….. softly, but persistently.

Inspector Rajeev pushed open Aryan's office door ….. his breath a shade too quick,

his eyes tight with something he hadn't had time to bury.

"Sir……." He didn't bother to sit.

"We just got a call. A body's been found."

Aryan's pen froze mid-stroke.

He stood slowly from his chair.

"A body…..again?"

His voice was steady,

but the word seemed to pull the air out of the room.

Rajeev nodded once ..... sharp, clipped.

"A passerby saw it. Phoned it in a few minutes ago."

"Where?" Aryan asked, already reaching for his jacket.

"Side street, just off the highway.

A car pulled over to the curb.

The victim's outside."

For a moment, neither of them spoke.

The wall clock ticked ..... too loud.

Too slow.

Aryan exhaled.

The weight settled on his shoulders like something he already knew would grow heavier.

"Why now.....?" he murmured.

Then, quieter:

"Okay. Let's go."

Rajeev didn't answer.

He didn't have to.

This case.....

It had always felt like a thread.

Delicate. Elusive.

And every time they thought they'd found the starting point ..... something they could finally pull, something that might lead them out of the dark ..... it broke.

Snapped mid-tug.

Slipped from their fingers like it didn't want to be followed.

And worse ..... it never unraveled cleanly.

It twisted back, tangled tighter,

pulled them into knots of questions that answered nothing.

Each breakthrough led to another wall.

Each clue ….. a circle.

A dead end dressed like hope.

Behind them, the caseboard waited ….. covered in photos, scribbled notes, and fading hope.

Maybe it was waiting for a new thread to follow.

Or maybe……. it was just waiting for the next body.

Chapter 21

The sun beat down on Chandrapur like judgment. Dry wind scraped across the narrow street, lifting dust and dread in equal parts.

Then came the scream.

And the town stirred.

Two police jeeps raced in, sirens splitting the silence. Inspector Aryan stepped out first.....his jaw locked, his eyes already scanning. Rajeev followed with a team of constables. Behind them rumbled the forensic van.

A crowd had formed like fire around oil.....eager, loud, uncertain.

Camera flashes. Media vans. A chorus of voices:

"Rai house driver..."

"Wasn't he at the pooja?"

"Narayan?"

Aryan stormed forward. "Keep everyone behind the barricade! Rajeev.....lock this place down. No one enters until we're done."

"Yes, sir."

yellow-and-black tape stretched across the mouth of the street. Uniformed officers moved fast, firm. The crowd was pushed back like a tide held at bay.

And there.....on the ground.....lay the body.

Face turned to the side.

Motionless.

Dust already clinging to the skin.

Aryan's voice dropped low, but its weight hit hard. "Who found him?"

A constable stepped up, pointing shakily to a man near the crowd…..young, helmet still hanging from his wrist.

Rajeev led him forward.

"He's in shock," the constable murmured.

Aryan's phone buzzed.

The SP.

"What the hell is going on, Aryan? There's pressure from every side. If this blows up….."

Aryan's voice was taut. "We're on it. Just give us some time."

"You don't have time," the SP snapped. "If this spirals, the ACP takes over."

Aryan ended the call.

He tossed the phone onto the dashboard and leaned back against the jeep, shoulders tight, jaw set.

This wasn't just a murder.

It felt deliberate.

Like someone was toying with them.

"We're not close," he muttered to himself.

"We're nowhere near the truth."

The air inside the Rai house still held the warmth of ghee lamps. Incense floated lazily. Karishma scrolled through pooja photos, grinning at silly guest poses. Anjali rearranged silver trays, peaceful in the soft rhythm of routine.

Then Kunal's phone rang.

He answered, nodded once…..and the colour drained from his face.

The phone slid from his hand and clattered onto the floor.

He dropped to his knees.

Anjali rushed forward, wheeling herself as fast as her hands could push. "Kunal?!"

He couldn't speak. Just stared at the floor.

Karishma and Vikrant appeared from the hall.

"What happened?" Karishma asked.

Finally, Kunal forced the words out. "Narayan... they found his body."

The room froze.

Time cracked.

Vikrant stepped back like he'd been slapped. He saw Narayan's face…..not lying still, but laughing beside him, guiding his hand on the steering wheel, shielding him from his father's wrath.

He didn't say a word.

He grabbed the car keys and ran.

In a shaded corner of the courtyard, Usha gently ran coconut oil through Anika's hair. The world outside was chaos. Here…..there was calm.

Roopa rolled out dough in the kitchen.

The scent of flour, heat, and haldi hung in the air.

Just then, a woman stepped in from the main gate…..smiling, holding a red bridal lehenga wrapped in plastic.

"Roopa didi, stitch this for my daughter. Shaadi's next week," she beamed.

Roopa nodded, wiping her hands.

The woman's tone changed. "Have you heard? A man from Rai house. Found dead. Police all over."

The bottle slipped from Usha's hand. Oil splashed across the cracked floor.

"Whose body?" she asked. Her voice had cracked. "Did they say who it was?"

The woman shrugged. "No name. But my son saw police. Said it was someone close to the Rai family."

Roopa's hands trembled as she took the fabric. "We'll stitch it. Come in 5 days."

Usha walked inside, without another word.

Anika followed. "Didi?"

Usha leaned against the wall; her eyes full. *"I don't know what's wrong with me... why I feel this way."*

She whispered like a confession,

"Please... let it not be him."

Vikrant.

Not just the man from the pooja.

Not just the one she had argued with.

Something more.

Something unspoken.

And that... scared her most of all.

The forensic team was working fast. Gloves. Swabs. Photos.

Aryan stepped beside the man who had called in the body. His voice was steadier now.

"Tell me everything. Start slow."

The man nodded. "I was riding my bike, heading for groceries. Saw a car. Then I saw him. I thought.....maybe he fainted. But...but when I checked..."

His voice dropped. "He wasn't breathing. So, I called the police."

Then came the screech of tires.

Vikrant.

He pushed through the barricade. "Where is he?"

Aryan didn't answer.

Rajeev stepped in. "Vikrant... when was the last time you saw Narayan?"

Vikrant's voice was hollow. "Today. This morning. He was at the pooja. He helped with everything. Afterward, he spoke with Maa... then said he'd drop Pandit Ji home."

Aryan's eyes narrowed. "Another Pandit?"

Vikrant nodded slowly.

That name again.

Rajeev met Aryan's gaze. "Same link. Again."

Aryan didn't answer.

His gaze moved..... not to the body, not to Vikrant..... but toward the forest. Toward something only he could feel.

Something was being threaded. And this time... the knot was tightening.

Chapter 22

The ceiling fan above Inspector Aryan creaked in slow, tired circles. Its rhythmic hum only made the silence sharper.

The board in front of him looked like a map of grief. Threads of red stretched across silent faces.....Anas. Rakesh. Pandit Keval. And now, Narayan.

Each name was no longer just a file. Each thread tugged like it was pulling at his own chest.

His jaw clenched.

"Rajeev," he called, voice tight.

Rajeev entered, already reading his expression. "I've pulled the data. Narayan's phone pinged at three towers. No calls and no activity."

Aryan didn't blink. "The Pandit. Was he dropped home?"

Rajeev shook his head. "No confirmation yet."

Aryan's hand gripped the desk edge. Then he exhaled. "His ex-wife. She's here?"

"Yes. Waiting outside."

Aryan rose slowly, his eyes still locked on the board.

In the corridor, a woman sat stiffly under the harsh glare of fluorescent light. Her saree.....once vibrant red.....had dulled into something lifeless. A streak of Sindoor still ran through her hair parting. The Mangalsutra around her neck caught the light and held it, like memory refusing to dim.

Aryan approached and sat beside her.

No badge.

No questions.

Just presence.

She looked up. Her voice trembled.

"We were divorced... but I still wore this," she said, fingers gently brushing the Mangalsutra.

"I kept putting Sindoor in my hair…. maybe because that meant I was still his. Not on paper. But somewhere… I….I still was."

Her voice cracked.

The words didn't flow…..they fell. In pieces.

"He said it was because I couldn't…. give him a child. That maybe I was cursed."

She exhaled shakily.

"We argued. I thought the silence between us would heal. But it didn't. It stayed. Grew."

Her hand trembled as it reached her face.

"Still… he was here. In this city. Breathing the same air. And that… that was enough for me."

She wiped her eyes.

Then broke.

A quiet sob…..small, but full of everything she never said aloud.

"And now… even that has been taken. What's left of me now?

A woman who couldn't give life….. and now has no one to carry hers forward."

Aryan couldn't speak.

His hands were steady.

But his eyes weren't.

He stood slowly, voice just above a whisper.

"You were never cursed. You loved."

He paused…..long enough for the silence to settle again.

Then, quietly:

"We'll find who did this. I promise."

And he left.

His steps heavy….. but his resolve heavier.

She didn't move.

Her eyes stayed fixed on the floor.

As if searching for words.

Or maybe…. angry that the earth couldn't hold them for her.

They never gave her a place.

Not in festivals.

Not in conversations.

Not even in grief.

To them, she wasn't a complete woman….. because her womb stayed quiet.

They never said it to her face.

But she heard it….. in their invitations that never came, in the way they whispered cursed when they thought she couldn't hear.

As if she was a shadow that might spoil something sacred.

Now, even her husband was gone.

And suddenly…..the Sindoor meant nothing.

The Mangalsutra was just a thread.

Her tears, just water.

Her eyes wanted to scream….. to ask, What am I now?

To shout, Was my love not enough? Was I never enough?

But she didn't say it.

She never had.

A few tears slipped down, silent and slow.

But she never looked up.

And she, still stayed quiet.

The flowers had wilted. The lamps had cooled. The fragrance of sandalwood had turned into something hollow.

Karishma sat cross-legged on her bed; a medical book opens on her lap. But her eyes didn't move. Her mind was miles away, stuck between the echo of footsteps and the memory of Narayan's laugh.

Downstairs, the silence was louder.

Anjali wheeled herself into Kunal's room. The afternoon sun drew long shadows across the floor.

Kunal sat on the edge of the bed, unmoving. Anjali placed her hand on his, her voice soft as thread.

"He said, 'Ma'am, I'll just be back.'"

Her voice broke.

"And now... there is no back."

Kunal said nothing. But the paper in his hand crumpled slowly in his palm. A storm brewed behind his eyes.....rage, guilt, or something older.

Vikrant was alone in his room. The letter sat in his lap.

Ameet pushed the door shut behind him, shoulders sagging under a layer of flour and fear. Every step from the shop to the house felt heavier than the last.

At the table, Roopa worked her treadle machine, stitching pearls onto a bridal blouse. Clack clack clack clack.....the needle drove down like it was trying to pin the day in place.

Ameet's voice broke the rhythm. "Did you hear?"

He didn't lift his eyes. "Narayan... he's been murdered." A breath hitched. "They're coming."

Roopa's hands froze..... just long enough for the silence to echo.....then the needle started again, faster this time.

Usha stepped in from the courtyard, drying wet palms on a cotton towel.

"What do you mean, Papa? Who's coming?"

Before Ameet could speak, Roopa rose too quickly, chair legs scraping the floor.

"Your father's exhausted," she said, forcing calm into her voice. "Help Anika in the kitchen, Usha."

But Usha stayed where she was. Her gaze fell to Ameet's hands.....hands that had kneaded dough a thousand mornings, now trembling ever so slightly.

The house seemed to hold its breath.

Something's coming, Usha thought.

She didn't know what.

Only that it was already at the doorstep.....close enough to taste in the thick, uneasy air.

The sun dipped lower, the gold bleeding into red.

Outside, Chandrapur had gone quieter than usual. Shops closed early. The chai stalls didn't clink with glasses.

People whispered instead of speaking.

In their homes, curtains were drawn.....not for the sun, but for what they feared might come next.

The city was not mourning a death.

It was waiting for another.

Chapter 23

The knock was heavy. Not loud…..but final.

Karishma, halfway through pouring tea, set the kettle down with a clink and rushed toward the front door.

Standing under the amber porchlight was Inspector Aryan Jha. His expression was unreadable, but the fatigue in his shoulders said everything.

"I'm Inspector Aryan," he said, voice firm but quiet. "I need to speak with your family. It's regarding Narayan."

Karishma nodded slowly. "Please… come in."

She led him into the dining hall. The air inside the Rai mansion still held the fading scent of incense, the memory of marigolds, and the ghost of a pooja that now felt like it belonged to a different world.

Soon, Kunal sat on the edge of the sofa, Anjali rolled in silently, and Vikrant stood behind them, arms folded tightly. Karishma remained standing; her fingers twisted in the edge of her dupatta.

Aryan looked around. His voice carried the weight of someone who'd said too many hard things today.

"I won't take much of your time. But we must move forward now. If you noticed anything strange with Narayan…..anything at all…..please tell me. A change in behaviour, arguments, tension... anything."

Anjali's voice broke the silence, thin and brittle.

"He was fine… he was helping with the pooja… I asked him to drop Pandit ji."

She blinked.

"He said he'd be back in a bit."

Kunal spoke next, slower.

"He was quiet. Kind. Loyal."

He exhaled. "We've had business issues, yes. Rivals. But Narayan was…. just a driver."

He paused, voice thinning. "Have you found the cause of his death?"

He looked down, as if bracing for what he didn't want to hear.

Aryan answered, steady and calm.

"The report could come anytime today. We'll inform you as soon as it does."

Vikrant didn't speak at first. But when he did, it cracked through the stillness like glass.

"He was more than that. He raised me. Protected me. Taught me to ride, to drive, to lie when I was caught... and now….."

His voice faltered. He turned away.

Aryan gave them a breath before continuing.

"You said Pooja, have you recorded the pooja?"

Vikrant nodded and left the room. He returned moments later with a pen drive.

"It's all in here. Crowd footage too. I don't know if it helps."

Aryan took it and stood.

"Thank you. We'll be in touch again."

The door closed quietly behind him, but the echo stayed longer.

Aryan slipped into the front seat of his jeep. He didn't turn the key yet. His phone rang before he could.

Rajeev's voice came through on the line.

"Update from Hyderabad. It's bigger than we thought."

Aryan straightened.

"Go on."

"Both Anas and Rakesh's mothers…..Fatima and Rajeshwari…..were receiving money. Monthly deposits. From Pandit Keval Lal's account. For almost three years."

Aryan blinked. "How long ago?"

"About eight to ten years. The payments stopped after that."

Aryan swore under his breath.

"We wasted time checking the last year's activity. This thing goes way back."

"There's more. Rajeshwari and Pandit were classmates. Same college. Same batch."

"And Fatima?"

"No known connection. But Hyderabad's team still checking her background."

Aryan's voice dropped.

"We're not chasing a single killer. We're chasing a legacy."

"Still no lab reports."

He ended the call, started the engine….. and drove into a silence that wasn't just outside,

but growing inside him too.

Karishma stood at Vikrant's door.

He sat at his desk, the same old letter open again. It looked worn now creased from rereading; edges softened like an old scar.

Karishma stepped inside, sat beside him.

"Bro… this letter. I don't think it was a prank."

He glanced at her.

"What if it's a clue? Someone trying to tell us something."

Vikrant nodded slowly. "Let's show it to Inspector."

Together, they opened the pooja footage again. Dozens of faces flickered across the screen.

Karishma leaned closer.

"Everyone looks normal."

Vikrant whispered, "Then it wasn't about who was watching. It was about who already knew."

✦ ∞ ✦

The room was quiet, except for the gentle flipping of pages.

Usha paced the floor, arms folded.

"Anika… something's wrong."

Anika looked up.

"With what?"

"With Papa. And Grandmother. I overheard them whispering today… Daadi said, 'they're coming.' Papa looked… scared."

Anika frowned.

"You think it's about the today's news?"

Usha paused. "I don't know. But it felt like… the past."

Anika's voice was cautious.

"Maybe they're just being careful. This town is scared."

But Usha couldn't shake the feeling…..her father's eyes hadn't looked scared.

They'd looked haunted.

✦ ∞ ✦

Roopa winced as Ameet passed her the medicine.

"You rest," he said. "I'll make tea."

Roopa swallowed the tablet, then glanced at him.

"Are you okay?"

Ameet looked at her, his eyes heavy.

"When I saw the body on the news… I couldn't breathe. I felt like it was starting again."

Roopa turned sharply.

"Shh. That time is gone. That chapter is closed."

A long pause.

Roopa whispered, "Let it stay buried."

Just then, Usha entered with a plate of fruits. She stopped, sensing the heaviness.

"What were you talking about?"

Roopa smiled too quickly.

"Nothing, beta. Your father was just being dramatic. He gets nervous during crime shows too."

Ameet gave a weak laugh.

"She's right. Too much emotion, I guess."

But Usha didn't believe it. Not fully.

She hugged her grandmother quietly. But her eyes stayed on her father.....who wasn't looking at her at all.

He was staring at the wall.

Like it remembered something he didn't want to.

But this time, silence didn't bring peace.

It brought the next page.

And somewhere, it had already been written.

Chapter 24

A dull thud broke the afternoon silence.

Aryan didn't look up. Not right away. He'd heard that sound before…..the weight of answers arriving late.

Rajeev stood on the other side of the desk, jaw tight, hand still resting on the freshly dropped file.

"Autopsy's in."

Aryan opened the folder, his eyes scanning line after line. Every page told the same story, just in different shades of cold.

Poison.

Traces in the bloodstream.

No signs of ingestion.

Just a sweet laced….. with death.

"Narayan died from consuming sweets containing the same compound as the earlier victims," Aryan said, his voice even.

Rajeev nodded, stepping over to the board behind him. Red threads stretched from photo to photo…..Anas, Rakesh, Narayan, Pandit Keval. A square forming. A pattern.

"Four men. Four deaths. All connected."

Aryan closed the file slowly.

"It's no longer speculation. It's a design."

Rajeev reached into a second envelope and pulled out a single folded sheet.

"This was found in Narayan's glovebox."

Aryan took the paper. As he unfolded it, his breath caught.

A Kundli…..a birth chart.

He read the name.

Satish Kumar.

"It's his," Rajeev said. "Verified by the local pandit who issued it. Real. Issued years ago."

Aryan stared at the parchment, its worn edges and inked markings.

"This isn't just revenge," Aryan murmured.

"It's ritualistic. Someone's following a belief... punishing through it."

Rajeev's voice dropped.

"Could it be a warning?"

Aryan shook his head.

"Warnings come before the act." "

This came after."

A beat.

"They didn't want fear. They wanted consequence."

The temple bells rang softly, their chimes caught in the folds of twilight. A few scattered devotees moved around the courtyard, their prayers floating with the incense smoke that painted the air gold.

Vikrant stood near a stone pillar, arms folded, gaze unfixed. His phone buzzed with updates…..headlines about Narayan, about the Rai family, about loss.

But none of it mattered.

He put the phone away like it was a lie he no longer wanted to read.

And then she appeared.

Usha. In a muted yellow kurta, the wind lifting the edge of her dupatta like a whisper. Her eyes searched his, calm but knowing.

"I heard about Narayan," she said softly. "I'm so sorry."

Vikrant didn't speak at first. His throat was tight. But her voice, her stillness…..somehow it made space.

"He wasn't just a driver," he said, voice barely audible. "He was... family."

Usha listened, letting the grief land between them.

"I never thanked him," Vikrant added, blinking quickly. "Not once."

She stepped closer, her hand resting gently on his arm.

"Then thank him now," she said. "Pray. Not because it'll fix anything. But because it'll tell your heart it's not too late."

He looked at her…..really looked…..and for a moment, the noise fell away. There was only the scent of ghee lamps, the echo of Sanskrit verses, and the quiet weight of sorrow.

"Yesterday we worshipped the Goddess," he whispered. "Today we will do funeral of a man who kept our family together."

Usha glanced toward the sanctum.

"Faith doesn't balance pain. It just helps carry it."

A breeze stirred between them, wrapping the silence in something almost sacred.

Then a voice broke the moment.

"Usha…" Karishma called softly from the steps.

Usha turned, smiling faintly. "Hi, Karishma."

Vikrant gave her a quick nod, and the two siblings walked ahead.

Usha didn't follow.

She stepped closer to the sanctum, knelt, and closed her eyes.

The diya flame flickered. Her hands folded.

Her whisper barely rose above the temple chants…..but it was enough.

"For the Rai family.

For mine.

For the truth.

And for peace."

Outside, twilight deepened. And somewhere in the distance, the forest listened.

Chapter 25

Sunlight made its way through the half-closed curtains, a pale line across the room ..... like an old memory: gentle, fading, and never asked for. The decorations from the pooja still clung to the walls, limp and fading. No one had touched them. No one could.

Karishma sat at the dining table, a medical textbook open before her, but her eyes hadn't moved from the same line for twenty minutes. Her fingers mindlessly flipped a page. Her mind was elsewhere.

The soft creak of wheels broke the silence. Anjali entered, her phone in hand.

"Karishma... did your brother wake up?"

Karishma shook her head without looking up.

"No. He came in late."

Anjali's sigh was heavy, almost fragile.

"The pooja was supposed to bring peace."

She paused. "Instead... it feels like we've invited something darker."

Karishma glanced toward the staircase.

"Should I call him for tea?"

Anjali nodded.

"Yes. And remind him... today is Narayan's last rites."

The case board had become a battlefield of red thread.

Faces stared out under thumbtacks. Victims. Clues. Crossed-out names.

Aryan stood in front of it, arms folded, eyes narrowed.

"Report?"

Rajeev walked in, holding a file in one hand, weariness in the other.

"We confirmed Narayan dropped the Pandit at home. Pandit said they talked about the pooja. Nothing strange."

Aryan asked without looking,

"Any calls after that?"

Rajeev shook his head.

"No. His phone logs were clean. No shops, no homes, no cameras. Just an open stretch of road. His car was parked neatly."

"And the laddu?" Aryan asked.

"He either ate it on his own… or someone made it look that way," Rajeev replied.

"Could've been a friend. Someone he trusted."

Aryan turned back to the board.

His eyes stopped on a new name: Satish.

"And why was Narayan carrying Satish's Kundli?"

Rajeev's voice dipped.

"That's the part we can't explain. It was clean. Just his fingerprints."

Aryan sat slowly. His mind piecing together a puzzle without edges.

"This killer isn't reckless," he murmured. "He's methodical."

Just then, Rajeev's phone buzzed.

He looked at the screen, then up.

"Sir. That girl…..Satish's sketch? The tech team restored her face."

Aryan stood.

"Circulate it. Today."

✦ ∞ ✦

In the flickering light of the media room, Aryan sat with eyes fixed on a screen.

The video of the Rai family's pooja played…..colourful, noisy, serene. Guests smiled, priests chanted, Narayan bowed and helped with guests' shoes.

"It's too normal," Aryan muttered.

He paused on a frame. Usha, by the pillar. Karishma laughing. Narayan walking toward the mandap.

"Not one wrong move," Rajeev said beside him. "Whoever planned this… stayed invisible."

Aryan's gaze sharpened.

"That's the kind of killer who doesn't stop."

The cremation ground was heavy with smoke and silence. The crowd was small. The grief…..immense.

Kunal stood in white, unmoving. Karishma clutched her dupatta like it anchored her. Vikrant stared at the fire, his eyes raw and red-rimmed.

A priest chanted softly as the flames rose.

Anjali sat in her wheelchair beside them, her hand trembling on the armrest.

Across the field, Narayan's ex-wife Kalyani stood behind a tree, eyes filled with a storm she couldn't scream. Her Mangalsutra glinted under her faded saree, her vermillion smeared but still there. She wasn't part of the family anymore. But she had come. To see. To grieve. To say goodbye.

Vikrant whispered through clenched teeth,

"He didn't deserve this."

His voice cracked with a rage no words could soothe.

Kunal's eyes remained fixed on the fire.

Flashback —

A younger Kunal, laughing.

"I'm not going into that forest alone."

Narayan, grinning.

"I've got your back, sir. Always."

Back in the present…..he blinked once.

But he didn't cry.

✦ ∞ ✦

Both inspectors stepped into Satish's shop.

Aryan walked straight to the counter and tossed the file onto the table.

"Explain this."

He slid the Kundli across.

"Found in Narayan's car. It's yours."

Satish went pale.

Rajeev leaned in.

"You said you didn't know about the matter. Yet Pandit used your phone to contact them. And now your birth chart shows up in a dead man's vehicle."

Satish stammered.

"I… I don't know how. Maybe Pandit had it. Maybe he….."

Aryan cut in,

"Convenient. So, your shop, your phone, your Kundli—and still nothing is yours?"

Satish swallowed. Sweat beading at his temple.

"Sir, please… I didn't kill anyone."

Rajeev stood.

"You're not under arrest. Not yet. But stay available. And stay in town."

Satish nodded, silent.

Aryan watched him for a moment, then stepped out of the shop.

Rajeev followed.

"He's lying," Aryan said, flatly.

No doubt. No pause.

✦ ∞ ✦

Back at the police station, Rajeev returned ….. holding fresh files ….. and something unreadable in his eyes. "News from Hyderabad. Fatima and Rajeshwari…..Pandit's so-called acquaintances? "

They both confessed something.

Aryan looked up.

"What?"

"They both said… Pandit was their husband."

Aryan froze.

"That's impossible."

"Different times. No overlap. Neither knew about the other."

Aryan sat back, a chill running down his spine.

"The killer knew before we did."

Rajeev nodded slowly.

"And Pandit's suicide…..what if it wasn't guilt… but fear?"

"He tried to outrun the truth," Aryan said. "But someone already caught up."

Rajeev leaned in.

"Think about it. The killer force pandit to calls his son, Anas, and then same thing with Rakesh."

Aryan's fingers tapped the desk.

"But why bring them all to Chandrapur?"

"Because" Rajeev said slowly, "the forest matters. The town matters. The killer isn't just punishing people. He's building something. A ritual. A pattern."

Aryan looked up.

"And what if it's not finished?"

Suddenly, both phones rang…..sharp, urgent.

Aryan answered first.

His face shifted.

Tension. Then something heavier.

"Satish just found another body."

His voice was low. Strained.

Rajeev answered his call, and within seconds….. his expression matched Aryan's.

"Sir……..Hyderabad confirmed. Fatima and Rajeshwari. Both are gone."

Silence pressed between them.

The kind that doesn't end with words.

Outside, the fire carrying Narayan's ashes still crackled.

Soft. Ritualistic. Final.

But beneath the flames…..

something darker burned.

It didn't scream.

It didn't rush.

It moved quietly.

With precision.

With purpose.

And for the first time, Aryan felt it.

They weren't chasing just a killer.

They were walking straight into a storm

someone had been planning for years.

Chapter 26

The sky over Chandrapur hung low, bruised with storm-coloured clouds. Sirens shattered the stillness as they weaved through narrow lanes and screeched to a halt behind Satish's modest home.

A crowd gathered beyond yellow tape, murmurs rising like smoke. A woman's body had been found…..cold, twisted. Her face, half-hidden in the shadows, looked more like a question than an answer.

Satish stood in front of it, pale as ash. His shirt stuck to his back with sweat. His lips trembled as he spoke.

"I... I closed the shop. Walked home like always. I was just reaching the back gate…..and... she was just there. I didn't even see her face at first. I panicked. I called immediately….."

Aryan's eyes didn't blink.

"Do you think this is normal, Satish? All bodies connected to your shop, your calls, and now one behind your home? Start talking."

Satish's voice cracked.

"I swear…..on my children…..I don't know what's happening!"

Rajeev stepped in; arms crossed.

"Either you're cursed, or you're hiding something."

Aryan didn't respond. He turned to the officers behind him.

"Get a warrant. Search his shop. His house. Every drawer, every crack."

The forensic team moved in with gloves and silence.

The wind stirred, curling through the alley like a whisper of dread.

"That's three wives of Pandit Keval," Rajeev murmured.

"No," Aryan corrected.

"That's three sacrifices."

✦ ∞ ✦

The sewing machine's hum came to a halt as Ameet entered the house in a rush.

His shirt was untucked. His eyes troubled.

Roopa looked up from the hem of a red bridal lehenga.

"What happened?"

"Come inside," Ameet said quickly. "Now."

Anika and Usha were in the kitchen, cutting bottle gourd. They followed the sound of urgency, halting at the threshold of the closed room.

Inside, Ameet's breath was heavy.

He didn't take the water Roopa offered.

"They found Pandit's wife. Murdered."

The glass slipped from Roopa's fingers and shattered.

Outside the door, Usha and Anika flinched.

"Papa?" they both called, voice uncertain.

Roopa's voice trembled.

"It's starting again."

Ameet looked away.

"I can't stop remembering her face. How I buried her with my own hands... and now.....again.....more blood."

"That was buried," Roopa whispered. "It was over. It was over."

"No," Ameet said. "They're watching. Maybe waiting. Maybe punishing."

"Police said it's a serial killer," Roopa insisted. "Not the past."

But Ameet's eyes betrayed him.

And outside the door, both daughters felt it in their bones.

Something had cracked in her father's silence.

When the door finally opened, Ameet stepped out.

He looked at her daughters. No words.

He simply knelt and placed a hand on each of their shoulders.

"No matter what happens… I'll protect you both."

But protection felt far away now. But even as he said it…..it felt far away. Like a promise made too close to the edge.

✦ ∞ ✦

The marigold garlands still hung along the banisters…..dry, colour fading. What once marked celebration now looked like leftover grief.

Karishma paced Vikrant's room like a caged bird.

"First Pandit. Then Narayan. Now his wife. Vikrant, how many more before you admit this is serial?"

Vikrant sat on the edge of the bed, rubbing his temples.

"Let the police work. We don't know what connects them yet."

"We don't?" Karishma snapped. "Then what are we even waiting for…..someone else in our house?"

In the next room, Kunal stood at the balcony door, phone in hand.

He scrolled through old messages. Old photos. But he didn't dial.

Anjali entered, her hands on the wheels of her chair.

"Kunal. What are you thinking?"

He whispered, more to himself than her.

"It all started with Samar."

Flashback —

The forest near the Rai factory was denser then, uncut and wild.

Kunal and Narayan walked through tall grass, surveying land for a new road.

Narayan spotted something red on the ground. A handkerchief. Embroidered with S.Dev.

He paused.

"Sir… is this, Samar's?"

They moved closer, brushed away leaves and dirt.

What they uncovered stilled the wind.

A woman's body. Bruised. Bound at the wrists. Her mouth gagged with a piece of torn cloth.

Narayan looked at Kunal.

"Sir, we have to report ….."

"This is murder," Kunal said. "She deserves justice."

Narayan stepped back.

"And destroy the Rai name? This will burn everything."

Kunal looked down at the body.

A young woman. A life snuffed.

"We have to Bury it," Narayan said quietly. "For the family. For the name."

The shovel hit the earth.

Flashback Ends —

Kunal stood at his window; the curtains drawn halfway.

The world outside looked dim…..even in daylight.

Vikrant entered slowly, a folded letter in hand.

"This letter," he said. "We should give it to Aryan. It says… *It all starts from the factory.*"

Kunal took the letter, eyes scanning it.

Then, without a word…..he tore it in half.

Vikrant stepped back.

"What are you doing?"

Kunal's voice was flat. "This family has buried enough."

He left the room.

Anjali sat in silence, her hand slowly moving along the wheel of her wheelchair.

Vikrant stood with the torn pieces in his hands.

Outside, the wind picked up. And far away, smoke curled from a chimney…..another body burned, another truth buried.

But in the ashes, someone was still watching. And the fire was far from done.

Chapter 27

The light spilling into the station was dull and grainy, filtered through barred windows dusted with years of tired secrets.

Inspector Aryan stood before the updated evidence board. Red threads branched across it like veins in a dying leaf.....tracing from Pandit Keval Lal to Fatima, Rajeshwari, and the third wife. From them, threads led to Anas, Rakesh, and Narayan. The connections were no longer coincidence. They were deliberate.

Rajeev entered with a notepad in hand.

"Sir, the pattern's taking shape. First the Pandit. Then both of his sons. Then Narayan. Now his all wife..."

Aryan didn't turn.

"Which makes the next likely target....."

"Narayan's wife. Kalyani," Rajeev said solemnly.

Aryan nodded.

"Assign immediate protection. She's already lost everything."

"Understood. Also.....clearance just came through. We're searching Satish's home and shop today. Cyber's digging through his deleted call logs and device backups."

Aryan finally turned, pacing the room.

"Good. Any word from Hyderabad? Or that mute girl Satish mentioned?"

Rajeev shook his head.

"Lab results pending. No trace of her yet."

Aryan's gaze drifted back to the board.

"If this was revenge, it could've happened years ago. So why now?"

Rajeev's voice was tentative.

"What changed?"

Aryan's tone dropped, grave.

"Maybe the killer didn't want time to pass. Maybe they needed it…..to watch, to study, to make it personal."

✦ ∞ ✦

Anika stirred tea, the steel spoon tapping gently against the rim of the cup. The smell of ginger and cardamom warmed the kitchen, but something in the air stayed tense unspoken.

Usha stepped out of her room, adjusting the strap of her bag.

"Where are you going this early?" Roopa's voice came from the hallway, weary but alert.

"The temple," Usha replied simply.

Roopa frowned as she walked in, her hands still covered in soap suds.

"Not alone. Not after what happened yesterday. Take Anika. Stay together."

Usha paused.

Anika smiled softly, already wrapping her dupatta.

"Let's go before the street fills up."

Usha gave a small nod, but her mind was already elsewhere…..on shadows that refused to leave.

✦ ∞ ✦

The once-lively Rai mansion felt faded now. The marigolds that had adorned its walls for the pooja drooped in surrender.

Vikrant stood by the window; arms folded. The phone buzzed in his hand. Karishma sat on the couch, legs tucked beneath her, watching him.

"We need to give that letter to the police," she said. "It might be a small clue. But it's something."

Vikrant sighed.

"I tore it. But I took a photo before that."

He cut the incoming call and quickly dialed another number.

"Inspector Aryan? I have something. Can we meet?"

"Where?"

"I'm heading to the temple with my sister. We can meet there."

"Done," Aryan replied.

The temple wore silence like a sacred shawl. Bells echoed faintly. Incense coiled into the air, carried by the soft morning breeze.

Usha and Anika lit their incense sticks, each movement deliberate, their eyes fixed on the flame.

Aryan arrived, shoes crunching gently on the stone steps.

"Namaste, Usha ji. Anika ji."

His voice was soft—but inside, his thoughts tangled as he caught Anika's gaze.

The girl with the Bindiya.

Steady hands.

Eyes that held something—like dusk, like monsoon, like truths left unspoken but deeply felt.

He had once said it quietly, almost in passing:

The bindiya…. it only ever suited her.

Because it was hers.

That red dot wasn't just tradition.

It wasn't decoration.

It was her.

Like the moon resting quietly between the eyebrows –

like light caught between storm clouds,

like a moon alone in the night sky.

Something small.
Something still.
But impossible not to look at….
Aryan looked at Anika's face again – and time folded.
Noise dimmed.
Even the dead felt distant.
And in a voice no one heard but his own, he whispered:
Forget the cases.
Forget the killings.
Forget this entire town if I must…..
I just want this one moment.
Just her face.
Just her bindiya.
Just….. her eyes looking back at me.
And for a second,
he wasn't a police officer.
He wasn't a man chasing answers.
He was simply…. a man who had fallen silent in front of someone who made him feel alive.
And in that temple, surrounded by incense and fading light,
he looked at her again.
Not just with his eyes.
But with everything he had never said.
His heart…..usually composed, sharp, trained…..stuttered.
He imagined …..
the two of them sitting quietly beside a riverbank, feet dipped in cool water, no corpses, no forest, no vengeance. Just her laughter, and the way she would look at the sky while he looked only at her.
But then…..
"Is it true?" Usha asked gently, breaking the silence. "Pandit's wife was murdered too?"
Aryan nodded.

"We're waiting on the autopsy. But yes…"

Anika's voice was hushed.

"Why now? Why so many, suddenly?"

Aryan exhaled.

"That question haunts me too."

A soft smile passed between him and Anika…..fleeting, but real.

Usha watched them with quiet curiosity, her eyes shifting between the two.

Moments later, Vikrant and Karishma arrived.

Vikrant spotted Usha immediately. His posture stiffened…..but his eyes softened before he looked away.

"Hello, Usha," he said, measured.

"Inspector. Anika."

Karishma added, grinning,

"Inspector Aryan, my brother's finally decided to be useful."

Vikrant cleared his throat.

"We found something you should see. But… I'd like to talk privately."

Usha looked to Anika.

"Let's go, sister."

Anika glanced once more at Aryan.

"Bye."

"Take care," Aryan replied, his voice barely above a whisper.

As the sisters walked away, Vikrant said,

"There was a letter. Left during our party. Said 'It all starts from the factory.'"

Karishma added,

"A little boy gave it to him. We searched the video footage but couldn't identify the kid."

"Can I see the letter?" Aryan asked.

Vikrant opened his gallery.

"I tore the original. But I kept a picture. Sending it now."

He hit send. The phone buzzed in Aryan's pocket.

Behind them, Usha lingered.

She stepped back quietly….. but not quietly enough.

Vikrant turned, eyes narrowing.

"You were listening?"

She met his glare without flinching.

"I came back for my slipper. Someone took mine by mistake."

Then she looked past him….. to Aryan.

Her voice shifted.

Lower. Honest.

"But when I heard the word factory… I couldn't walk away."

Aryan tilted his head slightly.

"Do you know anything about the factory?"

Usha nodded once, eyes steady.

"Not exactly. But I've been reading a book by Samar Dev. It's about a forest tribe that vanished from Chandrapur… long ago. That factory was built over their land."

Karishma blinked, startled.

"Samar Dev…. That's my Mamu."

Vikrant stepped forward, something breaking in his expression.

"He vanished in a car accident. Years ago. No body. No closure."

Usha didn't blink.

Didn't soften.

"Maybe he left more behind than a story."

Suddenly, Vikrant's hand shot out…..gripping her wrist.

Too tight.

Too sudden.

"Why are you doing this?

"Why are you digging up ghosts?"

Usha winced.

But didn't cry out.

Karishma stepped between them, voice sharp.

"Bro...! You're hurting her!"

He froze.

Then let go— staring at the faint red mark on Usha's wrist.

His voice dropped. Regret creeping in.

"I didn't mean to...."

But Usha didn't answer.

She turned away, wrapped her dupatta tightly around her shoulders, and walked off without a word.

Her eyes shimmered.

But she never looked back.

Vikrant stood there, unmoving.

His fingers still curled as if holding something that was no longer there.

And the question returned..... louder than ever in his chest:

Why does it hurt... when I hurt her?

Why do I do this··· when I never wanted to?

He didn't know if it was guilt..... or something far more dangerous.

But the ache stayed.

And this time, it followed her all the way down the corridor.

Chapter 28

The rain outside had stopped, but the air in Aryan's office still felt heavy…..thick with humidity, unanswered questions, and the scent of dried fear.

Rajeev entered quietly, a thin file in hand.

"Lab reports just came in."

Aryan nodded, rubbing his temple. The weight of names on the board behind him had grown unbearable…..every thread now felt like a pulse.

He opened the file.

"Cause of death?"

"Poison," Rajeev replied. "Di methyl parathion. A nerve agent. Odorless. Fatal in high concentration. Absorbed through skin."

Aryan's brow furrowed.

"How was it administered?"

Rajeev passed another page.

"Perfume. The bottle was on her dresser. She wore it just before going out."

Aryan looked up, startled.

"Going where?"

Rajeev hesitated.

"To meet her lover."

Aryan froze.

"Lover?"

"Satish," Rajeev said softly. "Confirmed. Last few call records, text exchanges… over a year and a half of contact."

Aryan leaned back in his chair, exhaling slowly.

"Satish is married."

Rajeev scratched the side of his neck.

"And to a woman far more beautiful than people expect him to deserve."

Aryan gave a crooked smirk.

"That's the thing about desire, Rajeev," Aryan said, his voice low, reflective.

"We chase what isn't ours. We fall in love, yes—but once we have it… once it stays….we start to forget."

Rajeev glanced at him but didn't interrupt.

"What once made our hearts race becomes routine. The love we once begged for becomes background. And then… we start looking elsewhere. For excitement. For escape. For something new."

They sat in silence. Not as officers. But as men.

Questioning things they never dared say out loud.

"Satish has a beautiful wife," Aryan continued.

"She stands beside him, shares his world. But still…. he found himself staring at Pandit's wife."

Rajeev frowned.

"Is that love? Is that what we've started calling love now?"

Aryan exhaled.

"I don't know. Maybe it never was love. Maybe we just fall for moments, not people. And when the moment fades…. so does the feeling."

The silence returned…..not cold, but heavy.

Because they both knew….

this wasn't just about Satish.

"Anyway," Rajeev finally broke the stillness.

"Satish claims they were supposed to meet that evening…..in the abandoned house behind his. He closed the shop early. Texted her. Said they'd meet near his place."

He hesitated, then added,

"We found an old, rusted nameplate with his name there too. Faded…. almost forgotten. Like a memory he never buried properly."

Aryan's voice dropped.

"And she'd already applied the perfume."

"Exactly. The poison activated within fifteen to twenty minutes."

A pause.

Heavy. Still.

"So….she died alone," Aryan murmured.

"Thinking she was going to meet someone who cared."

Rajeev shifted, discomfort in his tone.

"We didn't find any gift receipt in her house. No perfume bill. It might've been planted."

Aryan nodded, fingers steepled in thought.

"Trace the source. Check all local stores, online orders. See if anything leads back to Satish…..accounts, phone numbers."

Rajeev continued, his voice a touch lower.

"There's more. During the search of Satish's old house, we found paintings. Dozens of them. Covering every wall."

He glanced at his notepad.

"Forests.

A man behind bars.

A factory.

A little girl's portrait.

And a woman….drowning."

Aryan leaned forward, eyes narrowing.

"Get them photographed. Catalog every piece. I want to know what story he's trying to paint."

Rajeev gave a short nod.

"Also…..Hyderabad confirmed. All three women. Same poison. Different methods. Different bottles."

Aryan stood slowly.

His gaze distant.

Voice low, cold, but heavy with meaning.

"Someone's turning death into poetry."

"And each verse.... is stitched with history."

The sun outside didn't reach Usha's room. Shadows clung to the walls like silence that overstayed. She sat near the window, fingers gently brushing her wrist.

The red mark from Vikrant's grip had faded..... but the sting hadn't.

Not on her skin.

Not in her memory.

"How can a man change in seconds?"

she whispered.

It wasn't the pain that hurt.

Not the grip.

Not the mark.

It was the moment.

The shift.

The way his anger found her without warning.....and without reason.

At the temple, his eyes had been soft.

Almost searching.

And then..... his words, sharp.

His silence afterward.....

colder than any apology could undo.

She closed her eyes, the ache building not in her wrist,

but somewhere deeper.

Quieter.

"You didn't just hold my wrist, Vikrant," she breathed.

"You shattered something I never told you I'd built."

Something fragile.

Something she had never dared to name.

Not even to herself.

Karishma stormed into Vikrant's room without knocking.

"You hurt her."

Vikrant didn't look up from his desk.

"It wasn't on purpose."

"But you did it."

"She kept talking about Samar. I don't want to hear his name."

His voice cracked.

"You don't know what that name means in this house. Every time Maa and Papa came close, it was Samar who tore them apart. I've grown up watching my parents break in silence."

Karishma's tone softened.

"But Usha didn't know that."

He looked away.

"She's still your….."

"Still what?" he snapped.

She held his gaze.

"Still your friend."

Vikrant tried to laugh, bitter.

"Your friend, maybe."

Karishma sighed, standing up.

"Ok, my friend. Now I am going to make a tea for Mr. Broken."

As she left, Vikrant clenched his fists.

"I'm sorry, Usha," he whispered.

"I didn't mean to leave that bruise… not on your wrist. Not on your heart."

Kunal adjusted his coat at the doorway.

Anjali wheeled in, stopping behind him.

"Where are you going?"

"The farmhouse."

She started to reply—then faltered.

"Tell Narayan to….."

And stopped.

The name felt like broken glass in her mouth.

Her hands trembled.

Her mind drifted.

Flashback —

A younger Anjali walked into the old Rai study, pre-accident. Her gait was brisk, voice still full of light.

Kunal and Narayan stood nearby, talking low.

"Samar is not innocent," Kunal said sharply.

"He's my brother," Anjali replied. "How can you say that?"

Kunal turned away.

"He's not one of us. Never was."

Narayan tried to ease the tension.

"Mam Sahiba, these things... they're not worth the fights. I'm here to protect this family. To protect him."

Anjali stepped closer.

"Tell me, Narayan. What did Samar do?"

Narayan looked at Kunal. Then looked down.

"Nothing, Ma'am. Nothing. But you don't need to worry. I'm here."

Flash fades —

Anjali wiped her cheek gently.

"Samar," she whispered, "you were still my brother."

And somewhere in the shadows of her memory, a fire crackled burning what no one ever dared speak of.

Chapter 29

The storm outside had passed, but inside Aryan's office, it still raged.

The board was a constellation of tragedy now…..faces of the dead, red threads stitching their lives together with invisible ink. Aryan stood in front of it, arms folded behind his back, eyes tracing the pattern again and again.

Rajeev entered quietly, holding a fresh file like it was burning in his hands.

"Perfume shop report," he said, placing it on the table. "We cross-checked every cosmetic outlet near Pandit's neighbourhood. One match. The CCTV confirms…..his wife bought the same perfume a month ago."

Aryan didn't turn.

"And it was half-used?"

"Yes. So, the poison wasn't in the original bottle."

"Meaning it was tampered with. Someone added the poison later."

Rajeev nodded.

"Here's the twist. Same perfume…..sealed, unused…..was found in Satish's cupboard."

That got Aryan to turn. His gaze sharpened.

"Send it to the lab. Trace analysis for dimethyl parathion. Immediately."

"Already in process."

Aryan's voice dropped as he turned back to the board.

"Three women. Three deaths. All tied to the Pandit. And Satish? He's the common knot between them."

Rajeev folded his arms.

"Still no hard evidence. Just… threads."

Aryan's voice was a whisper.

"Threads lead to fabric. And fabric hides bodies."

✦ ∞ ✦

Evening shadows slipped through the windows like secrets, curling at the corners of the Rathi home.

Anika sat near the balcony, pretending to read. Her fingers played absently with the corner of a page while her eyes watched Usha pace behind her.

"Didi," Anika said softly, "do you ever wonder… how hard it must be? Being a police officer?"

Usha paused.

"You mean their work?"

Anika nodded, slowly.

"The pain they see… and the people they can't save."

Usha came and sat beside her, brushing a strand of hair from Anika's forehead.

"They are trained for that. Just like you will be trained to become a doctor…..learning to save lives, fighting disease, holding hope."

Anika's voice cracked.

"And what if we're too poor to dream that far?"

Usha took her hand.

"Dreams don't have price tags, Anika. They just need two things: your courage… and someone who believes in them."

Anika looked at her with tears in her eyes.

"Then I already have both."

✦ ∞ ✦

Karishma entered Vikrant's room with quiet steps and two cups of tea.

"For you," she said, handing one over. "Don't worry. No emotional lecture today."

Vikrant gave a faint smile.

"Thanks."

They sat in silence. The curtains fluttered at the window, letting in dusk and dust.

"You're still thinking about her, aren't you?" Karishma asked.

Vikrant kept his eyes on the floor.

"You said you wouldn't bring her up."

"Sorry," Karishma murmured.

"She doesn't matter," he insisted.

Karishma let out a quiet scoff.

"Then why is your face arguing with your voice?"

He exhaled, not answering.

"Police are questioning Satish," he muttered. "They found Narayan's wife... behind his house."

Karishma sat straighter.

"Satish? But.... He's innocent, right? "Karishma asked softly.

Vikrant gave a slow shrug.

"I know he is. But the police... they don't."

She placed her hand gently over his…..steady, warm.

"You trust him. Like you trusted Narayan."

He nodded once.

The weight of that name still lingered in his breath.

"And I know you miss Usha," she said, voice even softer.

Vikrant's jaw tightened.

His gaze dropped.

"She doesn't belong in this mess," he murmured.

"She should've walked away."

Karishma's voice lowered to a whisper, but her words carried more than sound.

"But you do. And she walked into it…. because she cared."

She hesitated.

Then added…..

"And maybe… somehow, it's all connected. She's following pieces that trace back to us. To things we never dared to."

Vikrant didn't speak.

But his silence trembled….. just slightly.

Like a man standing in a place where truth met guilt,

and both had her name.

Aryan sat at his desk, exhausted but wired. The case had grown limbs. Too many.

Rajeev entered again, this time with urgency in his step.

"Hyderabad police sent something strange."

Aryan looked up.

"Go on."

"Just hours before Rajeshwari and Fatima died, a doctor and a nurse visited both homes. CCTV confirms. They didn't visit a single other house."

Aryan's brows rose.

"What the hell?"

Rajeev opened a file.

"Rajeshwari inhaled poison from a joss stick laced with botulinum. Fatima ingested fluoroacetate in her cough syrup. Both are fast-acting neurotoxins. Symptoms started within minutes. Both were dead within two hours."

Aryan leaned back slowly.

"They were poisoned… in their own homes. And someone disguised as a doctor and nurse delivered it."

"Yes. And they weren't real."

Aryan stood and faced the evidence board.

"This was precise. Surgical. Someone orchestrated this like music…..notes of faith, family, guilt… and poison."

Rajeev nodded grimly.

"So, what now?"

Aryan's eyes settled on the photo of Pandit Keval Lal.

"Now? We follow the music. All the way to the one holding the baton."

Chapter 30

The dining hall of the Rai residence shimmered under the golden glow of the chandelier. Silverware clinked gently against porcelain, and the air carried the faint aroma of cumin and ghee. But the mood at the table was hushed…..stretched taut like the silence before a monsoon storm.

Kunal Rai cleared his throat, breaking the stillness.

"Beta… you remember Samina?"

Vikrant, mid-bite, looked up slowly.

"Samina?"

His voice was neutral, but his eyes hinted confusion.

Karishma smiled faintly.

"Samina, she is my bestie, Bro. We played games in the driveway every summer."

Kunal leaned forward, folding his napkin with care.

"Her father called today. We're considering a proposal…..for your engagement."

The spoon in Vikrant's hand hovered for a moment before he set it down.

"Papa… all of a sudden?"

"Listen," Kunal continued, measured but firm, "our stock value is unstable. Raichand's name carries weight. Political ties. Business growth. This alliance could bring calm to the waves."

Anjali, adjusting her shawl, added softly:

"She grew up in this house. Ate from this table. She's still ours."

"Studying in Oxford. Polite. And you both were close," Kunal said. "We're not forcing anything. Just meet her. It's only an engagement."

Vikrant leaned back, running a hand through his hair. He offered a faint smile…..a practiced one.

"Do whatever you want," he said flatly, picking up his spoon again. "Ugh… it's spicy."

Karishma looked into Vikrant's eyes—searching, silent for a moment.

Then she smiled softly.

"Maybe Bro deserves some Jalebi?"

Vikrant nudged her under the table, murmuring,

"Stop it. I know what you're hinting at."

Karishma grinned, unbothered.

"And I know you know."

For a moment, the table breathed again…..half laughter, half longing.

The kind of ease that only exists when hearts remember what it's like to feel light again.

In the modest kitchen of the Rathi house, the sounds were simpler…..steel tumblers, sizzling ghee, and soft voices.

Usha wiped her hands on a cloth, glancing at the quiet figures of Ameet and Roopa at the dinner table. Across the room, Anika beamed.

"Papa, want to try my kheer?"

Usha's face lit up.

"You made kheer? Why didn't you tell me earlier!"

Ameet chuckled.

"Ok. But don't give any to your grandmother. Sugar is her enemy."

Anika smirked.

"I made sugar-free. She's not escaping dessert tonight."

Roopa laughed, gently swatting Anika's arm.

"She takes care of me better than I do myself."

Usha leaned against the counter, a faraway look in her eyes.

"I wish….I wish Maa was here… She would've loved this."

Roopa's smile faltered. Her eyes moved toward Ameet…..who looked down, quietly pressing his palms together. His eyes carried a weight that had learned how to stay silent. But a smile still managed to cross his face.

"Kheer is sweet," he murmured.

And just like that, the room filled with warmth. Outside, darkness waited. But inside, there was only the comfort of familiarity and food, and the scent of cardamom weaving around memories not yet spoken.

A lone tube light buzzed softly above Aryan's door. The room was quiet, save for the mosquitoes dancing at his ankles. He stood with one hand in his pocket, the other holding his phone to his ear.

"Rajeev," he said.

"Sir? All good?"

Aryan swatted a mosquito.

"Just the buzzing. Anything from Hyderabad?"

Rajeev's voice was low.

"Still nothing concrete. Forensics are crawling through records. They say maybe tomorrow."

Aryan nodded to himself.

"Alright. Let me know the second anything shifts. I don't know why… but I feel like something's close. Like a door we've been walking past is finally about to open."

"Yes, sir. I'll stay on it."

The call ended with a click.

Aryan looked up at the night sky through the window of his room.

The stars were faint tonight….. as if the clouds had swallowed their courage.

But the air was still.

Heavy.

Holding the scent of something unfinished.

He could feel it in his chest.

Not panic.

Not fear.

Something quieter.

A truth was coming.

Not loud.

Not sudden.

Slow.

Steady.

And alive.

Like a shadow that had waited long enough to be seen.

Chapter 31

The morning drifted into the Rai house with the quiet fragrance of incense and the soft clink of bangles. Golden sunlight filtered through sheer curtains, gently brushing the marble floors. In Vikrant's room, however, the brightness felt like intrusion.

He sat on the edge of the bed, hair tousled, brows knitted.

Karishma entered without knocking, holding a pooja thali in one hand and her phone in the other.

"Good morning, Mr. Broody. I come bearing divine blessings... and childhood flashbacks."

Vikrant rubbed his temple.

"Not now, Karishma. And that pooja smoke gives me a headache."

She rolled her eyes dramatically, then waved her phone in front of him.

"Look! Samina. Mom gave me this old photo. Remember? You two built a sandcastle together and declared it a kingdom."

Vikrant glanced at it and looked away.

"Yeah, we were seven. Doesn't mean I should marry her now."

Karishma's voice dropped, more curious than teasing now.

"Then why are you agreeing to the engagement?"

He didn't answer at first. His fingers tightened around the bedsheet.

"Because it's what Dad wants. What this house needs."

She sat beside him.

"And what about what you want?"

Vikrant's voice was lower now.

"There's no space for that."

Karishma stared at him for a long moment, then asked carefully,
"You don't have feelings for anyone else? Not even...?"

He stood up.

"Drop it. I must get to work."

She smirked, rising too.

"Fine. But breakfast's ready. And..."

She turned to leave the room.....but his voice stopped her.

"You still have Usha's number?"

Karishma paused, surprised.

"Why?"

Vikrant looked at her, his voice low.

"I just... I just want to say sorry."

Karishma's grin widened, teasing.

"That's all? And......?"

He didn't answer.

"Okay..," she smirked.

"Want me to cancel the engagement? Honestly, I wouldn't mind. I never liked it anyway. I just want you to do what your heart says.

"Karishma!" he snapped, flustered.

"This isn't about that. It's just....I did wrong. I hurt her. And I need to say sorry. That's all."

Karishma didn't reply right away.

Her eyes drifted to the pooja thali held gently in her right hand.....the cotton wick still burning, flame flickering against the wind trying to put it out.

She slowly moved the thali inward, close to her chest..... as if protecting something sacred.

Something only she understood.

She murmured something under her breath.

Soft. Inaudible.

Words only the flame heard.

And maybe....

only the heart that was breaking beside it."

✦ ∞ ✦

Aryan pushed through the station's creaking door, sleeves rolled and hair unkempt. His face wore the exhaustion of too many sleepless nights.

"Mosquitoes. Government lodges are basically camps for them," he muttered, flopping into his chair.

Rajeev entered, holding a USB and a folder.

"No rest for us, sir. Cyber team pulled deleted files from Satish's phone."

Aryan inserted the drive. A series of images flashed.....sketched over, red Xs drawn crudely over pandit face.

Rajeev pointed.

"Satish says it was nothing.....just trying to keep Pandit's wife happy."

Aryan's brows drew together.

"Or he's rehearsing something darker."

Rajeev nodded; voice grim.

"I don't believe him."

Aryan leaned back.

"Neither do I."

✦ ∞ ✦

Usha sat near the window, her mother's silver chain looped around her fingers like memory. The soft rustle of the neem leaves outside whispered through the cracked panes.

Her phone buzzed.

"Sorry for yesterday. — Vikrant"

She stared at it for a moment, jaw tight.

Now, you remember softness?

But her fingers hesitated.

"It's okay."

A second buzz. A simple smile emoji.

She stared at it longer than she should've. And despite herself…..smiled back.

Just then, a knock.

She opened the door. Inspector Aryan stood, polite as always.

"I need to speak with you. About that book you mentioned."

"Of course," she said.

She led him to the veranda. Inside, Anika stepped out of the bathroom, wet hair clinging to her cheeks, no dupatta in sight. She froze.

Aryan stood immediately.

"I…..I'm sorry. I didn't mean….."

"My dupatta's on that chair," she replied, flustered but graceful.

He stepped aside awkwardly.

"Of course. I didn't realize."

As she walked past, Aryan whispered to himself.

"Anika….. all I want is to get lost in your rain-wet hair, in the quiet of your love….

But look at me…..still tangled in these case files, still drifting through unanswered questions. "

Usha returned with the book, unaware of the quiet shift in air.

"Here. This is Samar Dev's work. He wrote about a tribe… and in this chapter…..he mentions a reporter. Rekha. She disappeared on October 1st years ago."

Aryan's eyes scanned the pages.

"October 1."

"I don't know," Usha said, her voice lower now. "But that date… it has meaning. Every time we, our parents'

Before she could speak more, Anika returned, locking eyes with her sister. There was something in that glance…..protective, or warning.

Usha hesitated.

"Nothing. Maybe… coincidence."

Aryan didn't push. But he knew what silence sounded like when it was hiding something.

He tucked the book under his arm and gave a short nod.

"Thank you. If anything, else comes to mind... let me know."

He glanced once more at Anika before leaving, the scent of jasmine and questions lingering in the veranda.

And as the sisters stood in that quiet space, Usha felt it…..deep and certain.

Truth isn't something you can bury forever.

You can hide it…

but it slips…..through glances, through silences,

through the cracks between words.

And maybe…. hiding truth was never meant for people like her.

People who carry their wounds in their eyes, and their questions in their breath.

Chapter 32

The fan above Aryan spun lazily, unable to cut through the heat or the weight in the room. At his desk, Aryan leafed through Samar Dev's worn book again…..its pages browned at the edges, the ink faint in places, but its contents haunting. Scribbled margins. Sketches of trees with hollow eyes. A phrase underlined in red:

"People found ghosts here long ago….. and the forest still holds them.

Just then, Rajeev entered, holding a manila folder with urgency.

"Hyderabad police found the van. The one used by the fake doctor and nurse."

Aryan looked up sharply.

"Did they catch them?"

"No. Faces covered. CCTV from the lane outside shows them entering, but the angle doesn't capture them leaving clearly."

Aryan closed the book with a soft thud.

"Keep pushing. They couldn't have vanished. Check rental agencies. Nearby hospitals. Even uniform suppliers."

Rajeev nodded.

"What's the book about?"

Aryan shook his head.

"Don't know. Just get a photocopy made. I want full details on the author and the publisher. And find out where Samar lived…where he wrote… and where he disappeared."

He paused, then added quietly,

"And one more thing…..October 1st, 2003. A reporter named Rekha went missing in Chandrapur forest. I want every article ever written about it. No more blind spots."

Rajeev blinked.

"You think it's connected?"

Aryan's voice was calm but resolute.

"It might not be. But the last time someone ignored a missing girl… she disappeared from memory too. That won't happen again."

The bell rang…..sharp and clear through the marble hall.

Karishma opened the door and squealed before the face even came into view.

"Samina!"

And there she was….. Simple, radiant.

Eyes like pearls kissed by the morning sun.

A smile so natural, it felt like the word smile had been made for her.

Beauty didn't just suit her….. it surrendered to her.

The soft green dress she wore fluttered slightly in the breeze, as if the air, too, had paused for her arrival.

Karishma smiled…..wide, breathless.

And then… she moved.

The two embraced, tightly.

Laughter spilled out of them like it hadn't been years.

Like no time had passed at all.

Behind them, Anjali appeared, wheeling herself forward, joy lighting up her face.

"Samina is here!"

Samina stepped in with grace…..confident, but eyes carrying a softness that hadn't aged.

"Finally," she smiled. "It feels like nothing changed. Except... this chandelier looks bigger."

Karishma giggled.

"It's the same. You're just older."

She tapped a call to Vikrant.

"Bhai! Guess who just walked in?"

His voice, gruff on the other end.

"I have meetings, Karishma. Cut the call."

He hung up. But his screen still glowed…..with a message from Usha: "smile emoji"

For a moment, his expression broke.

Downstairs, Kunal welcomed Samina with warmth, though something shifted in his eyes when she said:

"Remember how Vikrant used to steal my toys and give them to Narayan to hide?"

Kunal's hand paused mid-gesture.

Flashback – Years Ago

In the dusky silence of the forest near the factory, Kunal and Narayan stood by a pit, burying a woman's body wrapped in cloth. Kunal handed him a satchel.

"Make sure this never comes up again."

Narayan nodded, loyal. Silent.

Back to Present —

Kunal murmured under his breath.

"Yes... Narayan always hid things well."

Anjali noticed his distant look but chose not to press.

"Samina, come. Let's get you settled."

✦ ∞ ✦

The aroma of cardamom drifted from the kitchen, warm and familiar. Anika stirred the kheer gently, while Usha dried the plates beside her.

"Why did you tell Inspector Aryan our parents were hiding something?"

Anika's voice broke the silence…..soft, but pointed.

Usha looked up, caught off-guard.

"I didn't say that. I only meant… sometimes, people speak more freely to outsiders. Especially when the truth is too heavy for home."

Anika's eyes clouded, her hands pausing mid-stir.

"No. Parents tell the truth to people they love."

Usha wiped her hands, stepped closer.

Her voice quiet…..measured.

"Or they lie…. to protect the ones they love."

She hesitated, then added….. "I used to think silence meant peace. But now…. I wonder if it's fear."

Their eyes met.

Two sisters, standing on opposite shores

of the same storm.

✦ ∞ ✦

Dry leaves crunched beneath Aryan's boots.

Rajeev followed closely, his breath heavy, uneven.

The trees stood tall and silent…..witnesses to things unsaid.

But the air carried more than just silence.

It carried memory.

Guilt.

Something almost… breathing.

"What are we even looking for?" Rajeev asked, brushing away a low-hanging branch.

Aryan didn't answer immediately.

He stepped into a small clearing, where the light barely touched the ground.

"They were all brought here," he said at last.

"The Pandit's sons. Narayan. All of them."

He knelt, his fingers grazing the earth as if trying to feel what words never said.

"This forest…..it's not just a place. It's a language. A ritual."

His voice dropped, almost to a whisper.

"They could've been killed anywhere. But they were brought here. Like someone wanted the soil to remember. Like they were trying to rewrite history….with blood."

Rajeev swallowed, unsettled.

"So…. what now?"

Aryan rose slowly, his gaze fixed ahead…..not on a path, but on something just beyond it.

"We go deeper."

A pause.

"Something connects all of it. Satish. The Rai house. The Pandit family. The silence in between."

And not far behind….. someone watched them.

Hidden in stillness.

Breathing with the forest.

Waiting.

Chapter 33

The sound of the main gate creaking open echoed faintly into the drawing room. Vikrant stepped in, shoulders heavy, tie half-loosened. He was expecting silence…..but found warmth.

Samina sat cross-legged on the sofa, a porcelain cup of tea in hand, laughter in her eyes as Karishma chatted beside her. Anjali was folding napkins. Kunal skimmed through the day's paper, but his ears were clearly tuned to the reunion.

"Hello, Viku," Samina said with ease, her voice laced with nostalgia.

Vikrant stopped mid-step.

"It's Vikrant now," he replied…..though his voice lacked edge. It was more memory than correction.

Karishma burst into laughter.

"You used to scream if anyone didn't call you Viku. And don't act like you've forgotten how we used to tease her with *Sam.*"

Even Anjali chuckled from her chair.

"That poor girl once ran into a cupboard just to escape your pranks."

Vikrant's lip twitched…..then gave in to the faintest smile.

The kind that barely shows…. but means everything.

Samina watched him quietly.

Not just the smile…..but the restraint behind it.

The way he held back, like something in him wasn't ready to move,

but remembered how it once did.

Karishma caught the glance between them.

Her laughter faltered…..just for a breath…..then returned like nothing had shifted.

She looked away, reaching for the tray on the table, adjusting plates that didn't need adjusting.

It was something to do with her hands.

Something to keep them from folding into silence.

Inside her mind:

Bro… I know you still carry her. Usha.

So why act like this moment is anything else?

She didn't wait for an answer.

Didn't need one.

She already knew how to bury questions that were never meant to be asked.

The sound of casual conversation resumed behind her.

Laughter. Footsteps.

But her back stayed to the room.

And if anyone noticed the way her shoulders stiffened for just a second…..they said nothing.

Because some silences…

are practiced.

The yellow bulb flickered overhead as steam curled from Anika's teacup. She sat on the floor in her pajamas, a heavy medical textbook open across her lap. Across from her, Usha lay sprawled on a cushion, her eyes studying her sister, not the book.

"Tell me one thing," Usha asked suddenly.

Anika didn't look up. "What?"

"You and Inspector Aryan?"

Anika nearly spilled the tea. "Aryan? What do you mean…..me and him?"

Usha raised an eyebrow. "Your eyes blush before your cheeks does. And he stares at you like the world slows down."

Anika rolled her eyes, cheeks heating. "There's nothing. And how do you know what he feels?"

Usha smirked. "So now you want to know what he feels?"

Caught.

Anika sighed, setting the cup aside.

"Those books. The entrance prep ones. They weren't just some random deliveries. He sent them. Didn't admit it, but... I know."

Usha gasped, hands to her chest.

"Stop. This is officially romantic. Let me write this story: Medical Girl and the Mystery Cop."

Anika threw a pillow at her, but laughter filled the room like wind through curtains…...soft, sudden, freeing.

For once, it felt like nothing was broken.

Rajeev was mid-laugh, his voice warm as he ended a call.

"Okay, okay. I'll bring the ghee laddoos next time, promise. Love you."

He clicked off the phone as Aryan entered, a slight smile tugging at the inspector's usually unreadable face.

"Who knew our stone-faced Rajeev was such a romantic?"

Rajeev stood awkwardly. "Sir…...uh... that….that actually was my wife."

Aryan chuckled.

"Relax. Come on. Let's escape this station's terrible tea before it poisons us both."

Rajeev grinned. "Samosa?"

"Samosa," Aryan agreed.

Under flickering fairy lights, the air smelled of hot oil and masala. The samosas sizzled in the pan, and Aryan and Rajeev stood by the wooden counter, sipping tea from glass tumblers.

"Sometimes I think we'll retire with samosas in one hand and unsolved murders in the other," Rajeev said, munching thoughtfully.

Just then, two familiar figures walked by.

Usha nudged her sister. "Your Samosa Inspector."

Anika blushed. "Lower your voice!"

But Aryan had already spotted them…..and promptly coughed as a crumb went the wrong way.

Anika rushed to the counter.

"Here…..water." She handed him the glass, concern in her eyes.

Aryan took it, still choking slightly, and gave a grateful nod.

"Thanks. I wasn't expecting…..well, anyone to see me like this."

Usha leaned in, teasing under her breath.

"Anika G… you've got a handsome one."

Aryan blinked.

Anika's mouth fell open. "Usha!"

Rajeev, mid-bite, choked on his samosa and nearly dropped it into the chutney.

Laughter broke out between them ….. sudden, unfiltered,

a crack of light in a town stitched with murder, secrets,

and forested silence.

For a moment, grief had no seat at the table.

There was only laughter,

soft glances,

and threads of something new.

Something delicate.

Something healing.

Something that might just stay…..if they let it.

Chapter 34

The sky outside was still soft with morning haze, but Aryan's office felt heavy with dust and history. The board in front of him was layered.....photos, red threads, yellowing notes.....all converging at one silent corner of the past.

Rajeev entered, holding a folder and a fragile newspaper that seemed to exhale time itself.

"Archives team found this," he said. "Dated 1st October 2003. A missing person report. And this....." he unfolded the clipping, ".....an article draft by Rekha."

Aryan took the file, his eyes locking onto the photo clipped to the top: *a young woman, fierce-eyed, proud. A journalist. Rekha.*

"She was a social activist from Goa," Rajeev said quietly. "Came here for a break but used the time to research. Wrote about tribal land rights, forest evictions, survivors of sexual violence. Brave voice, ahead of her time."

Aryan flipped through the thin pages. The edges were torn, but words still stood upright on the page.

"She went missing on the same day."

"Yes," Rajeev nodded. "Her friend, Alina, left a week later. Rekha's mother came back year after year. Filed police complaints, knocked doors, lit candles in the forest."

Aryan paused.

"And?"

"She passed away in 2012. Still waiting."

There was a long silence.

"We reached out to Alina. She lives in Berlin now. We're trying to speak with her."

Aryan closed the file gently, like laying flowers on a grave.

"A girl who stood for everyone... and no one stood for her. Except her mother. Until her last breath."

His voice was barely a whisper.

✦ ∞ ✦

Sunlight spilled into the dining room, casting soft gold over the breakfast spread. The house was alive with conversation, but there was a newness to the air…..Samina.

"Karishma, call Vikrant," Anjali said, pouring tea.

"May I?" Samina asked cheerfully.

Kunal smiled. "Of course, beta. Go."

She walked upstairs, paused outside Vikrant's door, and knocked lightly.

"Karishma, just five more minutes," Vikrant called, adjusting his collar.

"Not Karishma," came the playful reply. "It's me. Viku."

He turned. "Samina?"

"Breakfast's ready. And I made your favourite."

He forced a smile. "I'll be down."

Later, At the table, he took a bite of aloo paratha. Warm, crisp. Nostalgia in every chew.

"It's good," he admitted.

"Told you," Karishma grinned. "Samina is good at cooking."

Anjali beamed. "We should speak to the pandit soon. Fix an engagement date."

Vikrant froze for a beat.

"The paratha is good," he said slowly, "but that doesn't mean I said yes."

Kunal looked up; brows drawn. "What are you thinking?"

Vikrant smiled faintly. "Nothing. Just... a little spicy."

Karishma, watched him …..quiet, unreadable.

Steam curled from Anika's teacup as she flipped through her notes, but her focus had clearly fled. Across from her, Usha had a grin that spelled trouble.

"You called Aryan my handsome man in the middle of a market?" Anika asked in disbelief.

Usha giggled. "It slipped! But... come on, was I wrong?"

"Stop making things awkward!"

"Your cheeks were redder than the tomatoes you bought."

Anika looked down, lips twitching.

"You're impossible," she muttered.

Usha leaned closer.

"You didn't deny it."

Anika sighed. Her heart had quietly begun scribbling his name on its pages…..and Usha could read it like a book.

Rajeev walked in with a flicker of triumph.

"Hyderabad police caught one of the fake doctors."

Aryan straightened. "Alive?"

"Yes. Interrogation has started."

"And Alina?"

"Found a contact in Berlin."

Aryan's eyes lit with quiet admiration. "Tell her I want to talk. Whenever she's ready."

Rajeev hesitated… then smirked.

"By the way, when are you confessing?"

Aryan raised an eyebrow. "Confessing what?"

"That you're becoming a little too fond of a certain future doctor."

Aryan chuckled, shaking his head. "Usha sees everything."

"She does," Rajeev nodded. "And she's never wrong."

They laughed…..but Aryan's gaze drifted to the board once again. Rekha's photo watched him.

A girl who vanished in the name of truth.

A girl who still whispered through forest wind and yellowing paper.

Chapter 35

Sunlight filtered through the gauzy curtains of Vikrant's room, painting golden streaks across the floor. The warmth touched everything…..but not him.

He sat at the edge of the bed, motionless. Yesterday he'd smiled. Shared a meal. Let himself laugh. But the taste of joy was temporary, like a song half-remembered. What lingered was Usha. Her voice, her silences, her gaze that still lived somewhere inside him.

The door creaked open. Karishma stepped in with a towel over her shoulder, her hair damp from a recent shower.

"Bro," she said with feigned brightness, "Still stuck to that bed? Samina's parents are coming tomorrow, and you both need to visit the temple. Panditji will fix the engagement date."

Vikrant didn't move.

She watched him, her tone softening. "You, okay?"

He didn't respond.

"Or is your mind wandering to someone else?" she added gently. "Someone who made you feel more than just responsible."

Vikrant's jaw clenched. "Don't start."

"I won't," she said, sitting beside him. "But if you're going to marry one person while dreaming of another… it's not a wedding. It's a slow funeral."

He stood and brushed past her.

"We don't always choose love, Karishma. Sometimes we choose responsibility."

Karishma watched his retreating back. And softly, almost to herself, said,

"Then stop looking at her like she's the only thing you ever truly wanted and lost."

✦ ∞ ✦

The hum of ceiling fans buzzed faintly as Rajeev entered with a worn folder. Aryan looked up, still thumbing through Samar's book.

"Sir. We've got something."

Aryan closed the book. "Tell me."

"I spoke to Alina.....Rekha's best friend. She remembers everything. Rekha wasn't just a journalist. She was a force. Raised funds for survivors. Published essays cn consent and tribal rights. Brave, brilliant."

Aryan leaned forward, listening.

"Her mother was from Chandrapur. Rekha visited with Alina once, but then she kept returning on her own. She wanted to write about the forest, its stolen stories. And then on October 1st... she vanished."

Aryan's voice was barely a whisper.

"Forest..."

Rajeev flipped to another report.

"Also... we confirmed something else. Satish's sister.....Naina. She was in a relationship with Samar Dev. And she was pregnant."

Aryan sat upright.

"We searched her room. Found her diary. Sketches, love poems... grief between the lines. A note said: *Our love symbol died at Maheshwari Clinic.* We traced it.....records wiped. But we found a former nurse, Shamli. She remembers."

"The pregnancy was aborted... forcibly. Naina's family didn't approve. Shamli said Naina broke afterward. Mentally. Emotionally. She began painting obsessively. Then one day... she stopped showing up."

Aryan stood slowly; eyes locked on the wall where Rekha's photo still hung.

"She was erased."

"Both were," Rajeev said. "Rekha. Naina. For truth. For love."

Aryan picked up Samar's book again. His fingers trembled slightly.

"We're going to the Rai house," he said. "They buried something long ago. But the roots are growing back."

The smell of cumin and ghee lingered as Usha stirred the dal gently. Anika sat at the corner table, silent, eyes unfocused on the pages of her medical notes.

"You, okay?" Usha asked.

Anika looked up, then away. "Do you think Aryan will ever... see me as more than just a girl chasing her dream?"

Usha leaned against the wall, folding her arms.

"He already does. He just hasn't found the courage to admit it."

Anika's lips curved faintly. She turned the page of her book, but her thoughts stayed on the man with the quiet strength and unreadable eyes.

In her silence, a flower of hope unfurled.

The wind brushed gently against Vikrant's face as he stood on the balcony. Below, the house shimmered in light and laughter—engagement preparations unfolding like clockwork.

His phone buzzed.

"I'm excited. We're getting engaged! :)" — Samina

He stared at the message for a long moment.

Then lifted his gaze to the stars…..silent, scattered truths.

And in their light, he saw something.
Not Samina's smile.
Usha's silence.
Not the sound of temple bells.
But the echo of a whisper in the rain,
a laugh that lingered,
a pain that softened something inside him.
He closed his eyes.
And let himself feel it.
He didn't name it yet.
But it was no longer avoidable.

Chapter 36

The sun filtered in gently, lighting up the Rai mansion with a honey-coloured glow. Curtains stirred in a soft breeze, and chandeliers reflected slivers of gold on the marble floor. But today, the sparkle wasn't just from the glass and light ….. it was from anticipation.

Samina moved through the hall like she belonged in a painting. Her peach dupatta fluttered behind her like it had a heartbeat of its own.

Today, her parents were arriving.

Today, the engagement would begin to take shape.

In the living room, Anjali adjusted the flowers one last time, her hands lingering on every petal.

Karishma dusted the photo frames, eyes darting to the clock more often than the corners.

From his study, Kunal stepped out dressed in a white kurta ….. a man rebuilt, or at least pretending to be.

"This isn't just a proposal," he murmured to Anjali. "It's redemption. The Raichands are legacy. If Vikrant agrees, the Rai name won't just rise ….. it'll return."

Before Anjali could speak, Samina's voice rang down the hallway. "They're here!"

The front gate opened like a curtain lifting on a grand act. Mr. Raichand entered first ….. tall, iron-haired, all poise and pedigree. His wife followed; grace wrapped in emerald silk.

"Raichand sahib," Kunal greeted, arms extended. "Too many years."

Their hug was practiced but warm, like two powerful men rehearsing friendship. Anjali offered her smile. Karishma brought folded hands. Samina searched the stairs with expectant eyes.

"Viku must still be upstairs. I'll get him."

Upstairs, Vikrant was a statue in front of the mirror ..... buttoning his collar with mechanical precision. The tie didn't feel like fabric today. It felt like a noose.

The door opened. Samina stepped in, her perfume trailing before her.

"Viku," she chimed. "Mom and Dad are downstairs. Come."

He didn't turn.

"You look handsome," she said with a smile. "How do I look?"

He glanced once.

"Beautiful."

She lit up. He didn't.

"Okay! I'll wait."

As she left, Vikrant remained still. His eyes dropped to his phone.

A message. Just a single smile emoji from Usha.

He closed the screen, but not the ache.

The drawing room now echoed with laughter, the chime of teaspoons against porcelain, the rustle of silk. Sunita Raichand complimented the flower arrangement. Kunal beamed. Samina sat beside her mother, her fingers unconsciously fixing her bangles.

Vikrant descended, crisp and composed.

"Uncle. Aunty."

Raichand stood, clapping his shoulder. "You've grown into your name, son. Samina always said she'd marry no one else."

"Thank you, sir," Vikrant replied, perfectly polite, perfectly detached.

Karishma entered with a tea tray, her eyes scanning Vikrant's face. He smiled at the Raichands, but she saw it ….. the absence behind the smile.

"We'll go to the temple later today," Kunal announced. "Panditji will choose an auspicious date."

Vikrant nodded, mechanically.

Karishma, watching both Vikrant and Samina, thought silently: *Say her name. Say Usha. Or stop pretending you're happy.*

But he said nothing.

And Samina was glowing.

The morning buzzed with quiet life. Roopa was finishing a wedding dress, her fingers slightly sore from the needlework.

"Anika, make tea," she called. "My head is spinning."

"Yes, Daadi," came the reply.

Usha stepped in, drying her hands. "That dress is stunning, Daadi. Those pearls... like dewdrops."

Roopa narrowed her eyes. "Don't touch it! You made pakoras. You'll ruin it."

"My hands are clean!" Usha laughed. "I'll wash again just to admire it."

Roopa opened the dress fully now, proud of her craft. From the kitchen, Anika glimpsed it ….. and paused.

The stitching. The colour. The rhythm of the cloth.

She was suddenly somewhere else. Her own wedding day. The betrayal. The silence of not being chosen.

She blinked the memory away and stirred the tea harder.

Then, a knock at the door.

"Must be Kamla," Roopa said. "Usha, get it. Anika, one more cup."

Usha opened the door ….. and froze.

"Inspector?"

Aryan stood there; his expression soft. "Good morning. I came to return a book."

"Oh, Did it help?"

"This one helped," he smiled. "And yes, I was also hoping for tea."

"Anika's inside," Usha said, stepping aside. "Daadi thinks you're Kamla. Come in."

Inside the house, Roopa called out, "Come in! Why are you standing at the door?"

Aryan stepped in slowly.

Roopa turned…..and froze. Her expression shifted.

"You? What are you doing here?"

Aryan raised a hand gently. "I swear, I'm not here with questions."

He held out the book. "Just this."

Roopa squinted at it, then at him. "Even the police need novels, huh?"

He laughed nervously, his eyes scanning the room, searching for something to distract him. His gaze landed on the chair.

"Dupatta is not on the chair," Anika said softly from behind him, her voice calm but piercing.

He chuckled awkwardly, a forced sound, and sat down, the weight of her words lingering in the air. The space between them felt heavier now.

She walked in with a tray. Wet hair. Barely composed. But holding two cups of tea.

"Not this one. Daadi's sugar-free," she said, offering the other. "Yours has two spoons."

Their fingers brushed. A current passed between them.

Usha leaned back against the wall, a knowing smile playing at her lips.

Roopa watched all three with narrowed eyes.

"You both always talking in codes. Naughty girls," she muttered.

Aryan took a sip. Looked at Anika.

"Perfect."

"What?" Roopa asked.

"The tea," he replied. "Sweet. Strong. Balanced. Just how I like it."

Usha giggled behind her hand. Anika turned, her face pink.

Then Aryan's phone buzzed. He answered.

"Sir, any updates on the case?" Rajeev's voice crackled.

Aryan didn't look away from Anika.

"No updates. Still waiting… for a reply."

Anika froze.

Usha grinned.

"Yes," Anika blurted.

Roopa blinked. "Yes what?"

Usha jumped in. "She meant, yes to me. She'll help with the sewing."

Aryan stood, his voice low.

"It's a yes from my side, Rajeev."

He ended the call…..quiet, deliberate.

Roopa blinked, watching him closely.

He turned toward the door.

"Alright, I should get going now…."

But his eyes paused on Anika….. long enough for the silence to say the rest.

Outside, he slipped on his sunglasses.

The door clicked shut behind him,

but something stayed in the room.

Roopa whispered under her breath, "Mata Rani knows."

Anika smiled.

Not because she was told.

But because she knew.

Because sometimes, the quietest confessions

are the ones meant only for the one who understands them.

Chapter 37

The soft creak of Anjali's wheelchair echoed down the marble corridor, breaking the stillness of the house. The pooja had ended hours ago, but the air still carried a trace of sandalwood and marigold.

A knock at the door pulled her attention.

"Ramesh," she called. "See who it is."

Moments later, the house help returned.

"Inspector Aryan, madam."

Anjali's eyes narrowed slightly, but she nodded. "Send him in."

Aryan entered, straight-backed, measured. He glanced around briefly before speaking.

"Mrs....?"

"Rai," Anjali said, finishing his sentence. "Anjali Rai."

Aryan nodded politely.

"I was hoping to ask Mr. Kunal a few questions."

"They've gone to the temple," Anjali replied. "But you can speak to me. I know most of what matters."

He nodded, settling across from her. There was no small talk.

"I wanted to ask about Samar."

The name sat heavy in the air. For a moment, Anjali said nothing.

"My brother," she said finally. "Kunal never forgave him. There was a rift... something about business accounts. He was blamed for betrayal. But I kept meeting him. Quietly. Until the accident."

"Accident?" Aryan asked.

"He was with me. The car lost control. I survived. He didn't. At least... that's what we believed. His body was never found."

Aryan nodded slowly. "Do you know anyone named Naina?"

Anjali frowned. "Who?"

"Satish's sister. She was reportedly in a relationship with Samar."

She shook her head. "No. That's new to me."

Aryan stood, politely.

"Thank you, Mrs. Rai. I'll speak to Mr. Kunal directly next time."

Anjali watched him go, her mind tracing back through memories that suddenly didn't feel so familiar anymore.

Temple bells chimed in rhythmic waves, their sound cutting through the murmur of prayers and the rustle of silk sarees. Panditji folded his hands and stepped back from the havan kund.

"Tomorrow," the pandit announced.

"Auspicious for new beginnings."

Kunal nodded, pleased.

"Perfect. We'll finalize the engagement."

Samina smiled brightly, standing close to Vikrant.

Her eyes danced with hope.

Her bangles chimed like celebration itself.

Then the pandit added, flipping a page softly,

"There's another date….. two months later."

Samina looked at Vikrant, her voice warm, light.

"Maybe we can decide together?"

Karishma nudged Vikrant slightly.

"Bro?"

"I have no issue," Vikrant said.

Even. Measured.

But Karishma saw it.

His voice agreed.

His eyes….didn't.

And then….. as if time itself wanted to interrupt….. Usha and Anika stepped through the temple gate.

"Usha!" Karishma called out, her voice lifting.

She turned quickly to the family.

"Uncle, this is my friend Usha. And this is her sister, Anika."

Pleasantries passed like wind…..gentle, polite.

Samina extended a warm hand to both.

Karishma added, voice soft, almost careful, "You must come tomorrow. My brother is getting engaged to Samina."

Usha looked at Vikrant before replying.

Her voice was calm…..perfectly so.

But something flickered in her eyes.

"Congratulations, Karishma. And to you, Vikrant."

Vikrant held her gaze for just a second too long.

Long enough for the weight beneath the words to show.

Was her smile real?

Or was it…..like his had been all morning….. something practiced. Something worn, not felt.

Karishma watched them both.

Then looked at Samina…..who smiled, radiant, unaware.

And quietly, in the smallest whisper…..one only the flame of the diya might've heard….. Karishma looked at her and said:

"I don't want my brother to marry you…not ever."

The air around the temple shifted.

Not with words.

But with something deeper.

The kind of silence that arrives when truth is held in the throat but never let out.

Aryan strode into the police station's backroom, where threads of evidence stretched across corkboards like an unfinished puzzle. Rajeev was already waiting.

"Updates?" Aryan asked.

"Yes, sir. We finally spoke to the man posing as the doctor. Turns out …..he's a truck driver."

Aryan's brows furrowed. "Truck driver?"

Rajeev nodded. "He says he was paid to drive a medical van and wear a coat. Thought he was just helping a nurse. Said he got paid well. His job was just to act like a doctor…..nothing more."

Aryan leaned in. "And the nurse? Any sketch? Any ID?"

Rajeev handed over a rough profile.

"Matches the same girl Satish described. Half her face was covered. But the details line up. And…. she wasn't mute."

Aryan's jaw tightened.

"So, she was pretending."

"Yes, sir. And this woman…she wasn't just assisting." Rajeev's tone shifted.

"She planned everything. Where to go, what to do, what to wear. If she's not the killer ….. she's the closest to whoever is. We need to check for any link between her and Satish."

Aryan stepped back from the board, eyes narrowing.

"Maybe we've been looking at this wrong. We thought she was a pawn…."

A pause.

"But maybe she's the one moving the pieces."

Rajeev nodded.

"Or maybe Satish is using her as a shield."

Aryan's voice dropped.

"Keep eyes on Satish. Tighter than before."

"Already in place, sir."

The board behind them rustled softly under the ceiling fan.

And in that stillness, something shifted.

A new pattern began to emerge….. Not of the victims.

But of the puppeteer.

Chapter 38

The sun had dipped low, casting long amber shadows through the lattice windows of the Rai mansion. Upstairs, in a room that once held boyish laughter, Vikrant sat by the window motionless. Outside, birds chirped in the distance, but inside him, everything was quiet. Heavy. Still.

The scent of rose incense floated up from the hall, faint but lingering, like a memory you never chose to keep.

Karishma stepped in quietly, holding a brass plate with dry fruits and a cup of tea. She didn't speak right away. She placed it on the table, then looked at him.

"Tomorrow is your engagement," she said, voice low. "And I need to ask you…..are you… happy?"

He didn't move. His eyes stayed fixed on the horizon.

"Why do you ask that?" he murmured.

"Because I know you," she said gently, walking toward him. "You've always been quiet when you're hurting. And right now… I think you're fighting something. Or someone. Maybe even yourself."

She paused. "You….you love someone else. Don't you bro?"

Vikrant exhaled a slow breath and gave a faint, empty smile.

She sat beside him and gently took his hand.

"Close your eyes."

"Karishma, please ….."

"Just do it."

He sighed, but relented. His eyes slowly shut.

"Now," she whispered,

"Tell me the first face you see."

His lips parted….. but the silence lingered.

Too long.

"The face you always wanted to see….." she said, almost like a prayer.

He opened his eyes.

"No one."

Her voice snapped…..sharper than before.

"Liar."

She stood, anger flickering just beneath her calm.

"You're lying to me. And to yourself."

He looked away, his jaw clenched.

"She doesn't feel the same."

Karishma crouched in front of him, catching his gaze with hers.

"Did you ever ask her? Or are you just scared? Scared that silence is safer than hearing what you don't want?"

He didn't speak.

But his silence….. said everything.

"Did she smile," she asked, softer now,

"when she heard you were getting engaged?"

A faint nod. Nothing more.

Karishma's tone lowered, almost tender.

"Maybe she smiled because she doesn't know what you feel"

"Or maybe…. she's pretending too,"

His eyes clouded, conflicted.

The kind of quiet ache you only see in people who still hope…..

but don't know if they're allowed.

Karishma pulled out her phone.

"You won't say it? Fine. I will."

"What are you doing?"

"Calling Usha…..."

"Karishma….. stop."

"Too late."

✦ ∞ ✦

The sunset painted the sky a bruised purple, like something soft breaking apart. In the kitchen, Anika poured tea while Usha stood by the window, staring at the wind-touched curtain. Her silence was different tonight…..heavy with waiting.

"That dress Karishma wore was lovely, na?" Anika offered.

Usha gave a slight nod.

Anika saw it…..the smile that didn't reach her eyes.

"Are you okay?"

Before Usha could answer, her phone buzzed.

Karishma.

"Hello?"

"Usha!" Karishma's voice bubbled through the line.

"My brother wants to talk to you."

"What…..?"

A pause.

Then—his voice.

"Hi."

"Hi…."

A soft silence followed, wrapped in awkward air and years of unsaid memories.

A crow cawed somewhere outside.

From a nearby window, a dusty old music player hummed a forgotten Udit and Alka's love song.

"How are you?" he asked.

"I'm… good. You?"

"Good. I….."

But before he could finish, Karishma's voice returned—gentle, but clear.

"Forget his awkwardness. Usha…..do you love him?"

Vikrant froze.

So did Usha.

"What?" Usha whispered.

"You heard me," Karishma said, softer now.

"Do you love my brother?"

Usha didn't answer right away.

There was a pause….. long enough to mean something.

Then she said quietly,

"He's getting engaged tomorrow."

"That wasn't an answer."

But before anything else could be said ….. the line clicked.

Vikrant had ended the call.

Karishma turned to him, disappointed.

"You didn't let her speak."

He didn't respond.

Just stared at the floor, jaw tight, chest still.

Karishma looked at him.

Her voice lowered.

"But I heard her voice."

She paused.

"And I think….. I know what she would've said."

At the doorway, Samina stood.

She had heard everything.

She turned quietly, went to her room, and closed the door behind her.

The silence inside the room pressed against her chest.

She walked slowly to the mirror.

Her reflection stared back ….. composed, radiant…

unreal.

A bride, almost.

A woman on the edge of a day she had waited her whole life to reach.

She had waited for him.

Since they were kids.

Since laughter was louder than love, and love was just a word she didn't yet understand.

But even then…..her heart had chosen.

And it had never looked back.

She waited through years.

Through changes.

Through every silence he never explained,

through every glance he never held long enough.

Still, she stayed.

Still, she hoped.

"Tomorrow,"

she whispered,

"I was supposed to be his. Completely."

She opened the ring box.

Gold shimmered beneath the soft light ….. like a promise trying to survive.

But everything had changed.

The room.

The air.

Him.

"If he loves someone else…" her voice cracked,

"why does this hurt so much when I always knew?"

A single tear slipped onto the velvet lining—quiet, deliberate.

Not just for tomorrow.

But for every yesterday that had waited for it.

"Maybe love isn't about holding on, " she whispered.

"My heart always breathed for him…. always waited to be seen by his. My soul only ever moved in his direction. "

She paused ….. her voice breaking into silence.

"But today……..his breath chooses to whisper in another heart. "

She pressed the ring to her chest, holding it like a memory she hadn't prepared to lose.

Her smile cracked ….. porcelain, breaking under the weight of truth.

The tears came.

Not dramatic.

Not loud.

Just deep.

Honest.

Something inside her folded inward.

And broke.

There was no scream.

No sob.

Only silence….. the kind that wraps around a woman

who waited too long for a love

that never arrived.

A silence full of questions.

Of ache.

Of goodbye.

And still, she stayed quiet.

The living room buzzed with soft conversation and tea.

Raichand and Kunal discussed politics and business….. words like deals, growth, legacy.

Sunita and Anjali admired Samina's engagement Saree, fingers grazing over silk, eyes glittering with plans.

But above them ….. in a room where a mirror held a broken reflection, something was quietly coming undone.

Not loudly.

Not visibly.

But thread by thread ….. something was unravelling.

And no one heard it break.

✦ ∞ ✦

Usha's eyes stayed fixed on the chain by her bedside, the small silver infinity pendant swaying in the draft. The tiny loop of metal seemed to know more than she dared say.

Her fingers pressed to her chest, as if she could pin the ache in place.

"He's getting engaged," she murmured. "And I smiled."

Her pulse kept a steady rhythm, but every beat felt bruised, pushing against ribs that suddenly seemed too tight.

The silence in the room hummed with all the words she wouldn't let out.

She drew a long breath, held it, let it go.

Still nothing moved on her face.

In the room beside her, Anika sat with a book in her lap, smiling faintly at her phone. A note from Aryan.

Short.

Simple.

Thoughtful.

Yet her hands trembled just enough to betray her.

And the smile…..it stayed longer than expected.

✦ ∞ ✦

Aryan sat alone at his desk, the case file before him, but his mind elsewhere.

His fingers hovered over his phone.

He wasn't thinking about murder weapons, sketches, or forensic reports.

He was thinking of a girl who brewed the perfect tea.

And who wore silence better than poetry.

Behind these stirring hearts and uncertain truths...
The killer still waited.
Still watched.
And somewhere deeper in the shadows....
someone else was planning what would come next.

Chapter 39

The kitchen pulsed with the warm scent of cardamom and bubbling sugar. Anika stood by the stove, carefully lifting thin spirals of jalebi from the hot oil. The air hissed gently, but her fingers trembled…..not from heat, but from something quieter, heavier.

"Usha," she called, "Karishma's called you four times. She left messages too."

From the other room, Usha's voice came, low and distracted.

"I know. She invited me." A pause. "And you're coming too."

"Why would I go? It's you they want there."

"No," Usha replied as she entered, adjusting the earring on her right ear. "I don't know why, but... I need you with me. I feel like I might do something stupid."

She didn't say it, but the thought curled deep inside her…..Vikrant's engagement is today. Why did Karishma say all that? What if it meant something... or nothing at all?

"This one's sugar-free," Anika said, lifting a separate batch and gently placing them into a small box. "For Anjali aunty."

Usha, dressed in a modest bottle-green suit, nodded. "Did you pack it?"

"Yes."

"Good. And you're not staying back."

"Usha…"

"No buts. It's Karishma's brother's engagement. Besides….." her voice dropped, a teasing glint appearing, "Inspector Aryan might be there."

Anika turned; cheeks flushed. "That's not why I'm coming."

"Of course not," Usha grinned, picking up the box and linking her arm through her sister's. "Come on, doctor-to-be."

The Rai mansion shimmered with quiet grandeur. Marigold garlands draped across doorways, the scent of rosewater perfumed the air, and the faint rhythm of shehnai wove through the conversations of arriving guests.

In one of the upstairs bedrooms, Karishma adjusted the folds of Samina's peach lehenga, carefully pinning a pleat over her shoulder.

"You look beautiful," she said, though her voice faltered halfway through.

Samina met her eyes in the mirror. "You think so?"

Karishma hesitated, then nodded. "Of course... you do."

But behind Samina's eyes, something dimmed. She had seen the way Vikrant had been looking.....not at her. She had heard the silence in his voice. Felt it in the spaces between them.

She exhaled slowly.

Smile. she told herself. Just smile. You've always been strong.

Karishma wrapped her in a gentle hug, whispering,

"You always look beautiful."

Samina nodded.....but didn't answer.

Her hands held the fabric of her dress a little tighter.

Her smile stayed, but something behind it flickered.

Inside her, a thought echoed softly:

Beauty means nothing.... not when the heart isn't seen.

She glanced at Karishma.....just for a second.

And then, without moving her lips, she whispered.....

not aloud,

but in that quiet space only the heart can hear:

"I know you don't want me to be engaged to Vikrant."

"I know he loves someone else."

"But then…. why am I standing here in this dress?"

"Why does my heart still carry hope…. that maybe, just maybe, he'll look at me the way I've always looked at him?"

Her eyes shimmered. Not with tears.

But with the weight of knowing…..and still hoping.

"He may never love me,

but I….. I will continue to love him.

Even if I can't say it loud.

Even if no one ever knows.

I will….. forever."

Vikrant descended the stairs, crisp in an ivory sherwani, the gold stole draped over one shoulder. His face was still. Too still.

"Here comes the groom!" Karishma called out cheerfully.

Guests clapped politely. Samina turned toward the stairs. She held her breath…..just for a second…..hoping maybe this time he'd look at her like she wasn't a formality.

Then she saw it.

Usha.

Standing at the edge of the hall with Anika, holding the jalebi box.

And she saw the change in Vikrant.

No smile. No gasp.

Just a flicker.

But she saw it.

She always saw it.

The courtyard gleamed under gold-draped canopies. A velvet-dressed table stood in the centre, holding two ring boxes, flower trays, and the weight of two families' hopes.

Panditji chanted slowly, his voice folding into the rustle of guests and camera flashes.

Anika stood quietly near the back with Usha, holding the box of jalebi.

"Give this to Karishma when there's a break," Usha whispered.

Anika nodded silently.

Panditji looked up. "It is an auspicious hour. Please bring the rings."

Karishma stepped forward with the boxes, glancing briefly at her brother…..her heart tight with a thousand doubts.

Samina stepped forward too. Her hands were steady. Her smile, trained.

Vikrant reached for the ring.

He hesitated.

Just for a second.

Then…..A gasp broke through the ceremony.

"What happened?"

"Mom!" Karishma screamed.

Her body slid from the wheelchair. Her hand, clutching a single jalebi in a napkin, fell to the stone floor with a dull thud. The jalebi box tumbled near Anika's feet, the oil seeping through the cloth.

"Anjali!" Kunal's voice cracked as he dropped to his knees. "Anjali, look at me!"

Guests swarmed in confusion.

Samina rushed forward, skirts trailing, forgetting everything.

"Aunty, please… please get up," she cried, cradling Anjali's head in her lap. Her voice broke. "Aunty…"

Karishma stood frozen, both hands over her mouth.

Usha shouted, "Call a doctor!"

"Move!" Anika said, pushing through the crowd. "I've studied emergency response…..please move!"

Everything blurred. The music had stopped. The bells no longer rang. Even the marigolds seemed to wilt in silence.

Samina sat motionless beside Anjali, her bangles clinking faintly against the marble.

She wasn't thinking about the ring.

She wasn't thinking about Usha.

She was thinking about a woman who used to braid her hair, call her second daughter, and kiss her forehead when no one else was looking.

Now that hand lay motionless, the half eaten jalebi untouched.

Its sweetness had turned into silence.

Chapter 40

The grand hall, once dressed in marigold and festivity, now held a silence that felt heavier than stone. Where laughter had echoed, now there was only the soft rustle of grief.

Anjali Rai lay motionless.

Her saree, once proudly pleated, fanned around her like fallen petals. Her bangles were stilled. Her smile had gone somewhere far.

Kunal sat beside her, crumpled, holding her hand like he could still convince the warmth to return. Karishma was on the floor, her forehead pressed to her mother's shoulder, whispering, "Wake up, Maa... please..."

Samina crouched beside them, her own tears slipping quietly. She had forgotten her role in the celebration. At this moment, she was just a daughter losing another mother.

In the background, an ambulance screeched into the driveway. Doctors rushed in, but their hands were not hopeful. One turned after a moment and shook his head.

"She is no more."

At the door, Usha gripped Anika's hand tightly. Both stood frozen, tears balanced in their lashes. Around them, the world was still moving ..... but inside, something had stopped.

Aryan entered with Rajeev, the weight in his chest heavier than his badge.

"Rajeev," he said quietly, "no one leaves the premises. Lock it down. Call the forensic team."

"Already on it, sir. Five minutes out."

Aryan stepped through the stunned crowd. His voice rose calmly, firmly.

"Please… we need space."

But love doesn't always follow instructions.

Karishma clung to her mother's still body. Samina tried gently to pull her away. Kunal wouldn't release her hand.

The forensic team arrived with soft steps and metal cases.

"We'll need footage," Aryan said. "Someone must've been recording. Get it. Start filming now too. Every face. Every angle."

"Fingerprints?" Rajeev asked.

"Not yet. Focus on immediate family."

Aryan looked to Kunal, who was still kneeling. His voice softened.

"Who saw her collapse?"

Ramesh, the butler, stepped forward.

"Sir… she had a jalebi. From that white box. Just one. Then… she collapsed."

A voice from the forensics team echoed across the courtyard.

"Poison suspected. She consumed jalebi seconds before collapse. We'll confirm, but… it's likely."

Aryan's gaze narrowed.

"Who gave her the jalebi?"

Ramesh hesitated. Then pointed.

"That girl."

Everyone turned.

Eyes searched for someone to blame.

Aryan's gaze landed on Anika.

The girl whose laugh once lived between his ribs.

"Anika," he breathed.

Not as an officer…..but as a man

stunned into disbelief.

He had waited to see her again.

But not like this.

Not in this silence,
where everything soft turned sharp.
Kunal stood, grief now igniting into fury.
"Arrest her! She poisoned my wife!"
"She didn't do this," Aryan said…..quiet, but unwavering.
But Anika….. Anika broke.
Her body folded in on itself,
tears falling fast,
as though the whole world had picked her up
only to throw her down again.
Usha ran forward, arms out like a shield.
"She didn't, uncle. She made the jalebi at home. She even tasted it—please."
From the crowd, someone whispered— sharp, cruel, loud enough to sting.
"That girl…. She's cursed. The Pandit died at her wedding, and now this. Wherever she goes, death follows."
The words landed like knives.
And Anika….
she heard them all.
Every syllable.
The world had said it before.
And now, it said it again.
Not as truth….. but as a sentence.
One she'd carried quietly for far too long.
Usha turned…..desperate…..toward Vikrant.
She believed if anyone could see through it,
it would be him.
She looked up at him, eyes wide,
already filled with unshed grief.
"Say something," she whispered,
her voice trembling like a thread stretched too thin.

"My sister is not….."
But Vikrant's gaze dropped to the floor.
The silence that followed stretched like glass.
Fragile.
Cracking.
When he finally spoke,
the words came out low,
as if even he hated them.
"Please…. arrest her."
The sentence landed like a whip crack.
Usha flinched…..
as though the sound itself had torn through her skin.
A hot sting bloomed across her chest…..
shame, disbelief, betrayal.
All at once.
All from him.
She didn't scream.
She didn't argue.
She didn't fall.
She just stood there…..
heart splintering
in a room that once felt safe.
Because sometimes, it's not the world that breaks you.
It's the person you thought never would.
And still, she stayed quiet.

Aryan, Usha, Rajeev, and Anika sat in silence inside the police station. The air was still…..thick with tension, unspoken questions, and a truth waiting to surface.

Then Aryan stepped forward, his voice steady but gentler than before.

He looked directly at Anika…..no hesitation, no doubt.

"I believe you," he said.

"Help me prove it."

Anika nodded, eyes glistening but her voice calm.

"Even if the world hangs me tomorrow… your belief is enough today."

Aryan held her gaze.

"Tell me everything."

Anika's voice trembled, but her words were clear.

"I made jalebis. A sugar-free one for Anjali aunty. Usha told me to give the box to Karishma. But aunty saw me. She asked. I gave it directly."

"Did you taste them?"

"Yes."

Rajeev added, "Sir, I suspect Ramesh. He pointed too fast."

Aryan nodded. "Let's get footage. Interview staff."

They reviewed footage on Aryan's office monitor.

Fast-forwarded.

Rewound.

Faces blurred.

Nothing obvious.

"Maybe the jalebi was switched later," Rajeev said. "In the kitchen. Or… even during the ritual."

Suddenly, Usha rushed in, breathless.

"Sir ….. switch on the news. Now!"

The screen lit up.

The news played on the TV in the corner.

"I'm the cameraman of today's event. I gave her the poison. I saw her eat the jalebi."

Aryan froze.

A breath left him…..sharp, heavy, like he'd been holding it for hours. Relief washed over him, raw and overwhelming.

He turned on his heel and walked straight to the holding room.

No hesitation.

No pause.

Anika looked up as he entered….. eyes tired, uncertain, afraid.

Aryan stopped in front of her, voice steady.

"He confessed."

A beat.

"I know you were innocent."

Tears welled up in her eyes.

But she didn't speak.

She didn't need to.

For the first time in days, she believed she might finally breathe again.

Anika stood slowly, her eyes brimming.

"When they all turned on me…. you stood still. For me."

Aryan met her gaze.

"Your eyes never lied," he whispered.

"Even if I…I saw you do it…. I'd still believe you didn't."

They embraced– quiet, full, the kind of embrace that doesn't need apology or explanation.

Outside, in the hallway, Usha closed her eyes and whispered to the wind:

"Mata Rani……you saved my sister.

Always.

Always bless her…..the girl who never stopped believing in love,

even when the world stopped believing in her."

Anjali's body was taken away.

Karishma curled into Vikrant's shoulder, broken.

She didn't speak.

She just wanted to hold her… just once more.

Vikrant held her.

Numb.

Across the house, Samina sat in silence, running her fingers over the gold engagement ring.

Sunita and Raichand walked in, faces set.

"We're leaving," Raichand said. "This family feels cursed. I thought Rai was safe, but I was wrong."

"Dad, please," Samina answered, standing her ground. "I'm not going anywhere."

Sunita tried again. "Samina, you deserve better than this place."

Samina's voice trembled, but her eyes blazed with resolve as she shook her head. "No," she said, breath catching, "I'm staying here."

✦ ∞ ✦

Kunal sat alone in the hallway.

The walls around him echoed nothing back.

His face was hollow…emptied of anger, pride, and everything that once made him loud.

"Come back," he whispered into the cold.

"Please….come back."

His voice cracked… not from shouting,

but from holding in everything he should have said when it mattered.

"I thought I was protecting you."

"I thought silence would save us."

He paused, swallowing grief.

"But all it did… was steal you from me. "

His hands trembled.

And his heart…shattered in the quiet.

"You always wanted answers from me. "

"But I stayed quiet.

Every time.

I thought it was strength….. but it was fear. "

He looked down at his hands… empty now, useless.

"Come back… I want to share you with the world, with truth, with everything I once hid. I want to give you the words I buried. "

"But now…. It's too late, isn't it?" And the silence answered him.

Not with mercy.

But with finality.

✦ ∞ ✦

Anika opened the door slowly.

"Papa? Daadi?" Usha called behind her.

No answer.

They stepped inside.

The house was still.

Empty.

"Where are Papa and Daadi?" Usha murmured, glancing around.

Something in her voice trembled…just a little.

And then Aryan's phone rang.

He answered quietly.

"Sir," Rajeev said on the other end,

"Anika's father came to the station asking for her. You'd already left. We're bringing them home now."

Moments later, the door opened again.

Roopa and Ameet entered …. and without a word, they pulled both girls into a long, trembling embrace.

No apologies.

No explanations.

Just arms that finally let go of fear.

Rajeev stepped in behind them, blinking in confusion.

"Where's sir?"

"In the kitchen," Usha replied.

"Making tea."

"What?!"

Just then, Aryan walked in …. holding a tray with cups.

"You're back," he said simply.

Roopa blinked in disbelief.

"Inspector…. made tea?"

And for the first time that day, Anika laughed.

Light, honest, and alive.

"I'll make more," she offered, reaching for the tray.

"No," Aryan said gently.

"You rest. I can manage."

Ameet stepped forward, took Aryan's hand in his.

"You protected my daughter."

A pause.

"For that……..thank you."

✦ ∞ ✦

Rajeev drove. Aryan stared out at the city lights bleeding into the road.

"Update on the cameraman?" Aryan asked.

"They found him, sir."

A pause.

"He's dead."

Aryan closed his eyes.

"Poison?"

"Yes."

"He was made to confess. Then silenced."

"But… why clear Anika's name, then kill him?"

Aryan looked ahead.

"That's what we need to find out next…"

He didn't say it aloud, but the truth pressed against his ribs:

Someone is killing... but someone else is protecting.

And now...

The game was no longer about death.

It was about why.

Chapter 41

The ceiling fan above Aryan's desk turned slowly, slicing the silence like a dull blade. The room was thick...not with noise, but with the weight of too many answers still buried in the dark.

Aryan sat forward, elbows planted on a desk littered with folders, crime scene photos, autopsy notes. The evidence board ahead of him looked more like a war map now...threads of red connecting lives that had nothing in common but death.

Rajeev stepped in, two clay cups of chai in hand.

"You didn't sleep," he said, placing one down.

Aryan didn't deny it. "No time left for sleep, Rajeev. Every step we take... someone resets the board."

He stood, eyes drifting to the pinned photographs.

"First, we chased Pandit's secrets. Then Anas and Rakesh. Then Narayan. Then his wives. And now Anjali Rai. Just when we think we're close to the centre, it shifts."

Rajeev's jaw tightened. "Higher-ups called. Ten days. That's the deadline, or CID takes over."

Aryan didn't flinch. He sipped the tea slowly. "This isn't a case anymore. It's a narrative. Someone is writing it... and we're reading it too late."

He took the folder Rajeev handed him. The edges were warm. Fresh.

"Anjali's toxicology?"

Rajeev nodded. "She didn't die from what she ate directly. The poison...slow-acting, rare...was strongest on her right hand. Forensics found residue on a Cameraman's mobile phone she was holding. The poison wasn't in the jalebi, Aryan. It was on the device she touched while eating it."

Aryan froze.

"She touched the phone… then the jalebi," he said softly. "The timing wasn't accidental. Someone handed her that phone at the exact moment she would trust it."

"Cameraman," Rajeev said. "Same guy who filmed the pooja. Same guy who went on live TV. Same guy who turned up dead hours later."

Aryan's eyes narrowed. "So, he wasn't just filming. He was delivering."

Rajeev hesitated. "But why frame Anika… and then save her? Was it remorse? Or something else?"

Aryan looked up; his voice low but sharp. "Maybe the plan changed mid-way. Maybe she was always a piece on the board…but then something, someone, made them stop. Protect her. Confuse us."

Rajeev. "What about the Kundli."

Aryan stared at it.

"No," he said. "Now I think… it was a performance. A symbol. The killer wanted us to think like that. He dressed the crime in ritual, so we'd chase meaning while he bought time."

Rajeev exhaled. "And we did."

Aryan turned to the board again. "Every move has a mirror. They framed her, then saved her. Burned a clue, then planted a new one. It's not chaos…it's choreography."

"And we're dancing to their rhythm," Rajeev murmured.

Aryan stared out the window.

The sunlight was golden. But inside him, something colder moved.

✦ ∞ ✦

Sunlight spilled through the curtains like it was apologizing. But nothing brightened the shadows in the Rai home.

Vikrant hadn't changed out of his clothes. His dress was crumpled, his hair uncombed. He hadn't spoken in hours. He sat by the window, watching a world go on without the woman who had held it together for them.

On the bed, Karishma lay curled like a child, one hand clutching a half-wet handkerchief.

Downstairs, Kunal stood near the entrance as white-clad mourners trickled in. Raichand spoke quietly beside him.

"We should prepare for the agni sanskar. The sooner… the easier the release."

But Kunal didn't respond.

Because how do you release someone who never let go of you?

Anjali's body lay in the centre of the hall. Draped in white, head framed by flowers. The faint scent of incense rose like grief in the air.

Guests murmured condolences, but no words could touch the stillness that clung to the furniture, to the walls, to the bones of the house.

In a modest room where sunlight came in soft and slow, Anika and Usha lay sleeping, arms looped around each other in wordless trust.

Roopa peeked in gently.

"Girls… get up. I've made tea. You didn't eat anything last night."

Anika stirred. "Papa…?"

"He went to the shop early," Roopa said, voice soft. "Come. You both need food."

Usha sat up; her voice hoarse. "We're okay, Daadi. Just… tired."

Roopa reached in and tucked a blanket closer around them. "It's alright. There's no race to healing. Come when you can."

She left quietly. And in that silence, something settled…a comfort that asked for nothing.

✦ ∞ ✦

Aryan's sleeves were rolled up. His eyes hadn't left the board in hours.

"Rajeev," he said, "we're thinking too small. Forget the poison. Forget the weapon. Think about the setup."

Rajeev leaned in. "How did the cameraman get that job?"

"Exactly," Aryan snapped. "Who recommended him? Which studio? There's a thread there…we've just missed it."

"I'll check all local bookings," Rajeev said.

"And one more thing," Aryan added. "Put someone near the Rathi house. Quietly. I don't care who is the killer right now…I care who they're planning to use next."

Rajeev paused. "Sir, we got a message from Alina. Rekha's best friend. She wants to know if we're reopening the case."

Aryan's eyes moved to the photo of Rekha, still pinned like a ghost among fresher faces.

"I don't have the luxury of old ghosts right now," he said. "But if she wants to help….tell her I'm listening."

Rajeev nodded.

As he left, Aryan sat down again.

He didn't look at the board this time

He closed his eyes.

And whispered, "Show me your next move."

Because whoever the killer was….They weren't done. Not yet.

Chapter 42

The sun had just begun its descent, brushing the sky with a soft amber hue, as if it, too, was grieving.

At the gate, a courier waited dust on his shoes, fatigue in his posture.

"Letter for Miss Anika Rathi," he said, handing over the sealed envelope.

Usha took it with a distracted nod, wiping her damp hands on her dupatta. The air smelled faintly of fried cumin and drying clothes. Inside, the house hummed with the quiet rhythm of recovery….after days of grief, silence had become a strange sort of guest.

"Di!" Usha called, stepping into the living room. "A letter. For you."

Anika emerged from her room, her hair loosely tied, her face bare of expression. She looked… still……..like a breath held too long. She took the envelope, tore it open with shaking fingers.

"Medical college…" she whispered. "It's an admission form."

Usha blinked. "Wait… what?"

Anika stared at the paper, as if it might vanish. "I didn't. We couldn't afford the fees…"

Usha stepped closer, the realization blooming in her voice. "It's Aryan. He did it."

Anika's voice trembled. "But it's so expensive."

Usha took her sister's hand. "To someone who loves you… your dreams aren't expenses. They're promises worth keeping."

There was silence between them, the kind that doesn't fall heavy….but rather, gentle. Reverent.

Just then, Roopa walked in, drying her hands with the edge of her saree.

"What are you two whispering like old women?" she asked, her tone half-annoyed, half-curious.

Anika quickly folded the letter, hiding the tremor in her hands. "Nothing, Daadi."

Roopa squinted suspiciously. "Come make tea, then. Let's whisper over that."

The fragrance of sandalwood lingered long after the final chant had faded.

In the hall, Anjali's photo now rested amid marigold garlands, her smile frozen in a moment too far gone. The silence in the house was deep…not empty, but full. Full of unsaid things. Of steps that would never echo again.

Upstairs, in a room that once shimmered with silk and celebrations, Samina sat with her parents.

"We should cancel the engagement," Raichand said plainly. "We'll tell Kunal it's not the right time. She'll return to England."

But Samina looked up sharply, her voice thin but unshaken. "No."

Sunita blinked. "What?"

Samina rose. "I'm not going. If you both want to leave, leave. But I'm not running. Not from this house. Not from these people. Not when they're breaking."

Raichand sighed. "Beta, this isn't about…."

"It's about feeling, Papa. And we don't break when they need someone to stay."

She didn't wait for response.

She simply turned…. And stepped out of the room.

Steady. Silent. Certain.

✦ ∞ ✦

Kunal sat like stone. Anjali's framed photo rested in his hands, the garlands clinging to the glass like vines desperate to hold on.

His voice, when it came, was a murmur. "Without you... this house is just walls and wood."

He closed his eyes.

Flashback —

A younger Kunal and Anjali stepped into the house...newly married, full of light.

Anjali spun in the living room, her laughter ringing through the walls like music.

"This is a beautiful house," she said, smiling wide.

"It wasn't," Kunal replied, eyes on her.

"But now...with you....it is."

Back to the present —

The same room stood still.

Too quiet.

Too empty.

The silence didn't feel peaceful anymore.

It felt like betrayal.

Like absence.

And Kunal realized....the house hadn't lost her.

It had lost its beauty.

✦ ∞ ✦

Karishma brought in a cup of tea and set it beside her brother.

"You haven't eaten," she said quietly.

He didn't move.

"I miss Mom," she whispered, tears trailing down her cheek.

He nodded, unable to speak. The guilt had swallowed his voice whole.

Just then, Samina stepped in, urgency in her voice. "Anika didn't do it. The cameraman confessed. He's the one who poisoned Anjali aunty. It wasn't her."

Vikrant looked up sharply. "What?"

"She's innocent."

Karishma gasped. "Then she… she didn't….?"

Samina nodded. "She didn't. And Aryan knows it. He stood by her."

Vikrant sank into his seat, his head falling into his hands.

His voice cracked,

barely more than a breath.

"I… I told them to arrest her sister.

I told the world she was guilty."

He stared down at his hands…. the same ones that had once held Usha's.

The same ones that didn't reach for her

when she needed him most.

"I didn't point at a stranger," he whispered.

"I pointed at the sister of the woman who trusted me."

A pause. A tremble.

"I don't deserve forgiveness."

"Not from her. Not from anyone."

Kunal was just locking the gate when Aryan arrived.

"Heading somewhere?" Aryan asked.

Kunal didn't turn. "Maybe. Maybe not."

"Just two questions," Aryan said. "Who hired the cameraman?"

Kunal sighed. "Ask Vikrant. He was the one handling it"

"And do you think someone from your past is behind this? These murders feel... personal."

Kunal looked down. "It's your job to find out. Mine is to protect what's left."

Aryan's eyes didn't waver. "Then help me protect them too. Before the killer strikes again."

Kunal didn't answer. He got into his car. Engine silent. He didn't drive off.

He just sat there... alone, breathing through the regret that had wrapped around his ribs like steel.

✦ ∞ ✦

Aryan met Vikrant at the base of the stairs.

"Our team traced the poisoned phone. It was handed to Anjali by the cameraman....Sanjay. He confessed."

A pause.

"He's dead now."

Vikrant froze.

"Satish referred him. Word of mouth. I didn't know anything more."

Aryan nodded, focused.

"We're heading to Satish's house now. If he's just a pawn, it's time to find out who's holding the strings."

He pulled out a Sketch and held it up.

"Have you seen this girl before?"

Vikrant looked closely, then shook his head.

"No. Who is she?"

"We're still finding that out," Aryan said.

"Could be a pawn. Could be the killer. Either way... she's connected."

He stepped back, his tone final.

"Thanks for your time. I have to go."

✦ ∞ ✦

Aryan and Rajeev stood shoulder to shoulder, a whiteboard covered in photos and ink lines before them.

"Satish says he referred Sanjay to several houses. Took a small commission. Claims he didn't know he'd do this," Rajeev said.

"And the sketch girl?" Aryan asked.

Rajeev's face turned grim.

"Hyderabad police traced her. Her name is Ruhi."

Aryan's voice lowered. "Ruhi….."

Rajeev nodded, then continued.

"She was studying chemistry, working part-time at a private medical lab. And... she was an orphan. An NGO took her in. They supported her education, raised her like family."

He hesitated.

"She was just 13 when they found her. But for the past year…. she's been missing."

Aryan's eyes narrowed.

"What more can we find on her? Any leads, any recent data?"

"They said she lived in a group home while attending college. She was quiet….kept to herself. A good student, but emotionally distant. She vanished without warning, and no one's seen her since."

Aryan stepped back, thinking aloud.

"She wasn't working alone. Someone was guiding her…or using her."

Rajeev's expression darkened.

"The NGO did everything they could. Raised her like their own. But she was always…. somewhere else. Not emotionally connected. Not open. No one really knew her."

Aryan turned toward the whiteboard, hands behind his back.

His voice dropped…measured, sharp.

"So, she lived a life... but no one ever really saw her."

"Exactly," Rajeev replied.

Aryan stared at the board.

"We're not chasing a killer anymore."

A long pause.

"We're chasing a story someone's trying to erase."

Chapter 43

The clinking of steel plates and soft rustle of chapatis being torn filled the modest dining room. It was a familiar sound. Comforting. But that night, beneath it, something quieter brewed…..an undercurrent of words waiting to be spoken.

Ameet sat at the head of the table, posture upright, hands slow and methodical as he tore his roti. Beside him, Roopa stirred her sabzi without tasting it. Usha and Anika sat across, quiet, mirroring each other in the way sisters often do.

Just as Anika spooned a second ladle of dal into her bowl, Usha cleared her throat and smiled faintly.

"Papa," she said, casually, but her eyes twinkled. "I saw a lovely man, for Anika."

Anika froze mid-motion. "What are you saying?"

Roopa looked up sharply. "Who?"

Ameet raised his brows. "Which man, Usha?"

Usha leaned in with a grin. "Inspector Aryan. And it's not just me. Anyone with eyes can see…they love each other."

Anika choked on her breath. "Usha!"

Roopa's spoon clanged against the plate. "Love?"

Ameet laughed, brushing it off. "Usha don't tease your sister. Just eat."

But Usha didn't retreat. "It's not teasing, Papa. I mean it."

Ameet turned to Anika. "Is she serious, beta?"

Anika stared down at her plate, silent.

Roopa's voice cut through the air. "Anika. Answer your father."

After a moment, her voice came, almost a whisper. "He... loves me."

Roopa's eyes narrowed. "And you?"

Usha nudged her leg under the table, and Anika nodded, eyes still lowered.

Ameet rose from his chair, slowly walking to Anika. He bent, gently cupping her face. "Is it true?"

Tears shimmered in her lashes. She nodded again.

And then, unexpectedly, Ameet smiled.

"Well," he said, "that's good news."

Usha laughed quietly and wrapped her arms around Anika's shoulders.

But Roopa stood, shaking her head. "You all have lost your minds. This is not how things are done."

Ameet looked at her with calm humor. "At least she fell in love with a man….not a ghost."

Even Anika chuckled faintly.

But Roopa wasn't done. "Did he say he wants to marry her?"

The table went quiet again.

Roopa's voice softened, but it turned colder. "Then it's not love. It's air. A floating thing. Nothing."

Anika looked away. Usha's mouth pressed shut.

The mood fractured.

Ameet, quiet all this while, looked off into the dark hallway…..his hands resting in his lap, eyes distant, as if something within had started whispering.

Usha placed her hand on his. "Papa... they love each other. Isn't love enough?"

Ameet didn't answer immediately. Then, quietly, "Falling in love isn't a sin. Staying true to it... that's what matters."

Usha watched his face. "You loved Ma?"

Ameet's eyes didn't blink. "More than anyone could. But..."

He paused. His voice faltered. "She never knew. I never told her. Not properly. Not the way she deserved."

And with that, he stood and walked silently into his room.

Roopa's face remained hard. But her hands trembled slightly as she reached for the water jug.

Usha sat still, watching the empty hallway her father had disappeared into.

She didn't know if it was grief or guilt that weighed heavier in the room….but she knew something had cracked.

✦ ∞ ✦

Upstairs, Karishma knocked softly. "Bhaiya... come down. Papa and Samina's parents are waiting. Don't sit here alone."

Vikrant sat on the edge of the bed, unmoving. "I'm not hungry."

Karishma crossed her arms. "If you won't eat, I won't either."

He sighed. "Why are you doing this?"

"Why are you?"

A long pause.

Then Vikrant stood.

"Fine."

Down the stairs, the table was dressed in silver platters, untouched food, and conversations that had dried before they reached the air.

Raichand spoke first. "We'll be leaving tomorrow."

Kunal looked up, surprised. "So soon?"

Raichand nodded. "The engagement didn't happen. The next auspicious date is months away."

Sunita added calmly, "Samina is coming with us."

Samina's voice was low but firm. "No. I'm staying."

Raichand stiffened. "You're coming. That's final."

Kunal raised a brow. "Is something wrong?"

Sunita smiled. "Of course not."

Just then, Vikrant entered. His dress from the previous night still clung to him like a costume left on too long.

"Samina," he said, voice dry, "maybe it's best you go."

Samina looked at him.

Just looked.

Not a word.

He had said,

"It's better if I go."

And that was it.

The air in the room grew still…. not heavy, but hollow.

Inside her, something folded inward.

Her soul whispered his name,

held him in the spaces he was already leaving.

She wasn't fighting him.

She was fighting herself….the part that still hoped.

Still loved.

Still stayed.

She said nothing.

Not a single word.

Her eyes dropped to the plate in front of her….. still empty.

She had waited all morning.

Waited for him to come down so they could eat together.

So she could start.

So she could belong.

But now….

how could she eat?

How could she even lift her hand to fill the plate,

when the one she filled her world with

was choosing to walk away?

She just stared.

At the plate.

At the emptiness inside it.

And in its silver curve, her own face looked back at her.

Still. Quiet.

Like someone learning what it means

to be left behind.

Kunal looked up from his untouched food. "Did Aryan ask you anything today?"

Vikrant replied, "Only about the cameraman."

Karishma looked between them, cautious. "Papa… are you hiding something?"

The air thickened.

Raichand placed his spoon down. "Tell them why the factory really closed."

Vikrant frowned. "You said it was financial losses."

Raichand's gaze slid to Kunal. "That's what he told you."

Kunal stood abruptly. "Enough, Raichand."

But Karishma pressed. "Papa… what happened?"

Raichand didn't blink.

"They found a young girl's body buried on the factory grounds. The police were called. But by the time they arrived….it had vanished. Your father shut the factory down. That's the truth."

Vikrant stared at him.

"Papa…..?"

Kunal rose from the table, his hands trembling.

He didn't say a word.

He just walked away.

Vikrant and Karishma froze.

The air around them held still….like it, too, had heard something it couldn't unhear.

But Samina….

Samina hadn't heard a single word.

Her eyes stayed fixed ahead, but she was somewhere else entirely.

Far from the room.
Far from the noise.
She wasn't hearing about bodies or factories.
She was hearing the silence Vikrant left behind.
Only her body remained in the chair….still, poised.
But inside…
she was lost in the feeling of him.
In the space where she once imagined his love might live.
And now, that space was just air.
Still.
Empty.
Unanswered.
She sat there quietly,
in the echo of a feeling
that had nowhere left to go.

Kunal sat alone in the dark.
Only a faint glow from the corridor spilled across the floor.
Anjali's photo rested beside him.
He held it like it was the last soft thing in a world that had turned
to stone.

Flashback —
The factory.
Narayan and Kunal stood in a half-dug pit.
A girl's lifeless body lay wrapped in a jute bag.
Kunal's voice shook.
"They were digging the wrong section."
Narayan wiped his brow.
"Manager told them Part B. They went for C."
Kunal gritted his teeth.

"Get the body out. I will handle it. Silence the workers. Pay them. Fire the ones who won't shut up."

Narayan nodded.

"Yes, sir."

Back to present —

Kunal clutched his wife's photo tighter, his knuckles pale against the frame.

"I buried her," he whispered.

"Not just that girl…

I buried every truth that could have saved us."

Outside the door……Karishma stood listening.

No tears.

No words.

Just her….. still in the hallway,

where silence sounded like a verdict.

Chapter 44

The night had fallen like a hush across the village. The forest beyond the Rathi house was silent….save for a lone owl calling from its perch, its voice cutting through the stillness like an ancient memory.

Inside, the small bedroom was wrapped in the dull hum of a ceiling fan and the gentle breathing of two sisters sharing a bed. Anika, eyes half-open, whispered into the quiet, "Usha… do you think Aryan loves me?"

Usha, lying beside her, turned and gently brushed a loose strand of hair off Anika's forehead. Her smile was soft but certain.

"Yes," she whispered. "I don't think. I know."

Anika's voice trembled faintly. "But will he marry me?"

Usha's fingers tightened around her sister's hand. "He will. Because he doesn't just love you, Di. He respects you. That's the kind of love that stays."

Anika slowly exhaled, her lashes fluttering closed. Her lips curved faintly into a smile….the kind that only comes when something heavy finally softens.

Usha watched her sleep for a long while.

The rise and fall of Anika's breath felt like proof….. that some storms could pass.

And then, barely above a whisper,

only to herself, she said:

"He stood when no one else did.

When they pointed at you. .blamed you….

he stayed."

A pause…….

Her voice cracked gently.

"Of course he'll be with you.

He saw you. "

She looked away,

toward the window,

toward the silence she'd never learned how to fight.

"And I...... "

A bitter breath.

"I watched another man break me.

Again.

And again.... "

A single tear slid down her cheek

and vanished into the pillow beside her.

No sound.

No sob.

Just silence that knew too much.

The wind outside had picked up, brushing dry leaves against the windows with a hushed rustle.

Karishma tiptoed into her brother's room. She found Vikrant by the window, arms crossed, his eyes lost in the cold dark.

"You're still awake?"

"I can't sleep," he murmured. "The factory... Mom... everything's a blur."

Karishma wrapped her shawl tighter around herself. "That story about the body... It's like the house itself is holding its breath. Like something wants to break out."

Vikrant didn't answer, but his arms dropped.

Karishma walked to him and placed her hand gently on his back.

"Whatever comes next, we'll face it. Together."

He nodded slowly, the lines on his face deeper tonight.

Outside, the wind howled.

Winter had arrived early this year.

✦ ∞ ✦

Kunal jolted up from his bed, drenched in sweat.

In his dream, the girl had returned…..mud-smeared, broken, her lifeless body walking again through the forest. This time, she reached for Karishma.

"No!" he shouted.

Karishma and Vikrant rushed in, startled. "Papa!"

Kunal sat on the edge of the bed; breath ragged. "It was just… a dream."

Karishma stepped forward; her voice steady but soft. "Papa, you're not sleeping. You're running. You're hiding something… and it's hurting you more than us."

Kunal closed his eyes. And for the first time in years….he spoke.

"1st of October, 2003."

He didn't look at them. His voice carried the weight of a man breaking in slow motion.

"There was a girl. An orphan. She was about twelve. Someone had left her near our factory years ago. I let her stay. Gave her food. She had nowhere else."

He paused. "Then one day… she was raped. Brutally. The man responsible was caught. Sentenced to 20 years. The factory workers were relieved. We had a small pooja to mark the *day of her justice.*"

His voice cracked.

"That same time in morning… Narayan and I went for a walk inside the factory grounds. And we found a body. Another girl. Older. Raped. Strangled. Left in the open near the forest's edge."

Karishma covered her mouth. Vikrant stood frozen.

"She had a notebook. Scribbled pages… about tribal history. About the forest. She was a journalist. Her name was Rekha. And near her body… was Samar's wallet. His handkerchief."

Kunal looked up at them.

"We panicked. The police would never believe us. It would've destroyed everything…..our name, the factory, our family. So, I told Narayan to help me bury her. Deep inside an unused part of the grounds."

Silence pressed into the room.

"But two days later, workers digging for a pipeline found the grave. Wrong section. They called the police. Narayan stalled them while I arrived. We bribed the workers. Fired those who didn't fall in line. That night, we shifted the body again… buried it deeper, in a safer corner. Then, few days later, we shut down the factory. Spread rumours of a ghost. And it worked."

Vikrant's voice was barely audible. "You buried a woman. And made her death a myth?"

Kunal's lips trembled.

"We took her notebook. She was researching tribes… the forest…collecting old artifacts and stories. She had gathered so much. So we turned it into something else. Wove it into a story….a myth. We added ritualistic symbols, twisted facts, fed the fear. We spread stories about the forest, and then we published it. All of it. As a book."

Another breath, heavier now.

"We called it History of the Forest…and put Samar's name on the cover."

Karishma's voice quivered, barely a whisper. "Why, Samar?"

Kunal's eyes dropped to the floor, his guilt pressing down like a storm he could no longer hold back.

"I knew he was involved in that rape. I wanted him gone. Out of our lives forever. I wanted to set things right… to punish him. But I couldn't. Not in this house. Not in front of the people who still trusted us."

He swallowed hard.

"And then…. the accident happened. Samar died. So I used it. I published that book under his name. Paid people to write ghost stories, blogs….anything to shift the narrative."

His voice dropped

"Anything to bury the truth. To bury him."

Another pause. One that felt like confession and relief, all at once.

"And I finally had a reason to hate him.

Openly.

Even after he was gone."

A beat.

The weight of what followed thickened the air.

"Rekha was a journalist….. and the pressure was mounting. The media wouldn't let go of her. She was everywhere—headlines, whispers, investigations. The police already knew she'd been in town. That she was working on something tied to the forest. So we twisted the facts. We added her name to the book. And we paid people to write blogs…. ghost stories….false articles tying Rekha to the forest. Said she disappeared because of the spirits there. At first, no one believed it. But then they saw her shoes. Her watch. Hanging from the trees like warnings."

A pause………..long, cold.

"Me and Narayan planted them. We made the forest bleed fiction….until it buried the truth. And they believed."

Karishma's body swayed with shock, her hand over her mouth.

"You buried the truth... and turned it into a lie."

Her voice cracked as she asked the final, heartbreaking question,

"Was that girl's body ever… given peace?"

Kunal's gaze remained locked on the ground, his voice barely audible. "She's still out there… buried deep."

Outside, the wind rose sharply….not just howling,
but listening, as if the forest itself had been waiting
to hear what had been hidden.
And somewhere within that silence……….
not in words,
but in the ache of what was never spoken………
one name echoed louder than the rest.
Rekha.
She tried to write the truth.
Raised her voice for women who had none.
She fought for what mattered– for justice, for memory, for stories no one wanted told.
But they silenced her.
Twisted her words into fiction.
Hung her watch from a tree…… and called it ghost.
Even as her truth was stolen….. Even when the forest became her grave… she never screamed.
She never begged.
She never got to speak again.
But her echo didn't die.
It whispered… low, through roots, through the wind, through the rustle of leaves that remembered her name
long after the world forgot.
They took her voice.
Her story.
Her body.
And still…. they couldn't take her truth.
It stayed behind.
Quiet.
Unyielding.
Heavy in the air.
Etched into the silence.

And still…… she stayed quiet.
In the air.
In the echoes.
In the forest.
In memory.
In night.
Waiting.
For someone to say her name.
To call her back.
To give her justice.
To give her peace.

Chapter 45

The morning sun filtered through the dusty glass windows of Chandrapur Police Station, casting long, golden bars across the floor. The air was quiet, almost reverent. But inside Aryan's office, silence carried a different weight....a heaviness that had nothing to do with time of day.

Aryan sat slouched in his chair, sleeves rolled up, face shadowed by exhaustion. The wall behind him was a chaos of red-thread connections, grainy photos, and handwritten notes. But now it all felt... insufficient.

Anjali's death had tilted everything. What once seemed like threads now looked like echoes...faint, fading, and circular.

Rajeev walked in, holding a thick, worn diary.

"Naina's," he said, placing it on Aryan's desk. "There's something you should read."

Aryan opened it to the marked page. The handwriting was uneven, like the thoughts were trembling on the page. He read aloud:

"And still, God stayed quiet."

He looked up, brow furrowed. "Now, what is this?"

Rajeev stepped forward. "It aligns with her earlier metaphors. You remember.....she called her abortion 'our love symbol Died at Maheshwari Hospital.' Maybe this is her way of saying even God watched in silence... while she was broken."

Aryan leaned back in his chair, eyes lifting to the ceiling as if waiting for it to speak. "Maybe she didn't mean God. Maybe she meant someone she once believed in. The Pandit."

Rajeev nodded. "Could be. Or Samar. Or Satish. Someone she thought would protect her but didn't. And now..."

"Now someone's doing it for her," Aryan finished quietly. "Satish."

Rajeev's voice dropped. "He's always on the edge of the story, never in it. Always helpful. Always there. But too invisible."

Aryan nodded. "Keep him under watch. Every move."

Rajeev hesitated. "That's not all, sir. These are the painting we found"

He placed a bundle of folded cloth on the desk. They began opening them, one by one.

The first canvas revealed a forest…..thick, heavy with vines. Dark, endless. Familiar.

Aryan's voice was barely a breath. "This is here. Chandrapur forest."

The second canvas; Samar. A fierce rendering…..his face was twisted, distorted with anger.

Aryan's jaw tightened. "There's no confusion in this brushstroke. She hated him."

The third; a cold, grey building surrounded by a fence and trees.

Rajeev pointed. "That's the Rai factory."

The fourth painting stopped them. It was different. Softer.

A man behind prison bars….but his face wasn't harsh. His eyes were drawn in layers of sorrow and strength. There was something… almost sacred about him.

Aryan whispered, "Someone she respected. Or someone wrongly blamed."

Rajeev tilted his head. "Someone she hoped would be free."

They moved on.

The fifth; a young woman bathed in soft golden hues; a faint halo drawn over her head. Light surrounded her.

"She's in peace now," Rajeev murmured. "See the rings? Like angels. That's not just a person. That's a memory."

Aryan said nothing. His eyes lingered.

Then came the final canvas.

The same girl. But not in gold. This time, the background was fractured....stormy greys, slashing lines of black, crimson mist in the distance.

Below the painting, written in messy, urgent letters:

"She left behind only a rhythm the wind dares remember."

Aryan stood still. His hands were cold.

Rajeev leaned in. "It's a message."

Aryan replied, "It's not just a message. It's a dirge."

He turned the canvas around.

Another sentence was scribbled on the back:

"Rainy evening knock heralds arrival."

Rajeev's voice cracked in the silence. "Say that again, sir."

Aryan did.

Slower this time. "Rainy. Evening. Knock. Heralds. Arrival."

Then the realization fell.....hard, sharp, quiet.

They looked at each other.

Rajeev whispered, "REKHA."

The letters.

R. E. K. H. A.

Aryan closed his eyes. Goosebumps raced across his arms.

"She didn't just die," he said, voice low and hollow. "She left a trail. Buried inside her pain. Inside her silence."

Rajeev stared at the painting. "Sir... Naina didn't just suffer. She documented it. She left poetry. Warnings. Memories. Truth disguised as art."

Aryan's voice was no longer a whisper. "She wasn't waiting for help. She was planting clues."

The fan spun slowly above them. Outside, the wind rustled faintly against the glass.

Inside the room, there was no movement.

Only stillness.

And the heavy realization that the dead girl had never stopped speaking.

They had simply taken too long to listen.

Chapter 46

The air inside the station hung heavy, thick with a silence that hummed like a warning. Morning sunlight spilled through the blinds in streaks, slicing across the paintings laid out across the table…..Naina's haunting fragments of memory. Each canvas whispered something ancient. Something unfinished.

Aryan stood still, eyes fixed on the one with the forest….a tangle of brushstrokes that looked almost like veins, as if the land itself bled stories.

"She must've seen Rekha," Rajeev said quietly, breaking the hush.

Aryan nodded. "Or knew what happened to her."

"She didn't use words," Rajeev murmured. "She used symbols. Pain wrapped in colour."

Aryan's eyes didn't move from the forest. "Innocent girls. Rekha. Naina. Both tried to speak. Both silenced."

Rajeev clenched his jaw. "Satish… he's not working alone. We need to follow every move."

Aryan's fingers hovered over the spine of Samar's book. "He hid truths in fiction. But fiction borrows from fact."

Just then, Aryan's phone buzzed. He read the message once, twice.

Usha: I want to meet you. It's about Anika… and you. Waiting at the temple.

He slid the phone into his pocket, voice low but steady. "Rajeev, I'll be back. Lock these up. This case… it's not just about death anymore. It's about the lives left behind."

✦ ∞ ✦

Golden light crept across the marble floor. In the quiet bedroom, Karishma lay curled up on the couch, her breath even. Vikrant stirred, rubbing his temples as he sat up.

"Shit," he whispered. The clock read nearly eleven.

He rushed through a cold bath, towel draped across his shoulders as he stepped out….only to find Samina standing at the door, soft smile in place.

"I came earlier," she said. "Didn't want to wake you."

"Your parents left?" he asked, voice still groggy.

Samina nodded. "Yes."

Karishma stretched, sitting up. "Ugh, why didn't someone wake me?"

Samina chuckled gently. "Breakfast's on the stove. I'll heat it."

Vikrant paused, towel still in hand. "Why didn't you go with them?"

Samina's smile faltered. "Because… it hurts more to leave you than to stay."

She turned and walked away; her silence more telling than any confession.

Vikrant stood there, unmoving.

Karishma reached for his arm. "You're going to talk to Anika?"

He nodded. "I must. I have to say sorry."

Karishma held his gaze. "Then go. Don't carry it longer than she already has."

He stepped toward the door, each stride heavy with regret… and something else. A feeling once buried, now quietly blooming.

Love.

Sunlight kissed the temple steps in warm gold. The scent of jasmine lingered with each passing breeze. Birds cooed lazily from the trees, as if the day itself had paused to listen.

Usha sat on the edge of the courtyard, fingers fidgeting with the hem of her dupatta.

When Aryan arrived, the worry in her face softened.

"You, okay?" he asked gently.

She nodded, then hesitated. "I just… need to know something."

"Ask."

She met his gaze. "Do you love my sister?"

Aryan smiled…..tender, unwavering. "Yes. I do."

Usha breathed out, a small smile flickering. "Will you marry her?"

"When the case ends, I'll come with my parents. She deserves every bit of love done right. And your book… it helped me understand her better."

Usha's eyes shimmered. "Then finish this, Aryan. End it all. And marry her."

Aryan gave a gentle nod.

"We've connected a thread," he said. "Samar knew Rekha. Naina too. And now… Satish is hiding more than we thought. Naina is Satish's sister."

"Naina?" Usha's brows furrowed. "Satish once told me she painted him."

"She did. But their story was darker. Samar abandoned her after she got pregnant. She was forced into abortion. After that… she shattered. And now…..her brother is taking revenge."

Usha's voice thinned. "He always seemed so… normal."

"That's the danger. We think he's protecting someone… or avenging. And Anika…..she might've been a target… or a shield. When Anjali died, Anika was blamed at first because of that cameraman…..Sanjay. But someone cleared her name. Why?"

Usha went still. "You think he'll come after our family?"

"We've placed security. But clever men always notice. So… stay alert."

The bells chimed faintly in the background, while the world prayed and moved forward. But here, the past refused to rest.

"Did you find out why my pendant symbol was in that book?" Usha asked.

"We're not sure. But Naina left us one clue…. 'And still, God stayed quiet.' We think she meant the pandit. Or someone who knew and stayed silent."

Usha nodded slowly.

Aryan looked at her, something deeper in his tone. "You once mentioned your father. That Anika cut you off."

Usha lowered her eyes. "He worked in the Rai factory. Never shared much. But on October 1st…the day Narayan died…..he was terrified. Said, 'They're coming.' I think… he knew something."

Aryan's eyes sharpened. "That might be what ties it all. Rekha vanished on October 1st too."

Usha changed the subject softly. "By the way… Anika got the admission form. Did you….?"

Aryan grinned. "Of course. I want her to have everything."

Usha smiled. "She's lucky."

"I'll drop you home," Aryan offered. "Got a gift for her anyway."

She nodded, warmth returning to her face.

Vikrant stood outside the gate, heart pounding like a boy at his first confession. He knocked.

Anika opened it, surprise flashing in her eyes. "Vikrant ji…?"

"I came to say sorry," he said, eyes earnest. "I let fear guide me, not love. I'm truly… sorry."

She stood quietly, then stepped aside. "Come in."

He looked around, taking in the small home with soft reverence.

"It's simple… but it feels alive."

Anika smiled. "It's small."

"But it's a home," he said. "That's rare."

She moved to the kitchen. "Tea?"

He nodded. "Usha?"

"She went to the temple."

Just then, a car door shut outside.

Usha entered with Aryan, her eyes catching Vikrant's car. She smiled.

"Come in, Aryan. Anika will be happy."

"Only if she makes the tea herself," Aryan grinned.

They stepped in.

"Inspector," Vikrant said, surprised.

Aryan gave a nod. "Hope I'm not interrupting."

"Not at all."

Anika emerged with a tray. Her face lit up. "You came."

"I promised," Aryan said.

Usha teased, "Strong tea, please. He's had a long day."

Vikrant leaned toward her. "What's between them?"

Usha raised a brow. "Love. What else?"

He looked down, guilt rippling through him.

Aryan sensed the silence. "Let's just have tea. Forget yesterday."

But then….Aryan's phone buzzed. He picked it up.

"Rajeev?" His voice changed. He stood abruptly; tea untouched.

Everyone stilled.

"What's wrong?" Anika asked, her voice barely a whisper.

Outside, the wind rustled the trees. Shadows shifted. The warmth of the afternoon gave way to something colder.

Something had changed.

And something was coming.

Chapter 47

Rajeev's voice crackled through the phone, taut with urgency.

"Sir, remember you asked me to dig into the Rathi family's records at the start of the case?"

Aryan stood up slowly, his instincts alert. "Yes?"

"I rechecked the files this morning. Ameet Rathi's bank account.....holds over ten lakh."

Aryan's brows lifted. "Ten lakh?"

"Yes. It came from a woman named Namarta Parkash. I tracked the transfer."

Aryan's voice dropped to a whisper. "Namarta..."

"He saved the number under 'Namu' in his contacts."

"Namu," Aryan repeated, slower now.....like the word itself had teeth.

Behind him, Usha stirred, her voice rising above the silence.

"Namu... that nurse..."

Aryan turned. "You know her?"

Rajeev's voice still echoed through the speaker. "I'm tracing her location now. But this... this is connected."

Aryan ended the call and looked at Usha. His gaze was steady, but something in his voice trembled, curious and careful. "Tell me everything you remember."

Usha glanced at her sister, then folded her arms tightly, as if holding memory close.

"She was the nurse who saved us. The night me and Anika were born, it rained like the sky had broken open. No cars, no ambulance.

My mother went into labor at home. Our grandmother ran to fetch help…..and brought back a local nurse. Namu.”

Her breath hitched.

“She delivered us. But my mother… didn’t survive.”

Anika’s voice came soft, trailing behind her sister’s. “They never told us more. Every time we asked, they changed the subject. I always felt… something was missing.”

Aryan’s expression grew darker. “According to Rajeev, this ‘Namu’ …… Namarta…. once transferred ten lakh rupees to your father. And the strange part? There’s no other activity in that account. It’s like he opened it just for that one transfer….and he never even withdrew the money.”

Anika gasped, as if the truth slapped her breath away. “That’s not possible. We’ve struggled our whole lives. If Baba had that kind of money… we would’ve known.”

Usha’s voice trembled like a reed in wind. “What kind of secret is worth hiding from your own daughters?”

In the corner of the room, Vikrant had been silent, arms folded, eyes downcast. Now he spoke, voice low and strangely soft. “Sometimes, parents carry the weight of their past, so we don’t have to. Maybe they thought burying it would protect you.”

Aryan turned toward him, something sharper in his tone. “But you… you know something, don’t you?”

Vikrant didn’t answer. His silence was almost an admission.

Aryan’s voice deepened. “Why did your father shut down the factory, Vikrant?”

Vikrant hesitated, then spoke. “He said people claimed it was haunted. That Samar started those rumours to destroy our name.”

“Ghosts?” Aryan repeated, disbelieving. “You really believe that?”

“I don’t know what to believe anymore,” Vikrant murmured.

Aryan stepped closer. “What about Satish? How well do you know him?”

"He's my friend," Vikrant replied. "A good friend. But lately... he's stopped coming the shop. He's afraid."

"And you think that's a coincidence?" Aryan pressed. "Satish is behind this. He has reason….and he's not alone."

"No," Vikrant shook his head. "I don't blame him. I can't."

Aryan didn't let up. "Your mother is gone. Naina…..Satish's sister….died with a heart torn by betrayal. She was pregnant, and Samar left her. Your family buried her truth. Do you understand what that kind of silence does to a brother like Satish?"

Vikrant's breath caught in his throat. "No… that can't be true."

"It is." Aryan's voice dropped. "And worse. Satish is seeking revenge….and he's not doing it in the open. He's erasing, the same way Naina was erased."

Usha stepped forward. "Aryan, maybe we…."

But Vikrant raised a hand. "Let him speak. I want to hear this."

Aryan's voice steadied, carrying the weight of a gavel. "Samar didn't just leave Naina. He ruined her. And your father? He helped cover it. Her pain is painted across those canvases…..silent cries in oil and shadow. The factory, the forest, Rekha….everything leads back there."

Something shifted in Vikrant's eyes.

He staggered back a step, gripping the chair.

Aryan's voice softened to a slow, dreadful calm. "Your father didn't just look away from Naina's death… Your father killed her"

"No!" Vikrant shouted, the word breaking from his throat like thunder. "It wasn't my father. Samar killed Rekha."

Silence.

Time collapsed into a single, breathless second.

Aryan stood frozen.

Usha's eyes widened.

Anika covered her mouth with her hand.

Vikrant blinked….slowly, like waking from a dream.

"I… I didn't mean…." he stammered, realizing.

But it was already spoken.

The room, once thick with secrets, now gasped with truth.

The forest soil had held it. The paintings had whispered it. The wind had carried it from leaf to leaf.

And now, finally, the name was spoken.

Rekha.

She had waited for someone to speak for her.

And Vikrant Rai…..blood of the very family that buried her….was the one who finally did.

Chapter 48

The home felt altered….like it had exhaled something it held for too long.

Moments ago, this space had echoed with soft voices and cautious laughter. Now, it held its breath. Even the curtains, swaying faintly, seemed to still in reverence of the truth just spoken.

Vikrant stood frozen, a man caught between shame and shock.

"My father didn't kill Rekha... it was Samar."

The words, once unspeakable, now hung in the air like a slow-burning fire. No one moved.

Anika's hand flew to her mouth, her breath catching mid-gasp. Usha's eyes widened, her fingers trembling slightly as they clutched the cushion beside her. Aryan's gaze remained on Vikrant…..steadfast, sharp….but not unkind. Those five words had shaken every thread of their unravelling mystery.

"I… I didn't mean to say it like that," Vikrant stammered. But the weight of the truth was already falling.

Aryan stepped forward, his voice calm, controlled. "Rekha… she wasn't just missing, was she?"

Vikrant's silence was answer enough.

"She was dead."

A pause.

"Buried."

Usha sat slowly on the edge of the sofa; her knees no longer able to hold the gravity. Anika remained standing, silent tears glossing her eyes. The image of Rekha returned to them all…..fierce, defiant, unyielding. A woman who stood against silence. And was silenced for it.

Aryan's voice softened but held its edge. "Vikrant. I need you to trust me. What you say now…..what we learn here…stays within us. We'll investigate quietly. If your father wasn't part of it, we won't drag him through this. But we need the truth."

And then, slowly, painfully, Vikrant began.

He spoke of what his father once confessed……words shared in a late night, once dismissed as drunken guilt. It was October 1st, 2003. There had been celebration in the Rai factory, a girl had won justice after a long trial. People were gathered, hopeful. But amid the cheering, something dark was unearthed in the forest nearby….a girl's body, half-covered in soil. A notebook lay beside her.

"She'd been raped," Vikrant whispered. "Her body was… broken. But that notebook…..she'd written about land, tribes, old stories. Like she was trying to capture truth before it disappeared."

Usha's hand found Anika's and held tight. Neither spoke, but their silence screamed louder than grief.

"My father panicked. So did Narayan. They hadn't killed her—but they buried her. Hid her deep beneath the C-section of the factory. When some workers found the body later, he paid them off. Shut them up. He said… it was for our family's name."

Aryan didn't interrupt. He only listened. Steady. Focused.

Vikrant swallowed, his voice cracking. "They turned it into a myth. A ghost story. Said the land was cursed. Shut the factory. And Rekha….she vanished into superstition."

Anika choked back a sob, her lips trembling. Rekha had died in pursuit of justice. And justice, like her body, was buried under convenience.

"She fought," Aryan murmured, his voice like a vow. "She fought until the end."

A silence stretched. Sacred.

Then Aryan stood. There was no uncertainty in him now. "She will get justice. But before we reopen files, before we even find her body....we need to stop the one who's using her memory for revenge."

Vikrant nodded solemnly.

Then, after a pause, he said, "Maybe we should make a group chat. Just between us. Private. We can stay updated... stay connected."

Usha gave a small smile, the kind that surfaces in ruins. "That's actually... a good idea."

Anika whispered, "But... I only have a keypad phone."

Aryan smiled, something warm flickering behind the exhaustion in his eyes. "Well, your father has over ten lakhs in his account. I think we can arrange a phone."

Laughter trickled in like light after a storm. Small. Real.

"You're all teasing me now," Anika said, half-embarrassed, half-blushing.

"No," Aryan said, eyes softening. "Just happy to see you smile."

Usha bent forward, reaching under the table for a small green box wrapped with gold ribbon.

Anika blinked. "What's this?"

Aryan shrugged, grinning. "A gift."

"A phone?"

"Your first gift from Aryan," Usha added with a wink.

"No," Anika smiled shyly. "Second. He already gifted me books."

"Third," Aryan corrected, raising a finger. "I also filled your college admission form."

Usha laughed. "He's keeping track now."

Anika's eyes lowered. "I haven't given you anything."

Aryan tilted his head, gaze gentler now. "You gave me your trust. Your smile. And tea... with two spoons of sugar. That's more than enough."

Vikrant rolled his eyes. "Love turns everyone into poets."

Usha grinned. "You wouldn't understand. Ego man"

He raised a brow. "So, love is about gifts, is it?"

"Not gifts," Usha replied. "Gestures. One day, you pick up a letter, or a bracelet, or a phone… and remember. That's how love survives. It leaves footprints in time."

For a second, they were not detectives and suspects and survivors.

They were just people. Holding moments.

Aryan smiled. But behind it, his mind still worked.

Because the truth was unspooling fast.

And justice….it wasn't a distant idea anymore.

It was close.

Almost breathing.

Chapter 49

The evening sun spilled through the blinds in fractured slants, turning the floor into a chessboard of fading gold and shadow. The light moved slowly, like it too was listening.

Rajeev paced Aryan's office, files gripped tight in his hands, his footsteps echoing softly steady, tense, deliberate. Aryan stood by the evidence board, where strings stitched stories between faces and places. One corner was soaked in colour…..Naina's paintings. Stark. Fragile. Screaming in silence.

A single page from her diary sat beneath a glass paperweight. The final line inked in delicate scrawl:

"She left behind only a rhythm the wind dares remember."

Aryan's eyes lingered on that line for a moment, then shifted to Rajeev.

"We're close," he said, barely above a whisper. "But we move quietly now. No ripples."

He unlocked his phone.

WhatsApp – New Group Created

Members Added: Aryan, Rajeev, Vikrant, Usha, Anika

Rajeev nodded, his jaw tightening. "Understood." He glanced at the phone and asked, "Sir, is it safe to share information within the project group?"

Aryan closed the phone and placed it back on the table. "We need information. To get it, we'll have to share a little. Gain their trust. It's the only way to uncover what their parents are hiding."

Rajeev smiled. "Smart, sir. That's a solid move."

Aryan turned back toward the board. "We know Samar killed Rekha. And Naina... she knew. She didn't write it. She painted it. Her silence wasn't surrender....it was a different kind of voice."

Rajeev's brow furrowed. "That one painting. The man behind bars. I keep going back to it. I think she was trying to tell us something else. That the wrong man went to prison."

Aryan's voice dropped. "You mean....someone else took the punishment for Samar's crime?"

"Exactly. He raped that orphan girl in the factory... and someone else was jailed."

Aryan's hands curled into fists. "If that man's out now....after twenty years in hell for someone else's sin....he could be part of Satish's plan. And he wouldn't just be angry. He'd be burning."

He turned, sharp. "Vikrant said the factory held a celebration in 2003....for justice delivered. A girl had fought her case for a year. So the crime happened late 2002 or early 2003."

Aryan's eyes narrowed. "Check court records from 2002 to 2003. Especially verdicts around October 1st, 2003. Look into assault or rape cases—find out who the inspector was. They can't cover up something this big without help from the police."

"I'm on it," Rajeev said, scribbling furiously. "Also, I'm digging into Ameet Rathi and Namu. That transfer... it doesn't feel clean."

Aryan's gaze hardened. "Ten lakhs. From a nurse. For what?"

Rajeev flipped open a folder. "I contacted the bank. Tracing it. We'll find her."

In the warm spill of kitchen light, Karishma chopped tomatoes with determined rhythm, a messy apron tied around her waist. Each slice came down with a little more force than necessary.

Vikrant stepped in, surprised. "Whoa. What's going on here?"

Karishma looked up. "Ramesh's wife is sick. He's off today. Samina's in charge. I'm playing assistant."

"From medicine to tomatoes, huh?"

She smirked. "Honestly? This is harder. These tomatoes don't sit still like frogs in anatomy labs."

"Do you know what tomorrow is?" She asked.

Vikrant blinked. "Uh...my meeting?"

She rolled her eyes. "Samina's birthday."

"Ohhh," he muttered. "Where is she?"

Just then, Samina entered, wiping her hands on a dish towel.

Vikrant shifted. "Happy early birthday."

Karishma crossed her arms. "He forgot."

Samina smiled softly. "That's okay."

"Let's do something," Vikrant said. "Not a party. Just... us. Simple. Quiet."

Samina hesitated. "Anjali aunty just passed. It feels wrong."

Karishma reached over gently. "Not a celebration. Just cake. A little warmth. I want to... for you."

After a moment, Samina nodded. "Okay."

Karishma lit up. "I'll bake her Favorite!"

Kunal appeared at the doorway, his presence calm. "She's part of this family. She's your life, Vikrant."

Samina's eyes flicked to Vikrant's. He didn't speak. But he didn't deny it.

Ameet stepped through the main door, weary from the day. Roopa sat in the living room, eyes red and dabbing at them with a handkerchief.

"What happened?" he asked.

"Maha Pooja at Meena's. So much smoke. My eyes are burning."

Usha entered, holding eyedrops. She knelt gently beside Roopa, steady hands administering the medicine.

From the kitchen, Anika called, "Dinner's almost ready!"

Then....ding. A sharp notification tone pierced the quiet.

Roopa frowned. "What was that?"

Usha stiffened.

"Sounded like a ringtone," Ameet muttered.

Roopa stood, following the sound into the bedroom. Moments later, she returned, holding a sleek smartphone.

"Whose is this?"

Usha and Anika shared a single glance...then Usha stepped forward. "Anika's."

Roopa's eyes narrowed. "Looks expensive."

Ameet chuckled. "Let me guess. Inspector Aryan?"

Roopa's jaw fell. "He's just giving her phones now?"

Before the storm could rise, Usha stepped in. "He loves her. He wants to marry her. What's the issue?"

Roopa's voice turned sharp. "Everything is the issue!"

Ameet raised his hand. "Enough. We'll talk tomorrow. Usha, go help your sister."

He walked over, plucked the phone from Roopa's hand, and passed it to Usha. "Change the ringtone, will you? It's irritating."

Usha let out a faint smile and walked to the kitchen.

"There are two messages," she told Anika. "From someone named Love Aryan. Seriously?"

Anika turned bright red. "Let me see!"

Usha held the phone just out of reach. "Let me guess... romantic confession?"

She tapped and read aloud. "Preparation books for your exam."

She laughed. "Well, not the steamiest love letter."

"He's mad," Anika murmured, smiling.

Usha leaned against the counter. "Maybe. But mad people love with their whole hearts."

From the hallway, Roopa called out, "Why are you both giggling?"

They giggled louder.

For a moment, beneath the layers of secrets, grief, and a woman's forgotten grave….two sisters laughed.

And in that laughter, love quietly breathed. Just enough to keep them going.

Chapter 50

The morning light spilled gently through the curtains, brushing the wooden floor with the calm hush of a new day. In the dining area, the table was half-set, the air fragrant with toasted bread and cardamom tea.

Vikrant descended the stairs in a crisp grey half-sleeve shirt, adjusting his wristwatch. "Good morning, Father."

Kunal looked up from behind his newspaper, reading glasses resting on the edge of his nose. "Good morning, beta."

Karishma appeared next, still half-asleep, tying her ponytail with one hand and yawning. The quiet hum of clinking cups came from the kitchen.....Samina was already up, her soft bangles chiming as she poured tea.

"Happy, happy, happy birthday once again!" Karishma squealed, throwing her arms around Samina from behind.

Kunal smiled as he folded his newspaper. "Happy birthday, Samina."

Vikrant pulled out a chair, nodding. "Happy birthday."

Samina turned, offering a modest smile. "Thank you."

Karishma slipped onto the chair beside Vikrant and leaned in. "I have to buy something.... something nice for her," she whispered.

Vikrant reached for a sandwich from the plate and took a bite. His brows lifted. "Wow. Who made this?"

Karishma grinned. "Who else? The queen of quiet flavours," she gestured toward Samina.

Vikrant glanced at her. "It's really good."

Karishma poured him tea, the steam curling between them. "So? What's the plan today?"

Vikrant looked over at Samina. "What kind of gift do you want?"

Kunal raised an eyebrow over his glasses. "That's not how it works. You don't ask. You know. That's the point. Otherwise, it's not a gift....it's a transaction."

Karishma grinned at Samina. "I have to find something beautiful."

Vikrant sighed, theatrically. "Fine. I'll surprise her."

The hallway was hushed. Ameet had already left for the shop. Roopa sat back on the divan, a cool compress resting over her swollen eyelids. A faint trace of sandalwood lingered in the air from the previous night's pooja.

Usha sat beside her, gently tilting her mother's head to check her eyes. "Did you use the drops last night?"

Roopa nodded faintly. "Yes. It's just the smoke. It'll pass."

Anika entered, balancing a kettle of warm water. "You should still see a doctor."

"No need, beti. Let the medicine work. Now go warm some water for yourselves.....the morning's caught a bit of chill."

The sisters moved into the kitchen. As the kettle began to hum, Usha leaned closer. "Should we ask her about Namu?"

Anika shook her head. "She'll get upset again. Let her rest today."

Just then, Usha's phone buzzed on the counter.

"Message," she murmured, unlocking it.

Anika peeked. "From the group?"

"No. Vikrant."

The message read:

"What kind of gift do you like?"

Usha frowned. "What's he playing at now?"

Anika laughed. "Trying to win you over, obviously."

Usha typed: *"I don't need anything."*
Another message came instantly.
"Can I gift you a bracelet?"
Usha rolled her eyes. "Bracelet? Really?"
"Why the sudden interest in gifts?" she replied.
"To say sorry."
Usha showed the screen to Anika, who burst out laughing.
"Sorry accepted," she typed, half-smiling.
"Then let me gift something."
"No."
"Okay, bangles?"
"I hate bangles."
"Red sari?"
"I hate red."
"Which colour do you love?"
"Why should I tell you?"
"General knowledge."
"Old trick."
"Okay. Then the gift's a surprise. Bye!"
"Angry emoji."
Anika was laughing freely now. "You didn't say no, though."
Usha rolled her eyes. "I didn't say yes either."

✦ ∞ ✦

The fluorescent lights buzzed faintly above Aryan's desk. The windows were half-open, letting in a breeze that toyed with the edges of a case file left carelessly ajar.

Rajeev entered, his stride brisk, a folder in hand.

"Sir. Namarta's bank statement."

Aryan took it, flipping through quickly.

"Zero balance?"

"Completely. And something else....she wasn't a nurse."

Aryan looked up sharply. "What?"

"She was a doctor. Full name: Dr. Namrata Parkash. She held a private license. No major hospital records. We're trying to find her clinic. Phone's off. Cyber is tracking her last ping."

Aryan stood, tension returning to his posture. "Get me everything on Ameet Rathi….his calls, financials, employment. I want every thread traced. And push Cyber Unit to isolate Dr. Namrata's last digital footprint. There's a gap somewhere. And it's important."

He picked up his phone and typed into the group:

Her full name is Dr. Namrata Parkash. No balance left in her account. We're tracing her last location.

He stared out the window, eyes fixed on a point only he could see.

Outside, the day moved on….cars honking distantly, footsteps passing the station door….but inside Aryan's mind, it all quieted.

Because the past had begun to speak again.

And this time, he was ready to listen.

Chapter 51

The door creaked open as Vikrant stepped into the Rai mansion, his arms weighed down with glossy shopping bags. The scent of new packaging, and gift paper followed him like an announcement.

Karishma looked up from the sofa, one leg tucked beneath her, phone in hand. She raised an eyebrow.

"Gifts for the birthday girl!" she said, grinning as she stood. "Samina, come on..."

From the kitchen, the soft clang of a spoon paused for a second. Samina was stirring noodles in a saucepan, the aroma of garlic and spring onion curling into the hallway. She didn't turn, but she had heard.

Vikrant placed the bags on the table, brushing his sleeve and scanning the room.

"I bought something for her. Where is she?"

Karishma replied, still smiling, "She's in the kitchen. And I've already wrapped a special gift from my side."

"Good," Vikrant said, nodding.

He looked around. "Where's Dad? He messaged me earlier.....said he wanted a specific gift for Samina. I got it too. Here it is."

Karishma took the box from the bag, inspecting the label with curiosity.

Then Vikrant pulled out another box.....wrapped in silver and blue, tied with a deep navy ribbon. "This one's from me," he said softly. "For Samina."

She glanced at the another gift box he held and tilted her head. "And that one... is it for me, brother?"

Karishma raised both eyebrows now. "Or two gifts for Samina?"

Before Vikrant could respond, a quiet footstep interrupted them.....Samina had arrived.

She had entered the room unnoticed, wiping her hands on a towel. Her eyes flicked to the boxes, her smile blooming for a moment......until Vikrant spoke.

"No," he said softly, shaking his head. "That one's not for Samina."

Her smile faltered. Just slightly.....but enough. She turned, murmuring something about tea, and disappeared into the kitchen.

Karishma smirked. "Oh, I know who that one's for."

"Shut up," Vikrant muttered, snatching the green-wrapped box and heading upstairs.

Warm light filled the kitchen as the comforting smell of coriander and garlic mingled with the sound of soup gently simmering. Usha ladled broth into a bowl for Roopa, who sat nearby with a shawl around her shoulders, her eyes still red from the morning's irritation.

Anika was chopping carrots nearby, humming an old tune under her breath. Usha's phone buzzed on the counter.

She wiped her hands, glanced at the screen. "Vikrant."

Anika leaned in. "Again?"

Usha turned the screen. *A photo of a green-wrapped gift box, sitting on a polished wooden table.*

Anika grinned. "Your admirer is texting again."

Usha rolled her eyes, but her lips betrayed a smile. "He's probably still trying to redeem himself for that mess of a night."

"Or maybe," Anika said, placing the knife down, "he just wants to make you smile."

Usha's fingers paused over the screen. She typed:
"What's in it?"
The reply came quickly.
"When we meet, I'll hand it to you myself."

She sent a laughing emoji.

He responded with a row of hearts. Then more emojis.

She sent two more.

He replied with three laughing faces.

Upstairs in the Rai house, Samina walked softly toward Vikrant's room, a tray of tea in her hands.

She wasn't expecting much…just to ask if he wanted some.

Just to be kind.

But as she reached the open door, she paused.

Vikrant was sitting on the bed.

Phone in one hand, a green-wrapped box in the other.

His face….

relaxed.

Slightly flushed.

Eyes soft with something unspoken.

Something not for her.

She didn't step in.

Didn't call his name.

Didn't interrupt.

She simply turned around.

Silently.

Steadily.

Her steps calm….but the storm had already begun inside.

He loves her.

That's all right.

I don't need to feel jealous.

Just… respect their bond.

Pray for it.

Her mind whispered reason.

But her heart…..heart broke a little.

Quietly.

In a place no one could see.

✦ ∞ ✦

Karishma slurped her noodles, scrolling through Instagram. She held up a gift box.

"Should I post this with a birthday tag? Add some hearts, tag you?"

Samina shook her head gently. "No… Anjali aunty just passed. It would look wrong. People might say we're celebrating."

Karishma's smile faded. "True. If only Mom was here… this would've felt so different."

Samina moved closer, her fingers brushing the tag on the gift:

HBD Samina – From Vikrant.

She traced the Birthday note of his name slowly. A whisper stirred in her chest:

It's not mandatory that he loves me. But it is mandatory that I will love him. And I will. Quietly. Till the end.

Karishma, still on her phone, slowly erased the message she had written:

"Happy Birthday 🖤 🖤 🖤 🖤*"*

The post never went up.

Samina turned and walked back into the kitchen.

A hush followed her footsteps.

Not loud.

Not heavy.

Just …. The kind that stays.

✦ ∞ ✦

The soft buzz of the station mixed with idle murmurs and footsteps echoing down the hall.

Aryan leaned against the break counter, sipping tea beside a lady constable.

"Marriage is tough," she said, shaking her head. "My husband thinks I flirt with everyone here."

Aryan smiled. "And why would he think that?"

She shrugged. "Probably because he flirts with everyone."

They laughed together, the rare sound briefly warming the walls.

Rajeev entered, breaking the moment. His face was serious, files under one arm.

"Sir. We need to talk."

Inside the office, Aryan sat, listening intently as Rajeev laid out the sheets.

"There's an official death record for Namarta. She died in a car fire…with her husband and newborn baby. Two days after delivery."

Aryan's eyes narrowed. "Burned?"

Rajeev nodded. "Her body was found completely charred. Her husband's only partially. The baby too… gone."

Aryan closed his eyes for a moment. "Who was the husband?"

"Inspector Manoj Prakash. Same officer who handled the orphan rape case in 2003. Kunal's family friend."

Aryan straightened in his chair. "Manoj? Same day Rekha died?"

Rajeev nodded.

"Yes. October 1st, 2003."

Aryan leaned forward, the weight of it settling.

"That day again…. And if Namarta is dead….then who sent money to Ameet?"

Rajeev cut in, voice quick. "Sir, there's more. The victim….the orphan girl….was only twelve. She lived inside the factory. A caretaker looked after her."

A pause.

"On July 26….she was found in the forest. Raped."

Aryan's jaw tensed.

"The verdict?"

"A man named Afzal. From a nearby village. Convicted under POCSO. Got twenty years. Released early last year for good behaviour."

Aryan frowned.

"Afzal….. that name…" he pointed to the painting.

"That means…. in Naina's sketch—the man behind bars…that's him?" Rajeev said.

Aryan stood abruptly, crossing to the board. He pulled the painting down, eyes dark.

"If Afzal was innocent," he said slowly, "then someone used the law to bury their sin." He turned to Rajeev. "And now? Afzal could be out for revenge."

A beat.

"And Satish…. he might be helping him."

Rajeev nodded.

"We're checking prison records. Visitors, timelines, who he connected with. We'll have his current location soon."

"Age?"

"Fifty-four."

Aryan turned to the window.

Evening had started to stretch across the sky.

"Find him. Fast."

He picked up his phone, opened the group chat.

And then, he typed:

Namarta's husband was Inspector Manoj. They died with their newborn on Oct 1, 2003.

Same day as Rekha.

Same day the orphan case verdict was announced.

Afzal might be innocent.

Team is tracing his movements post-release.

Keep this confidential.

He hit send.

Outside, the breeze moved low through the trees.

Shadows stretched their fingers across the fading light.
In one house,
a gift waited quietly on a bed.
In another,
a heartbeat surrendered without a sound.
And somewhere…. just beyond reach…someone watched
as the threads began to tighten.
Waiting.

Chapter 52

The house lay under the hush of night, its edges softened by the warmth of home and the hum of secrets. In Roopa's room, a rosewater-soaked cloth rested over her swollen eyes. She breathed deeply, surrendering to exhaustion in the hush of her pillow, her breath the only sound beside the slow ticking of the wall clock.

In the dining area, the light above flickered now and then, buzzing faintly like a tired memory. But beneath it, the table glowed with warmth. A simple steel-framed setting, plates of dal, rice, and chapati spread out. The food was ordinary, the silence surrounding it….anything but.

Ameet reached for a roti, dipped it slowly into the steaming bowl of lentils. "How are her eyes now?"

Usha stirred her rice absently, the spoon circling like her thoughts. "Still red. She had soup earlier and just wanted to lie down."

Anika added, her voice softer, "She's had her medicine, but it doesn't seem to help. We should really take her to an eye hospital."

Ameet sighed. The crease between his brows deepened. "You know how much those places charge? Just an appointment costs more than a week's groceries. And your father earns twenty thousand a month."

Anika paused mid-bite. She looked up, her eyes steady. "You have more money in your account."

The room went still.

Ameet's hand froze mid-air, a piece of roti between his fingers. He looked at her.

Usha jumped in, gently intercepting. "She meant…maybe you saved something. For emergencies. For her wedding, even. Maybe this counts."

Ameet slowly set the roti back on his plate. His jaw tightened, then relaxed. "I'll call a friend. He knows a doctor nearby. We'll start there."

Just then, Usha's phone buzzed on the side. She glanced at it. A second later, Anika's screen lit up too.

Ameet raised an eyebrow. "Both of you? Getting messages at the same time?"

Usha forced a casual smile. "It's a soup group. Winter recipes."

Ameet laughed. "Make sure to save the garlic one for me."

They smiled back, too quickly.

As they returned to their food, the silence returned too….this time filled with something unspoken. A shared secret, stirring just beneath the surface, waiting for the spoon to reach the bottom of the bowl.

The living room glowed faintly; golden fairy lights strung above like delicate threads of memory. There were no balloons, no music….only soft shadows and family. A chocolate cake sat quietly at the centre of the table, surrounded by warmth and restraint.

Samina stood beneath the lights in a red saree edged with gold thread. Her hair fell to one side, earrings brushing against her cheeks. She looked composed, but there was something faraway in her eyes…as if part of her stood in another room, watching.

Karishma, bright in a peacock blue suit, waved her phone. "Samina! Come, selfie."

They laughed softly. Kunal adjusted his kurta and beamed. "Family photo!"

They huddled close, warm shoulders and soft smiles. Then Kunal said, "One with Samina and Vikrant."

Samina hesitated.

Vikrant walked over, a polite distance between them. They posed stiffly.

"Closer," Kunal said, frowning. "You're not strangers."

He chuckled. "You look like mannequins at a wedding showroom."

Vikrant took half a step in. The photo clicked.

Later, as the cake was cut and the candles flickered out, Samina began unwrapping the gifts.

Kunal's gift was a soft beige silk dress....modest, elegant. Karishma's gift shimmered: a French perfume, a gold chain, and a note folded in the shape of a red heart.

Samina smiled and nodded. "Thank you both. These are beautiful."

Then Vikrant handed her the silver and blue box.

She unwrapped it slowly. Inside lay a necklace....simple but exquisite, clearly expensive. Her fingers brushed the delicate links.

"This is... beautiful," she whispered.

Vikrant stood suddenly, too quickly. "Oh! That was a mistake."

Kunal blinked. "What?"

"The shopkeeper switched the gift box," Vikrant said quietly. "That one wasn't meant for Samina."

A silence spread across the room like ink on cloth.

Samina's hand hovered over the necklace. She nodded, the smile already slipping. "It's fine," she said quietly, placing the box back on the table. "Thank you, though."

Karishma stepped forward quickly. "Actually, he bought two. This must be the other one."

Vikrant returned moments later with a green-wrapped box.

Samina opened it gently. Inside was a slender bracelet, delicate and silver toned. Her smile was softer now smaller.

"It's lovely. Thank you."

Kunal said nothing. He only watched.

✦ ∞ ✦

Anika stood at the sink, sleeves rolled up, her hands submerged in warm water. The clink of utensils, the splash of soap….everything soft, everything real.

Usha scrolled through her phone at the kitchen table.

She paused. "Namarta... she's Inspector Manoj's wife."

Anika turned. "What?"

Usha looked up, stunned. "Aryan messaged. That doctor... Namu... she was married to that inspector."

Before Anika could react, another message buzzed in. Usha opened it.

It was from Vikrant.

A photo. The silver necklace, unboxed, catching light under the warm glow of his bedroom lamp.

Anika peeked over. "It's beautiful."

Usha typed:

Thanks.

But her finger hesitated over the send button.

She stared at Vikrant's profile picture. The thought of Samina, her eyes, her silence.

She erased the message.

Typed again:

I can't accept this. You should give it to Samina.

✦ ∞ ✦

In Vikrant's room, he stared at his screen. A red heart emoji blinked in the message box. And his thumb hovered over the send button….but before he could press it,

a message from Usha appeared.

"I can't accept the gift."

He paused.

The room around him suddenly felt smaller.

Still.

In the side Room, Samina sat on her bed, the bracelet cradled gently in her palm.

She brought it to her lips.

Kissed it once…quietly.

A gesture no one would see.

"This is everything," she whispered.

Her gaze drifted to the window, eyes tracing stars no one else was looking for.

She smiled softly— but it wasn't for anyone in the house.

It was for something far away.

Something she held on to, even as it slipped from her fingers.

The gift had a name on it.

But it wasn't hers.

And somewhere… beyond the walls,

beyond the lights, beyond the leftover cake…. the night began to peel itself open.

One layer at a time.

The truth was rising.

Not with a whisper this time…. but with a shout.

Chapter 53

The kitchen carried the soft scent of cardamom and slow-brewing tea. Morning sunlight filtered through half-drawn curtains, striping the walls in gold and warmth. Usha and Anika sat at the dining table, their fingers wrapped around ceramic cups, the silence between them gentle and familiar.

Not empty. Just known.

Roopa entered quietly, her shawl slipping off one shoulder. She moved slowly, but not with pain…..just caution.

Usha rose instantly.

"Maa, you should be resting. You only just started feeling better. If you need anything, just call us, okay?"

Roopa smiled, that tired softness returning to her face.

"I'm fine, beta. I told you….it happens. The drops are working."

Anika added gently, "Still, you need rest."

Roopa exhaled, the way one does when they've already lived through too much.

"I was feeling lonely in that room. Thought I'd sit with you for a while. That's all."

Usha nodded and picked up the pooja thali.

"I'm heading to the temple."

Roopa cupped her hands.

"Go, daughter"

And as Usha stepped outside, into the light of a morning that felt no different….she didn't know that something long buried was about to stir again.

✦ ∞ ✦

Upstairs, Vikrant stood near his window. Still. Unblinking.

Outside, the world was just waking up....but inside him, something had been awake all night.

His phone screen still held Usha's last message: *"You should give this to Samina."*

The necklace lay inside the drawer. Still in its box. Not because he gave it to Samina.....but because Samina had opened it, mistakenly, last night. She had touched it. She had smiled. And then, she had cried.

And he... had let her.

Not out of love.

Out of guilt.

The necklace lay inside the drawer, still resting in its opened box.

Untouched.

Unclaimed.

Vikrant sat nearby, eyes fixed on nothing—but his mind stayed on Usha.

"She's not accepting it...."

he murmured, almost to himself,

"just because I'm getting engaged to Samina."

A pause.

His voice lowered, softer now...not angry, not bitter. Just.... aching.

"She's walking away.....because of a bond that never had a name.

"He picked up his phone and typed:

Where are you?

Moments later, the reply came:

Going to the temple. Why?

He stared at the blinking cursor, then replied:

"Okay."

Then he stood up, closed the necklace box, and walked out...truth tucked under his arm like unfinished confession.

Kunal sipped chai at the breakfast table, bright-eyed and already making plans.

"Panditji said engagement can happen now. Marriage, two months later. So... should we fix a date?"

Vikrant reached the bottom of the staircase, his steps pausing. He didn't answer.

Samina sat quietly beside Kunal. Her eyes were lowered, but she heard the silence in Vikrant's breath. It wasn't hesitance.

It was truth trying not to break.

Finally, Vikrant spoke...softly.

"I have to go out. We'll talk later."

And just like that, he left...without glancing back, the wrapped truth still in his hand.

Samina's gaze followed him until the door closed.

She stood up slowly and walked into the kitchen. Her body moved, but her mind wasn't there. She felt numb. Tired.

She looked down at her wrist. The bracelet Vikrant had given her last night was still there.

Not the necklace.

Not the one meant to touch her heart.

Just the bracelet.

She touched the beads gently, like they might fall apart if she pressed too hard. Her voice came out low, like she was afraid someone might hear the truth in it.

"Hey, bracelet... he gave you to me. But today... he didn't even look at you."

Her chest tightened. One tear escaped, running quietly down her cheek.

And then she smiled. Not a happy smile. The kind of smile you give yourself when there's no one left to explain how broken you really are. The kind of smile you wear to survive.

She wiped the tear away. The bracelet caught the white kitchen light and sparkled like it meant something.

Inside her, she was quiet.

So quiet…. it almost hurt to breathe.

She loved him.

Deeply.

Fully.

Every part of her wanted to belong to him.

To be seen.

Chosen.

But she said nothing.

Asked for nothing.

She just stayed.

Loved him in silence.

Because that's what love looked like to her…not loud,

not demanding, just present.

Even when it hurt.

Even when it made her feel invisible.

And maybe…..

maybe that was selfish too.

Because even if he never looked back, even if his heart belonged elsewhere— she still couldn't stop loving him..

The Temple courtyard was washed in morning sun and incense smoke. Bells chimed faintly from somewhere deep inside.

Usha's steps were light, but her mind was heavy.

Then she saw him….standing outside the temple.

Gift box in hand.

Waiting.

She stopped.

"Now I know why you messaged me," she said.

Vikrant nodded.

"You already knew."

Her smile was dry.

"So, you're here to give me that necklace?"

"Yes," he said, gently.

She let out a breathless laugh… not joy, just ache.

"But you're someone else's now.

Give it to her."

Vikrant lowered his eyes.

And silence fell… colder than the wind,

sharper than anything they dared to say.

Usha's voice came again,

a little harder now.

"There's someone waiting for you.

There's a path.

Why are you standing here?"

He whispered,

"Because."

She stared.

Her voice shook.

"Because?"

More silence.

She shook her head.

"You still won't say it. You can't."

She stepped past him, into the temple.

Her pooja thali steady in her hands….but her heart trembling,

like a prayer left unspoken.

Behind her, Vikrant stood…frozen.

Remembering the ease of messages.

The teasing emojis.

The rhythm they once shared.

But now…with her in front of him, when it truly mattered…

his voice collapsed.

Why does the truth steal my words?

Why does silence feel louder than sound when I look at her?

Something cracked inside him.

At last.

He stepped forward.

And shouted… raw, unguarded: "Usha!"

She stopped.

Turned.

Their eyes met… and this time, his didn't flinch.

The temple air held its breath.

Incense curled through the silence.

A bell chimed.

Somewhere, a chant echoed.

Vikrant walked up to her.

Held out the box.

A gift.

Not just expensive… but honest.

She didn't take it.

"Why are you giving me this?" she asked softly.

"Because I wanted to," he said. "For you."

She stepped back slightly.

Her voice was gentler now…. but firm,

like truth that had waited too long. "No. You're hiding something."

"I'm not," he said.

"You are."

Her eyes didn't move.

"You think silence protects.

You think if you say nothing,

nothing breaks.

But you're already breaking.

I can see it.

So why can't you just say it?"

Vikrant's thoughts (internal):

I tried to lock it away.

Bury it beneath duty, guilt, and the weight of everyone else's expectations.

I thought maybe... if I committed to Samina....this ache would fade.

But it didn't.

It grew louder.

Angrier.

Sadder.

And now I'm standing here...

unable to pretend anymore.

He took a breath...deep, trembling...and looked her in the eyes.

Finally.

"I'm not getting engaged to Samina."

Usha stiffened.

Her breath caught.

"I told myself I would.

I thought maybe if I did.... I'd stop feeling this way."

He swallowed hard.

"But I can't.

I won't lie to her.

Or to myself.

Or to you."

Usha's lips parted.

Sunlight spilled through the temple doorway, falling across their faces.

A hush..... sacred, thick,

holy.

She reached out….and took the box.

Not for the necklace.

But for what it meant now.

She held it to her chest, like memory, like confession.

Her voice cracked.

"Why, Vikrant?

Why would you try to force your heart away from me?

Why make your love hate me?"

He shook his head, voice breaking.

"I don't know. I used to hate love. Hate what it did to people…..made them weak, made them foolish."

He stepped closer, trembling.

"But now….."

His voice dropped.

No louder than a prayer.

"Now I just want to scream it.

To the gods.

To the sky.

To you."

A beat. A breath.

"I love you, Usha.

I love you so much………

it terrifies me."

She gasped…. not with drama,

but with release.

And then…. she stepped into him.

They fell into each other's arms.

No spectacle.

No noise.

Just home.

His face buried in her shoulder.

Her fingers gripped the back of his kurta

like she was afraid the moment would vanish.
Tears fell... his into her shoulder,
hers into his silence.
And beneath ancient temple bells,
bathed in soft golden light....two souls stopped pretending.
And started believing again.

Chapter 54

The room was steeped in a tired quiet. The air smelled of paper dust and burnt coffee, heavy with memories. On the far wall, red threads crisscrossed between photos and notes…..like veins on a heart that still refused to beat the truth aloud.

Aryan stood in front of it, arms folded, eyes locked on the web of connections. Somewhere in the silence, the past was still speaking.

The door creaked open. Rajeev entered, holding a thin file like it carried the weight of a ghost.

"Sir," he said, voice clipped but burdened, "I've got updates. About Afzal."

Aryan turned slightly, just enough to listen.

Rajeev continued, "He worked at the Rai factory. Had a wife…Noor…and a son, Daniyal. Fourteen when Afzal was arrested. Noor was pregnant at that time, when Afzal was arrested. After the sentencing… they vanished. Sold the house. No forwarding address. Nothing."

Aryan's gaze didn't shift. "Society must've pushed them out. Judgment stains deeper than guilt."

Rajeev nodded. "Yes Sir, Locals say she was harassed. Threats. Slurs. The whole family went underground. And Afzal? In prison, he stayed silent. No outbursts. No trouble. Helped inmates. But the day he was released… gone."

He placed a few worn photographs on the table. Aryan's fingers hovered over Daniyal's image. The boy's eyes…..young, yet already weary…..felt like they were staring back through time.

Aryan leaned in slightly, his eyes still fixed on the board. "Any update about Satish?"

Rajeev lowered his voice "he was still in his home, but there's more. I checked the hospital archives. Namarta Prakash gave birth to a baby girl on the night of September 29th. Discharged on October 1st. That same night, she, her husband….Inspector Manoj….and the child… were found dead. Burned. Inside their car."

Aryan inhaled sharply. The fluorescent lights above flickered, as if the room, too, flinched.

He stepped back from the board. "Then… someone used her bank account to send money. To Ameet. On July 15, 2004. But she died on October 1st, 2003. How?"

Rajeev nodded grimly. "We need to look at Ameet more closely."

Aryan's eyes slid to Anika's picture….pinned beside Usha's. A quiet storm gathered in his chest.

"I know what you're thinking," Rajeev said. "It could break her. But this can't stay buried."

Aryan dialled. After two rings, a soft "Hello" answered.

"Anika," Aryan began gently, "We'd like to speak with your father. We believe…. he may know something."

Silence. Then her voice returned, quieter now. "Okay. Do what you must. I believe in you."

He ended the call.

"We'll talk to him," Aryan said. "Not as officers. As sons trying to protect what's left."

Rajeev's jaw tightened. "If Afzal is alive, he's the architect of a long, slow revenge. His accomplices? Noor. Daniyal. And maybe…"

Aryan finished it: "The orphan, Ruhi. Maybe she is with Afzal."

"But what about the other child?" Rajeev asked. "Noor was pregnant. That was twenty years ago."

Aryan stared at the board; voice low. "October 1st. A day of endings......and beginnings. The sentencing. The fire. A vow for revenge. But why wait two decades?"

Rajeev's expression darkened. "Maybe they were waiting. For Afzal. To finish what they began."

Aryan's thoughts connected like lightning across the strings. "Pandit. Narayan. Anjali. One by one."

Rajeev added, "We couldn't trace factory records. But Anika and Usha said Ameet was a labourer."

Aryan narrowed his eyes. "Then why lie to his daughters?"

Rajeev said quietly, "Fear. Or guilt."

Aryan's jaw tightened. "Then I'll ask him myself."

✦ ∞ ✦

Anika sat on chair inside the kitchen, fingers curling around the soft ends of her dupatta. Her mind replayed her father's silences, the way he flinched at simple questions. As if truth was a wound, he never stopped bleeding from.

In the room, Usha held the necklace Vikrant had given her, its metal still warm from her touch. She didn't wear it for beauty......it was memory in disguise. A promise forged in silence.

Anika leaned against the doorway, watching her sister's quiet glow.

"So," she teased, "you've finally surrendered to love?"

Usha's smile was soft, reverent. "He's not getting engaged to Samina. He... he chose me."

"Did he say it?"

"More than in words," Usha whispered, clutching the necklace tighter. "I've always known. Today, he just stopped hiding it."

Anika's voice gentled. "Do you...do you love him?"

Usha nodded slowly. "It's not the kind of love that shouts. It's the kind that aches. When he's hurt, I feel it. Like… like he stitched himself into my soul."

They hugged, a shared quiet between them. A sisterhood stronger than any storm.

Then Anika's tone shifted. "Aryan called. He wants to talk to Papa. About… Namarta."

Usha straightened. "We should ask Daadi. Maybe… maybe she knows something."

They walked to Roopa's room together. The old woman sat by the window, her gaze miles away, drifting in a sky that no longer belonged to the present.

Roopa turned as they entered. "My girls," she said with a faded smile, "what is it?"

Usha sat beside her. "Daadi, we need answers. Honest ones. Please."

"I'm tired," Roopa whispered. "Let's talk tomorrow."

"No, Daadi," Anika insisted. "We're drowning in secrets. And we need air."

Roopa's eyes faltered.

"Why does Papa have so much money?" Anika asked.

The question hung like a sword.

Roopa stood, gripping the windowsill. Her voice cracked. "How… do you know that?"

"Aryan found it," Anika said gently. "But he's not judging. He wants to protect us."

Roopa turned. Her eyes….once sharp….now glistened with fear.

"You told the inspector?"

"No," Usha replied. "He told us. But Papa's innocent, and if someone is using him…please help us protect him."

Anika stepped forward. "Who is Namu?"

"She… she was a nurse," Roopa said weakly.

"Or a doctor?" Usha pressed.

The air shifted.

Anika's voice dropped to a whisper. "Namarta Prakash."

Roopa sat down heavily, as though her legs gave in to the weight of memory.

"How do you know that name?" she asked, barely audible.

Usha knelt beside her. "We're not here to blame you. Just tell us."

Roopa's eyes welled, then overflowed. Tears rolled down without permission, like a flood she could no longer hold back.

Anika's voice cracked. "What happened on October 1st, Daadi? What is it that's been haunting you?"

Usha echoed, softer, "What happened twenty years ago?"

Roopa looked away, her voice a hush against the fading light.

"I've buried it for two decades. Prayed it would never return. But... memory doesn't die. It waits."

She stared out the window again.

"And now," she whispered to no one, "it's come home."

Chapter 55

The light filtered softly through Karishma's window, dappling the floor with sleepy golden squares. She sat cross-legged on her bed, textbook open, highlighter poised....but her mind wandered between definitions and dreams.

The door creaked. Vikrant stepped in.

He wasn't carrying his usual heaviness. Something had shifted.....his eyes lighter, like they had finally stopped arguing with the heart.

Karishma glanced up.

"You look... suspiciously light," she said, narrowing her eyes. "Spill."

Vikrant's grin gave him away.

"I told Usha," he said. "And she said yes."

Karishma's book snapped shut, forgotten. She leapt to her feet, squealing.

"Are you serious?"

"Completely."

She shook her head, laughing. "You? The guy who mocked every love song? You're in love?"

"Hopelessly," Vikrant said, and for once, it didn't sound like a joke.

Karishma's smile softened. "Then you need to tell Papa. And Samina. She deserves honesty, not silence."

Vikrant nodded. "I know. I'm going now."

✦ ∝ ✦

The kitchen hummed with quiet clinks of utensils and the soft chop of vegetables. Samina stood by the counter, sleeves rolled, movements steady.

Too steady.

Vikrant stepped in, paused, watching her.

"Hi," he said.

She turned, offering a warm smile. "Hi. Ramesh's wife is unwell. I told Uncle I'd help."

He nodded. "You're doing this alone?"

"It's not too much work. And Karishma's coming….she'll help me."

His eyes drifted to her wrist.

"You're wearing the bracelet."

Samina's smile grew faint. "Yeah. You noticed?"

"Yes."

A silence settled. Familiar, yet distant.

She broke it gently. "Want some tea?"

Vikrant shook his head. "No… I need to say something."

She knew. She'd known from the moment he walked in.

Don't say it. Don't say what I already know. Just stay a little longer in this silence. Let this be our moment. "

"I love someone else," Vikrant said.

"And I want to marry her."

A clean cut.

Irreversible.

Like a sentence that ends more than a moment…..

it ends a hope.

The knife slipped from Samina's fingers.

A thin, crimson line bloomed across her skin.

Not deep.

But deep enough to feel like truth.

She didn't flinch.

Didn't cry out.

Just stared.

Because some pain doesn't scream…. it simply stays.

"Samina!" Vikrant rushed toward her.

"Your finger…"

He grabbed her hand, pressed a cloth to the wound.

His hands trembled.

Hers didn't.

"You're bleeding. Hold on…I'll get a bandage."

He left the room.

And for a moment,

she sat there,

watching the blood rise.

He touched me.

He cared.

Not the way I hoped…….

But he cared.

She stared at the wound.

And a part of her…. the part that still clung to the dream…..

wanted it to never heal.

She wanted the pain to stay.

To mark her.

To remind her

of how it felt… to almost be loved.

He returned.

Wrapped her finger gently,

like she was something fragile

he never intended to break…..but did anyway.

His eyes didn't meet hers.

"I'm sorry," he whispered.

"For what?" she asked, voice soft.

"For everything."

She smiled.

A small, broken thing
held together by grace.
"You don't owe me an apology. Just…… love her well."
A pause.
"She's lucky."
Vikrant stared.
"What?"
"Nothing," she said, looking away.
He left.
Quietly.
As if leaving louder would've made it worse.
Samina raised her hand.
She looked at the bandage.
Then slowly, gently…. she peeled it off.
The skin beneath was still raw.
Still red.
Still hers.
And she kissed it.
Not the bandage…. but the wound itself.
A whisper against pain,
like one last thread tying her to what she never had.
"Sorry," she whispered.
Her eyes shimmered.
She closed them.
And then…almost like a prayer:
"I don't want you to heal."
"I want you to stay. Forever."
"I want to live with the memory……
because it's all he left me with."
"Let it sting when I wash dishes.
Let it throb when I'm alone.
Let it remind me……."

that for one moment....he touched me. "
"That once... he cared. "
She folded the used bandage in her palm,
like it held more weight than gold.
Then gently pressed it to her heart.
Sorry, finger.
Don't heal too fast.
Stay broken for me.
Stay aching.
Let me carry something.... even if it's just this.

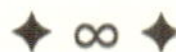

He stared at his stained fingers. Blood still clung to his skin.
Not his.... But it felt like it was.
His chest ached, hollow and hot.
I hurt her..?
I should've told her earlier...
The silence of his own delay echoed louder than her footsteps walking away.
He walked down the hall
and knocked softly on Karishma's door.
She looked up from her book.
He didn't sit.
He just said it. "I told her."
Karishma blinked.
Then smiled... gentle, knowing. "Really?" A teasing grin touched her lips. "Finally, my brother listened to his heart?"
But his face didn't match hers.
"Karishma," he whispered, voice cracking,
"I was mad. I should've told Usha long ago that I love her. I waited... but I didn't even know what I was feeling."
He sat down now, slowly.

A man exhausted…..by delay.

By regret.

"Why did it take so long to know it was love? Why?"

Karishma gently set her book aside.

Her voice wasn't light this time.

It was soft.

Steady.

Laced with memories she never shared.

"Love doesn't arrive on a schedule, Bhai.

It doesn't knock with warning.

It arrives in silence.

In feeling."

She breathed in.

"When your heart whispers their name into empty rooms.

When you find yourself caring without trying.

When your eyes search for one face….even in crowds.

When their smile becomes your anchor.

When their pain……

becomes your pain."

Vikrant watched her, stunned.

"When you hurt just imagining losing them.

When they're the dream behind your closed eyes.

When you'd give anything…. Everything…..just to keep them safe.

Just to keep them smiling."

She paused,

but her eyes were full of things she didn't say.

"That's love."

Vikrant nodded slowly,

his voice quiet.

Almost a confession.

"I feel that for Usha."

A beat.

"But…. how do you know all this?"
Karishma smiled faintly.
A little too fast.
A little too practiced.
"I read.
And I feel."
He stood to leave.
She reached for her phone the moment he turned….
as if her truth could only live in silence.
When your heart starts pumping thoughts instead of blood…
When your breath feels borrowed from someone else….
That's love too.
She kissed the phone.
Soft.
Secret.
Like something only she was allowed to know.
And sometimes….
love just stays quiet.
So the one you love can speak.

The scent of turmeric drifted through the air. Usha and Anika moved quietly in the kitchen. Roopa rested outside, humming to herself.

A knock at the door broke the stillness.

Anika whispered, "Aryan?"

But it was Vikrant.

"I'm Vikrant Rai," he said to Ameet, standing stiffly. "I want to talk to Usha."

Usha blinked. "What?"

Ameet turned to her. "Vikrant!"

Anika stifled a laugh behind her palm.

Usha's thoughts spiralled…..Is he mad? Composing herself quickly, she spoke with forced cheer, "Yes, Papa. Actually… I think Karishma joined that recipe group, maybe she wanted to talk with me."

Vikrant nodded, a small smile tugging at his lips. "Yes. She wants to meet her. She needs help with dinner."

Ameet frowned. "But at this hour?"

Usha turned to Vikrant, trying to end it gently. "I'll call her and ask what she needs…."

Vikrant cut her off, eyes locking with hers.

"No. I need you…. I mean, she needs you."

Ameet looked between them, sighed, then shrugged.

"Alright. But just this time."

Vikrant added under his breath,

"Father's already upset.

If Usha doesn't show up, he'll take it out on Karishma again…

all because of Usha's 'boring' recipe."

From behind, Anika burst into laughter.

"What?" Usha frowned.

Ameet shook his head, half amused, half exasperated.

"Why did you even suggest someone who's a beginner?"

He waved her off.

"Now go. And come back soon."

The city lights blurred past as Vikrant drove, Usha burst into laughter. "We were almost caught… but that was a good lie you made up."

Vikrant smiled, his eyes softening. "I wanted our first dinner to begin with laughter."

✦ ∞ ✦

Karishma hugged Usha. The room buzzed with warmth. Samina appeared, said hello, then slipped back into the kitchen.

She didn't need to be told. She understood.

Kunal entered as Vikrant stood.

"Papa," he began. "I love Usha. I want to marry her."

Silence fell like snow.

"You're engaged to Samina," Kunal said.

Karishma stepped forward. "But they love each other."

Kunal raised a hand.

Samina's voice came from the doorway. "He's right."

All heads turned.

"I'm not happy," she said. "My parents pushed me. But... he loves someone else. And she deserves that love. Completely."

Kunal looked at Usha.

"You're the same girl from that night? I am sorry"

"No Uncle, don't," she said quietly.

He shook his head. "If my son is happy, I have no questions."

Anika sat on her bed, arms wrapped around a photo of her mother.

Usha entered, sat beside her.

"You always hold that when you're sad," she whispered.

Anika nodded slowly.

"Aryan came. He asked Papa about the money. About Namrata"

Her voice lowered.

"And Papa.... he just said he didn't know. Aryan asked again.....calmly. But Papa told him, 'If you want to arrest me, go ahead. I don't know her.'"

Her voice cracked.

"And Aryan... didn't. He walked away. Alone."

She broke then.... the weight of silence and loyalty crushing her all at once. I don't deserve him.

Because of me, he stayed quiet.

He didn't come here as a police officer.

He came here…. as a son."

Usha pulled her close, held her tight.

"Don't say that.

You are loved.

You are seen.

And you are never a curse."

They stayed like that.

Two sisters.

One sorrow.

Bound by silence.

Holding on to each other….because no one else ever did.

The wind howled softly through the partially open window.

Aryan stood motionless, arms folded, the chill biting at his skin, but he didn't care.

Outside, darkness blanketed the world. But inside him, a darker war brewed.

His eyes stared into the night, but all he saw were two paths:

Anika. Her eyes. Her promise. Her pain.

Justice. Truth. The case.

The killer hiding in plain sight. His badge lay on the table. Heavy. Honest. But tonight, his heart was heavier. And as the cold air stung his face, Aryan didn't close the window.

He let the wind hurt him. He wanted it to. Because pain was easier than choosing between love and law.

Chapter 56

The morning air held a quiet thrill, the kind that makes heartbeats echo louder in the chest. Sunlight poured through the windows like blessing itself. Today wasn't just a day....it was a beginning.

Vikrant stood before the mirror, adjusting his collar for the third time. A faint blush bloomed on his cheeks...an unfamiliar softness for a man usually composed. Love had undone him in the most beautiful way.

Behind him, Karishma entered with arms folded and an eyebrow cocked.

"Oh ho," she teased, "someone's grinning like a Bollywood hero on his wedding poster."

Vikrant turned, caught mid-swoon. He laughed, half shy, half proud.

"She said yes, Karishma. Today we make it official."

Karishma's expression softened. "I know. And she's perfect for you."

Samina moved with quiet precision, chopping vegetables in rhythm with her thoughts. Her face was calm, but her heart waged silent wars. Kunal stepped in, pausing by the counter.

"I thought you were leaving for Mumbai," he said.

Samina offered a gentle smile. "I was... but I wanted to stay. My childhood friend is getting engaged today."

Kunal nodded, his eyes kind. "Thank you, beta."

She returned to the vegetables.

She didn't speak much these days….her silence had learned how to hold back the storms. Her grief didn't shout anymore. It sat quietly in the room with her, like an old companion.

Vikrant and Karishma descended the staircase, dressed in soft tones of celebration.

Karishma turned to her father. "We're ready."

Kunal straightened his watch, nodding. "Let's go then."

Karishma glanced at Samina. "Will you come with us?"

Samina shook her head. "I'll stay. Papa said he might call. I'll wait for that."

Vikrant looked at her, trying to read what hid beneath her calm. But Samina had become an artist of silence. She stared at her phone, pretending to scroll, though the screen was still dark.

Let the feeling go, her heart whispered. *Bury it deep, and never let it bloom again.*

A single tear dared to fall. She wiped it before it could reach her cheek and walked quietly to her room.

✦ ∞ ✦

Files lay open in front of Aryan, but he wasn't reading. His eyes flicked across pages without seeing. Outside, the world moved. Inside him, everything was still.

Rajeev entered briskly.

"Sir, update from the bank."

Aryan looked up, weary but alert.

"Namarta came in personally. Transferred her entire final salary to Ameet's account."

Aryan leaned forward. "Wait… she didn't die in 2003?"

Rajeev nodded. "She was alive. Months later."

Aryan's voice dropped. "Then why fake her death? Why vanish? And if Ameet knows... why lie?"

Rajeev met his eyes. "We'll find out. We're close."

He stepped back, leaving Aryan with thoughts that felt like splinters under skin.

His phone buzzed. A message from Anika.

"I'm sorry... because of me, you went alone again. You stood for me... again. But I'll find the answers. I promise."

Aryan stared at the screen, heart aching. Then replied with only three red heart emojis.

Nothing else.

It said everything.

✦ ∞ ✦

Anika held her phone close, her thumb lingering over the last message. A faint smile curved her lips, and yet, her eyes betrayed the heaviness beneath.

In the kitchen, Usha was practically glowing. She'd received Vikrant's message....they were on their way.

When the Rai family arrived, Roopa welcomed them with warmth and grace. The family gathered in the veranda, the scent of cardamom tea rising with laughter.

Usha and Anika brought out tea and biscuits.

Vikrant grinned. "Papa, Anika makes amazing tea."

Kunal took a sip. "Mmm. She does."

Eyes met. Smiles were exchanged. Love passed between Usha and Vikrant not as words, but as glances that held more weight than any vow.

"Where's Usha's father?" Vikrant asked.

Roopa answered, "At the shop. But he's sent his blessings."

Kunal turned to Roopa, "Then it's settled. With your blessing, his, and these two lovely sisters… let's plan the engagement."

Laughter echoed through the veranda. Joy, unrestrained, finally allowed to live in the open.

Vikrant sent a message to Satish.

"Thank you, brother. We're bonding forever now."

Satish replied instantly. 

"Always, my friend."

✦ ∞ ✦

After the visit, the Rai family stopped at a temple, its courtyard bathed in golden light. Kunal handed over their Kundlis to the priest and requested an auspicious date.

Diyas were lit.

Hands joined in prayer.

Eyes closed in silent gratitude.

Outside, the breeze turned gentle. Not cold, not warm….just right.

A day wrapped in gold.

A moment without weight.

The first page of a new chapter, fluttering open like the petals of marigolds at their feet.

Chapter 57

The dining room glowed under a soft golden chandelier. The air was thick with laughter and the scent of cumin and saffron. Plates clinked, spoons stirred, and for once, the world outside did not exist. It was only family. Together.

Kunal sat at the head of the table; his gaze proud but kind. Karishma nudged Vikrant from across the table, her grin teasing.

"I still can't believe it," she said, shaking her head. "Vikrant Rai....who once cringed at Valentine's Day....fell in love. And proposed!"

Vikrant tried to hide his blush behind a glass of water. But his smile gave him away.

Kunal chuckled. "All that matters is he followed his heart. That's how marriages should begin."

Samina laughed along, her tone light, playful.

"Oh come on, look at him," she said, gesturing with her spoon. "He's glowing. Blushing like a boy who's just written his crush a poem."

Everyone laughed....everyone except the voice inside Samina that trembled.

She didn't look at Vikrant.

She hadn't for a while.

But she felt everything.....the way he leaned ever so slightly toward Karishma's side,

the quiet shift in his breath

when Usha's name was mentioned,

the sparkle in his eyes he didn't even know was there.

Her laugh echoed in the room.... light, practiced.... but it fell hollow in her own chest.

The girl who once called him Viku

no longer used his name.

Not out of anger.

But out of surrender.

Her silence was eloquent.

And it said only this:

I still love you.

But I won't stand in the way of someone else being loved.

Kunal's phone buzzed. He wiped his hands and answered.

"Yes, Panditji? Hmm........ Alright. Thank you."

He ended the call and turned to the table with a grin that carried more than news....it carried a twist.

"So... there's no suitable date for the engagement anytime soon."

A ripple of confusion passed over the table. Faces tilted. Forks froze.

"But..." Kunal continued, smile widening, "there is an auspicious date for the wedding. In two days."

Silence broke into gasps.

Karishma nearly dropped her spoon. "What! A wedding? In two days? This is insane....I love it!"

Vikrant's eyes widened for a second, caught between disbelief and delight.

"Two days..." he murmured. Then a slow, warm smile took over. "Perfect."

Samina nodded calmly. "Then we begin preparations tomorrow. Guest list, outfits, invites. I'll start drafting everything."

She spoke like she always had.... efficient, dependable, gentle.

But the bite of food held no taste.

Her hands moved out of habit, her face calm, her soul....numb.

Say it, her heart whispered.

Say the love you never said.

But she swallowed that voice

like a bitter seed…. one meant to grow, not in light, but in silence.

Karishma clapped her hands. "Okay! I'll handle the decoration. Samina, Shopping list is yours."

Vikrant pulled out his phone. His fingers moved quickly.

"Usha. The wedding is in two days."

✦ ∞ ✦

Dinner was quiet, but not tense. A kind of calm lived there….like dusk settling on an old roof.

Ameet, Roopa, Usha, and Anika sat at the table. Each carried a different kind of weight. But when Usha's phone buzzed, the entire room noticed her cheeks colour.

Ameet looked up. "What happened?"

Anika read the message aloud, smiling faintly. "The engagement is cancelled. The wedding is in two days."

Roopa blinked. "Two days?" Her voice wavered less in worry, more in memory.

But then her face softened. "So be it. Mata Rani's blessing is on this union. Let's make it happen."

Ameet nodded. "I'll speak to the shop owner."

Roopa raised an eyebrow. "Don't say speak. Tell him your daughter's getting married. If he refuses….tell me. I'll talk to his wife."

Laughter broke out….light, airy, needed. The heaviness eased. If only for a moment.

Anika smiled. "Papa, you're on full leave tomorrow. No debates."

Ameet lifted his hands in surrender.

For the first time in days, peace sat at their table. Usha and Anika exchanged a look…of hope, of quiet joy.

A wedding was coming.

And the storm that had hovered for so long… stepped back, just a little.

✦ ∞ ✦

The investigation room wore its usual stillness, but tonight it felt heavier. Photographs, red strings, maps of death and decisions lay across the board like an unfinished puzzle.

Aryan stood before it all, arms folded, expression unreadable. A cup of chai sat beside him….cold, untouched.

Rajeev entered; his face unusually light. "Sir. Did you see the group chat? Vikrant and Usha are getting married. In two days."

Aryan allowed a half-smile. "Yeah. I saw."

"They're really in love."

Aryan didn't respond at first. Then quietly, "And love… is dangerous when you're chasing a killer."

He stepped back from the board, scanning the web of names and faces.

"We've been looking for answers," he said. "But maybe we've been asking the wrong questions."

Rajeev frowned. "What kind of questions?"

Aryan's voice was low. "Why them? Why not even Kunal?"

Rajeev stepped closer. "The killings started the moment Afzal came out. His family vanished. They killed the inspector from the rape case… then the driver… one by one."

He paused. "But the Pandit's death still doesn't fit."

Aryan nodded. "Exactly. Maybe the Pandit wasn't just a witness. Maybe he was involved. What about Satish?"

"We've observed him. He's present around every event. But never directly. No record. No evidence."

Aryan's voice dropped again. "Then why did he hide Naina's pregnancy? Why protect Samar's memory? Why keep her painting?"

Rajeev sighed. "He said it was to forget. That she was his sister."

"And Kunal?"

"No motive. He exposed Samar. Told Vikrant the truth himself. Doesn't add up if he were hiding something."

Aryan's jaw clenched. "And Ameet?"

Rajeev hesitated.

"Strange timeline," he said. "Moved here in 2004. Started working immediately. But nothing links him to Namarta. No documents. No job records. No interaction."

Aryan stared at the board. "But she transferred her entire payment to him. That's not a coincidence."

Rajeev nodded. "And yet… he looks innocent. But his silence isn't guilt. It's pain."

Aryan turned away from the board. "We're going through the files again. All of them."

Rajeev raised an eyebrow. "What are we looking for?"

Aryan's eyes didn't blink.

"Not answers. The right questions."

They sat. The case files opened like scars. And somewhere between the lines, truth waited….not to be found.

But to be heard.

Chapter 58

The house breathed wedding air.

Curtains danced to the breeze, the scent of marigolds trailed through every hallway, and soft music played from someone's forgotten playlist. It was the day before the wedding.....and the house had transformed into a palette of joy, nerves, and whispered dreams.

In the drawing room, sunlight spilled across bundles of fabric, shimmering bangles, and velvet boxes lined with gold and pearl.

Samina sat cross-legged on the carpet, a deep red saree draped over her lap. Her fingers moved gently along the zari work, tracing each thread like it held a memory. She looked up.

"Karishma?" she called, voice steady, almost serene. "What do you think about this one?"

Karishma, hunched over a tray of bangles, glanced up.

"It's beautiful.

Red always suits Usha.

And green.....green suits you.....always"

Samina nodded softly, folding the saree with care. Around her were six neatly arranged sarees...three she had chosen for Usha, two for Karishma, and one for herself.

She didn't speak about the ache. The one that lingered beneath her smile, between the folds of every fabric she touched. She kept her fingers moving.....across colours, borders, clasps....as if beauty could quiet grief.

She didn't need to say it out loud: *What if this had been my wedding? What if this red had been mine?*

Her smile flickered. Not for the world to see. Just to stop the tears from rising.

✦ ∞ ✦

The sunlight filtered through sheer curtains, spilling onto an unmade bed and half-packed bags. Vikrant stood in front of the mirror, straightening his kurta collar before picking up his phone.

He clicked a photo of the room and typed:

Tomorrow, this room is ours.

He laughed at himself. A soft, lovesick laugh. His cheeks pinked like a teenager.

And for the first time in years, his room didn't feel like just his. It already felt like theirs.

✦ ∞ ✦

Across town, Usha kissed her phone screen, blushing like a flame caught in wind.

Anika caught her mid-motion. "Oh ho! Save it for tomorrow. No one's stopping you from kissing him for real."

They both burst into laughter.

The dining table was scattered with handwritten notes, guest lists, and saree catalogues. Excitement buzzed in the air like static before rain.

"Come on," Anika said. "You're the bride, not a daydreamer. We've got twenty hours and fifty tasks."

"I'm here," Usha grinned. "Fully present."

But her heart was already tomorrow.

✦ ∞ ✦

The mood in the station was anything but celebratory. Aryan stood before the investigation board again....red strings, scrawled timelines, names that had become too familiar.

The board hadn't changed.

But something inside him had.

Rajeev entered quickly, holding his phone like it carried the final clue.

"Sir," he said, slightly breathless. "That surveillance car we parked outside Satish's shop... I checked the dashcam footage."

Aryan turned to face him.

Rajeev continued, "There's a tube light above Satish's shutter. It's off in most clips. But on in one. The night before Anjali's murder."

Aryan's eyes sharpened. "Check the night before Pandit's wife died. And Narayan too."

Rajeev nodded. "We didn't have surveillance back then... but my friend has a shop across the road. His outdoor CCTV covers Satish's storefront. I called him already."

Two hours later, Rajeev returned with the footage.

They reviewed it, frame by frame.

Tube light - on.

The night before every murder.

Aryan exhaled. "He's been signaling. That light was never a coincidence. It was a code."

Rajeev's face darkened. "No wonder we found nothing in phone records. The orders were visual."

Aryan stepped back from the board, eyes narrowing. "Satish was the hub. The messenger. He lit the fuse."

Rajeev nodded slowly. "Then his accomplices never needed calls. Just.....the signal."

A tense silence stretched between them.

Aryan's voice dropped......calm but resolute. "Shadow him. No alerts. No group updates. Only us."

Rajeev's reply was quiet but firm.

"Understood." Aryan's voice dropped to a rare softness. "Good work today, Rajeev."

He nodded; pride restrained but present.

As Aryan turned back to the board, something shifted. The lines no longer blurred.

The story was speaking now.

Not through evidence.

But through silence, flickers of light, and the ache of those left behind.

The board, for the first time, was starting to bleed the truth.

Chapter 59

The Rai house glowed like a temple under preparation. Tomorrow was the day …….. Vikrant and Usha's wedding. And every corner of the house throbbed with a different kind of devotion.

Kunal was stationed by the phone, flipping through lists and confirming caterers, decorators, and priests. His voice rang with command, but his eyes betrayed joy. Karishma, clipboard in hand, darted around the veranda, scolding the lighting team while laughing mid-sentence.

Outside, under strings of half-hung fairy lights, Samina was preparing the mandap stage…… the sacred circle where Usha and Vikrant would take seven vows. Her hands placed marigold garlands around the arch, setting their names side by side.

She stood back, examining it. "Romantic, isn't it?" she whispered.

Just then, Vikrant approached. He had been watching her from the doorway.

"Nice work," he said casually.

Samina looked at him with her practiced smile. "Of course. I'm good at making things beautiful. Look at your name and Usha's …. don't they look made for each other?"

Vikrant chuckled. "Yes… Thanks."

Samina tilted her head. "Why the thank you?"

"You were the one who told Papa you didn't want to continue this. You helped us both. So, thank you."

Samina said nothing at first. Then, with a shrug, "No worries. Just don't forget to smile tomorrow. Have you picked your outfit?"

"Yeah, Usha helped me choose. I sent her some options."

"Romantic," she replied, eyes fixed on the garland.

Vikrant laughed, cheeks flushing and walked off toward Karishma who was battling a tangle of fairy lights.

What Vikrant saw was just a fraction of her. The smiles, the nods, the cheerful suggestions. But not the parts that mattered.

Every word she said came from the heart …… not the one she lived with, but the one she hid.

Every breath was a negotiation between what she wished for and what she accepted. Every moment beside Vikrant was a quiet war she fought alone.

Sometimes, she controlled the soul. Sometimes, the soul controlled her eyes. Sometimes, her eyes betrayed it all. But she always knew how to pull back ….. like a master of silence.

Love that deep doesn't vanish. It transforms. It stays buried in marrow and memory. Even when the world applauds someone else's name beside his.

There weren't any glittering drapes or chandeliers at the Rathi house, but there was love ……. and plenty of hands to prepare for tomorrow.

Ameet was rolling out dough in the kitchen, preparing puris with Anika. Roopa sat with a phone in hand, inviting a handful of friends. Usha was tidying the bedroom, folding fresh bedsheets and wiping every glass pane twice.

They had no grand guest list, no lavish tents, but they had joy ….. and a daughter getting married tomorrow.

Rajeev entered Aryan's office, face tense. "Sir…sir bad news. The tube light is ….on."

Aryan froze. He turned back to the board.

"Tomorrow is the wedding," he said grimly.

Rajeev nodded. "Which means Satish has triggered the signal."

Aryan paced slowly. "The attack will be tomorrow. We don't know if….if it's Vikrant, Usha, Karishma, or Kunal… but someone is the target."

Rajeev leaned closer, voice low. "I've already arranged a team. Undercover. Dressed as guests. All armed."

Aryan gave a slow nod. "Good. No communication with the Rai house. If the killer senses anything, they'll vanish. Or worse."

A brief pause. Then Rajeev asked quietly, "Should we arrest Satish?"

Aryan shook his head. "No. If we pull him out, the killers might execute a backup plan."

Then he paused, thinking. "There's one more person inside. Samina. She isn't family. If she's not involved, maybe she can help us."

Rajeev hesitated. "What if she's part of it?"

Aryan's voice cut through the room, sharp and controlled. "Get me her records. Now."

Later that Night at the police station Rajeev returned, his tone even but eyes scanning Aryan for reaction. "She's clean, sir. Samina Raichand. Daughter of Raichand and Sunita. Childhood friend of Vikrant. Studied in Mumbai. Currently enrolled in Oxford."

He paused…just a breath…before adding, "She was briefly engaged to Vikrant. It ended… by mutual decision. No criminal records. No visible flags. But she's not easy to read."

Aryan nodded. "Call history?"

Rajeev showed the file.

Aryan tapped his fingers. "I'll go to the Rai house. Pretend it's a friendly visit. Observe Samina closely."

✦ ∞ ✦

Later that night at the Rai house most workers had left. Karishma was taking pictures of the stage. Samina was arranging dinner plates.

Then Aryan arrived in plain clothes.

Kunal looked at Aryan, raising a brow. "Why are you here? At this hour?"

Before Aryan could respond, Vikrant stepped in. "He's a friend. I invited him for dinner."

Aryan joined them with casual ease, his tone light. "The decorations are beautiful."

Vikrant smiled. "All thanks to Karishma and Samina."

Aryan's gaze shifted to Samina. "Impressive work."

Samina nodded with a soft smile. "Just trying to help."

Aryan watched her through the evening. From a distance, everything appeared normal. Too normal. Samina's smile was steady, her gestures measured....nothing gave her away. Whatever once stirred beneath the surface had long been buried. And no one....not even an inspector trained to read silence—could trace what she was hiding.

Until Vikrant said, "Samina, can you make tea?"

Then added with a faint smile, "No one makes tea like her."

In that fragile, flickering moment...no longer than three seconds....something slipped.

Aryan saw it.

A tremor in her eyes. A softness that hadn't entirely hardened.

The tears she never let fall.

The hope she never voiced.

The love she never dared to claim.

And just as swiftly, she tucked it all away masking it with a playful grin.

"See, Karishma? Finally, some recognition."

But Aryan knew.

In that single unguarded blink, he had seen the truth she thought no one could find…. She still loved Vikrant.

Moments later, Aryan stepped into the kitchen, where Samina was busy making tea. She looked up, confused and slightly afraid, unsure why he had followed her in.

"I told them I'll make another type of tea like of best tea. So, I came here to contest with you."

Samina chuckled. "Alright."

Then Aryan said softly, "Do you love him?"

She stilled. A beat passed before she answered. "He's my childhood friend… so yes. But not like that.

Aryan's voice shifted. "Samina, I need your help. Tomorrow someone might be attacked. Vikrant, Usha, Karishma… we don't know who. But it's planned."

Her hands trembled.

"Why would someone….?"

"Shh," Aryan whispered. "Just listen. Takes this phone. Hide it. I'll contact you. We might need your eyes."

Samina stared at the device. Then, slowly, she took it and tucked it into her waistband.

"I'll help."

Aryan smiled faintly. "Now, make sure there's extra tea from his side…and let's get back to our tea war."

Later Vikrant leaned back, his voice calm. "Samina's is better."

Samina's hand paused mid-air.

What?

She had brewed the tea hurriedly, keeping it simple…..plain, even. Not out of laziness, but intention. She wanted Aryan to win. He was helping her… helping Vikrant's family. And somewhere deep down, she'd hoped that this small gesture….stepping aside…might mean something. A quiet thank you to a man who had walked into the fire with her.

But now... Vikrant had chosen hers.

She looked up slowly, trying to read his face, but it gave nothing away. No flicker. No message behind the smile.

And that's what unsettled her most.

Why mine?

Was it just habit?

A childhood reflex?

Or... was it something else?

Was this his way of saying thank you?

Of course, Vikrant wouldn't say it outright.

Not to her.

Not anymore.

So maybe this was it. This quiet choice, this simple comment…..maybe this was all he could give. Maybe it was his version of gratitude... for everything she had done, for staying silent, for holding back.

She looked down at her cup and swallowed the knot in her throat.

Then, forcing a casual smile for the table, she said, "See, Karishma? I still have fans."

Later at night, Samina sat on the edge of her bed, the soft fabric of her wedding sari spilling onto her lap like the final pages of a story she would never write. She had laid out three saris for Usha, two for Karishma, and one for herself.

Her fingers grazed the beaded hem, and then her eyes shifted to the second phone resting beside her pillow. The one Aryan had given her.

Its screen light on.

She picked it up quickly.

Any stranger face might arrive tomorrow in disguise. You need to always keep the earphone in one ear. Look for anything: someone near the stage, someone offering sweets, someone hovering too long near the family. We will be there. But your eyes are our best chance."

Samina stared at the screen, then typed back:

"I will protect him. I will protect them all."

She locked the phone and slid it into the secret pocket sewn into her lehenga. Then leaned back against the bed frame.

Tomorrow, she would not stand behind the curtains– but out in the open, and watch the man she loved

marry the girl he chose.

Maybe her destiny had always meant

for her to remain silent….. to always protect her love, like a cotton wick that burns itself just to spread light.

And today– today, she had something.

Some small, quiet way to love him more.

Because when you love someone– deeply, with heart, madly….

you learn to fight.

Not just for yourself.

But for them.

Even if they never know.

Even if they never will.

She whispered softly to the night:

"Tomorrow…..

I won't let anything happen to you.

Not to Usha.

Not to anyone. "

Then she turned off the light.

Curled into bed

with her dupatta pressed to her chest….

not for comfort, but for courage.

Like a shield.

Like a hope.

And as the house slipped into quiet dreams,

She stayed awake.

Eyes open.

Heart steady.

Holding on to something greater than heartbreak.... the will to protect.

Chapter 60

The sun had barely broken the horizon. Pale gold trickled through the frosted glass panes of the police station, bathing the cold walls in reluctant light.

Inside, the air was heavy with tension. Not the kind that explodes…. the kind that coils, silent, breathless, waiting.

Ceiling fans hummed. Files rustled. A mobile crackled somewhere in the distance. And in the middle of it all, Aryan and Rajeev stood, eyes rimmed red, minds racing.

Rajeev rubbed his temples and said, his voice low and sharp, "We can't take chances anymore, Aryan. Today's the wedding. If the killer acts now... we lose everything. But at least…..now we know who's involved."

Aryan leaned back in his chair, jaw tight, arms folded. "So, what's your plan?"

Rajeev didn't hesitate. "We pick up Satish. Quietly. No warrant. No mess. Pull him from his house. We make him talk."

Aryan's eyes narrowed. "And what if he doesn't talk? What if he has a backup plan in place…… someone else watching, ready to act the second he disappears?"

Rajeev countered, "That's unlikely."

Aryan stood, tone rising. "Unlikely isn't good enough today."

They walked toward the back interrogation room, yellow light flickering above, shadows dancing around them like secrets whispering through cracks.

"I have another option," Rajeev offered.

Aryan turned. "What?"

Rajeev's voice lowered. "We arrest Kunal. Fake charge. Halt the wedding. Disrupt their plan. The killer panics…… makes a mistake."

Aryan stared at him, long and hard. "No. That's exactly what they want….chaos. We give them that, they'll shift targets or worse."

He paused.

Then quietly, "There's someone else. Ameet."

Rajeev exhaled. "He's not talking. He's already said everything he's going to."

Aryan looked at his phone. Then murmured, "Sometimes… the only way to win against monsters is to play like one."

Without another word, he typed:

"Sorry."

The mandap shimmered under soft sunlight. Strings of marigold swayed gently in the wind. Drums played faintly in the background. Guests were beginning to gather.

Anika, busy greeting relatives, hadn't checked her phone. Usha helped Pandit-ji arrange the havan things. Ameet moved from one group to another, his smile gentle, his eyes tired.

Then Aryan arrived.

"I need to speak with you, Uncle" he said quietly, stepping in front of Ameet.

Ameet's smile didn't falter. "Enjoy the food. And yes, Give Usha your blessings."

Aryan's voice dropped. "It's ….. it's important."

"I've told you before….. I have no answers."

Aryan stepped closer, hand in his pocket. "Ok….Then I'll announce it now. Announce About Anika. About her pregnancy."

Ameet froze.

Aryan's voice was calm, but deadly quiet. "You want me to say it here, in front of all guests? Or outside?"

✦ ∞ ✦

Ameet sat still, hands in his lap, staring through the windshield.

Aryan broke the silence. "Anika's pregnant. She's carrying my child."

Ameet's lips trembled. His chest rose in a stifled breath. Tears clung to his lashes.

Aryan didn't stop. "Don't cry. If someone sees us like this, it becomes a full sad story."

Ameet wiped his face, barely able to speak. "You never even loved her."

"No," Aryan said truthfully. "I didn't. But if you help me now..... give me the truth.... I'll protect her. I'll marry her. I'll fix this."

It was all a lie. But the kind told for something greater.

He remembered what Samina once said: "Sometimes, love means holding your pain until the fire cools down."

Ameet stared at the decorated lawn, where lives played out in laughter..... and lies.

"If I speak," he whispered, "the truth might save them. But silence... will destroy... destroy everything."

He turned slowly.

"What do you want to know?"

Aryan's voice was steady. "You and Namrata. Tell me everything."

Flashback – 20 Years Ago

There was nothing extraordinary about that morning.

The sky over Chandrapur hung dull and tired,

the streets looked like dust settled in the folds of forgotten pages,

and the city was calm—like unspoken words waiting for meaning.

Ameet, 27, stepped off the bus with the weight of failure pressing between his shoulders.

He had come looking for work.....any work.

Even if it meant sweeping floors or sorting shelves.

He wasn't a man of loud dreams.

He was quiet. Gentle.

The kind of man who knew how to disappear into a crowd without ever being noticed.

Ameet found a job at a bookstore.

And that day…..fate noticed him.

The bookstore smelled of old paper, ink, and the ghost of distant rain.

He was folding newspapers when she walked in.

A yellow saree.

A doctor's apron.

A delicate silver anklet.

A stethoscope tucked loosely against her collarbone.

And around her neck…an infinity pendant that caught the light when she moved.

Namrata.

She didn't look at him.

She asked for a poetry book…..Gulzar.

He found it quickly.

She paid.

Left.

And something ….something inside Ameet…. stayed.

Love didn't arrive that day with rain.

It arrived in silence– in the hush of turning pages, in the rustle of a yellow saree disappearing through a door.

He didn't know her name.

But he knew her presence…. like a name written on a fogged window.

Fading.

But unforgettable.

He began waiting for her.

Not intentionally at first.

But soon, his hands folded paper faster.

His breath paused when the door creaked.

And some weeks, she didn't come at all.

Yet her absence filled the room

as if she had never left.

He learned her name from a receipt:

Dr. Namrata.

One day, she walked in wearing a white coat.

That was when he noticed the badge.

And for the first time,

he didn't see her as a stranger……

but as someone…someone impossibly out of reach.

A doctor.

Beautiful.

Confident.

Educated.

And him?

Just a man behind a counter.

Then one day, she returned……graceful as always, but not alone.

Beside her stood a man in uniform.

Tall.

A badge glinting against his chest.

Inspector Manoj Prakash.

She smiled……..polite, distant.

And turned to the shop owner.

"This is my husband," she said.

Just like that.

Ameet felt something shift inside him— something …. something heavy,

like a heavy stone falling through still water.

She was married.

He didn't speak.

Didn't flinch.

But something inside him dimmed.

Quietly…..like a house losing its last light.

He had no right.

No promises.

No dreams ever spoken aloud.

But it still felt like loss.

A loss no one saw.

He watched her leave.

That night, he walked home slower than usual…

as if even time had grown heavier.

He tried to forget her.

He failed.

It was dark. October 1st, 2003.

Ameet was walking home under the flickering amber glow of a tired streetlight.

The cicadas buzzed louder than usual, like the night was humming a warning.

The forest near the road…..usually filled with the sound of rustling leaves and distant movement….had gone quiet. Unnaturally quiet.

And then……he saw her.

Stumbling out of the shadows.

Blood smeared across her forehead.

Hair stuck to her damp face in tangled strands.

Eyes wide…..not with fear, but something worse.

Like her soul had touched death.

"Namrata?"

Ameet's voice broke the silence.

He stepped forward.

She turned sharply, panic flashing across her face.

"Who are you? How do you know my name?"

"I……I work at the bookstore," he stammered.

"And, I saw your badge once. That's all."

She blinked.

Her breathing began to slow.

A flicker of recognition surfaced in her eyes.

But it faded quickly.

Then her gaze shifted…… into the trees.

Ameet followed her line of sight.

And he saw them.

Bodies.

Scattered beneath the trees like broken pieces of a story no one should witness.

Some twisted.

Some perfectly still.

Blood soaking into the ground.

He couldn't speak.

Couldn't move.

The forest had stolen his voice.

And Namrata….She didn't scream.

Didn't cry.

She just whispered—barely audible, almost to herself:

"I……I killed my husband. "

And the night……

The night never let him forget.

Not the silence.

Not the blood.

Not the weight of what he saw.

Some bodies.

A woman.

A man in uniform.

And a boy.

Blood darkening the soil

as if the forest itself was trying to bury what had happened.

Namrata looked at him, her voice shaking.

"I killed."

Ameet froze.

She stared at him— eyes hollow, searching, waiting for fear.

For judgment.

For him to run.

"Why are you still here? she asked.

"Why haven't you run?"

Ameet swallowed hard.

"I don't know," he said quietly.

"But I won't leave you."

She looked at him like he couldn't be real.

A stranger in the middle of a nightmare....who didn't ask questions, didn't run, didn't reach for the law or the past.

He just stood there.

Maybe she didn't fall in love with him.

But that night, someone stayed.

Someone didn't care what was right or wrong.

Someone simply asked:

"What can I do?"

And that....

was enough.

enough for her.

Her lips trembled.

Her voice cracked.

She...., she had just killed.

Her husband.

Her partner.

So she didn't speak.

Not at first.

She just stood there.

Broken.

Breathing.

Silent.

And still, she stayed quiet.

And then…..for the first time that night…..she began to speak.

Namrata, her husband Manoj, and their newborn twins were driving back from the hospital that night.

The roads were quiet.

The forest was still.

Then….a boy appeared.

He ran into the road, breathless, wild with fear.

"My mother….she's pregnant. She's in pain. She can't walk. Please."

Namrata didn't hesitate.

She was a doctor.

It was instinct.

Manoj protested. Said it could be a trap.

But she had already stepped out.

Under the banyan tree, she found the woman….half-conscious, clutching her swollen stomach.

Her face pale. Her pain obvious.

And then—her eyes widened.

She looked past Namrata.

Straight at Manoj.

"This man…." she gasped.

"He helped them. He destroyed my family."

Namrata froze.

What?

But Manoj…. he understood.

His face went pale. His hand trembled.

And then….without warning….he slapped the woman.

She cried out.

He reached for his gun.

"No!" Namrata screamed.

But it was too late.

A gunshot rang out.

The boy….the one who had begged them for help….grabbed a stone and hurled it.

It struck Manoj hard across the temple.

He fell to the ground.

But he didn't stay down.

Manoj staggered back to his feet, blood on his face, gun still in hand…..raising it again.

Namrata was screaming now.

Screaming.

Shaking.

Trying to wake from something that wasn't a dream.

And then she saw it.

A branch.

Heavy. Splintered.

She picked it up.

Swung it with both hands….just as the gun fired again.

One bullet.

Two bodies fell.

Manoj.

The boy.

And then….

Namrata collapsed too.

On her knees.

The branch still in her hands.

Blood on her hands.

Breath caught in her throat.

And then Namrata heard it.... the voice of the mother, fighting through her final breaths.

The bullet had torn near her heart.

Blood was already soaking into the soil.

She was slipping.

But even in that moment.... with her husband dead, bodies around her, a nightmare unfolding under the forest sky... Namrata didn't turn away from her duty.

From her oath.

She was still a doctor.

Still a woman who couldn't walk away from life.

The twins hadn't even opened their eyes to this world.

They hadn't seen the night.

They hadn't felt its weight.

Namrata tried.

She tried everything.

But in the end.... she could only save one.

A girl.

The mother, bleeding and fading, reached out with what little strength remained.

Her hand brushed the newborn's face.

Her eyes met Namrata's.

She wanted to say something.

Anything.

But the words....

never came.

Her voice disappeared into the night.

Just like her life.

Namrata sat frozen.

Covered in blood.

Holding a child who would never know the full truth of that night.

And Ameet….. he stayed.

A tear slipped down his cheek.

He looked at her.

And inside, he said what his heart had always known:

"I'm proud I loved a woman like you.

"I'm proud I love a doctor like you. "

Then aloud….without hesitation,

without fear,

without silence—he said:

"You didn't do wrong.

You saved a life."

The forest was quiet.

But the silence wasn't empty.

It was full of echoes.

Full of what was lost…. and what was left behind.

Namrata hugged her daughter….sleeping in the back seat of the car, unaware of the storm outside or inside her mother.

She didn't cry anymore.

Her tears had dried somewhere between shock and surrender.

She held the surviving child…Anika…against her chest like a lifeline.

The only proof that something pure had made it out alive.

She looked at Ameet.

"Can you raise these girls?"

Ameet swallowed.

"I won't separate a daughter from her mother," he said quietly.

He looked at the blood on her hands.

The fear in her eyes.

The fire still in her breath.

Then he said it...soft but firm, "You can go. I'll go to the police. I'll say I did all of this."

Namrata's eyes widened.

"Why would you do that? Why would you sacrifice yourself for me?"

Ameet didn't answer right away.

He just stood there, silent....like he had been since the beginning.

Then finally, he spoke "I don't know. But my heart, my mind, my soul...everything in me.....is telling me to do this for you."

A few tears slipped from her eyes.

But she didn't speak.

Not at first.

Then, finally...."No," she said. "I can't let you do that."

They stood like that for a while....two broken people holding onto each other in the dark.

After everything.... after so much silence....

Ameet finally said,

"Then come with me, Namu.

With a new name. A new life.

We'll raise them together."

She didn't respond.

Not immediately.

But then....she nodded.

And so, Ameet took them both.

Usha, and the woman's surviving daughter....Anika.

Two girls bound not just by blood,

but by the same night of ash and silence.

The woman's son.... the boy who had run into the road,

who died trying to protect his mother....Ameet buried him himself.

Deep in the forest.

No prayers.

No name.

Just soil and sorrow.

A secret he swore would never leave the trees.

They placed the bodies in the car:

Manoj. The woman. The newborn girl who hadn't survived.

They lit the car.

Watched as the flames rose,

until the sky turned red and the world turned away.

The city believed it was an accident.

That Inspector Manoj, his wife, and child had died in a tragic blaze.

But there was something in the forest.

A presence.

Watching.

A rustle. A breath.

Something that didn't belong to the trees.

Namrata looked once.

Ameet looked too.

And for a heartbeat…..they both felt it.

Someone was there.

They didn't wait to find out who.

They walked.

Later, the police found the burnt car.

And the story was sealed:

Inspector Manoj.

His wife.

His child.

All gone in the fire.

But in truth….only ashes remained.

And somewhere, beneath the trees…

a secret watched.

And waited.

Flashback Ends —

✦ ∞ ✦

Back in the Car – Present

Aryan wiped his eyes. "You raised both girls?"

Ameet nodded, his voice barely holding. "Anika and Usha."

Aryan whispered, "And your wife?"

Ameet looked away. "I never married. I just... made Namrata my wife in dreams. But I never told her. Never said I loved her. Not even once."

A pause stretched.

"Where's Namrata now?"

A long silence.

"She stayed with me for a year," Ameet said quietly. "She couldn't sleep. Couldn't eat. She kept saying someone would come from the forest and reveal everything. She wasn't herself anymore. I looked after her, as best I could. But one day… she walked into the forest."

His voice cracked.

"She never came back. We found her body. Stab wounds. No suspects. No answers."

Ameet leaned back, eyes clouded with old storms.

"I gave Anika her mother's photograph….Noor. It was folded inside the boy's belongings. And Namrata… she gave her chain to Usha. Said she wanted her to have something real. Something of her."

Aryan nodded slowly. "Usha once told me her infinity pendant was hidden in a book. Did Namrata ever mention another chain?"

Ameet hesitated. Then sighed. "Yes… once. She said Manoj had ordered a similar one for Usha. Just like hers. But he lost it. Said it slipped from his pocket deep in the forest."

In Aryan's mind, the puzzle clicked.

The chain in the book... it wasn't the original.

Rekha found it.

And Kunal….he used it during the old ritual reenactments. Like a symbol. A ghost.

Aryan looked at Ameet and whispered, "You did this for love. You stayed quiet. Silently loved her. Never married, so you could raise her daughter. And not just hers…..but the other girl she saved too. You're not just a father… you're the definition of one."

He reached out, gently touched Ameet's hand.

"Anika's not pregnant," Aryan said. "It was a lie. I needed the truth. For them."

Ameet nodded slowly. "I knew. Not the lie. But… the love."

Aryan paused, then asked, "And the money Namrata sent you?"

"I never touched it," Ameet replied. "It was hers. I just… kept it. Like a part of her that stayed."

Ameet looked toward the wedding canopy outside the windshield.

And somewhere behind them, the sacred fire crackled.

A wedding was about to begin.

But in the shadow of joy…

Justice was finally waking up.

Chapter 61

The rain had long stopped, but Aryan remained still in his car. The windshield was dotted with remnants of a storm now passed, but inside him, the tempest raged on. Every revelation inched under his skin like cold needles …. sharp, deliberate, and unforgiving.

Namu.

The name echoed through his chest like the trace of a forgotten lullaby. Once Dr. Namrata …. healer, lover, mother. To Ameet, she was softened into "Namu," a name worn smooth by time and tenderness. But beneath that quietness had lived a blaze. And in that blaze were secrets that refused to die.

She wasn't just Usha's mother.

And she wasn't Anika's.

The truth struck like a blade, clean and final …. Usha was the daughter of Inspector Manoj and Namrata.

Anika… was Afzal and Noor's child.

Two girls raised as sisters, but never by blood. They were joined instead by sorrow …. by ashes, not birth. Their childhood was built not on fairy tales, but on the ruins of those who had failed them.

But Aryan's mind wasn't done asking.

Where was the orphan girl now?

Why was the Pandit silenced?

And what role had Satish played in this long game of grief?

His knuckles tightened around the steering wheel. The storm had passed, but its aftermath had just begun.

He dialled Rajeev.

✦ ∞ ✦

The courtyard glowed under marigold lights. The air smelled of jasmine and vermilion smoke. Soft shehnai notes weaved through the laughter, like a quiet promise.

Usha circled the sacred fire, her red bridal lehenga brushing against Vikrant's sherwani with every round. With each step, they walked deeper into a new life .... or so it seemed.

From the fringes, Samina watched like a sentinel. Her eyes scanned every face, every whisper.

Aryan arrived late, his face pale with thought.

"No suspicious movement," Samina said, her voice low. "No threats. Everything's clean."

Aryan didn't answer. His phone vibrated.

Rajeev.

"Aryan," Rajeev's voice was taut. "I have something."

"Go on."

"Remember Narayan's wife? When I questioned her, she asked to see my baby. My wife recorded the call. Later, when I slowed the footage....."

"What did you find?"

"In the corner of the screen, hidden... Ruhi. Hiding behind a curtain."

Aryan's pulse thudded. "You're sure?"

"She didn't realize the front camera caught her. It was her."

Rajeev continued, breathless, "I traced the phone location used during the murders of Rajeshwari and Fatima. It wasn't Ruhi's number. It belonged to Narayan's wife ....Kalyani."

Aryan's voice dropped into steel. "She's behind it."

"She's the architect."

"Arrest her. Now. I'm coming."

✦ ∞ ✦

The door creaked open.

Kalyani stood in a pale green saree. Her eyes were calm, too calm. Her smile barely touched her lips.

Rajeev stepped forward. "Kalyani Devi. You're under arrest."

Her smile froze. "What nonsense…."

Aryan met her gaze. "We know everything."

She twitched.

In one sudden motion, she pulled a blade from her waist and flung it.

Aryan ducked.

Rajeev leapt forward. "Sir!"

"I'm fine."

The knife clattered to the floor. Kalyani didn't resist the cuffs. As the lady constable gripped her wrists, she laughed ….a hollow, bone-deep sound.

"You can put me in chains," she whispered, "but the game's already begun. And you're too late."

Rajeev and Aryan exchanged a glance.

And in that silence, the air turned cold.

The fan overhead groaned with every spin. Kalyani sat with folded arms, face impassive. A constable stood by the wall.

"She hasn't spoken," the constable whispered.

Aryan walked in; his eyes fixed on hers. "We know who Ruhi is."

Kalyani smiled. "The orphan."

Rajeev's voice was sharp. "You couldn't have children. So, you raised her. And twisted her into your weapon."

The smile faltered.

"So, you know," she muttered.

Aryan leaned forward. "We know the poisons. The distractions. The rituals. We know you created chaos and called it justice."

Her eyes didn't blink. "Justice is never given," she said. "It is taken."

"You murdered people," Rajeev hissed. "Innocents."

Kalyani's voice turned sharper. "I was shunned. I came from Hyderabad. Married into this village. I couldn't bear children. My husband left me in silence. The village called me cursed. They stopped inviting me. I moved into the forest... ..forest ..where no one could curse me more than the silence already had."

Her gaze drifted, staring at something only she could see. A life long gone.

"Naina was kind…she came often. Shared stories. Her presence softened the forest's cruelty. But one day she told me…..she was pregnant. Unwed. Blessed with what I was denied."

Her jaw tightened.

"She was the cursed one, not me. I never saw her again. And then, I saw Namrata with Ameet… burning bodies in the forest. That night, I learned everything."

Her voice cracked…..like a flute snapped in half.

"I raised that girl. Sent her away to Hyderabad. To learn. To grow. To survive. She was Ruhi. My shadow. My daughter by choice."

She didn't stop.

"We started with the Pandit. He knew what Samar was doing. Knew the sin. And stayed silent. I found his family, traced his lies, blackmailed him. He called his sons to the forest. That night, I handed him a poisoned cigarette. Two minutes. That's all it took. And with guilt, he burned."

"I found Anika's kundli by accident. I burned it. But the police started drawing patterns. Reading rituals. We had to confuse them."

"Ruhi killed Rajeshwari. And Fatima. I went to Pandit's wife… slipped poison into her perfume bottle. Fitting, wasn't it? Dying in Satish's arms."

She smirked faintly.

"Ruhi wanted Afzal to live. He helped her... when Samar..." her voice caught, then hardened. "But Narayan wanted him dead. So, I killed Narayan. Laced the ladoos with poison. Pretended it was a prayer offering."

Aryan whispered, "The photographer?"

Kalyani's eyes gleamed. "He was noise."

Rajeev's voice cracked. "But his confession..."

"Scripted," she snapped. "Ours."

Aryan's eyes narrowed. "How did you turn off Satish's tube light?"

She chuckled. "Smart automation. Controlled from my phone. VPN paid. Untraceable."

Aryan's jaw clenched. "Where is Ruhi now?"

Kalyani leaned back. Her smile returned. Cold. Certain.

"She's finishing our final act."

Rajeev stiffened. "What act?"

Laughter spilled from her lips....slow, hollow, cruel.

"You destroyed lives," Aryan said, voice quiet but thunderous.

Kalyani's voice softened into something terrifying. "No. I avenged one."

Outside, the skies had cleared.

At the Rai house, the scent of incense lingered. Rose petals lay scattered like fragile dreams. Music danced through the air as if nothing was wrong.

But somewhere beyond the garlands and vows,

In a place untouched by celebration.....The last piece had already moved.

And the woman in the shadows...

Had not yet played her final note.

Kalyani's last move was still in play.

Chapter 62

Mist clung to the windows like breath against glass.

The scent of damp files and sleepless coffee haunted the room. The investigation board glowed under a flickering bulb…..names, faces, red threads webbed together like veins of the dead.

Rajeev stared at it.

What will be Kalyani's last move?

And then….something clicked.

He turned sharply. "Sir, I'm stepping out."

Aryan looked up from his notes. "Everything alright?"

Rajeev didn't answer fully…..just nodded once. "Something I need to check."

He left swiftly. The hallway felt colder than before.

He walked past the empty rooms, past the silence, until he reached the cell.

The room where Kalyani Devi had sat calm, shackled, yet undefeated.

Now empty. Shadows lingered where she once breathed.

Two hours later.

Rajeev burst into the war room, chest heaving. "Sir….Ruhi. No sign. Still no trace."

Aryan didn't turn. He stood facing the board, eyes dragging across fading photographs and tangled strings like they might whisper answers.

"She's still out there," he said. "This isn't over. I want full-scale surveillance. No one moves alone."

Rajeev hesitated. "There's more. We found Afzal's body. In Kunal Rai's farmhouse."

Silence.

Aryan's fists curled at his sides. "Even now... even after her arrest... Kalyani kept playing. Every move a thread. Every death... deliberate."

He shut his eyes for a breath, the weight of too many ghosts pressing down.

Then opened them with steel.

"Bring in Kunal. And find out what the hell Afzal was doing there."

The metal chair scraped against the tiled floor.

Aryan didn't speak at first. He just sat across the table, elbows resting, fingers laced. The hum of the overhead light buzzed like tension in the silence.

Across from him, sat Kunaal.....nervous, tired, or maybe just trying to seem both.

Aryan finally leaned forward.

"Let's not waste time," he said quietly. "You already know why you're here." Rajeev stood by the door, unreadable. "You're being charged with the murder of Afzal."

Kunal jolted. "What? That's insane!"

Aryan stepped in....quiet, precise. "We found Afzal. On your land. Beaten. Dead. Explain."

Kunal's voice cracked. "I don't know! I swear! After he was released, Narayan was looking for him. I told him......find him, talk to him, scare him maybe... but I didn't.........."

He stopped.

Then whispered, "Did... did you find someone else there?"

Aryan narrowed his eyes. "Someone else? What do you mean?"

Rajeev shook his head. "No guards. No one. Just Afzal. Dead."

Aryan exhaled slowly. "Ruhi is still missing."

They stepped into the hallway. The lights buzzed above them.

Rajeev's voice dropped. "Sir… this feels wrong. Too clean. Like it was planted. Kalyani may have staged this too…..framed Kunal. Laid it all out like a final performance."

Aryan's gaze was distant, his voice low. "Without Ruhi, all we have is a body.

And Kunal…"

A pause.

"……..is still guilty of silence."

The mansion shimmered in lights and joy. Usha, radiant in red, returned with Vikrant, laughter trailing behind like silk.

"Where's Papa?" Vikrant asked, glancing around.

Samina approached with a smile. "With Aryan. He'll join soon. Come, both of you must rest."

Karishma led Usha up the stairs, anklets chiming like bells in a forgotten temple. The bridal suite shimmered with golden petals and soft candlelight ……..love written in flame and fragrance.

Downstairs, Samina's smile faltered. Her phone buzzed in her palm.

Aryan exhaled, his voice steady but strained. "We've caught Kalyani. But Ruhi is still missing. Her last move… could be tonight. Stay alert."

Samina listened again.

Her breath caught.

Aryan called her, voice steady but grim. He told her everything……Kalyani's confession, the bodies, the final act yet to unfold.

Samina didn't speak for a moment.

Then softly, "I'll protect them."

She hung up……and froze.

Her mind spiralled.

Pandit. Manoj. Namrata. Afzal. Every death, every ritual… a thread tied to Ruhi's past.

And then……

A cold truth pierced her chest like steel.

Namrata's daughter… is Usha.

And Kalyani's last move… is to destroy her.

With trembling hands, Samina redialled Aryan.

"Sir," she whispered. "I need to do something. Please… trust me.

And if I can't… you have to do my last work."

She turned from the hallway, heart pounding, and found Karishma laughing softly near the marigold-strewn archway.

"Karishma…" her voice broke on the name.

Karishma turned, catching the look in Samina's eyes….confused at first, then searching.

"Sam?" she asked. "What… what's wrong?"

Samina's eyes shimmered. A single tear slid down.

Without a word, she stepped forward and embraced her tightly.

"I know you're bold," Samina whispered into her hair. "And tonight… you have to be bolder than ever."

Karishma stiffened. "Sam, what are you saying? What happened?"

But Samina didn't explain. Couldn't.

She pulled back slowly, wiped her tears, and forced a smile that didn't reach her eyes.

"You look pretty," she said, her voice soft, breaking. "More than pretty."

She turned away.

Walked down the hall.

And just before she disappeared behind the corner, she looked back one last time.

Their eyes met.

Samina's gaze lingered, heavy with everything left unsaid.

Then she was gone.

Karishma stood still, her smile fading. The music around her felt distant. Faint.

Something hollow bloomed in her chest.

An ache.

A warning.

A whisper that the night was about to change.

Samina walked softly into Usha's room, a glass of juice in hand. Her voice was barely a whisper against the stillness.

"Drink this. You must be exhausted."

Usha smiled, tired and trusting. "Thank you… I am."

She drank without question.

Minutes passed. The air hung heavy with unspoken love.

Then her eyes began to dim. Her limbs softened. Her breath slowed.

Samina caught her as she stumbled, arms trembling, tears rising like a tide she could no longer hold back. She cradled Usha gently…. like a sister, like someone who'd promised to guard what the world had tried to destroy.

With careful hands, she undressed her. Folded her bridal saree aside.

And then……Samina wrapped it around herself.

Every pleat a prayer. Every thread a vow.

She locked the door behind her, whispering a promise through the wood.

"Sleep, Usha. I'll take the night for you, for your love, for my love"

The pills would keep her safe.

Unharmed. Unreachable.

Far from the storm.

In Vikrant's room, Samina sat silently on the edge of the bed. Her face veiled. Her heart bare. Her soul already burning.

Tonight…..She was the bride.

And the shield.

The fire outside was for celebration.

But the fire inside her……

Was for war.

✦ ∞ ✦

The music faltered. Then drowned.

Panic swept in like a storm breaking through silk.

Outside, a reporter screamed into the chaos……

"BREAKING - Kunal Rai arrested in connection with factory murders and the death of Afzal!"

Gasps echoed like shattered glass.

Guests froze mid-step. Phones buzzed. Mothers clutched their children.

Laughter dissolved into dread.

On the stairs, Karishma ran…….barefoot, breathless, her heart pounding before she even knew why.

But someone else had already reached the top.

Ruhi.

A gun in her hand.

Her eyes empty. Focused.

Her steps…..calm, deliberate, silent as snow falling on graves.

She didn't speak.

She didn't tremble.

She walked down the corridor like the night itself had chosen her.

Toward the bridal room.

Toward vengeance.

Toward the final page.

A single second.

A single bullet.

And silence.

Samina fell.

Not in fear.

Not in regret.

But with grace.

With purpose.

With love stitched into every wound she took.

She fell like someone who had already said goodbye.

Like someone who knew.........that a heartbeat could be louder than a gunshot

if it carried enough love inside it.

Chapter 63

"Usha?!" Vikrant's voice cracked through the chaos.

He rushed forward, heart thundered in his ears.

He pulled back the veil with shaking hands..... And the world collapsed.

"Samina..."

She lay cradled in his arms, trembling.

The red of her bridal saree was no longer the colour of joy.... but of wounds, of silence, of sacrifice.

Her eyes fluttered open. Just enough.

Enough to see him.

Enough to say goodbye.

A smile found her lips.....fragile, cracked, but real.

Like a candle refusing to go out.

"I always wondered..." her voice barely a breath, "if I'd die alone."

She coughed....wet, final.

"But look at me now... in red... in your arms...

like a bride...

like a miracle."

Her fingers grazed his as though trying to memorize one last touch.

"I loved you," she whispered, "with no promise... no name... no right.

But I loved you with everything I never said."

Her breath caught.

"I didn't just save Usha... I saved my love.

That's my forever."

She blinked slowly, tears resting at the corner of her eyes.

"And now… I know my love is happy."

Vikrant shook, clutching her hand like a drowning man.

"No… please… don't go…"

She smiled faintly.

"Even if I couldn't be your bride…

I became your story."

And then……….she was still.

Gone with a tear.

A smile.

And a silence so full of love… it echoed.

The red she wore didn't fade.

It burned.

Not as a symbol of death— but as a legend

of the woman who wore love

like armour.

Usha wept; her arms wrapped around Samina's lifeless body.

But in truth— Someone else had died with her.

Karishma.

She walked out of the Rai mansion barefoot.

Each step echoing like a memory she could no longer carry.

The world around her buzzed with confusion, but her world… had ended with a single shot.

She never told anyone.

That Samina was her hush.

Her moon.

Her heartbeat stitched in shadows.

That every time her eyes closed, it was Samina's laughter that lingered. Her touch. Her absence.

But Karishma had always lived quietly.

And silence… was all she ever allowed herself.

Until now.

She stood at the edge of the cliff where the wind howled like grief itself.

Tears streamed freely, mixing with the storm.

Her chest ached with the weight of unspoken things.

She stepped forward......

"Karishma!" Aryan's voice sliced through the wind, urgent, raw.

She didn't turn.

Didn't flinch.

"I know," he said softly behind her. "You loved her."

Her voice broke like glass.

"For what should I live now?"

Aryan stepped closer.

He held something in his hand.

A phone. Glowing. Ticking.

A voice played.

Samina.

"If you're hearing this........

it means I'm no longer alive.

Karishma....

I know.

I always knew.

That you loved me ... more than anyone ever has, more than you loved yourself.

I felt it .... in your heartbeat when you hugged me, in your eyes when you looked at me.

You knew me better than I knew myself.

You made my favourite things your favourite too.

You loved me in silence···

and I heard every word of it.

And I'm sorry.

I'm sorry I couldn't love you back the way you deserved.

But please....

Don't end your story here.

You have to live.

For you.

For me.

For us.

Live….. so I can live in you.

And Karishma….

you looked beautiful in green too."

Karishma collapsed.

Her knees struck the earth.

And something inside her cracked wide open.

She stared at the ground, but her eyes…….. they were seeing Samina.

Tears rolled freely, but they couldn't blur her face.

Not in memory.

Not now.

She looked up at the sky.

Her lips trembled…..she wanted to scream her name, to shatter the silence, to fall and never rise again.

But she didn't.

She whispered.

She touched her chest, and whispered

"I will live…. and love.

Always.

This is not my life anymore…. I already died when you did.

This life now…….

It's yours.

And I'll live it for you. "

She wiped her eyes.

Not to stop crying… but to see clearly.

To begin.

She ran to Aryan…. no words.

Just need.

She clutched the phone to her chest

as if she were holding Samina…. not for the last time, but as if she never let go at all.

The storm paused…… for her grief.

And today, the silence spoke.

The cliff heard it.

The sky heard it.

And somewhere….

Samina did too.

Because sometimes…

the bravest love

is the one that never asked for anything.

But stayed anyway.

Chapter 64

Aryan closed the final case file.

His eyes lingered on the last photograph.

A single tear slipped down and landed on the page….. the last drop of a long storm.

Across the room, Rajeev stepped forward.

"Sir… thank you. You finally closed this case."

Aryan didn't look up. "We did it. Our team. You, me… we held every thread until the whole story showed itself."

Rajeev nodded, a tired smile on his face. "Yes, sir."

Aryan's phone buzzed on the desk. Anika's wallpaper lit the screen….soft, smiling, hopeful.

He stared at it. Smiled faintly. Slipped it back into his coat pocket.

Then he murmured, "Rajeev… I'm still confused. Why did Kalyani save Anika? And how… how did she kill Afzal?"

Rajeev hesitated.

He didn't answer.

But inside him, the memory rewound like an old reel…. The truth Aryan never saw.

"Well?" he asked.

Rajeev exhaled slowly. "Yes, sir. Still no idea why Kalyani saved Anika. Maybe… it was to distract us. She always did that well."

Aryan smiled faintly. "Yes… she always did."

Rajeev glanced at the window.

"Oh, and Satish stopped by. Said thanks. For not revealing his truth with Pandit's wife."

Aryan nodded. "He helped us. He wasn't the villain. He was just protecting Naina's memory. Hiding it from a world too cruel to forgive."

He paused.

"But Samar… is still missing. Somewhere. In the forest."

Rajeev stared out the window, voice barely a breath.

"…Yes, sir."

But in his heart, the truth lay buried.

Along with the bodies.

Along with the final bullet.

Along with the story Aryan would never read.

Justice came not with vengeance, but with quiet resolve.

Rekha got the justice.

Not because the world was kind…. but because her truth could no longer be buried.

Even in death, she was heard.

She stayed quiet.

But the truth didn't.

Ruhi and Kalyani were sentenced. Their names etched coldly into the records. Aryan only wrote what the law needed. Not everything. Not the truth about Naina. Not Samar. Not the little boy buried under a forgotten sky.

Some truths, he knew, weren't meant to stain paper.

They were meant to live softly… in memory.

Anika approached him days later, her voice carrying the weight of new roots.

"I know now," she said, eyes uncertain, "that I'm Afzal's daughter."

Aryan said nothing. Sometimes, silence was the kindest answer.

"But I'll still call Ameet my father," she smiled softly. "Because blood makes a connection. But love… makes a family."

Usha, too, found her anchor in truth.

And when someone asked, she simply replied:

"I am Ameet's daughter. And Anika is my sister……..my twin flame in this life. Nothing else matters."

The past no longer defined them.

Only love did.

Chapter 65

The Funeral That Felt Like Silence

Samina's funeral was unlike any other.

No piercing wails clawed at the sky.

No overdrawn speeches tried to capture what couldn't be contained.

Only stillness.

Only wind.

The banyan tree swayed above her pyre, its old limbs whispering secrets to the sky....as if nature itself bowed to a woman who had never asked for the world yet gave hers away.

Aryan stood near the fire. Eyes red, jaw tight.

"She didn't die for duty," he murmured, voice coarse. "She died for love. She didn't just save Usha... she saved what love should feel like."

And with a soldier's dignity, he raised his hand in one final salute.

A farewell between warriors.

✦ ∞ ✦

The Rai mansion, once veiled in secrets and shadows, began to breathe again.

Laughter didn't return all at once. It tiptoed into rooms, like a cautious guest.

But slowly, light seeped in.

Pain still lived there....in the cracks of walls, in quiet corners. But time, like morning sun through sheer curtains, warmed even the coldest memories.

Each morning, Vikrant woke with Usha beside him….her breath steady, her presence his peace.

But some mornings…

When the wind was softer than usual,

When the light touched the bed like a prayer……He would feel something.

Her.

Samina.

Not in flesh.

But in the spaces only hearts can sense.

In the pause before Usha stirred.

In the hush that fell just before dawn.

In the way the curtain lifted when no one touched it.

He never spoke of it.

Never dared to.

But sometimes… he'd whisper into the air, a name no one else heard.

"Samina."

What is love?

It's not always loud.

Not always mutual.

Not always easy to name.

Sometimes, love is sacrifice.

Sometimes, it's sitting in the shadows just to make sure someone else gets the light.

It's pouring out everything you have…..without needing to be chosen.

Samina never wore Vikrant's ring.

Never wore the Mangalsutra bearing his name.

Never filled her hairline with sindoor as his bride.

Never got a title, or a place in history.

But she loved with such unshakable grace…

That the world had to remember her.
Some people die and become names on paper.
Others die........and become legend.

✦ ∞ ✦

Beneath the old banyan tree in the Rai compound,
where incense still clings to the air,
a small brass plate rests........quiet, unmarked by time.
Samina.
The one who never asked to be loved…
but loved anyway.
Each morning, someone places a marigold garland there.
Sometimes a diya flickers beside it,
its flame small but steady.......like the love she left behind.
The wind moves gently through the leaves above.
The temple chimes sing her song.
And if you close your eyes…..
and listen, truly listen……….
you might still hear her voice.
Not in pain.
Not in longing.
But in peace.
Saying:
"Even in death…… I loved till the end."
And in that love,
Samina became something eternal.

✦ ∞ ✦

Karishma's world had changed.
She now lived in a university hostel ……new walls, new
timetables, new books.

But nothing truly felt new.

Every morning, she whispered:

"Morning, Samina….."

She made tea, just like she used to – and whispered to herself:

"Samina…. you made it better."

Every night, she whispered into her pillow.

And every night, her eyes spilled quiet tears.

She lived—because Samina had asked her to.

But she grieved like someone who had lost their own skin.

In the cafeteria, she smiled politely.

In lectures, she answered clearly.

But when the sun dipped behind the clouds…..

when the dorm grew quiet….

Karishma took out Samina' s voice recording.

Just to hear her love again.

Just to remind her soul why it was still breathing.

Karishma never told anyone that her first and last love had been a woman.

She didn't need to.

Because some loves don't ask to be spoken aloud.

They live in glances, in rituals, in the way you hold a cup of tea as if someone's still there.

Her love lived in the quiet…. not because it was less, but because the world wasn't gentle enough to hear it.

But she loved.

And she still does.

In silence.

In memory.

In breath.

She loved a woman quietly.

She loved a woman in silence.

She never told anyone.

She never even told herself.

But her heart always knew.

And in the story of red.......where one woman died in bridal crimson, and another lived carrying that love ...... a quiet kind of forever was born.

Not the kind that fades.

Not the kind that shouts.

But the kind that endures.

Not every love has a name.

Not every love needs one.

Some are made to bloom in silence ..... not because they are small, but because they are sacred.

And still........ she loved.

And that love – quiet as it was .... was brave.

Epilogue

The sun filtered softly through the curtains, spilling gold onto the small living room where time had begun to move gently again.

Anika stood near the table, her bag packed. Today, she would leave for Mumbai ..... not just for a scholarship in medicine, but for something far older: a promise carved into memory.

Her mother .... the one who raised her ..... had always lived with quiet dignity, and her dream had always been simple:

to serve. To heal.

But Anika now knew what many didn't.

Her real father's love had belonged to Namarta.

And though Namarta never raised her, her name would live on.

Anika would become a doctor.

And one day, the hospital she opened would carry the name: Namarta Memorial.

She adjusted her duffel on the table with care.

Amit was ready by the door, silent, watching her fingers move.

"I know," he said finally, voice hushed, "some days it still feels like everything is unraveling. That for all these years, you lived as Ameet's daughter... and now you know you weren't."

Anika turned to him, her expression calm, but not without weight.

"It doesn't matter who I was born from," she said. "I had Ameet. I had Usha. I still do. And that's more than most ever get."

She paused, her voice trembling, but firm.

"But I also know... my blood father was murdered. And one day, justice will find the one who did it."

A silence followed .....not empty, but full of everything unspoken.

Flashback —

The interrogation room. Kalyani sat still, spine straight, her silence biting like frost.

Rajeev leaned in. "What's your final play, Kalyani?"

No answer.

"If you won't tell me," he said, measured, "I'll go to Ruhi. She deserves to know."

That cracked her.

"What did you say?" Her voice was low, breaking.

"I know you love her," he said. "You'd kill for her. You already did. Your husband… remember?"

A shadow passed across her face. Regret, maybe. Or the ghost of it.

"I found Ruhi's old box," Rajeev went on. "Letters she wrote to Afzal. Photos. She loved him. Because he stayed. Because he wasn't the monster everyone made him out to be."

Kalyani's fingers coiled tightly around the steel cuffs.

"You were afraid," he whispered. "Afzal would be released… and she'd leave you. You couldn't lose her. Not again. So you did what you always do ….. you silenced the threat."

Her lips trembled. Her voice, when it came, was nearly a plea.

"I didn't…"

"You don't have to admit it," Rajeev said gently. "But if you don't speak now, she'll hear it from me. And she'll hate you."

Kalyani shattered.

Tears…. not from fear, but grief …..began to fall.

And she spoke.

She told him the truth.

That it wasn't Afzal ….but Samar ….who was the monster.

That Kunal, wracked with guilt, had captured Samar.

That Samar was still alive.

"I knew he was alive…… but I didn't know where Kunal had hidden him.

So I sent a letter to the Rai house …. hoping Kunal would panic.

Hoping they'd move Samar….and I could track him.

And it worked."

She looked straight at Rajeev.

"The day you came to my house, asking about Narayan ….I knew then…. Kunal had sent him. That's when I started digging."

"I found out Narayan and Afzal were last seen at the farmhouse.

That meant….. Samar was likely there too."

She paused. Her voice steady, but quieter now.

"Kunal was trying to give Afzal justice.

To balance the sins.

He was waiting for Afzal to return ….. so he could face the man who had destroyed him."

And then, Rajeev asked the final question:

"How does Anika fit in?"

Kalyani swallowed.

The air turned still.

Even the room seemed to hold its breath.

"Anika……Anika is Afzal's daughter."

Rajeev froze.

Kalyani continued.

"I took her.

In the chaos of the wedding, I brought her to the farmhouse."

"I told her… the man inside is her father.

And that there's another …… the one who started it all.

I gave her a photo of Noor…. her mother.

Told her to go inside."

Rajeev didn't wait.

He turned and left for the farmhouse.

Immediately.

✦ ∞ ✦

At the farmhouse.......

He found Anika on the floor, knees drawn, eyes blank.

In her hand, a gun.

In the room, two bodies.

Afzal.

Samar.

Both dead.

Rajeev dropped to his knees. "Anika…"

She looked up, tears breaking through.

"I killed him. I killed Samar. He murdered my father."

"Did anyone else see you?"

She shook her head.

"Give me the gun."

Her fingers loosened, but her voice cracked. "I need to tell Aryan. He'll understand. He loves me."

Rajeev's hands held hers. Gentle. Steady.

"He'll love you always. But don't tell him. Not this. Not now."

She didn't reply. Just looked at him, shattered.

"I've seen how he looks at your photo," Rajeev said. "That smile in his silence. Let him keep seeing you like that.

Not through glass.

Not across court benches."

Anika wept. And nodded.

Rajeev buried the bodies himself. Deep. Silent. Forever.

Flashback ends—

Now, back in the room bathed in gold – Anika turned to Ameet again, her hand reaching for his.

"I love you," she whispered.

More than I ever thought possible."

He held her hand tighter, though she didn't look at him just yet.

Her eyes drifted to the still corner of the room ….. to that quiet space where the past seemed to sit, invisible…. but not absent.

Someone had stayed silent for her that day.

For friendship.

For justice.

For love.

And now, with so much still left unspoken ….. this was her beginning.

And still…… she stayed quiet.

Acknowledgements

Every story begins somewhere…. and this one began with a few unforgettable characters who quietly shaped my heart long before I wrote a single word.

To **Surbhi Chandna**, who played *Anika* in *Ishqbaaz*….. thank you. Watching your character made me feel something I couldn't explain. It was in your strength, your softness, your storm. Somewhere in those episodes, I found the courage to imagine my own Anika. And that's where this novel truly began.

To **Sumbal**, who helped this manuscript ….. thank you for your care, for your time, and for being part of the final step that brought this story into the world.

To **Anas Ali**, for walking beside me through deadlines, detours, and dreams. Your friendship and support at Deakin meant more than I can ever explain.

To **Shabana** and **Dileep Kumar** …. thank you for being my family away from home. Your doors have always been open, your meals filled with comfort, and your presence a quiet reminder that I'm never truly alone in this city.

To **Tara** and **Kevin** …. though you're far across the ocean, your belief still reaches me. Thank you for being part of the roots I carry, even from miles away.

To my **friends** and **family**…..thank you for being patient with me when I disappeared into pages.

And finally, to you…. the **reader**.
Thank you for carrying this story.
For listening between the lines.